CW01652728

NEWTONS CURSE:

THE AFTERMATH

All characters and names in this book are fictional; any resemblance to actual persons, living or dead, is purely coincidental. This book is not suitable for young children. It contains graphic sexual/trigger warning content.

ISBN: 978-1-4467-9554-5

First printing: 2023

Printing publisher Lulu.com
Lulu Enterprises, Inc.

About The Author

Ana M R - Nunes

Born in January 1968 in St Helier, Jersey, Ana, half English, half Portuguese, moved to England when she was just a small child. She is one of a twin and the third oldest in line with eight siblings. Her childhood was spent in children's homes and then four foster homes. During her early twenties, Ana married a musician in the British army, spent twenty years moving around the UK, and lived in Germany briefly. After a divorce, she now lives peacefully in County Durham with her three children living close by.

OTHER BOOKS BY ANA M R-NUNES

ELVES OF TWO LANDS:
HOPE WITHIN HEART

BETWEEN THE EYES OF A KILLER

NEWTONS CURSE: LIFE AND DEATH (part one)

NEWTONS CURSE: SEAPORT SOUTHERN SHORE (part three)

NEWTONS CURSE:
THE AFTERMATH

Part Two

Ana M R-Nunes

Prologue

'When you think you've seen and been through all, something more will always fill the void afterward.' That is my husband's saying, King Elensar, a Shalimar/Elf who, despite having a mother who hated Humans and Newtons, loved me for who I was.

My story began over a thousand years ago when I embarked on a journey into my current realm. It's a world brimming with joy, illumination, and affection. I didn't stumble upon this realm by mere luck but rather through a quest initiated by my late mother.

I arrived through a portal in Cutton Folly's forest, stepping into an unfamiliar realm. It was a time filled with people and perils I did not know of. It was an entirely different era, consumed by wars, deaths, dragons, and beasts. If you've read my first journal, you'll be aware of the special powers I possessed, known as Newton's power. I kept this power hidden, using it to restore balance and normalcy to the realm of the Shalimar.

You may already know that I passed away while giving birth to our daughter, Star. And you have also come to know that Elensar was not Star's biological father. My foolishness led her birth father, Elrohir, and his wife, Arien, straight to our doorstep, resulting in them taking her away from us. Looking back, I realize how ignorant and naive I was then. My vision and understanding of the world were so limited.

The days that followed Star's departure were filled with months and years of anguish and sorrow that I can't even begin to put into words. Even after a thousand years have passed, the mere thought of her still brings tears to my eyes. All I can do now is continue living, believing we will be reunited one day. But let me tell you, my story is far from over.

My story is still unfolding, evolving with each passing day. I assure you that I will always have the courage to venture into uncharted territories, encounter unknown faces, and embrace extraordinary experiences. I go by Amelia, and this is the tale of my life thus far. Join me as I invite you to walk alongside me, embarking on yet another captivating journey through my existence.

Volarie Castle Present Day

Lenith looked up from the book he'd just read and saw the three faces of his siblings with open mouths, "Well," spoken in a Scottish accent. "I can tell by these expressions that you're all dumbfounded!"

"Our mother is a mixed breed!" said Sarath, still looking astonished at what they'd just all heard, "All those things mother said, the way she came into our world, the way she met father," as Sarath continued to speak, her voice trembled with shock and curiosity. "Our dearly departed sister Star, the war, the fake gods! The affair with Uncle Celahir!"

"It appears so," Etheryn nodded to his younger sister, "We all know most of it because it's in Volarie's history books."

"It's all starting to make sense now," whispered Sarath, her eyes widening. "Our mother's mixed-breed heritage explains much about our family's history and the unfolding events." She paused for a moment, trying to gather her thoughts.

"But what does it mean for us?" questioned Lucy, their older sister, her brows furrowed with concern. "Are we also part of this mixed breed lineage? And if so, what powers or abilities might we possess?"

Sarath nodded, her mind racing with possibilities. "Perhaps our mother's mixed bloodline has gifted us with unique strengths," she pondered aloud. "Maybe that's why Star has always had an uncanny connection with nature, or Uncle Celahir possesses such incredible knowledge of ancient lore."

"And what about the war and the fake gods?" interjected Etheryn, his voice filled with determination. "Could our mixed heritage hold the key to unravelling the truth behind these written words?"

Sarath's eyes widened as Etheryn's words struck a chord within her. The war that had ravaged their land for generations and the false gods worshipped by the masses all seemed interconnected somehow. She had always felt a deep sense of unease whenever she thought about the state of their world, as if hidden layers had been waiting to be uncovered. Her mind raced with questions. What if their mixed heritage was not just a coincidence? What if it held the answers they had been searching for all along? With determination burning in her eyes, Sarath turned to Etheryn and said, "There's a lot missed out," said Sarath, "What if all we heard happened again? Who's to say those robot things in the sky don't decide to wipe us out!"

"You worry too much," answered Lucy.

"I worry for a good reason," said Sarath, "So should you! Think about it," Sarath continued, her voice filled with concern. "We've already seen how quickly things can change in the story Lenith just spoke about. One moment, everything seems normal, and the next, chaos ensues. Who's to say history won't repeat itself?"

"She's right; it could happen again," a voice answered from behind a bookshelf, "At any time of the day or night." That male voice made them turn around in the circle to see their older brother walk out and then lean against a bookshelf.

"Lathlorn!" said a shocked Etheryn, "When did you arrive?"

Lathlorn chuckled softly, his eyes twinkling with mischief. "Oh, I've been here for quite some time, my dear brother. I was enjoying the peace of this library until I couldn't resist joining in on your conversation."

Sarath raised an eyebrow at her older brother's sudden appearance. "And what do you mean by *It could happen again*?"

Lathlorn's expression turned serious as he pushed himself off the bookshelf and walked towards them. "I'm sure you'll find out soon enough if you have the other book. Do you?"

Lenith nodded, his curiosity piqued by his brother's cryptic words. He showed the book as evidence to him.

"And I'm guessing you'll read that too?" Again, Lenith nodded. "Then perhaps I should let you know I'm not the only one here; Alexander's here too."

"Alexander!"

"Yes, Etheryn, my dear twin brother," another brother stepped out from the bookshelf behind Lathlorn.

Lenith's eyes widened in surprise as Etheryn emerged from the shadows of the bookshelf. The resemblance between his twin brothers was uncanny, their features mirroring each other perfectly. But while Alexander possessed curiosity and intrigue, Etheryn exuded an aura of mystery and wisdom.

"I didn't hear you both enter," said Lucy, "And my hearing is normally pretty sharp."

Alexander chuckled and replied, "Well, Lucy, we have ways of being stealthy when we want to be."

Lathlorn grinned mischievously and added, "Indeed! We thought it would be fun to surprise you. Besides, sneaking up on you all is always a good way to evaluate your sharp senses."

"And perhaps the real reason you didn't hear them, Lucy, was because you were engrossed in the story too, which, I might add, is very unlike you, little sis," said Etheryn, smiling at her.

"I'll agree to that," laughed Sarath. "She normally hates these sorts of books."

"What would you know about what books I like to read? Been nosy again, have we Sarath!"

"No, I haven't."

"Well, stop sounding like you think you know me!"

Etheryn chuckled and shook his head. "Oh, come on, Lucy. We've known each other our whole lives. By now, we have a pretty good idea of each other's preferences."

Lucy crossed her arms and raised an eyebrow at Sarath. "And what about you? What do you know about my reading habits?"

Sarath smirked mischievously. "Well, let's see. You used to despise anything that wasn't a fantasy novel or a mystery thriller. But lately, I've noticed you branching out into different genres—"

"See, I knew it," Lucy scowled, "Bloody nosy parker you are!"

Sarath interrupted her with a playful grin. "No, I'm just observant—"

"Don't start bickering, you two," said Lenith, "Or I'll be knocking your heads together!"

"Go on; it might make one of them see more sense," laughed Etheryn.

"You," Lucy retorted, crossing her arms defiantly and sneering at him, "Can shove it as well!"

Etheryn raised an eyebrow at Lucy's defiant stance, his playful grin turning into a mischievous smirk. "Oh, I see," he teased, his voice dripping with sarcasm. "Lucy here thinks she knows better than all of us."

Sarath clapped her hands together sharply. "Lathlorn," she looked over to him, "You're the oldest; sort her out."

"I'm sure Etheryn can sort it out himself," Lathlorn started to walk over to them, followed by Alexander, "But if it gets out of hand, I'll stay to sort it out."

A mischievous glint appeared in Etheryn's eyes as he leaned forward, his voice dripping with amusement. "Oh, I don't mind sorting it out myself," he said, his tone laced with a challenge.

Lucy's defiant stance faltered momentarily as she glanced between Etheryn and Lathlorn. She knew that Etheryn was skilled in the art of verbal sparring, but Lathlorn had always been the one to keep them all in line. She was about to say something to Etheryn when Lenith said something instead.

"Lathlorn," Lenith laughed, "You're only really staying to hear the rest of the story, aren't you," nodding to the books on his lap.

"Would you be surprised to know," Lathlorn said as he sat down, "I've already read them?"

Lenith chuckled, his eyes sparkling mischievously. "Well, I suppose I shouldn't be surprised. You always were the one with an insatiable thirst for knowledge."

Lathlorn grinned, his gaze shifting toward Lucy momentarily before returning to Lenith. "And you, my dear brother, have always been the master of storytelling. I couldn't resist staying to hear your captivating words once again."

"Lathlorn," Sarath said, surprised, "When did you read them?"

"Ah, little sister," his gaze had wandered over to her seated figure, "It was a very long time ago."

"A long time ago?"

"I don't want to spoil your talk, but I was reading here," said Lenith, tapping a book's cover with his finger.

"I'm sorry," laughed Lathlorn, "Is it the second one?"

"The second book of doom, you mean," said Lucy boringly.

"But it's not all doom and gloom," Lathlorn interjected. "The second book holds secrets, hidden knowledge that could change everything we know."

Lucy rolled her eyes, unimpressed. "Oh please, not another one of your conspiracy theories, Lathlorn. We've heard enough of those."

Lathlorn chuckled, "Well, Lucy, you might be surprised. Sometimes truth is stranger than fiction."

Curiosity piqued, Lucy couldn't help but ask, "Alright then, what's so special about this *book of doom*?"

"Let's read it and find out, shall we," said Lenith, opening the book up. *"Newtons Curse: The Aftermath,"* he started reading aloud. *"'What,' said Andrin, stopping in his tracks, his head bent forward, eyes staring at the ground, 'On earth is this?'"*

Chapter 1

A Cold Adventure

"What," said Andrin, his head bent forward, eyes staring at the ground, "On earth is this?"

"That good friend," said Lenith, walking to his side, "Is what the humans call snow."

"I've never seen, felt it before."

"Touch it; it won't bite you."

Andrin stepped closer, uncertainly reaching out his hand. When it contacted the cold, strange substance, Andrin felt a wave of awe. At first, the pressure felt nice, calming on his skin. But then, as he let his hand rest for a moment longer, its intense, sharp coldness took over. He quickly withdrew and watched as it fell back to the ground.

Lenith chuckled a little, "That's snow, Andrin. It's a rare and magical phenomenon in many areas. It's here one day and gone the next. I've heard it's only seen a few times yearly near this place."

Andrin became spellbound by the transformation the white fluff created in his environment; he felt like he was in a tale told by an ancient storyteller. It was a feeling of awe and wonder that he'd never forget.

"It feels pleasant to the touch," he saw Lenith kneel beside him, slip fingers into the snow, and cup a small handful of it. "Taste it," a hand filled with the snow held out to him, "It's fresh, natural."

Andrin hesitated, his gaze shifting between Lenith's expectant face and the snow-filled hand. Then he said, "I am not doing it."

"It's not going to kill you. Watch," Andrin popped some into his mouth.

"What are you doing?" Andrin's eyes widened, "Are you mad?"

Lenith swallowed the snow; his lips formed a grin, "Now it's your turn."

Andrin crossed his arms defiantly, refusing to give in to Lenith's absurd request. "I don't think so!" The idea of consuming it seemed unbelievable, especially considering the freezing temperatures.

"Stop being a kin," he scooped another handful of snow. "I'm still alive, am I not?"

Andrin stood up, "What if we catch some sickness," his friend rose to stand before him, "It's not as if we can get help here if we get ill."

"Your concern is rubbish," another pinch of snow popped into his mouth, "As long as it's pure white, there's nothing to worry about."

Andrin looked at the snow around his feet and scuffed it with a dark leather foot. "I don't know." His foot pushed the snow aside, revealing damp old leaves rotting under it. "It might be unwise; it might—" His words were interrupted by noise; more noises caused him to swiftly raise his head to level a frightened gaze at his friend.

Lenith was now about ten to fifteen paces away from him, hand clasped to his throat. He was gagging, spitting, choking. Andrin's heart raced as panic gripped him, his mind struggling to comprehend the sudden turn of events. The cacophony of noises continued to assault his ears, drowning out any coherent thought.

With wide eyes, he watched in horror as Lenith's face contorted in more agony, desperately gasping for air. Without a second thought, he sprang into action, propelled by adrenaline. Closing the distance between them in mere seconds, he reached out instinctively to help Lenith. His trembling hands fumbled to find a way to alleviate the choking grip that held his friend captive.

Frantically searching for a solution, his mind raced through many possibilities. Should he attempt the Heimlich maneuver? Or try to dislodge whatever was obstructing Lenith's airway. Lenith's arm reached out to Andrin; he wasn't in time. Lenith's body silently fell, hitting the snow with a slight thud, arms spread out, and his head fell to the side.

Andrin stood frozen, his heart pounding as he watched Lenith's lifeless form lying motionless in the snow. The world around him seemed to fade into a blur, and time slowed as he tried to process the gravity of what had just happened. A wave of guilt washed over Andrin, consuming him entirely. He could have prevented this tragedy if he had reacted faster and reached out quickly. He couldn't bear the weight of his inaction; it felt like a heavy burden crushing his spirit.

Tears welled up in Andrin's eyes as memories flooded his mind - memories of laughter shared with Lenith, adventures they embarked on together, and dreams they once nurtured side by side. How could all of that be gone now? How could fate be so cruel? Andrin knelt beside Lenith's lifeless body with trembling hands, gently brushing away the snow that clung to his friend's face.

"What did I tell you!" said Andrin, crying out in fear. "You wouldn't listen." He knelt closer; his long, dark brown overcoat splayed out upon the ground behind him. He reached out a trembling hand. "You never listen," he felt Lenith's heart; he thought he felt no beats of life. "Valar, no!" he cried. "Not here, not now," his hands moved the chest, desperately seeking a heartbeat. "Listen to me; listen, Valar!"

"He's not going to hear you, brother."

Shocked and angry, Andrin started to his feet and glared at him, "Lenith!" he growled as Lenith stood up. "That's not funny!"

Lenith raised his hands placatingly, his eyes widening with surprise. "Andrin, I didn't mean to upset you," he said earnestly. "I apologize if my words came across as a joke."

Andrin's anger simmered beneath the surface, his fists clenched tightly. He took a deep breath, trying to calm himself before responding. "It's not just about this one comment, Lenith," he said, his voice tinged with frustration. "It's about everything lately. You always seem to enjoy my struggles and belittle my efforts."

Lenith's expression softened as he realized the depth of Andrin's feelings. He stepped closer, concern etched on his face. "Andrin, I never intended to undermine your efforts or make light of your struggles," he explained sincerely. "I may have a different way of coping, but that doesn't mean I don't take your challenges seriously. It was only a bit of fun," Lenith said, slapping him on the back.

"That's not a joke you'll play again on me!"

"As if I would!" Andrin's black eyebrows arched in doubt of his words. "Seriously, brother, I won't if it upsets you."

"Then don't!"

"You take things so gravely. Come," said Lenith, "Times shifting on," flinging his hood over his long golden hair, he turned back to him, "We better get going; we only have five hours here."

"You're wasting it," said Andrin, covering his head. "Not me."

"I'm not wasting it; I just thought I'd get your heart pumping."

"It is alive now, thanks to you."

"Then come, let's get going."

Now, these two young male Shalimars were what we call elves, but they were not elves like the size of garden gnomes. They are human-sized elves/Shalimar. Unlike the mischievous woodland creatures often associated with elves, these Shalimars exuded an aura of wisdom and power. Had you seen them from a distance, you would have assumed they are just like you and me, but there are quite a few differences between a human and a Shalimar. So, what are the differences?

Their ears, delicately pointed and finely tuned, allow them to catch even the faintest sounds. It is said that they can hear the rustle of leaves from miles away, a skill that eludes our human senses. Their acute hearing grants them an unparalleled awareness of their surroundings, making them masters of stealth and evasion. But it is their noses that truly set them apart. Longer and more refined than ours, their olfactory prowess is extraordinary. They can detect scents precisely and accurately discern an aroma's type, age, and origin. Their sense of smell is so heightened that it becomes a sixth sense, guiding them through the world in ways we can only imagine. And then there are their eyes, windows to a world beyond our comprehension. For those blessed with exceptional vision, their sight extends far beyond what our feeble eyes can perceive. They can spot movement on the horizon or observe intricate details from great distances. Their faces' bone structures are oval and sharp, not one shape different from the other as ours are. Upon their pale faces, no hair, not even a whisper of a beard, was emerging, leaving their smooth skin unblemished and pristine; it was as if nature had deemed them too perfect to require such earthly adornments. Their arms, these are a little longer, stronger than ours are. Their torsos, unlike ours, are muscular, fat-less, and lacking hair. The only hair they hold is long upon their heads, eyebrow hairs. Their legs are longer, running 150 miles when fully exerting their pace. Tallness in height, tall they are, perhaps their longer breathing years have something to do with it. Their physical attributes, so distinct from ours, hint at a different evolutionary path. Could their longer arms and muscular torsos result from adapting to a more demanding environment? They may come from a world where survival requires exceptional strength and agility. The absence of body hair suggests an adaptation to a warmer climate or the need for efficient heat dissipation during intense physical activity. It's fascinating how evolution can shape beings in diverse ways tailored to their needs. The length of their legs is genuinely remarkable. Running 150 miles at total exertion implies incredible endurance and stamina. Are they natural-born runners, or has their society greatly emphasized physical fitness and athleticism? It raises questions about the role of sports and physical activities in their culture. Their towering height is striking, making them stand out among us. Is their elongated stature a result of prolonged exposure to lower gravity conditions? Or it could be an outcome of genetic factors unique to their species.

Now that I have talked of their outward appearances, I should speak of their inner self-emotions. Their possessiveness comes not from fear of loss but their love for their chosen one. Their protectiveness reveals itself in danger, toiling in the land of their ideas and views. Love is the driving force behind their actions, permeating every aspect of their being. They nurture and cherish a fleeting emotion and a deep-rooted connection. Their love is not possessive in a negative sense; rather, it stems from a genuine desire to care for and protect their chosen one. In their eyes, you can see the intensity of their affection, a reflection of the depth of their emotions. It's as if their gaze holds the power to heal wounds and ignite passion simultaneously. Their eyes speak volumes, conveying unspoken words of adoration and devotion. When they warmly wrap their arms around you, it feels like being enveloped in a cocoon of safety and warmth. Their touch is gentle yet firm, providing solace in distress and reassurance during moments of doubt. In that embrace, you can feel the strength of their love radiating through every fiber of your being. Their inner self-emotions are like a symphony, playing harmoniously in the depths of their soul. Their infectious and genuine laughter fills the air with joy and lifts the spirits of those around them. It is as if their happiness is contagious, spreading like wildfire and igniting a spark within others. In times of sorrow, their empathy shines through as they offer a shoulder to lean on and a listening ear. Their understanding nature allows them to truly comprehend the pain that others may be experiencing, providing comfort without judgment or expectation. They possess an innate ability to soothe troubled hearts with their mere presence. Their compassion knows no bounds; it flows freely from their heart, enveloping everyone they encounter. They have an uncanny knack for recognizing when someone needs encouragement or support and readily provide it without hesitation. Their words of encouragement are a balm for wounded souls, mending broken spirits and instilling hope where it was once lost, but enough of this; I must get back to the story.

Chapter 2

The Shalimar Portal

It was a freezing day when William, a young-hearted male of thirty years of chestnut brown hair shoulder-length, eyes the colour of dark brown, height five feet ten inches, decided to embark on an adventure. One he had been planning to take for the last few days.

William put on his warmest clothes and started his journey. He walked through the snow-covered forest, his feet crunching in the snow with each step. William felt a chill in the air while looking around. The sun was setting, and he could feel the temperature dropping as he continued his journey. The dense forest seemed to hold its breath as if whispering secrets to the wind. William pulled his coat tighter around him, trying to shield himself from the biting cold. The once vibrant green canopy above was now a tapestry of skeletal branches adorned with delicate snowflakes that glistened in the fading light.

As he trudged deeper into the forest's heart, William couldn't help but feel a sense of unease creeping up his spine. The silence was deafening, broken only by the occasional creaking of ancient trees and his laboured breaths. Shadows danced on the ground, elongated by the setting sun, casting an eerie glow over everything. William's mind wandered back to why he had embarked on this journey in the first place. He'd found old pieces of journal hidden under his kitchen floorboards, written in elegant calligraphy, speaking of a hidden realm deep within these very woods. It was as if the writer had left behind breadcrumbs for a brave soul like William to follow. With each step forward, William's imagination soared. He envisioned a world untouched by time, with mythical creatures and enchanting landscapes. He yearned to uncover its secrets and unravel the mysteries that lay hidden within its boundaries, but he had also come to spread the news of a terrible warning to those who would listen to his words.

As William walked further, he saw two frozen twisted beech trees shaped like a bowed archway surrounded by tall trees. Right smack in the middle of them was a swirling mass of white and black energy starting to grow bigger with each footstep he took. As William approached the frozen, twisted beech trees, a sense of curiosity and caution washed over him. The archway they formed seemed almost ethereal, as if nature had carefully sculpted it. The surrounding tall trees stood like silent sentinels, their branches reaching out towards the heavens. But the swirling mass of white and black energy captivated William's attention. It danced and twirled within the archway, its contrasting colours intertwining in a mesmerizing display. With each step he took, the energy seemed to pulse and expand, growing more vibrant and powerful. Intrigued yet apprehensive, William hesitated momentarily before deciding to venture closer. A gentle breeze rustled through the leaves above as he cautiously approached the archway, whispering secrets only nature could comprehend. The air crackled with an otherworldly energy, sending shivers down his spine. With each passing moment, the swirling mass grew larger and more intense.

William's heart raced with a mixture of excitement and trepidation. He had never encountered anything like this before, and the unknown held both allure and danger. As he stepped closer to the archway, he could feel the pull of its enigmatic power, drawing him in like a moth to a flame. The once gentle breeze transformed into a gust, swirling around him with an almost sentient force. It seemed as if the air was alive, whispering ancient secrets that danced on the edge of his consciousness. The hairs on his arms stood on end as if charged by an invisible electricity. His eyes widened in awe as he beheld the spectacle before him. The swirling mass that had initially caught his attention now took on a mesmerizing form. It appeared to be a portal to another realm or dimension beyond human comprehension. Its colours shifted and morphed, blending hues that defied earthly logic. A strange sensation washed over him as he cautiously approached the swirling portal, a sense of being pulled, then finally dragged into it.

William's surroundings transformed into a chaotic blend of colours and shapes. The sensation was disorienting, like being caught in a whirlwind of emotions and thoughts. He tried to make sense of his surroundings, but grasping any tangible form or structure was impossible. Time seemed to lose all meaning as he travelled through the depths of the portal. Fear and curiosity battled within him, each emotion amplifying the other. Questions flooded his mind: Where was he going? What awaited him on the other side? Would he ever return? Suddenly, as abruptly as it had taken hold of him, the swirling portal released its grip. William found himself standing on solid ground once again, but everything around him had changed.

William was now in another realm, a snowy place. The crisp air was biting, causing William's breath to form small clouds before him. He looked around in awe, marvelling at the untouched beauty surrounding him. The trees stood tall and proud; their branches weighed down by the heavy blanket of snow. The ground beneath his feet was a pristine white canvas, interrupted only by the occasional animal tracks. As he ventured deeper into the snowy forest, William couldn't help but feel a sense of tranquillity wash over him.

For a second, to gain awareness of what just happened, he took a deep breath of the chilly air and said one sentence aloud. "Well, this is going to be one unforgettable adventure," he sighed again and stepped a foot forward.

The silence was almost deafening, broken only by the soft, crunching sound of his boots on the icy ground—each step he took left a temporary mark before the ever-falling snowflakes quickly swallowed it. The forest seemed to stretch endlessly before him, with no signs of civilization or human presence in sight. It felt as though time had stood still in this wintry wonderland. As William continued his exploration of the forest, he noticed peculiar signs of life hidden amongst the snow-covered landscape. Delicate animal tracks crisscrossed the ground, leading him to wonder what creatures called this mystical forest their home. He imagined foxes gracefully leaping through the underbrush and deer cautiously nibbling on the few remaining patches of grass. The tracks seemed to disappear into thin air as if the animals had vanished into another realm altogether. Intrigued by this enigmatic phenomenon, William's curiosity propelled him further into the heart of the forest. As he ventured deeper, a soft rustling sound caught his attention. He turned his gaze towards a cluster of tall evergreen trees, their branches heavy with snow. There, perched on a low-hanging branch, was an owl with piercing yellow eyes that seemed to hold ancient wisdom. Its feathers blended seamlessly with the snowy backdrop, making it almost invisible to an untrained eye. The owl hooted softly and spread its wings, gliding effortlessly through the forest canopy. Mesmerized by its graceful flight, William followed its path until he stumbled upon a hidden clearing bathed in sunlight.

"What are you doing here?"

The muscular voice in a Scottish accent startled William, causing him to turn around abruptly. Standing before him was a tall figure clad in a thick fur hooded cloak, his piercing blue eyes fixed on William with curiosity. The stranger's presence exuded an air of authority and mystery. William stammered, caught off guard by the unexpected encounter, "I—I came through the portal."

The man's stern expression softened as he observed William's confusion. "Aye, I can see that. This is private land."

William's frown deepened as he took in the sight of the peculiar being standing before him. Its eyes, a piercing shade of icy blue, seemed to hold an otherworldly wisdom that sent a shiver down his spine. The voice was firm and commanding, resonating with an authority that demanded respect. "I apologize if I have trespassed," William replied, his voice laced with a hint of defiance. "But I was not aware that this land was private. There were no signs or indications."

The man's expression remained stoic as he crossed his arms over his broad chest. "Private or not, this place is off-limits to outsiders," he declared firmly. "Only those who possess a receipt of entrance may enter."

Confusion washed over William's face as he tried to comprehend the man's words. "Receipt? What receipt are you talking about?"

The man sighed, his breath forming a misty cloud in the chilly air. "A letter from the Queen of Volarie."

William looked closer. Is this one of the fairytale beings from the document? Do you have something to do with those documents? You could be. He examined his face and his pointed ears. *Yes, you're a Shalimar/Elf creature. Okay, here goes.* "Look, I need to speak to whoever is in charge." As William uttered those words, a sense of anticipation filled the air. He couldn't believe he had stumbled upon a real-life fairytale being, a Shalimar/Elf creature. The realization sent shivers down his spine, but he knew he had to gather his courage and find out more.

The creature's eyes widened with surprise as it processed William's request. It seemed taken aback by his directness and determination. "I'll take you nowhere!"

"If you send me back, more will come here."

"You can't pace steps in this land," the Shalimar grabbed his arm. "Don't make me exercise force on you!"

"But I've something of urgency to say."

"Pronounce your words; I'll pass them on."

"No, you don't understand; these words must come from my lips, a human's lip," he touched the Shalimar's arm. "It's something to do with a child taken from my world." The Shalimar looked confused, "Look, I need to speak to your leader before it's too late."

"Too late, too late for what?" questioned the Shalimar, his eyes filled with concern.

"Too late to stop anything from happening," William replied urgently.

The Shalimar dropped his hand away from his arm and stepped back. "I'll need proof before we take you anywhere," he said cautiously, unsure whether to trust him.

"We?" William inquired, raising an eyebrow in surprise.

The Shalimar nodded solemnly. "I can't leave my position," he explained.

"I understand your caution," William said, his voice filled with determination. "But we don't have much time. Lives are at stake, and everything will be lost if we don't act now."

The Shalimar sighed, his eyes filled with conflict. "I know the gravity of the situation," he admitted, his voice heavy with responsibility. "But my duty to protect this realm has always been my priority."

William's gaze hardened as he stepped closer to the Shalimar. "And what good is protecting this realm if there's no one left to live in it?" he challenged, his words laced with urgency.

The Shalimar's brow furrowed, his mind grappling with the weight of William's words. His gaze shifted from William to the vast expanse of their thriving kingdom, and then he turned back to William. "As I told you, I cannot break from my position. However, Lenith will take you only if he feels it's right."

William looked around. "Lenith, where's this, Lenith?"

The Shalimar turned his head and shouted, "Lenith!"

With his name called aloud, William saw a Shalimar emerge from the forest and walk gracefully forward; his movements seemed effortless like they were flowing with the wind and had life experiences far beyond William's; then he stopped a few feet away from them both.

This Lenith was tall, with bright golden hair, long in length, tied back into a ponytail with a twig-like fastener. His facial features were fair in colour. His blue and bright eyes were stern-looking, black eyebrows slightly arched above them. His tall, lean figure gave the impression that he was careful about what he ate.

"Yes," this Lenith spoke in a language William couldn't understand. "I told you to be silent when standing on guard."

"This human says he must converse with someone of authority."

William saw him, eyeing him with caution. "Does he have a good cause in requesting it?"

"I cannot determine the true intentions of this human," the other male replied, his tone cautious yet firm. "But if he claims to have a valid reason to speak with someone of authority, it is our duty to investigate further, is it not."

Lenith walked before William and said in the human tongue, "Do you have proof?"

"I've no physical proof, but my words should be enough."

"Words can be deceiving," Lenith replied, his voice laced with scepticism. "We cannot afford to let our guard down based solely on what someone says."

William nodded understandingly, acknowledging Lenith's valid concern. "I understand your hesitation," he said earnestly. "But what I must say is of utmost importance and could potentially save countless lives here in this realm."

Lenith glanced at the other male before stepping forward to address William directly. "If your words hold such weight, then you must understand our need for verification," Lenith's voice was firm yet tinged with a hint of curiosity.

"I completely understand your need for verification," William replied, calm and composed. "I anticipated this very concern. I have no proof, but there will be truth if you listen to my words."

"Very well," Lenith said, his voice steady. "We will listen to your words but know that we are not easily convinced."

William nodded, his eyes focused and determined. He took a deep breath before beginning his explanation. "I understand that my claims may seem extraordinary, but I assure you they are rooted in truth," William paused for a moment, then started again, his voice steady but tinged with a hint of urgency. "I come from another world, realm. In my world, an imminent threat threatens your realm."

Lenith's eyes narrowed as he listened intently, his curiosity piqued. "What kind of threat?" he inquired, his voice laced with scepticism.

"Someone took a child from my world. I think she's known as Amelia, the Newton? But you should also know more people will be—"

"Amelia?" the other male's mouth opened, an interrupted sentence said in shock, "There is only one with that name here—"

"And you will remain silent about it," William heard Lenith angrily interrupt the male's words; anger flared, and his voice grew colder, cutting through the tension like a blade. "We cannot afford to let this information spread," Lenith declared firmly. "The consequences could be catastrophic."

"That's why I must seek someone who knows about this."

The other male, his voice trembling, addressed Lenith. "What do we do now?" he asked cautiously.

Lenith's eyes narrowed as he pondered the question, his mind racing to find a solution. He knew their next steps would be crucial in preventing any potential disaster. After a moment of contemplation, he finally spoke, his voice laced with urgency. "Then your words are proof enough; I'll take you to meet someone else," Lenith grasped William's arm. "Can you fly a horse?"

"Fly!" William's eyes widened in surprise at Lenith's question. "Fly a horse?" he repeated, his voice filled with confusion and excitement. The idea seemed preposterous yet intriguing at the same time.

Lenith nodded; his expression was severe but determined. "Yes, fly a horse," he affirmed. "We don't have much time, and traveling by conventional means won't get us there fast enough."

As the realization sank in, William's mind raced with possibilities. He had always been fascinated by mythical creatures and tales of extraordinary abilities. The thought of soaring through the sky on the back of a majestic creature ignited a spark within him. "But how?" William asked, his voice tinged with anticipation. "How can we make a horse fly?"

Lenith's gaze shifted to the distant mountains, where dark storm clouds were gathering ominously. "We don't have time for this," he said impatiently. "We have a mission to complete, which doesn't involve discussing how or why they fly. Our priority is to deliver this message to the Queen before it's too late. Lives are at stake." William saw Lenith walk away and enter the forest behind him, returning moments later with another Shalimar and horse. "You shall ride with me," Lenith said, walking the horse toward him. "Gliath, Andrin will linger with you," he saw him leap swiftly onto his horse, a hand outstretched to him. "You, outsider, take your seat upon Firthion so he may spread his wings and take flight."

William hesitated for a moment, unsure of what to do. He had never ridden a horse, let alone one that could fly. But the urgency in Lenith's voice and the determination in his eyes convinced him that there was no time to waste. With a deep breath, William approached Firthion cautiously. The magnificent creature stood tall and proud, its wings folded neatly against its sides. Its glossy coat shimmered under the sunlight from high above. Lenith extended a hand towards William, urging him to climb onto Firthion's back. Gathering his courage, William grasped Lenith's hand and hoisted himself onto Firthion's back. The horse shifted slightly beneath him, adjusting to his weight. It felt strange as Firthion began to move; William's heart raced with excitement and trepidation. The horse's powerful muscles rippled beneath him, propelling them forward with a graceful stride.

With each step, William could feel the energy coursing through Firthion's body as if they connected mysteriously. As they ventured deeper into the unknown, William marvelled at the realm unfolding before his eyes. The wind whispered through his hair, carrying the scents of wildflowers and distant forests. The landscape stretched out endlessly, revealing breathtaking vistas that seemed to exist only in dreams. Over a village called Lurth - a tranquil nest among two sprawling hills with thatched roofs of cottages they flew. He saw grazing farm animals and crop masses stretching out as far as the eye could see. Over the forbidding, barren Jarin Plains - with its cracked, sandy ground and lifeless, pale bones of thirsty fauna, he took a long look from high above - they took in the breathtaking view of the rocky Rokey Mountains, its snow-capped peaks reaching high and the secrets of its hidden caves holding great mystery. Next, they flew over Neatles Plain, basking in a tranquil, sunlit expanse with plenty of water, shade, and lush vegetation to the horizon. But amidst the awe-inspiring beauty, a sense of unease crept into William's mind. He couldn't shake off the feeling of venturing into uncharted territory physically and emotionally. It was as if Firthion flew him across vast landscapes and towards an unexplored realm within himself.

"Not much further now," Lenith had turned his head slightly and called out to William, "You see those two hills ahead," Lenith's voice broke through William's mesmerized state. "We're almost there."

William squinted, trying to make out the two hills in the distance. Firthion's wings beat rhythmically, carrying them effortlessly towards the hills. William could feel a surge of energy coursing through his veins as if the air around him was charged with an otherworldly power. He couldn't help but wonder what awaited him beyond those hills. William noticed a large, tall, majestic building between the two hills as their horse flew closer. Its towering spires reached towards the heavens, casting long shadows over the surrounding landscape. The building seemed to emanate an air of mystery and power, captivating William's imagination.

"That," Lenith called out to William as the same building started to loom in front of them, "Is Volarie Castle our intended location," with a slight movement of his body, Lenith made their horse begin to descend, turning in flight to towards a well-tended pasture behind Volarie's majestic castle. Moments later, the lush green grass welcomed them as they dismounted and allowed their horse to graze freely, and now William was walking in double quick steps to keep up with Lenith's heading towards the castle's back entrance. "Once we enter," Lenith said, his voice filled with determination, "You must not speak unless spoken to."

William nodded, his heart pounding with anticipation. As they approached the towering castle walls, Lenith led the way through a hidden path that wound around the castle's perimeter. The sound of their footsteps echoed as they neared the back entrance. William couldn't help but feel excitement and nervousness coursing through his veins. As they reached the door, Lenith paused momentarily, his eyes scanning their surroundings for any signs of civilization, the palace guards, and servants. Satisfied they were alone, he opened the heavy wooden door, revealing a dimly lit corridor. The two stepped inside, their footsteps quiet on the stone floor beneath them. The air smelled musty and old, hinting at the passage of time and neglect. The endless corridor stretched before them, its walls adorned with symbols and carvings. The flickering torches lining the walls cast eerie shadows that danced along the ancient stone, creating an atmosphere of mystery and intrigue. As they ventured further, Lenith took them into another corridor, then up a twisted stone stairwell to a passage with five doors. William followed Lenith's hushed footsteps as they walked through one of the old wooden oak doors. Into another corridor, they entered, this one much more different than the last one. Its velvety texture the deep plush carpet beneath their feet, made them feel like they were walking on clouds.

Lenith paused before a door, his hand resting on the brass door handle, "Remember what I said, don't speak unless spoken to."

William nodded silently, his heart pounding with anticipation.

Chapter 3

An Introduction to the Queen.

Lenith turned back to the door and opened it swiftly. The door closed just as quickly behind them. Standing right beside them as they entered was a guard; his vision had been looking forward into the room before their entrance, and now he was looking at them.

Prince Lenith and William exchanged a glance, then, with a calm yet authoritative voice, Lenith addressed the guard, attempting to conceal the urgency in a language William couldn't understand. "Good evening, sir. We seek an audience with grandmother. It is of utmost importance that we speak with her immediately."

The guard, taken aback by the unexpected presence of the prince and his human companion, quickly straightened himself and slightly bowed respectfully. "Apologies, Your Highness," he stammered, speaking in a tongue William didn't understand either. "I was not informed of your arrival. Please allow me to announce you to Her Majesty."

Lenith nodded, grateful for the guard's cooperation. "Thank you, sir. We appreciate your assistance."

They followed the guard across a room adorned with intricate paintings and stunning sculptures, furniture finely crafted, a marble floor polished to a shine, and a large fireplace blazing in the centre of the room, with a luxurious rug in front of it. William couldn't help but say to Lenith in a whispering tone, "Are you some sort of high noble?"

"Why do you ask?"

"The guard bowed his head slightly before speaking."

Lenith glanced at William, a small smile playing on his lips. "I suppose you could say that," he replied cryptically. "But let's focus on the task at hand for now."

William couldn't help but steal glances at their surroundings as they followed the guard. The luxury of the room was unlike anything he had ever seen before. The paintings came alive with vibrant colours and intricate details, each brush stroke telling its story. The sculptures stood tall and proud, capturing the essence of grace and beauty. The furniture, adorned with plush cushions and delicate embroidery, exuded an air of elegance that made William feel slightly out of place. William marvelled at the craftsmanship of creating such pieces, wondering who could afford such luxury. The marble floor beneath their feet felt cool and smooth as they walked out into a hallway, then stepped further until the guard reached an ash door and promptly stopped in front of it.

"The Queen is in here," he whispered, his voice barely audible. The guard raised his hand and gently knocked on the door, waiting for permission to enter; a faint response from inside the room answered him seconds later. With a nod of approval from Lenith, the guard turned the ornate doorknob and pushed open the heavy ash door. It creaked as it swung open, revealing a dimly lit chamber beyond.

Before Lenith and William entered, words were directed at the guard by Lenith, "Listen well, for I'll only speak these words once. Send more protectors to the portal."

"Why?"

"No questions, just do it."

The guard nodded, his expression a mix of curiosity and obedience. He understood that Lenith's orders would not be questioned, especially concerning the portal. With a final glance at Lenith and William, he turned on his heel and hurried off to fulfil his task.

As the heavy door closed, Lenith and William entered the dimly lit chamber. Their footsteps echoed softly against the stone floor as they went further in. Lenith's eyes scanned the room, taking in every detail. There was another lit fireplace, dancing flames of orange and gold. William moved closer to a wall to examine an exceptionally detailed tapestry; Lenith drew his attention toward a large wooden desk near the centre of the room covered in scattered parchments and ancient books, their pages yellowed with age. The desk seemed untouched for centuries, as if waiting for someone to unlock its secrets. To the right-hand side of this was another door, a guard standing watch over them, eyes following their every move. Lenith didn't seem to care he was there or that another one was standing by the door they had entered. He was more interested in the settee to the left of the desk and who was lying upon it. With a deep breath, Lenith approached the couch and gestured for William to stay where he was.

Lenith's heart raced as he neared the settee, his eyes fixed on the figure lying upon it. The room was filled with an eerie silence, broken only by the faint sound of his footsteps echoing against the cold stone walls. As he drew closer, he could make out the delicate features of a woman, her face pale and serene. The guard's watchful gaze intensified, his suspicion evident in his narrowed eyes. Lenith could feel the weight of that scrutiny, but he refused to let it deter him. With a gentle touch, Lenith brushed aside silk-like strands of white hair that had fallen across the woman's forehead. Her skin was cold, but it didn't shiver down his spine. He suddenly went down on his knees, kneeling before his grandmother. As Lenith studied her face more closely, he noticed a faint scar tracing her cheekbone. It seemed oddly familiar, stirring distant memories within him of a story of how that came to be upon her face; fragments of a forgotten tale began to resurface.

In her youth, before she had born any kin's, she had been a keen rider, a flyer on her horse; people even called her *'The Flying Queen'* until one day, it all stopped. Lenith's curiosity was piqued as he delved deeper into the fragments of the forgotten tale. He recalled his grandmother's words, spoken with a hint of sadness, about how her riding days abruptly ended. She had mentioned an accident, but the details remained hazy in her memory to tell the whole story.

Driven to uncover more of the tale, Lenith embarked on a quest to piece together the missing parts of his grandmother's story. He sought out those who had known her during her days as *'The Flying Queen*,' hoping they could shed light on what had transpired. As he traversed through villages and towns, Lenith encountered elderly folks who remembered her extraordinary horsemanship. They spoke of her grace and fearlessness, painting vivid pictures of her soaring through the air on horseback, captivating all who witnessed her rides. Then, one day, while visiting a remote village nestled amidst rolling hills, Lenith stumbled upon an old stable hand named Elias.

With his weathered face and calloused hands, Elias had spent his entire life working with horses. He had seen many skilled riders come and go, but Lenith's grandmother was different. The mere mention of the name, '*The Flying Queen*' brought a glimmer of nostalgia to Elias' eyes. Intrigued by the tales he had heard from his grandmother, Lenith approached Elias and struck up a conversation. As they sat on a wooden bench outside the stable, Elias shared his memories of Lenith's grandmother.

His words painted a picture of a woman with an unbreakable bond with her horses. "She was like no other rider I've ever seen," Elias reminisced, his voice filled with admiration. "Her connection with the horses was something magical. It was as if she could communicate with them without uttering a single word."

Lenith listened intently, captivated by every word that left Elias' lips. He yearned to know more about this extraordinary woman who shared his bloodline.

"But there was a terrible accident," Elias continued, his voice filled with a hint of sadness.

Lenith leaned forward, his curiosity piqued. "What happened?" he asked, his eyes fixed on Elias.

Elias took a deep breath before continuing. "One stormy night, while she was riding her favourite horse, a lightning bolt struck nearby where they were flying, the Rokey Mountains, a bolt that came from the ground up into the sky. The sudden loud crack startled the horse, causing it to rear up and lose its balance. They both fell to the ground, and she suffered a severe head injury."

Lenith's heart sank as he imagined the scene unfolding before him. "How did she ever survive that fall with just a small scar?" he asked bewilderedly.

"Valar knows only that answer," he shrugged his shoulders. "The accident left her in a coma for months; when she woke, all that was left of that terrible day was a faint scar upon her cheekbone. Perhaps the answer for her healing was lying in a coma state. But when she finally woke up, something else had changed within her. She had lost her ability to communicate with the horses."

"Lenith, my dearly beloved grandson, you've returned," Queen Catreen's voice, spoken in their tongue, brought Lenith back to reality, to the present day.

Lenith blinked, momentarily disoriented as his grandmother's voice penetrated his thoughts. He turned towards her, his heart swelling with a mix of emotions. It had been months since he last saw Queen Catreen, his grandmother, the matriarch of their kingdom. "Grandmother," Lenith whispered, his voice filled with reverence and affection while taking her hand in his own. "I have missed you dearly."

A soft smile tugged at Queen Catreen's lips as she gently squeezed Lenith's hand. "And I, you, my dear grandson," she replied, her voice tinged with joy and sadness. "Tell me, my dear grandson," Queen Catreen began, her voice steady yet gentle. "What troubles your heart? What challenges have arisen in your absence? Your thoughts hide something from me, but your eyes say different."

Lenith looked into his grandmother's wise, perceptive eyes, feeling comfort and vulnerability. He knew he could trust her with his deepest concerns but articulating them was another matter entirely. Taking a deep breath, he spoke softly, choosing his words carefully. "Grandmother," Lenith began, his voice quivering slightly. "Since I left our kingdom to explore the world beyond our borders, I have witnessed beauty and darkness where people suffer needlessly. It weighs heavily on my heart, but I am not here for those tales to be told."

Queen Catreen listened intently, her grip on Lenith's hand tightening slightly in support.

"I've brought a visitor to see you," Lenith turned his head, beckoned William to come forward, then turned his gaze back. "He's brought information he wishes you to hear."

William walked closer and stopped inches from him; his sight was upon a figure of a slim elderly lady dressed in a long dark blue flowing gown lazing on the couch.

"He's human!" Queen Catreen spoke as if she was offended that William was a human.

"He came through the portal with news for us to hear," Lenith lowered his other hand to her arm.

"Were you there?" She started to rise into a sitting position. "You know your father doesn't like it when you go to that place."

Lenith rose from his knees and stood before her. "Grandmother," he let out a small laugh, "You really shouldn't worry about me."

"You're still a youthful kin in my eyes."

Lenith smiled, turned to face William, and spoke in the human tongue, "Speak your name so I may introduce you to Queen Catreen of Volarie."

William bowed, stepped back, and said, "My name is William Defer."

"You, William," Catreen spoke in a Scottish accent. "You must have great courage to come here, or you're foolish."

"Your Highness, it's a long story; maybe you should be seated."

"I can withstand hearing words in an upright position."

"Would you like me to get father first grandmother?" The answer was a nod of her head; her body looked as if it were shaking out of fear. Lenith sat her down on the settee and stood before William. "Because I suspect you're the holder of bitter news, you'll not be going back to the human world. On the other hand, my father may let you survive, but only if he's in a good disposition. If not, you shall be lifeless by dawn." Lenith turned away from a stunned William and spoke to Grethorn, who was standing by the door in the room. "Make sure he stays."

"Yes, Your Highness." Grethorn saw William swiftly lower his gaze to the floor. The next sound Grethorn heard was the door closing, a long, drawn-out sigh coming from across the room. He saw William's head stay in that position for twenty minutes. Grethorn, intrigued by his peculiar behaviour, couldn't help but wonder what had transpired. As a seasoned castle guard, he was used to observing people from a distance, but this incident piqued his curiosity.

Remaining discreetly positioned near the room entrance, Grethorn observed William's head still bowed low, seemingly lost in deep contemplation. The air in the room grew heavy with anticipation as he awaited the Queen's question.

The silence stretched indefinitely until the Queen's voice finally broke through. "Tell me, dear human," she spoke gently yet commandingly. "What weighs so heavily on your mind that you find solace in staring at the floor?"

William's head slowly lifted, revealing eyes filled with sadness and resignation. His voice trembled as he began to speak, his words carrying an air of vulnerability that resonated throughout the room. "Your Majesty," he started hesitantly, but she stopped him.

"You," her hand pointed to William, "Tell me, human, where you came from; if there were snow there, how would you be rid of marks left by feet in it?"

William looked like he was thinking of an answer to the question. When the answer came forward, it went like this. "It's impossible."

"Just as I thought," sniggering aloud. "See how easily your mind dwells in one place. A human, you're all alike."

Grethorn saw William appear slightly angry, saying, "How would you be rid of marks left in the snow by feet? The sun's scorching rays would melt the marks." Grethorn, the castle guard, stood tall and proud as he listened to William's suggestion. His eyes widened with curiosity, intrigued by the simplicity yet brilliance of the idea. Using the sun's scorching rays to melt away footprints left in the snow seemed almost too good to be true. As he glanced at the Queen, Grethorn noticed a flicker of surprise in her eyes.

"Perhaps there's hope for you after all," the Queen replied. "I'm afraid it's too late for others."

William looked like he would say something; he didn't get the chance because Prince Lenith returned to the room with Cithern, another castle guard, by his side. "Grandmother," Lenith said as he entered the room. "I've sent someone to inform Father about William; he'll be here shortly."

Chapter 4

The Queen's Son Prince Elensar

In the drawing room, Queen Catreen, the human, the two castle guards, and Lenith waited for Lenith's father. They didn't have to wait long before he opened the door. The figure of Queen Catreen's eldest son, dressed in black leather trousers and a long white sleeve shirt, marched into the room. William looked at a Shalimar with stunning, handsome features making his way over to him—the physical stature of a well-kept athletic body. Long, soft, straight golden hair, piercing sea-blue eyes, and facial features reminded him of a young famous movie star he'd seen plastered on billboards. The same beautiful, sultry, graceful look stole your eyesight from the road and pavement for a few moments of surprise.

This Shalimar stopped in front of William. "I am Prince Elensar of Volarie," he introduced himself, again that Scottish accent was there, "You had better have a good reason for being here."

Woo, he thought to himself, Bloody hell! *Are you tall or what!* Prince Elensar's over-tallness in height made him retreat a step back as if afraid. And he was. He was the tallest Shalimar he'd seen, standing at seven-foot-two-three at least. William bowed his head.

"Look at me," said Elensar in the human language. "Why have you appeared in our land?"

William's eyes widened as butterflies twisted through him like a symphony, the most beautiful music he'd ever heard. He felt a strange mix of emotions as he stared into the depths of the prince's penetrating gaze as if they were connected frighteningly and thrillingly. He hadn't ever felt so strongly about another person before, and he found himself strangely spellbound by the prince's assertive presence, like a moth to a flame. He almost wanted to reach out and touch the young man, explore the contours of his face and body, but he knew that would be wrong.

"I said, why have you appeared in our land?"

"I—I bring a warning," William replied with a sense of urgency.

"What forewarning could you possibly carry?"

"Others will be coming," William said, looking around him as if he were worried these *'others'* were in the same room as him.

"Others?" his voice laced with concern, "Who are these *'others'* you speak of?"

William took a deep breath and removed a small bundle of rolled-up discoloured papers from his coat. "We found these," William said, his voice trembling as he handed the discoloured papers to the Shalimar before him.

"These are ancient," he saw Elensar's fingers tracing the worn edges of the parchments. "Who are we?"

"Tim and I—" he watched as Elensar opened one of the rolled-up papers; he saw the Queen get up from the sofa and walk towards them both. "But Tim, I'm afraid to say, took most of them; the rest left behind I brought with me."

William saw Lenith walk towards him, holding an annoyed gaze; his words sounded angrier. "You said you had no physical proof!"

William felt a knot tighten in his stomach as Lenith's accusatory words hung in the air. He hoped his explanation would appease him, but it fuelled his anger further. He struggled to find the right words to defend himself. "I—I know what I said, Lenith," William stammered, his voice tinged with regret. "But I never knew back then you were someone I could trust."

"Where were these papers hidden," Elensar asked.

"Someone concealed them under my kitchen floorboards," he replied, his voice steady despite his unease. "I kept them locked away for a while, thinking they were only old memories of a time long gone. I never imagined they held such significance."

Elensar's piercing gaze bore into William, searching for any signs of deception. The room fell silent as everyone awaited his response. Lenith's anger seemed to dissipate momentarily, replaced by a glimmer of curiosity mixed with caution.

"Why did you keep them hidden all this time?" Elensar asked, his voice laced with suspicion.

"Yes, why indeed?" asked the Queen, now she was standing next to her son, looking at the paper in his hand. "And what makes you think you have the authority to decide what should be hidden from us?"

William hesitated momentarily before answering them all, choosing his words carefully. "I kept them hidden because I believed, at the time, they were just old papers from a life long gone."

"So, what made you change your mind to seek us out?" asked Lenith, holding a frown upon his brow.

"An incident occurred, several ones, mainly at night. Words that spoke to me to seek you out, pass them onto you." William took a deep breath, his eyes darting between the curious faces of those around him in the room. "It started with strange dreams," William began, his voice filled with apprehension and determination. "Visions of a different time, a different place. I couldn't make sense of them at first, but they felt so vivid, so real." He paused, searching for the right words to convey the weight of his experiences. "In these dreams, I saw people who looked just like you all," he gestured towards them. "They were living in a realm torn apart by chaos and darkness caused by one individual." A murmur spread through the room as everyone exchanged puzzled glances. William pressed on, his voice growing more urgent. "But it wasn't just dreaming anymore. I started hearing whispers in my sleep—I began to see signs in my waking life too," he confessed, his voice barely above a whisper. "Voices coming from the cracks in my bedroom walls, flickers of light moving around as if by invisible hands."

"What did the words say to you?" asked the Queen.

William took a deep breath, his eyes darting around the room as if searching for an escape. "The words were cryptic, Your Majesty," he replied, trembling.

The Queen leaned forward, her expression a mix of curiosity and concern. "And did you understand these messages, William? Could you make sense of them, for you must have done to bring them to my doorstep, but I need to see them myself, this proof you bring with you," she snatched the papers from Elensar's hands and began reading them herself. As the Queen delved into the contents of the documents, her brows furrowed in deep concentration. The words on the page seemed to unravel a web of secrets and hidden intentions. The Queen's mind raced as she connected the dots between these papers and reacted with angry words. "Luthleadon!" she heatedly said, her voice filled with anger and disbelief.

Luthleadon, whom grandmother was talking about, came from their realm, the world of Shalimar. A being everyone had thought was a Shalimar. Even Catreen herself did not know his identity, yet this Luthleadon, who had lived in the Mirnith towers in the old dark lands with his father, held a secret; perhaps even he never knew he had. The mystery was that he was more human than a Shalimar. But to discover why Luthleadon holds human blood in his veins, the story must return to Luthleadon's father.

King Tarron, Luthleadon's father, ventured into the human realm, and after searching the realm and being awed by one beauty, Tarron finally settled on a woman who had captured his heart. He returned to his realm with her, hoping she would never want to return to the human world. To outsiders, the first year of Speantal and her relationship was going great. She would appear to her people in public with a genuine smile, and nothing seemed to be causing a problem between the couple. But these outsiders failed to realize that Speantal was facing a battle in her mind and heart, thinking she wasn't welcome in their realm, or at least that's what a voice inside her thoughts was telling her. In private, she struggled with doubt, insecurity, and betrayal that she had yet to overcome. She was anxious that the same issues would resurface the more her relationship progressed, and while she still loved her husband, she couldn't help but feel a lingering fear. Despite this, she put on a brave face and continued to smile in public, hoping that the feelings would one day pass. Still, she couldn't help but feel a sense of sadness deep inside.

During their second year together, Tarron's silent bride, Speantal, begged Tarron to let her see her world after she delivered their first kin, a stillborn. Tarron, sensing she only said this because their kin's loss saddened her, decided not to grant her wish; it didn't end there.

Tarron and his wife endured unimaginable pain and sorrow for seven years. During this time, she sadly bore him six stillbirths—the death of her babies. The grief of this loss caused her to no longer want to be bound by marriage and the life of a homemaker; she wanted to take a journey on her own, and Tarron's initial refusal of this wish only made her sad. However, the man's love for his wife exceeded his selfishness, and he agreed to let her go. He just wanted to make sure his wife was happy again so that he could have the smiling face of his beloved companion back in his life. Though the risk of her going alone was immense, Tarron took it nonetheless.

Months later, after her return, the news of Speantal's impending kin spread throughout the Shalimar population of Mirnith with anticipation and jubilation. The Shalimar, a mystical race with ethereal beauty and ancient wisdom, held great reverence for the birth of a kin, seen as a sacred event that brought hope and prosperity to their realm. The air crackled with excitement; preparations were next made to welcome the newest addition to their community. Elaborate feasts were organized and adorned with vibrant flowers and shimmering lights. The villagers eagerly shared stories of past kins' remarkable abilities and extraordinary destinies. Mirnith was abuzz with an atmosphere of celebration.

However, amid the general merriment, whispers circulated among a few curious souls who doubted Speantal's intentions. They speculated that her frequent trips to the human realm were not merely innocent visits but clandestine encounters with a long-lost lover. Such an accusation was indeed blasphemous in their eyes, and the mere suggestion of such a thing was punishable by exile. Thus, those who harboured such thoughts kept their silence to themselves for fear of being sent to the dungeons for voicing their ideas. When Speantal died while giving birth to the kin named Luthleadon, all these rumours and suspicions had already dissipated into the wind, but over time, those people's thoughts were forgotten, lost forever; now, back to the present day.

"Just as I thought—" the Queen's voice spoke heatedly. "Tell me, human, these letters, why do you think she did it?"

William's head rose a little more. "I can't speak for a person long gone," he saw the Queen's eyes narrow as if studying his expression, making him shift uncomfortably under the weight of her gaze.

"I can. That woman planned this to upturn our world. You have caused this commotion to let others come unnoticed."

William's heart raced as he watched the Queen's piercing gaze bore into him. He knew he had to choose words carefully, for his fate and those he cared about hung in the balance. Taking a deep breath, he continued, his voice steady yet filled with conviction. "Your Majesty, I understand your suspicions, but I assure you I am not part of any conspiracy. I stumbled upon this evidence purely by chance," he saw her turn away from him as if she wanted nothing more to do with him.

"Oh, Valar!" the Queen used a distressed voice, "That woman, that human, that traitor, Amelia!"

"Amelia!" Those words had come from a shocked Elensar.

"Yes, her, that foul thing," the Queen answered. "Where is she?"

A guard answered her question, "She's in Kimbrund, my lady."

The Queen's eyes narrowed as she processed the guard's response. Kimbrund is a place known for its treacherous alleys and hidden secrets. It was where shadows danced, and whispers echoed through the cobblestone streets and deep forests. Without wasting another moment, the Queen straightened her regal attire, looked over to one of the guards in the room, and ordered, "You will send for her now and be quick in your steps! I'll not have that thing thinking she can stroll wherever she wants!"

Looking like the Queen's sudden outburst had taken him aback, the guard quickly composed himself. "Yes, Your Majesty," he replied with a sense of urgency. Without wasting another second, he turned and hurriedly approached the chamber door.

"Mother," said Elensar. "This must be wrong?"

"I don't understand," the Queen sounded confused, "How could she breathe so long in our land? She's just as he is, a human."

"Mother, please explain—"

The Queen looked up, looked stunned. "I can't believe it; we had a human right beneath our noses!"

"Maybe she isn't," said Lenith. "Maybe this human deceives us."

The Queen turned her gaze to him. "I think William tells the truth. Besides, we all know Luthleadon's name, even you, Lenith. But human, now you will tell us every detail so my son and I can decide if you live or die."

Chapter 5

The Papers In Cutton Folly

"But now, human," the Queen said to him, "Now you will tell us everything, every detail, so I can decide if you live or die."

He sighed. Why was he here? Why did he have to see, talk to, and warn them? Well, here is why. William began right at the beginning, with Cutton Folly forest mentioned first.

In Cutton Folly's vast forest, a small house would've remained hidden if it had not been for its bright red roof sticking out through the foliage surrounding it. This red roof was the first to catch his eye as he flew over Cutton Folly in a small airplane. For the next half an hour, his sky flayer, a one-person solar-powered plane, circled in the air, trying to better look below at the scenery. Curiosity got the best of him the following day, and he drove joyfully through Cutton Folly's forest in anticipation of what the rest of the house would look like. When he arrived, he could not contain his excitement; the contrasting red and white for sale sign outside the home utterly captivated him to look for a phone number. He found it. To take in the beauty of the house's innards, he immediately began to search for his cellular phone, which he'd left in his jeep. Thankfully, after about thirty minutes, he successfully found it.

Within weeks of a phone call to an estate agent, he was the proud owner of an old English house that needed renovations that would roll into thousands of pounds before it was inhabitable. However, that information didn't worry him; he had the cash to do this work. No, he wanted a concealed place where he could live in silence, forget the endless questions he had to answer about his daughter's unexplained death; this place was it.

William had grand plans for his purchased house, dedicated to seeing them through. He started by building a new front porch and creating a garden, the walls plastered, strengthened, and painted, which kept him busy for three months. William stayed at Furn, a Cutton Folly village hotel, during this time. After a year of hard work, William moved out of the hotel and into his house, which he called Northline. He made it more homely one by one, checking off projects on his mental list: uncluttered the closets and kitchen cupboards, painted the walls a cheery yellow, added a side garden, and hung curtains with patterned prints.

Now, the Northline translation meant calm; on this day, the house had no peaceful atmosphere. Tim and William were finishing their DIY project: replacing the kitchen floorboards. As they removed the old floorboards, dust spread, contaminating every corner of the house and creating an incredible mess. However, despite the disturbance, the two were dedicated to the project and would usually stop at nothing to complete it, but Tim saw something that made him stop.

"What's that!" quizzed Tim. "It looks like a bundle of papers!"

William paused, wiping the sweat off his forehead with the back of his hand, and leaned over the gap. He squinted his eyes, trying to get a better look at the mysterious bundle. The papers were crumpled and yellowed, as if they had been hidden away for years. Without thinking twice, William reached out to grab the bundle. As his fingers brushed against the worn edges of the papers, a surge of excitement rushed through him. He carefully pulled them out from the gap, revealing a stack of handwritten letters, he began reading one of them aloud.

Today brought the end for us, yet what we have done is only a beginning to start beyond the 'Heart's' *twenty-first birthday. A new dawn will begin in Cutton Folly's forest—an opening to release power beyond anyone's dreams. Until then, goodbyes are not the end, for we will all recognize your face when you come home again.*

Please do not remove the necklace she wears, for this is the only thing keeping her alive.

William furrowed his brow and cast his sight to the written words again, hearing Tim say, "That's strange, even bossy-like."

"It is rather rude; at least it leaves no doubt about what they were asking for."

"Perhaps it was written in a rush," said Tim.

"It could have," replied William. "We'll never know, will we?"

"True," agreed Tim. "But the hasty writing style could also be intentional, to create a sense of urgency or convey a particular mood."

William nodded thoughtfully. "That's a valid point. Sometimes, writers deliberately capture the raw emotions and chaotic thoughts that come with rushing through the writing process."

"What about the others? Are they the same?"

"You study them. I want to examine this more," William was looking at the one still in his hand.

"But I can't read very well," Tim replied, his voice filled with frustration.

William sighed loudly, began unravelling the remaining papers, and read them to himself; a few moments later, he uttered, "This is even odder."

"What is?"

"What I just read," William replied, his voice filled with confusion and intrigue. William slowly walked towards the small workbench. He carefully placed the papers across the table, ensuring they spread evenly, then picked one up, half-torn. As William examined the torn page, his eyes widened with anticipation. The faded ink revealed fragments of a story written in elegant cursive handwriting. His mind raced with questions about the mysterious author and the secrets hidden within these pages. "Tim, these are from a journal!" William exclaimed, his voice filled with excitement.

"Really! Who do you think wrote it?" Tim asked, his curiosity piqued. "And what kind of secrets could be hidden within its pages?"

William's mind raced with possibilities. He imagined a long-lost explorer who had stumbled upon a hidden treasure or an enigmatic figure who had witnessed extraordinary events unfold. The elegant cursive handwriting hinted at someone with refined tastes and a penchant for storytelling. "I can't even begin to imagine," William replied, his voice barely containing his eagerness. "But one thing is for sure - we have stumbled upon something truly remarkable," he started to read aloud.

8th October 1966

Wednesday last week, these strange people knocked on my door. The first one asked me questions while he stood under my porch. The second, a very handsome young chap, became quite interested in each of my rooms' details. He said he was an inspector sent by the Housing foundation company to check each room's walls. I'm sure he's no such thing, for his poor knowledge of such things makes me doubt his profession. Then something weird happened not long after he'd gone. Someone left a baby on the front porch with a silver necklace on my twenty-fourth birthday. Now, why would anyone leave such a valuable item of worth? Indeed, they could've pawned the silver and made money to feed such a tiny baby. This piece of paper may give some evidence of where the baby came from, but it's written in such a way I need help understanding what it means.

17th October 1966

When I first read the message, I felt oddly like something wasn't quite right. After a while, I finally realized what it was trying to tell me. After I die, I must cast Heart, *this helpless girl left in my care, into the shadows of Cutton Folly's forest. I'm not sure why this is, and I'm not sure what will happen to this girl afterward. All I know is there must be a good reason for such a strange message. I'm still grappling with answers and a way to help* Heart, *but I'm still at a loss. If I can unravel the mystery, I can find a way to help Heart.*

18th October 1966

Tonight is a tough night for my daughter, Heart. *She is very fragile, and her sobs pierce the house's walls like a thousand shards of glass. I can't help but to go to her and find out what's wrong. But even then, what do I do? There's no way I can fix whatever is causing her grief. All I can do is hug her tight, feed her, and wipe her tears. It breaks my heart to see her like this. I tell her everything will be alright and that I'm here for her. I show her that I understand and sympathize with every emotion she is feeling. I stroke her hair and whisper sweet nothings into her ear until her tears dry up, but her sadness only seems to increase every hour.*

24th October 1966

I can't do this on my own. I can't raise a child that is slipping away from me. I can't find the strength to take on the challenge of caring for a child who may not live to see the next day. I can't stay strong in the hard times when I want to curl up and cry. I can't do this by myself.

26th October 1966

My promises for a future with Heart *are shattered. Nothing will return what's been taken away, no matter how hard I pray. I asked why God would allow such suffering and tragedy to befall me. Why me?*
Why Heart*? My questions remained unanswered and unfulfilled.*

Tim's eyes flowed with tears. "I can't understand."

William sighed. "Life gives and takes. That's the way it's—"

"You're not bothered by such words—I'd have thought with losing Annabelle so soon after your wife's anniversary—"

William interrupted Tim, "Tim, grief is a complex journey that we all navigate differently. Losing Annabelle was devastating, but it doesn't mean I'm immune to pain or unaffected by loss."

Tim's eyes met William's, searching for answers. "But how do you keep going? How do you find the strength to face each day when life seems so unfair?"

A sad smile tugged at the corners of William's lips as he took a moment to collect his thoughts. "It's not about finding strength, Tim. It's about realizing that strength already exists within us," he dropped the paper onto the table and picked up another.

Tim placed a hand upon his arm in a friendly gesture. "I meant no harm by my words."

William smiled reassuringly. "We all make mistakes. The key is to learn from them and grow as individuals. Now, getting back to those papers," William nodded to the ones on the table. "If the dates state the year 1966, this house is ancient."

"And very weird, they're in good condition," Tim's hand went down to the tabletop, delicately feeling one of the papers with fingertips, "Even the papers are good quality!"

"Indeed. It's quite intriguing how well-preserved everything is. Perhaps the previous owners took great care of their belongings."

Tim furrowed his brow, deep in thought. "But why would someone keep these papers for so long? And why are they hidden away in this old house?" As if on cue, a gust of wind blew through a cracked window, causing the papers to rustle and dance on the table.

William's eyes widened with realization. "Tim, we may have stumbled upon something extraordinary here."

Curiosity piqued, Tim leaned closer to examine the papers more closely. His fingers traced over faded ink and elegant handwriting that seemed to tell a story. "These documents seem like personal letters or journals," he mused aloud.

William nodded, "It appears so. How many are there?"

"At least twenty, if not more!"

"Perhaps we'd better get reading before the night hits us," William's hand returned to the table and tentatively picked up another yellowed paper, eyes drawn to a particular line. He spoke its contents aloud, his voice a low whisper of sadness.

29th March 1967

It's been five months since I buried Heart in the garden, and during these five months, I've been mourning, crying, and brought back to life once more by a man. Now this man, this being my new lover Luthleadon, he passes to me, sweet smiles which ease my heartache, make my stomach turn somersaults as if I were a young teenager again, but where does he come from? Where does he go at night? I care for no answers; I care only that he's here now and shall, I hope, remain forever here with me, giving kind words and love.

10th May 1967

Last night, my new lover, tall, gentle, caring, with shoulder-length golden hair, lay by my side and told me things I find hard to understand and believe. He said my deceased Heart *was a half-breed, half-Shalimar, half-Newton; very odd. Yet, I wonder if he also knows I am a Newton, for he keeps asking me questions about certain things. Who were my parents? How long have I lived here? Was my first husband from the same blood as I? Had I ever heard of a secret society called the*

Leeches? To someone else, these questions may have been frowned upon, wondered if the person asking them was insane. But they didn't to me, for I knew the answers to those questions.

The first one, Who were my parents? *That would be Isabela and Tristian from Scotland in the Highlands, both full-blood Newtons.*

The second, How long have I lived here? *It's been a few years in this house, but I think he asked me how long I lived in the human world; that would be all my life, for I was born in Galston, Scotland.*

The third question, Was my first husband from the same blood as I? *No, he was human; we married young, very young, barely eighteen we both were, but he passed away at the age of twenty from drowning not long after we were married; such a sweet, caring man, God rest his soul.*

The fourth is the secret society called the Leeches*; I had heard of them from my parents, who spoke of them in bedtime stories when I was a child. They were a society that looked after Newtons who needed their help and protection. But these Leeches were not Newtons; they were Shalimar, elf-like beings from another dimension, the Shalimar realm. So, did I tell Luthleadon all this information? Did I answer him truthfully? I did, for one; you shouldn't have secrets from a lover.*

23rd June 1967

We've been talking, my lover and I, about Heart *that was left in my care again. He helps me get through the pain and memories I still carry when I think about Heart because he knows about her or claims to. I'm not sure how he knows, and he hasn't told me everything yet, but he seems genuine with his words, so I'll take it as the truth, and we still have time for him to tell me more. Tonight, he told me Heart's mother was called Tilleryn, and her father was Prince. Luthleadon even told me* Heart *wasn't meant to live. Then he said I must name my unborn child after* Heart*, and I just laughed because having a child was the last thing on my mind.*

15th July 1967

Oh my god! I carry a child! Luthleadon's sweet, strange voice calls me, telling me his dear brother Lucian will soon visit us. He showed me a drawing of him. When I look at him, I'm struck by how utterly different he looks from his brother, Luthleadon. I can tell they have a strong bond because he speaks often of him, and I'm anxious to see how their reunion goes. I fear Lucian might not recognize Luthleadon as much as he's changed in the past months. I want to make Lucian's stay here comfortable, and I hope they have the chance to catch up and share stories. It's funny how the call of a family can tug at the heartstrings, no matter how different the brothers look.

19th October 1967

Lucian is here again, staying the night with us for a visit. Like his brother, Luthleadon, Lucian has pale skin and long, dark hair, but his eyes scare me. Ruby red, they seem like the devil himself. However, my sweet lover insists that Lucian is not such a thing and has a good heart. I haven't yet been able to agree, but I'm sure deep down he must have a kind soul. This visit could be a pleasant one; however, I am anxious at the same time. Ultimately, with more time and chances for bonding, I can agree with my lover and enjoy the visit with Lucian and his good heart.

20th December 1967

I can carry on no more. First, the husband of my younger days, with whom I had shared so much joy and love, died, leaving me alone and heartbroken. Then, I had to deal with the death of Heart*, a tragedy that affected me deeply. As if this wasn't enough, my young lover, whom I had felt with a connection I had rarely felt for someone before, deserted me, leaving me completely helpless. I feel like the broken pieces of a puzzle; my heart shattered into millions of fragments and spread across the universe. Nothing feels the same anymore, not even the most unconditional of love. My life has reached a standstill, and I don't know how to continue.*

20th April 1968

She is born. Such sweetness she does hold in her sparkling brown eyes. Even her hair matches the same as Heart*, but I know she shall never be her, so I shall call my child Amelia.*

10th July 1968

I've decided something that'll place me in a place that will probably burn my soul. My child Amelia shall go to a new home, back to where Heart *first came from, back to her people.*

"This is unbelievable!" replied Tim in a tone of surprise. "She replaced the dead child with her daughter!"

"It looks like it," said William, re-reading the last sentence to himself again.

"But why would she do such a thing?" Tim asked, his brows furrowing in confusion.

William sighed, setting the newspaper down on the table. "I'm not sure, Tim. Some people can be driven to extreme measures for various reasons; perhaps she couldn't bear the thought of losing her child and resorted to this desperate act."

Tim shook his head in disbelief. "But how did she manage to pull it off? I mean, wouldn't someone have noticed?"

"Perhaps she thought she could rectify the promise by sending one of her own instead."

"Where did she send her?"

William picked up the first paper. "It appears right here, into the shadows of the forest."

Tim furrowed his brow, trying to make sense of the situation. "But why would she send someone into the shadows of the forest?"

"I'm not entirely sure, but there must be something significant about those shadows. Maybe they hold a secret or a hidden passage only the writer knows about."

Curiosity piqued, Tim's eyes darted towards the window, where the dense forest loomed just beyond their reach at the bottom of William's garden. "Do you think we should go after her? Who knows what dangers lie ahead if she's ventured into those shadows?"

"Tim, this was hundreds of years ago; if anything, it would be skeletons we'd discover now!" William hesitated momentarily before saying, "But even if it were now, it's risky, Tim. We wouldn't even know what we'd be up against or what awaited us in there. But if we want to uncover why now, this time, we might have no other choice."

"Creepy," Tim moved closer. "Let me see more," William handed the paper over. Tim looked at the document. "I wonder if she did send her into the shadows."

"I don't know."

"I mean, what sort of world could exist in shadows? One of terror is all I can think of, but maybe—"

"Maybe there's more to it than just terror," William interrupted, his voice filled with curiosity. "Think about it, Tim. Shadows are always associated with darkness and fear, but what if there's something hidden within them? Something extraordinary that we've never even imagined?"

Tim furrowed his brow, contemplating William's words. "I suppose it's possible," he replied cautiously. "But how can we be sure? We're just two ordinary people caught up in this mysterious situation."

William nodded thoughtfully. "You're right, Tim. We may be ordinary, but sometimes extraordinary things happen to ordinary people. And if this document is any indication, we may hold the key to unravelling something that might change our view on the supernatural."

"And this other thing, a world of Shalons or whatever they're called; William, this is amazing. Do you realize how much the information in these papers is worth? I mean—I know someone who would pay dearly for these papers—"

"These papers are going nowhere." William interrupted, his voice filled with determination. "We can't sell these papers."

Tim looked at him, perplexed. "But think about it, William! We could be set for life with the wealth these papers could bring us. We wouldn't have to worry about anything ever again."

William shook his head, a solemn expression on his face. "It's not about personal gain, Tim—"

"But William, think of the press we'd get, the money; Jackson—"

"Jackson, your older brother?"

"Yes."

"He's in the army, isn't he?"

"Yes, he got promoted a few weeks ago; he's a colonel now; well, he's pretty good at finding things, places out; it's a new world we could explo—"

Tim's remaining words William didn't hear; he was reading another letter. William hadn't noticed Tim had slipped the paper away quickly and discreetly into his pocket.

"Well, it was a good idea, do you not think?" he heard Tim's following words. "Maybe we should go look in that forest for ourselves first. What do you think?"

William glanced up from his letter, catching the tail end of Tim's words. Confusion flickered across his face as he tried to piece together what he had missed. Something about a forest and a good idea? His curiosity piqued, and William's eyes darted towards Tim, who seemed unusually eager. As William pondered Tim's suggestion, doubts began to creep into his mind. The forest in question was notorious for its eerie reputation, shrouded in tales of mythical stories. It was the kind of place parents warned their children about, urging them to stay away. But Tim's enthusiasm was infectious, and a small part of William couldn't help but wonder if there might be some truth to the legends.

"Maybe we should go look in that forest for ourselves first," Tim repeated, his voice filled with anticipation. He leaned closer to William, lowering his tone conspiratorially. "You never know what we might find."

William hesitated, torn between scepticism and curiosity, then said, "Don't be silly. It's all fairy tales, make-believe. Besides, if it were true, don't you think someone would've said of it before now?"

"Maybe we should rip up more of these floorboards around this house, see if she's hidden anything else," Tim tapped the floor with his foot.

Willaim glanced up. "We're not ripping any more floorboards up."

"I'm only making a suggestion."

"If you want holes in floors, do it to your house."

"I don't have a house."

"Then move out of your mother's house," he moved away from the table. "You're a full-grown man still tied to your mother's apron strings."

"There's nothing wrong with living with your mother."

"I'm not saying it isn't, just stating that you're still living there."

"Well, maybe I have my reasons for living with my mother," he replied defensively. "It's not as simple as just moving out."

Willaim sighed. "Look, I'm just concerned about you. You're capable of so much more than this."

"I appreciate your concern, but it's not fair to judge my situation without understanding it," he said calmly. "Living with my mother has its benefits, both for her and me."

"Benefits? Like what?" William questioned sceptically.

"For starters, she makes great food," Tim followed William's footsteps across the open flooring. "And you can say fact away. At least my mother can cook, which is more than can be said of your home cooking."

"If you don't like my cooking, go elsewhere."

"You need a woman's touch to teach you how to cook. My mother could give you lessons. She makes a delicious steak and kidney pie."

William rolled his eyes at Tim's remark, unwilling to back down. "Well, maybe your mother's steak and kidney pie are good, but it doesn't mean I need a woman to teach me how to cook. I can handle my kitchen just fine."

Tim smirked, clearly enjoying the banter. "Oh really? Last time I checked your attempt at making spaghetti resembled a pile of mushy noodles. It wouldn't hurt to learn a thing or two from someone who knows what they're doing."

William stopped near the open floorboards again and faced him, crossing his arms defiantly. "That was just one time! Besides, cooking is about experimenting and finding your style. I don't need anyone else telling me how to do it."

Tim chuckled, then stopped in front of him. "All right, if you say so. But don't come crying to me when you serve another disastrous meal. Oh, that reminds me; Mothers invited you next Sunday for a roast lamb dinner with all the trimmings."

"Your mother invited me?" William asked, trying to hide the slight tremor in his voice. "I mean, I'd be honoured to come over for dinner, but—"

"My brother Jackson and my sister Mary will be—"

"Your sister Mary?"

"Well, actually, it was Mary's idea. Seems keen on you."

"She does, does she? Well, she's too young for my liking."

"She's only twenty, ten years younger than you! Besides, age is just a number," Tim chuckled. "And Mary has always been mature for her age. You might be surprised by how well you two get along."

William raised an eyebrow, contemplating Tim's words. He had known Mary for a year now, but he never really saw her in a romantic light; she was more like a friend he'd spend time going out with, drinking with. However, he couldn't deny the sudden curiosity that sparked within him, but he still replied, "It's thirteen years, actually, and I'm afraid that's too much."

"Well, if you say so," Tim's sight went to the open floor at their feet, "I still think we should get a few more floorboards up."

William sighed. "Look, I get it. We're desperate to find answers about the girl's disappearance, but tearing up the entire house isn't the solution. We need to think logically and consider other options."

Tim crossed his arms, a determined look on his face. "But what if there's something important hidden here? Something that could lead us to her?"

"Even if there is, destroying the house won't help us find it," William reasoned. "We should focus on gathering more information with what we have here in front of us."

Tim reluctantly nodded, realizing the validity of William's point. "You're right; we need a more strategic approach. But we've hit a dead end with all our efforts so far."

"I don't know," he watched Tim look down at the floor into the hole where the papers had come from. "What's the matter?"

"William, another bundle of papers is under your kitchen floorboards!" Tim was now on the floor, looking in the hole.

"Another bundle of papers!" William's eyebrows furrowed in confusion as Tim scrambled to retrieve the unexpected bundle of papers from the hole. Curiosity piqued, he joined Tim on the floor, examining the contents of the newly discovered bundle. As they unravelled the pieces, their eyes widened in astonishment. The documents contained more detailed information from a journal like before, and now William was excitedly exclaiming, "Oh my god! It's true! It's true!"

"What's true, William?"

"Everything," William exclaimed, his eyes gleaming with disbelief and exhilaration. "These documents confirm everything we needed to know, need to know!"

14th February 1986

Amelia sits with me now, but I'm afraid I'll have to cast her outside so I may veil these letters. If anyone finds them, they'll also find my Amelia, but you should see her now, the beauty she's become. She has her father's smile, charm, and even his walk, but this beauty shall be gone from my sight soon, for this sight of her is closing quickly.

18th June 1986

Well, I did it. I placed the papers well and truly hidden from prying eyes. I hope I've enough air to conceal this; explain all this worrying to Amelia before I leave this world. I'm sure she is suspicious of something because yesterday she asked me a question.

She asked why she couldn't walk into the woods at the bottom of our garden. Should I tell her? Should I tell her she'd enter a new realm and never return here? Oh no, I could do no such thing. I'll wait, wait until my dying breath to tell my child. Then, I will tell her the truth, just not all of it.

Chapter 6

Princess Amelia Orian

The sound of serenity filled the air at the beach. The full moon lit the night sky, casting its shimmery glow across the sand like a blanket. Flames danced in the night breeze, and two small fires burned on the beach. There was a calmness to it all; the heat from the fires was soothing and cozy. The waves, too, seemed to catch the rhythm of the night, steadily flowing in and out, their lapping sound a gentle reminder of the tranquil environment.

Three females sat around a tiny lit fire in this same area, the warmth of the fire making them feel at peace with the world. One of them, a blonde-haired woman, had a cup of hot cocoa in her hand. A contented smile spread across her face as she sipped the warm cocoa. Next to her sat another blonde-haired woman with a large bowl in her hand. In the bowl were crabs and seafood. She reached in, picked out a piece of crab meat, and handed it to the third woman, a dark-haired woman who eagerly bit into the juicy part of the crab. To the left of them sat another group around a lit fire, twelve guards from Volarie sent to protect the three females in a deep conversation. Each man wore crafted leather breastplate armour over a dark blue and green tunic with the colours and crest of Volarie of the prince's house emblazoned on the back.

"I don't know how many times you keep saying that," this was Amelia's voice. "But it's getting annoying now."

"I mean it," said Sarian. "Thank you for allowing it to happen."

"Stop it, or I'll tell them to cancel it!"

As the conversation continued, the excitement grew palpable. The impending vow wedding of Sarian and Andrin had been a long time coming. Sofia couldn't help but join in on the laughter as she imagined Amelia frantically cancelling all the preparations they had made so far. It would be a disaster, not to mention a waste of time and money. "Oh Valar, don't do that," laughed Sofia. "She's already ordered her dress and veil."

"I have; it's light brown and cream, and it's nearly ready—"

"I should hope so," laughed Amelia. "It's very soon."

Amelia's eyes sparkled with mischief as she joined in on the laughter. "Can you imagine the chaos if I did that?" she exclaimed, her voice filled with playful exaggeration. "All those hours Sarian spent choosing the perfect flowers, tasting countless cake samples, and now it would all go down the drain!"

Sofia nodded, still chuckling. "And don't forget about the music! She spent months searching for the perfect musicians, ones you've always dreamed of having at your wedding vows."

Sarian sighed dramatically, pretending to wipe away an imaginary tear. "Oh, my poor dream wedding," she said mock-sorrowfully. "It would be such a shame to let it go, but you know I wouldn't let that happen," she laughed out loud. "It's going to be so exciting," Sarian hugged Amelia. "And the forest, we couldn't have picked a better one to do it in."

"Okay, okay," again Amelia laughed. "Ease off with the cuddling." Sarian did. "So, is everything else in place yet?"

"Yes, we've got flowers, food, and music sorted. Just need to sort the drinks and marquee now."

"I know of someone who can provide the marquee."

"You do?" Sarian was looking at Sofia. "It has to be the right one, light brown and cream—"

"In the colours of the royal household, Froyen," sighed Sofia. "Yes, it's all you keep going on about, brown this, cream that—"

Amelia interrupted Sofia's rant, trying to diffuse the tension. "All right, let's not get carried away with the colours. You want everything to look elegant and sophisticated, right?"

Sarian huffed, crossing her arms. "But it's important! The Froyen family has a long-standing tradition of using these colours for special events. It symbolizes their heritage and prestige."

Sofia chimed in, trying to lighten the mood. "I understand Sarian. But let's remember that this wedding is about you and Andrin. You want it to reflect your personalities, too."

Amelia nodded in agreement. "Exactly! You should incorporate elements that represent both you and Andrin as well. Maybe you can find a way to blend the traditional Froyen colours with something more modern and unique."

"Hopefully, you've made her see sense now, Amelia," laughed Sofia, "Because I was thinking she'd want her drinks made in the same colour, too."

"I was thinking," said Sarian. "Porth, that's a nice shade of brown, isn't it? Oh, and how about Wearling? That's got a lovely shade—"

"See," again another laugh from Amelia. "Told you. Well, at least she's picked ones that aren't strong."

"For once, she's made a good choice," replied Sofia. "At least she won't have a drunken husband on her wedding night."

"No, that's not a good idea," said Sarian. "But I don't have to worry too much about that; he knows his limits."
"Wish I could say the same about Din," sighed Sofia. "Sometimes I despair with his drinking; I know he's still young and trying things out, but seriously, I must tell him so many times to slow down."
"He's just having fun," replied Sarian. "That's all. You remember when we were young; everything was so much fun back then—"
"We still have fun," said Amelia. "Just sensibly."
"Well, when Andrin and I have kin's," proclaimed Sarian. "I'm going to let them enjoy their youth and do what they want."
"Are you planning on having kin's soon," Sofia asked Sarian. "A bit early for that thought, isn't it?"
"Well, one day, yes, I will," she smiled at her. "But it's up to Andrin when he wants them too."
"Well," replied Amelia. "My four are more than enough, so no more for me, thanks."
"You're not?"
"No," laughed Amelia. "And if this conversation is going to lead where I think it is, like last night, then I'm going to say the—"
"It would be nice, though," she saw Sarian taking a sip of cocoa.
Amelia gave her a look of puzzlement, "To have another child?"
"Why do you always call them that, Amelia, child?" she asked Sofia, pulling a piece of crab meat from a bowl.
"I don't know."
"We say kin, call them kin," said Sofia.
"But why do you prefer to call them kin?" Amelia inquired, genuinely interested in understanding Sofia's perspective.
Sofia paused, carefully considering her response before she began to explain. "Well, calling them kin feels more personal and intimate," Sofia replied thoughtfully. "It signifies a deeper connection and sense of belonging. It's like acknowledging that we are all part of the same family, regardless of blood ties."
Amelia nodded slowly, absorbing Sofia's explanation. She had always admired how deeply connected Sofia seemed with others around her. It was as if she possessed an innate ability to forge meaningful relationships effortlessly. "I suppose I can see the appeal in that," Amelia admitted with a hint of admiration. "But for me, I call them by the name my dear departed Aunt taught me."
"Children?" asked Sarian.
"Yes."
"That's a funny name."
"It's not, now. Can we please get away from this subject?" Amelia pleaded, feeling a sudden unease creeping up within her. She didn't want to delve any further into the topic of names and relationships, as it brought back memories she preferred to keep buried.

"But it'd be nice to have another pair of small feet running around," said Sofia, "To hear a kin's small laughter again."

Amelia sighed. "Have you been talking to my husband?"

Sofia chuckled softly, her eyes twinkling with mischief. "Oh, you know how I am, always poking my nose where it doesn't belong," she replied playfully. "But, Amelia, can you blame me for wanting to see your family grow? You and your husband make wonderful parents."

Amelia's expression softened as she looked at her friend. She understood Sofia's genuine concern and affectionate nature. They had been friends for hundreds of years, sharing both laughter and tears along the way. Sofia was always there for her, offering support and guidance whenever needed. "I appreciate your kind words, Sofia," Amelia said sincerely. "But the truth is, having children is not something I'm thinking of right now," she suddenly laughed, "You're just as bad as my husband. He mentioned something like this before we went on this trip."

"What did he say?"

"To think about his question."

"Which was?"

"Another child." Amelia's heart sank as she recalled her husband's words. The idea of having another child had been a topic of discussion between them for quite some time now. But lately, Amelia had been overwhelmed with their current responsibilities, and the thought of adding another little one to the mix seemed daunting.

Sarian looked at Amelia sympathetically. "I can understand why you might be hesitant," she said softly. "Raising kin's is no easy task, and it requires a lot of time and energy, but you have maids that could assist you if you require more help?"

Sofia placed her now empty bowl onto the sand. "If I were you and had the chances you have, I'd be begging for another kin."

Amelia rolled her eyes and replied, "I've done my share of filling this world with children."

"Kin's you mean!" laughed Sarian and Sofia.

Amelia sighed and looked out at the vast ocean in front of them. "I understand where you're coming from, but having many children isn't for everyone."

"It would make his day," replied Sarian, not letting the subject go.

Amelia couldn't help but feel annoyed at Sarian's persistence. She had always admired her unwavering determination, but sometimes, it felt like she pushed her desires onto others. "I get that it would make Elensar's day, Sarian," Amelia said, her voice tinged with frustration. "But we shouldn't base our decisions solely on what would please someone else. It's important to prioritize our happiness and well-being too."

"Amelia, I understand where you're coming from," Sofia said, her voice filled with empathy. "But sometimes, making someone else happy can also bring us joy and fulfilment." Now, it felt like Sofia had joined whatever plan Sarian had devised to get Amelia's mind to change about having another child.

Amelia sighed, her frustration momentarily giving way to contemplation. "I don't want to deny Elensar the chance to have a child," she admitted reluctantly. "But I also worry about spreading ourselves too thin. We already have so much on our plates with things, especially Elensar and his royal duties and taking care of our other four children."

Sarian now piped in, her voice filled with understanding but prompting her to decide otherwise, "But Amelia, think about the joy a new kin could bring to your family," Sarian interjected gently. "Yes, you have a lot on your plates, but love has a way of multiplying rather than dividing. We all know Elensar is an incredible father," Sofia nodded in agreement, "And I have no doubt he will continue to be devoted to all of your kin."

"Exactly," Sofia's turn to speak up, her voice filled with conviction. "Adding other kin to your family doesn't mean you will have less love or attention for each of them. It can create a stronger sibling bond and bring more joy into your lives."

"We understand the concerns, Amelia." Sarian smiled, "It's natural to worry about how you will manage everything. But remember, you are not alone in this journey. Elensar has repeatedly proven to be a loving and supportive partner and father."

Amelia shook her head. "Elensar's put you up to this, hasn't he?"

"No," Sofia said rather quickly.

Sarian's reply was different. "He might have said something," then she gave an impression as if she shouldn't have said that.

Amelia narrowed her eyes, suspicion growing within her. Sarian's sudden change in demeanour only fuelled her curiosity further. She had always known Elensar to be mischievous and cunning, often roping Sarian and Sofia into his schemes. But what could he have possibly said to make Sofia react this way? "Come on, Sarian," Amelia pressed, her voice laced with determination. "I can tell when you're hiding something from me. Spill it."

Sarian hesitated momentarily, glancing around nervously, afraid someone might overhear their conversation. Finally, she let out a defeated sigh and leaned closer to Amelia. "All right," she whispered reluctantly. "Elensar did mention something about getting Sofia and me to change your mind at wanting another kin, but—"

"I knew it! That's why we've spent most of this retreat talking about it, isn't it." Sarian was sadly nodding; Sofia didn't reply. Instead, she held a look of pure calmness. "God, he'll do anything to get his way," her head shook.

"For Valar's sake, Amelia," begged Sarian, "Don't tell him, you know."

"Tell him; I'll kill him, even castra—" Sofia suddenly burst out laughing. Amelia looked over at her. "What's so funny?"

"Nothing," Sofia fell upon the sand.

"It's not anything when you're laughing like that."
"Oh, Amelia, we're pulling your leg."
"Have we?" asked a surprised Sarian as if she didn't get it.
"Yes, Sarian," Sofia rolled onto her side and winked, "Remember?"
Amelia raised an eyebrow, slightly confused by their responses. "Pulling my leg?" she asked, her curiosity piqued.
Sofia's laughter subsided as she sat up, brushing off the sand from her clothes. With a mischievous grin, she leaned closer to Amelia and whispered conspiratorially, "We've been planning a joke for you all day!"
Amelia's response was a livid one, "What!"
"Ah," Sarian was laughing; it didn't sound as genuine as Sofia's, "I got so wrapped up in it I was beginning to believe our lies."
Sofia nodded, unable to contain her excitement any longer. "We thought it would be hilarious to see your reaction to us asking again," she admitted, trying to suppress her laughter.
"You've been planning a joke on me? All day?" Amelia exclaimed, her voice filled with disbelief and annoyance. "About my husband wanting another child? Where is the joke in that!"
Sofia's laughter faded as she realized the gravity of the situation. She exchanged a worried glance with Sarian, realizing their well-intentioned prank had taken an unexpected turn. "No, Amelia, it wasn't meant to be a joke," Sofia said softly, her voice tinged with regret. "We didn't mean to upset you. It was just—A mistake."
Amelia's eyes narrowed, "A mistake? How could you possibly misunderstand something like that? You know how sensitive I am about having another child."
Sarian leaned forward, her expression apologetic. "Amelia, we never intended to hurt you. We thought it would be harmless fun, but we misjudged the situation. We're truly sorry."
Amelia crossed her arms and sighed heavily. "Sorry? It doesn't change that you both played with my emotions all day. It's not something to take lightly." Amelia turned to Sarian, who gave her an even angrier look. "I thought you were supposed to be one of my best friends."
"It's only done in the name of fun."
"How can you say it's fun when it upsets me? Friends are supposed to lift, not tear each other down."
"Fun is whatever you make it."
"No, it's not," Amelia repeated firmly, her voice tinged with frustration. "Fun should never come at the expense of someone's feelings or well-being. Friends should be a source of support and encouragement, not a catalyst for pain and—"
"If you two are going to argue," Sofia's voice interrupted them both. "I'm going to bed."
"We're not arguing," Sarian answered.

"You could've fooled me," now Sofia was standing up. "Don't you think we have better things to do?"

Amelia looked up at her. "Like what?"

"Like going to bed before dawn joins us?"

"Perhaps we should," voiced Sarian getting up.

"Mind you," Sofia sighed aloud. "How you expect me to sleep knowing we've got danger ahead of us soon?"

"Well, you know what they say," Sarian replied. "Even a little sleep can make fresh minds and bodies for the morning."

"I suppose you're right."

"I'm always right, Sofia," Sarian gave her a friendly slap across the back. "You just need reminding every so often." Her sight then went to Amelia, who sat by the fire. "I never meant to hurt you, Amelia," Sarian finally admitted, her voice filled with remorse. "I guess I didn't fully understand how my idea of fun affected you. I'm sorry."

"Don't worry about it," that was said with no emotion without looking at her, for Amelia's gaze had gone back to the fire in front of her.

"Amelia, are you okay?"

Amelia's gaze was watching orange and red flames dancing. Inside her mind, she remembered the night before she left to go on this trip. The same night, Elensar was strutting around the room, barely a stitch to cover himself while prearranging his dream visits to see her. Amelia couldn't help but feel nostalgia and frustration as she recalled that fateful night. Elensar, with his irresistible charm and enigmatic allure, had always managed to captivate her attention. She remembered how his mischievous eyes sparkled with anticipation as he spoke of the dreams he would weave when they were physically apart.

But now, sitting by the crackling fire on the beach, Amelia wondered if those promises were merely empty words. Elensar's dream visits had become scarce lately, leaving her feeling disconnected and longing for his presence. The flames mirrored the conflicting emotions swirling within her - the warmth of their shared memories contrasting with the cold reality of their current situation.

"She looks okay to me—" Sarian began, but her words were interrupted by Sofia.

"I think," her gaze fixed on Amelia, "She's preoccupied with thoughts." Sofia's brow furrowed deeper as she watched Amelia. Sofia couldn't help but feel frustrated by her apparent lack of awareness. It appears Amelia was utterly oblivious to the world around her, lost in her little bubble of thoughts.

Why does he always have to do that? Amelia was thinking to herself. *Strut around as if he's no self-consciousness of what he's showing. Oh, bugger! His prearranged visits!* She turned her gaze to Sarian and Sofia. "What's the date today?"

"23rd September, why?"

23rd! Oh god, that's tonight!

"Sofia, what's wrong with her?"

Oh my god! It's tonight. He's coming tonight!

"Sofia," Sarian shook Sofia's arm, "What's she thinking?"

"I think she's just overwhelmed," Sofia whispered. "Tonight, is a big night for her."

Sarian furrowed her brow, confusion evident on her face. "What do you mean? Who is coming tonight?"

"I don't think you want to know, Sarian," laughed Sofia.

"Go on; you can read her mind, so tell me what she's thinking."

Sofia glanced at Sarian, gauging her reaction before deciding how much to reveal. "Elensar is coming to visit her in her dreams, I think—"

"What did you say?" Amelia had asked that softly, looking up at them but not registering their words. Her mind was preoccupied with a whirlwind of thoughts and emotions, making it difficult to focus on the conversation.

"Nothing," replied Sofia, "Just saying it's getting late."

"Late?" Amelia's gaze had returned to looking into the flames, flames that blew against the wind as if it was an emotion that seemed more powerful than the wind itself—flickering and dancing with a beauty that seemed to captivate Amelia, who stared mesmerizingly.

"Look at that!" Sarian had said this unexpectedly.

"At what?" Amelia tore her eyes away from the mesmerizing flames and turned to Sarian, a puzzled expression on her face. She followed her gaze back to the fire, trying to understand what had caught her attention. "What about them?"

"The flames are blowing towards the wind!"

Sofia placed her finger in her mouth, pulled it out, and checked the coldness of the wind on it. "Okay, that's weird."

"What's making it do that?" Sarian furrowed her brows, perplexed by the unfamiliar spectacle. The wind was blowing fiercely, yet the flames seemed to defy its direction. She couldn't wrap her head around it. Curiosity getting the better of her, Sarian decided to investigate further. With cautious steps, she approached the flickering flames that danced in defiance of the wind's force. "It looks like someone's blowing it that way on purpose." As she drew closer, a tingling sensation enveloped her senses, like an invisible energy pulsing through the air.

"Don't be daft," Amelia said while standing, "It's the wind play."

"Wind can't trick flames into bending towards it," Sofia replied in a matter of fact-like tone.

"Well, whatever it is," said Amelia, "I wouldn't worry about it."

"You're right," Sarian said, standing back up. "It's not something to worry about, but intriguing. I mean, have you ever seen flames behave like that before?"

Amelia shook her head, her eyes fixed on the dancing flames. "No, never. It's almost as if the wind has a mind peculiarly guiding the fire."

Sofia joined them, her gaze focused on the mesmerizing sight. "Indeed," she agreed. "It's as if there's some unseen force at play here, manipulating the elements, but there could be an easy explanation for it; It could be a wind funnel."

"A wind funnel?" Sarian asked with a frown on her brow. "I've seen one before, but it never did that."

"Maybe it's because we're near the shoreline?" Amelia yawned. "More open space."

Sarian's frown deepened as she considered Amelia's suggestion. "But we've been near the shoreline countless times, and it never caused this distraction before," she replied with slight concern.

Amelia stretched her arms lazily and glanced out at the sea. "True, but maybe there's something different about today. Weather patterns can be unpredictable, you know."

"Perhaps it's not just the wind," Sarian mused aloud. "There could be some other force at play here."

Amelia raised an eyebrow curiously. "What do you mean? Like some supernatural phenomenon?"

"There could be," Sarian sounded convinced it was, "I mean, not everything in the world we live in is—"

Amelia laughed, "Seriously, my friend, you're over-tired; it has been a long day."

"I guess you're right," Sarian replied with a yawn. "It's been non-stop since morning, and my brain feels like it's running on fumes."

Amelia chuckled, her eyes crinkling at the corners. "Well, it's no wonder you're starting to see things that aren't there. Remember when you thought that squirrel was a miniature cow?"

Sarian blushed, recalling the embarrassing incident from last night. "Hey, in my defence, it was dark, and I only caught a glimpse of it out of the corner of my eye!"

Amelia playfully nudged her with her elbow. "Sure, sure. Remember to keep your imagination in check before you start seeing dragons flying across the sky." They both laughed heartily at the absurdity of the image. The exhaustion seemed to fade away momentarily as their laughter filled the air. Amelia stepped away from the fire. "Now, if you don't mind, I'm going to hit the sack," she turned to Sofia and hugged her. Next, she went to Sarian.

"Huggy time," Sarian squealed, hugging her tightly, "Don't you just love her smallness—"

"Yeah, it's like cuddling a dwarf," laughed Sofia.

"I am no such thing," Amelia angrily protested, hearing those words about her petite height, then pushed Sarian away in a friendly play manner.

"No, you're not," again Sofia's voice talking, "But your height suggests otherwise."

"Jesus Christ, woman," Amelia laughed while walking away from them both, "Leave my height out of it! Now, goodnight, you two lunatics."

"Well, that's nice, isn't it?" Sarian muttered sarcastically as she watched Amelia's retreating figure. She exchanged an exasperated glance with Sofia, who was still chuckling at the height joke.

Sofia playfully nudged Sarian, saying, "Come on, don't be such a grump. You know Amelia can handle herself."

"Yes, I can," Amelia called back in a laughing tone, "Now, goodnight, Sarian, goodnight—"

"Goodnight, sleep well," Sofia laughed and turned around to see the flames were now twisting towards the direction Amelia had left; she laughed, "Okay, that's odd!"

"What is," asked Sarian, still watching Amelia's departure across the sand away from them both.

Sofia turned to face Sarian, her eyebrows furrowing in confusion. "The flames," she replied, pointing towards the twisting fire. "They seem to be following her, Amelia."

Sarian's eyes widened as she followed Sofia's gaze. The flames danced and flickered, their orange glow illuminating the night sky. It was peculiar that they were moving in the same direction as Amelia's departure.

"But how is that even possible?" Sarian wondered aloud, her voice filled with curiosity and concern.

Sofia shrugged, a bemused smile playing on her lips. "I have no idea," she admitted. "But it's strange." They both stood there momentarily, silently observing the mesmerizing sight before them. The flames continued to twist and turn, almost as if they were alive, chasing after Amelia's retreating figure. "This is spooky, Sarian. You could be right; it's some supernatural phenomenon.

"I think, as Amelia said earlier," Sarian replied. "We're both exhausted, seeing things that aren't there."

"Perhaps," Sofia's vision went to see Amelia reaching the edge of the beach, walking toward the trees with guards following closely behind, "I guess so," Sofia's voice trailed off as she watched Amelia disappear into the dense foliage.

Amelia had reached a clearing within a dense wood. Within this small clearing stood five fabric tents: purple, two blue, and two yellow. The blue and yellow tents were quite plain, whereas the purple one was larger, with intricate gold trimmings, with Volarie's crown crest suspended over the doors. Amelia's footsteps went toward the purple tent, seeing a guard come to walk by her side in the same direction. "Ah, Gorthlian, did you place candles in there?"

"Yes, my lady," he drew back the cloth door for her to slip into the tent, "Do you wish me to light them now?"

"Please," she slipped into the tent, and the guard followed, "I can't see to walk, let alone see where to sleep," he shifted from her side.

Amelia stepped further into the tent, her eyes adjusting to the dimly lit interior. The guard swiftly moved to a small table at the corner of the tent, where a cluster of candles stood ready for illumination. He ignited each candle with a flick, casting a warm glow that danced across the fabric walls.

Amelia's gaze fell upon an intricately designed bed adorned with plush pillows and luxurious silk sheets as the light grew brighter. It was fit for a Queen, or in this case, a princess. She moved the inner netting to the side and slipped inside, "Thank you, Gorthlian," she voiced as he retreated from the inner tent.

Gorthlian had been a castle guard for years, faithfully protecting the royal family and their esteemed guests. He had always admired Princess Amelia from afar, captivated by her grace and kindness. But it was an unspoken love hidden deep within his heart. He slipped to one of the tent corners, picked up a jug, and poured water into a large bowl on a small table. The next thing he added was a small bottle of red liquid, only two capfuls of it. He moved away, headed for the main tent entrance; as he did, his sight fixed for a moment, he saw the silhouette of his future Queen, Princess Amelia, undressing inside the netting. It made him smile, shake his head, and slip out of the tent. Outside, Gorthlian silently grasped a tent pole. His stomach hurt, his body doubled over as if he were about to be sick, and his mouth opened. A mist spewed out; a swirling grey haze coiled toward the tent entrance.

Inside the tent, inside the netting, Amelia's last garment fell to the floor; her head rose, and she called aloud, "Gorthlian, are you there still?" She'd heard the tent door flap as if someone had just slipped through, whispering words she couldn't hear. "Gorthlian, is that you!" No reply: she called. "Gorthlian, are you there?" She shuddered, goosebumps appearing. *God, it's cold!* She shook her head, moved away from the bed, picked up a towel, and wrapped it around her.

She walked to the inner tent, pushed aside the netting, and peeped into the outer tent. *He must have gone.* Before slipping through the inner tent's net and into the peaceful solitude of her private sanctuary, she glanced around one last time and then made a beeline for the washing bowl. *I'm going crazy; nobody here, just you and my shadows.* Amelia shook her head and proceeded to wash. *That's right, Amelia, talk to the shadows,* she laughed. *Great, I'm talking to myself!* Amelia put the flannel onto her face and proceeded to finish washing quickly.

Amelia's next steps were running footsteps toward the bed. A sense of relief washed over her as she dived onto the bed. The softness of the silk sheets against her skin provided a comforting embrace, soothing away the weariness that had settled deep within her bones. With closed eyes, she let out a contented sigh, brown eyes starting to close for sleep.

Near the end of her bed, unseen to her sight, a swirling grey mist slowly transformed into a tall blonde-haired male figure that began walking towards her when fully formed. As the figure approached Amelia, warmth and tranquillity filled the room. With each step, the figure's energy seemed to intertwine with Amelia's dreamscape, bridging the gap between reality and imagination. The top sheet covering Amelia's now sleeping figure was peeled away by a masculine pale hand, leaving her naked to his sight. He crawled slowly upon the bed, over her naked flesh, leaving a trail of delicate kisses in his wake. With his piercing gaze and gentle touch, the mysterious figure continued to explore every inch of her exposed skin. His lips danced across her collarbone, leaving a trail of warmth that sent shivers down her spine. Each kiss was filled with an intoxicating mix of tenderness and desire, awakening a dormant passion within Amelia's sleeping form. Time seemed to stand still as he traced his fingertips along the curves of her body, memorizing every contour and dip. The sudden parting of her legs revealed a vulnerability that only fueled his longing. Amelia's body responded eagerly as his fingertips continued exploring that area, arching towards his touch.

Amelia stirred slightly in her slumber. She felt a surge of anticipation and a hint of fear inside her dream world as the figure's presence outside her dreams slipped his naked body between her open thighs. The intertwining energy seemed to envelop her, blurring the lines between what was real and what was imagined. The figure's features became more defined, revealing piercing eyes that belonged to her husband, Elensar, eyes that held secrets from centuries past. His commanding touch ignited a fire within Amelia. She surrendered completely to the dreamlike encounter as he entered first slowly, then with the usual hunger he would always release until the early hours of the next day.

Chapter 7

Awake To See Treelun

"Amelia, it's nearly morning; the birds are calling, so come on, wake up, you sleepy head," Sarian called to her from the tent entrance. "Sofia needs waking."

"I know," she stretched, waking every muscle up while she did it. "Just give me a minute; I ache and hurt so much."

"No, no minutes to spare. Get your backside out here now."

Amelia grunted and finally managed to drag herself out of bed, her whole body protesting every movement. She half stumbled towards a chest full of clothes, her eyes still heavy with sleep.

Sarian stood by the tent door, tapping her foot impatiently. "Come on, Amelia! We're already running late," Sarian urged, frustration evident in her voice.

Amelia sighed and rummaged through her clothes, trying to find something suitable. Her mind was still foggy from sleep, making it difficult to make any decisions. Finally settling on an outfit, she dressed quickly and joined Sarian by the door.

Twenty minutes later, she and Sarian stood outside Sofia's tent, giggling like small school children. Sarian poked her head through the tent door. "Get up, you lazy thing."

Amelia joined in, playfully nudging Sofia's side with her foot. "Yes, come on, sleepyhead! We have an exciting day ahead," Amelia called out, trying to rouse Sofia from her slumber.

"I'm not getting up yet," Sofia replied with a mumbling sound. "Go back to bed; let me sleep longer."

Sarian rolled her eyes, a mischievous grin forming on her face, and then she whispered, "Oh, but you're missing out on something incredible outside."

Sofia groaned in response, pulling the blanket tighter around herself. "I highly doubt that," her voice muffled by the fabric.

"If you don't get your backside out of there, we'll come in."

"Leave me alone."

Sarian chuckled softly, her eyes glinting with mischief, her voice dripping with playful persuasion. "Come on, Sofia. You know you can't resist an adventure. There's a whole world waiting for us out there."

Sofia peeked out from under the blanket, her eyebrows furrowing in scepticism. "I've had enough adventures for one lifetime," she grumbled, her voice still muffled by the fabric. "I just want some peace."

Sarian's head withdrew from the tent and turned with a wicked smile toward Amelia. "Shall we?" she nodded to the tent.

"Yes."

With that, Amelia and Sarian exchanged mischievous glances before bursting into laughter. They slowly opened the tent door more, trying to contain their excitement. Then they darted in, ready to pounce onto Sofia's bed. The next minute, their two figures crashed into the tent, bundled onto Sofia, trying to tickle her into a complete state of awareness. Sofia's eyes flew open, startled by the sudden intrusion and the onslaught of tickles. She let out a mixture of laughter and protests, squirming beneath the weight of her mischievous friends. The tent shook with their infectious giggles, echoing through the stillness of the day. Amelia and Sarian finally relented, releasing Sofia from their ticklish assault.

Sofia playfully scolded them, gasping for breath, trying to catch her laughter. "You two are relentless; what's the matter with you?"

Amelia flashed a mischievous grin, her eyes sparkling with excitement. "We couldn't resist giving you a proper wake-up call on this adventure-filled day!"

"Exactly!" Sarian chimed in, her voice filled with enthusiasm, "We have so many exciting plans ahead, and we wanted to ensure you were wide awake and ready to conquer them all."

Sofia couldn't help but smile at their infectious energy. "All right, all right, I give in," laughed Sofia. "I'll get up." They both removed themselves and sat on the bed, laughing. "You two are impossible," sighed Sofia. "I don't know why you find Treelun so charming; he's only got a bunch of boring flowers attached to his trunk."

"No, I think how the sun and moon would hit the petals would be beautiful," added Sarian.

Sarian knew there was much more to Treelun than what Sofia pointed out. For one, people said that the trees in that forest had their form of communication. Rumour has it that some could even move from place to place on their own accord. It was a bit difficult to believe, but Sarian had seen it with her own eyes, and as far as she was concerned, that was all the proof she needed. But try as she might, Sarian couldn't seem to get Sofia to look beyond the aesthetics of Treelun and realize his true beauty.

Sarian sighed again. "You, Sofia, are the one who is impossible," she said in an exasperated voice, shaking her head. 'I don't know why you two think Treelun is so frightening. He has so much more to offer than that. I've seen something similar to him with my own eyes." Sarian looked at her friends, hoping to drive the point home. "Are you two going to pass up the chance to explore these unique abilities? Think of all the possibilities!"

"Look, I never said I wasn't going; I just said it's dangerous," said Sofia, tutting at her. "And what about the River of Death? That's dangerous, too?"

"We'll have the guards with us," answered Amelia.

"Ah, Sofia," smiled Sarian. "Where's your sense of adventure."

"It's not where yours is."

"Come on; it's only a little bit of fun. Besides, how often do we have an adventure for ourselves?"

"Not very often by what you say, but if this is what you want, so be it. Remember, if it all goes wrong tomorrow, I'm not the one your family will come to."

"Nothing will go wrong; now let's get packing."

Three hours later, the trio excitedly entered a drinking house in a small village called Smiltern, instantly soaking in its warm and inviting atmosphere. The crackling fire, enticing aromas, and casual conversation set the scene for a relaxing stay. Amelia and Sofia led the way in the main room, studying the menu carefully, while Sarian kept to the shadows and observed the locals closely. After selecting a few drinks and snacks, the guards joined them. For roughly an hour, the group of nine enjoyed a pleasant interlude in the drinking house. From time to time, Amelia would make light conversation and chat with local community members. After a while, she would turn the conversation to the outside world, questioning the locals on the roads and other villages they had recently visited, and then she turned her attention back to her friends.

"We can't stay long." Sarian slipped along a long wooden bench with three drink mugs in her hand, "The sun's going to be up soon."

"We'll only have one more drink," said Amelia, helping herself to a handful of figs. "Then we'll go again," she saw Sarian set a mug on the table before her.

"That's right, fatten yourself!" said Sofia, "Treelun will love that!"

Amelia chuckled, popping a fig into her mouth. "Oh please, Sofia. Treelun loves me just the way I am," she replied with a mischievous glint in her eyes.

Sofia raised an eyebrow, playfully nudging Amelia's arm. "Well, who wouldn't? You're beautiful inside and out," she said sincerely. "But you know how much he adores eating flesh."

Amelia grinned, savouring the sweet taste of the figs as she continued to munch on them.

"I can't believe we're doing this," Sarian got a handful of figs for herself. "That we're going to see Treelun."

"Figs," Amelia's hand dropped to her side, secretly placed the third fig into her pocket, "Are not fattening Sofia."

"So why are you hiding that one away, Amelia?"

"None of your business!"

"Did you hear what I said? I said I couldn't believe—"

"We heard," Sofia interrupted, shaking her head. "You can't believe you're going to see Treelun."

"I said we'll see him," answered Sarian. "But I'll let you off."

"I'd prefer you let me off seeing him altogether," said Sofia.

"But just think," uttered Sarian, getting excited, "When we get back to Volarie, you can tell your Din that you've seen one of the oldest tree eaters in the world!"

"That's if we come out alive," said Amelia, trying to sound all suspicious and concerned, "All those evil seeing eyes, noises with no name; I haven't mentioned the darkness yet."

"And if Treelun's sprouted its young in the forest it lives in," laughed Sarian. "We've got no hope at all, Amelia."

"No, none at all," Amelia laughed that.

"Stop it," Sofia bashed her half-filled mug with beer on the table. "Your evil, both of you and you, Amelia; you don't even like the darkness, so why would you want to go into that stupid forest!"

"Sofia," Amelia apologized, "I'm sorry, really I am."

"Do you think we'd go," said Sarian, "If it were dangerous?"

"I hate it when you two wind me up," Sofia's anger simmered as she glared at her friends, Amelia and Sarian.

Amelia's eyes softened with remorse as she reached out to touch Sofia's hand gently. "We promise," she smiled at her, "We won't do it again."

"Yes, with all my heart," Sarian crossed her heart with a hand, "No more teasing."

Sofia pulled her hand away; her expression managed a weak smile. "If you've given me your word, I'll believe you both, but anymore, that's it. I'm going home and say what you both did."

"You wouldn't dare!"

"Don't dare me, Amelia, because I will," said Sofia with a straight face. Then Sofia erupted into a laugh that sounded wicked.

"That's an evil joke you just played," sighed Sarian, watching Sofia's laughter fill the room, her eyes sparkling with mischief. "Plain nasty, that is."

"Got you both worried there for a minute, didn't it?"

"And how much, you don't know." Amelia was up from the table, walking away. "Just don't do that again, please."

"Why?" Sofia followed in her footsteps. "I thought it was quite entertaining," Sofia continued, a mischievous glint still in her eyes. "Seeing the two of you squirm like that was priceless."

Sarian shook her head, clearly not amused. "It's not funny, Sofia. You know how easily Amelia gets worried."

Amelia turned around, her expression a mix of frustration and concern. "Exactly! I don't need unnecessary stress regarding my husband, especially from my friends."

"I thought you were in charge of your relationship with Elensar," said Sofia, still following.

"I never said I was." Amelia's voice quivered with a hint of vulnerability as she continued, "I mean, yes, I love Elensar, and we have a strong bond, but that doesn't mean I have complete control over everything that happens between us."

"Ah, I get it now, Amelia!" said Sarian, laughing.

"Get what?" Amelia's brow furrowed in confusion as she tried to make sense of Sarian's words.

"I always thought you were keeping away from us when we returned home. Now I find out it was Elensar's doing."

"Elensar? Keeping away? What are you on about, woman?" said Sofia with a frown of confusion.

"Amelia's disappearance for a few days," Sarian turned, looked at Sofia, and laughed, "You know when we get back home after these retreats."

"Woman, you drive me to—"

Sarian stopped her remaining words, "I bet he locks her up!"

"What!" said a shocked Sofia. Sofia's eyes widened in disbelief as she processed Sarian's words. She had always known Elensar to be possessive and controlling, but to lock Amelia up sounded a bit too far out there.

"I bet he hides that key well," said Sarian, taking the suggestion further, "That's why we don't see her for days, isn't it?"

"What!" As Sarian's words sank in, Sofia couldn't help but recall when Amelia mysteriously disappeared for days. Elensar always had an excuse ready, claiming that Amelia needed time alone or was busy with work.

"What does he do, Amelia?" Sarian looked at her, "Make you submit to his every whim?"

Amelia shook her head and laughed at her, "Sarian!" She looked down at her hands, fidgeting with her fingers, "I'm not going into anything with you!" Inside her head, she secretly giggled at a vision explaining her disappearance. Food would be laid out inside her bedroom, enough to sustain Elensar and her for days so they didn't have to leave the room, and why? It was, as Elensar informed her after the first time it happened, that this was to be a relink time. To her, it felt like an endless love-making session throughout the night and day.

"Then it must be true!" laughed Sarian, "You wait till I see him, the filthy scandal keeping you locked up like that!"

"Sarian, don't be so absurd!" Sofia slapped her on the back, "You've got a filthy mind that makes far too many untrue tales!"

"Stop with all this nonsense!" Amelia quickly dashed for the door, "Nosy parkers, that's what you two are!"

"You can talk!" Sofia and Sarian replied in sync, coming up after her, "You're the nosiest parker of all!"

And that was it; the group returned to the village's centralized well, where the horses waited patiently. Once everyone was mounted and ready to continue their journey, they took their leave of Smiltern and made their way in the direction Treelun lived in. As they rode through the countryside, the group marvelled at the picturesque landscapes that unfolded before them. Rolling hills adorned with vibrant wildflowers stretched as far as the eye could see while a gentle breeze whispered through the tall grasses.

As they approached the outskirts of Entree Lea's place, a sense of tranquillity washed over them. The surroundings transformed into a serene forest, with towering trees that seemed to touch the sky. Sunlight filtered through the dense canopy above, casting enchanting patterns on the forest floor. As they ventured deeper into the forest, enchantment enveloped them. Shafts of sunlight pierced through the dense canopy above, casting ethereal beams that danced upon the forest floor. The air was thick with an earthy scent, mingling with the sweet fragrance of wildflowers that bloomed along their path. Every step they took seemed to echo with whispers from unseen creatures, as if the forest held secrets waiting for someone to discover. Ancient trees stood tall and proud, their gnarled branches reaching out like skeletal fingers, beckoning them further into the heart of Entrée Lea.

When they finally dismounted their horses, the castle guards spent the next hour pitching tents in the forest. The guards worked swiftly; their years of training were evident in every precise action, each tent strategically placed to form a protective circle around a central clearing where a crackling fire would soon be ablaze. The forest's natural beauty embraced their presence as if offering protection and solace. Once the tents were anchored, they began efficiently unloading supplies from their saddlebags. While this had gone on, Amelia, Sarian, and Sofia walked to the River of Death with a spare guard.

"It doesn't look frightening," Sofia gazed into the pitch-black water. "More calming than scary, don't you think?"

"Looks can be deceiving. Watch this." Amelia's hand went to her pocket, pulled a fig, and dropped it into the water.

As the three friends stood by the River of Death, they couldn't help but feel a sense of unease. Despite its tranquil appearance, the water held an air of mystery that sent shivers down their spines. Sofia's initial perception of calmness began to waver as Amelia's demonstration unfolded. The fig disappeared into the river's depths, swallowed by the darkness. The silence was almost eerie as if the river held its breath in anticipation. Then, suddenly, a low rumbling sound emerged from beneath the surface. Bubbles rose to the top, creating a mesmerizing pattern that danced upon the water.

Sarian's eyes widened with curiosity as she leaned closer to get a better look. "What do you think is causing that?" she asked, her voice filled with wonder. She stepped closer to the riverbank edge. "Is there some sort of fish in there causing that?"

"Fish!" Amelia pulled Sarian back. "There's no fish in there."

Sofia asked, "What is it then?"

"Elensar told me it's something in the water, well not in it, it's part of it. It eats anything that falls into it."

"That's disgusting," Sarian shuddered.

"I think we should be leaving soon," a guard voiced concern while looking at the forest's horizon.

"He's right; otherwise, by the time we get there, Treelun will be awake, and you don't want to be around when it happens."

"Great, now another thing to worry about," sighed Sofia. "Can't we just have a normal retreat?"

"You wanted to come," said Sarian. "Besides, this is exciting."

Sofia rolled her eyes at Sarian's response. "Exciting? More like terrifying," she muttered under her breath. The thought of being caught in the wake of Treelun's awakening sent shivers down her spine. She had heard countless stories about the ancient forest guardian and its wrath; none were comforting.

As the group prepared to leave, Sofia couldn't help but glance back at the towering trees surrounding them. The forest seemed to be alive, whispering secrets that only it knew. It was beautiful yet eerie, enchanting yet dangerous. The guard's concern echoed in Sofia's mind as they went through the dense foliage. Every rustle of leaves or crackling branch made her heart skip a beat. She couldn't shake off the feeling they were being watched, unseen eyes following their every move. Sofia glanced at Sarian, who seemed completely unfazed by their surroundings. They crossed a bridge supported by dozens of long wooden poles that sank into the River Of Death's floor ten minutes later.

As they reached the middle section, a section arched more upwards than the rest, Sarian whispered into Amelia's ear, "Just as well we didn't bring the horses."

"Why?" Amelia asked, keeping a firm hold on the thick twisted rope that stretched from one end of the bridge to the other.

"Listen to it groaning."

"I can't hear anything."

"Well, you wouldn't. You haven't got the same hearing as me."

"If you did," Sofia piped in. "You'd have the sense to stop this silly trip instead of making us all do it. Oh, Valar! Just listen."

"Listen to what?" Amelia asked, her curiosity piqued as she strained her ears to catch any unusual sounds. The river's rushing was loud, but she could hear a faint creaking noise from the bridge. Amelia's grip on the rope tightened as she glanced nervously at the poles sinking into the river's floor. "Should we turn back?" Amelia asked, contemplating retracing their steps and finding an alternative route.

Sofia shook her head slightly, her eyes fixed on the path ahead. "No, we have come too far to turn back now," she said firmly.

They listened intently as the planks beneath their feet creaked and groaned a faint warning. Their hearts beat a little faster out of fear, as if just one wrong step would cause the bridge to collapse. Fortunately, the adventurers made it to the other side in one piece.

As they walked further on, Sofia couldn't help but notice Amelia's eyes sparkling with curiosity and a slight fear. "Can you believe we're here?" Amelia whispered, "This forest is said to hold ancient secrets and hidden treasures."

Sofia nodded, her heart pounding with slight fear. "I've heard tales of mythical creatures dwelling within these woods," she replied in hushed tones. "Legends speak of magical beings who possess extraordinary powers and wisdom beyond imagination."

"I know it sounds all great and that," Amelia gripped Sofia's hand, "But this darkness surrounding us now, it's quite frightening."

"You're not alone, Amelia," Sofia smiled down at her, "We're all here too, and you have that," she gently grasped Amelia's other hand, pulled up the sleeve, and revealed a thin bracelet made of gold, with amethyst, amazonian, and moonstone jewels. "You have that as protection, too."

"This? It's not a magical bracelet, Sofia," Amelia looked down at her bracelet. It made her smile thinking back to the time Elensar had given it to her with words saying, '*As real as I can be with you when we're apart.*' Amelia laughed at those words, not fully understanding what they meant until he said they'd never be apart if she wore this around her wrist. *Such a true romantic he is.*

"I thought it was," Sofia released Amelia's wrist, "I overheard Elensar say something to Andrin just before we left to go on this trip," Sofia continued, her voice filled with excitement. "He told him this bracelet has special powers, like it can connect two souls even when they are physically apart, and that Andrin should get one for Sarian, too." Sofia saw Amelia's eyes widen in surprise as if she had never heard Elensar mention anything about the bracelet's magical properties. "Or maybe he hasn't told you the real secret of it?"

Still recovering from her surprise, Amelia composed herself and asked Sofia, "What do you mean? What secret are you talking about?"

Sofia smirked mischievously before leaning in closer, her voice barely above a whisper. "Well, rumour has it that the bracelet not only connects souls but also possesses the ability to appear right in front of you, and I can bet you he's probably hiding right near us now somewhere."

"Don't be daft," the idea of a mystical bracelet with such extraordinary powers seemed far-fetched, yet an undeniable curiosity stirred within Amelia. "It's just a bracelet."

"No, you wait and see; he'll jump out on us, scare us to death," Sofia looked around herself, "Remember, unlike many, I know what he's like. He always played the teaser for as long as I can remember, even with me."

Amelia chuckled softly at Sofia's apprehension. "Oh, Sofia, you always let your imagination run wild," she said teasingly. "Elensar is not some sorcerer who will jump out at us from behind the trees. He's just a regular guy with a knack for surprises," she pulled her sleeve down, covering the bracelet. "Anyway, Elensar promised he'd stay in Volarie."

"Yes," Sarian chipped in, "Being all miserable and such. Yet I think it's cute that he's like that. Like a lovesick puppy."

Sofia frowned. "Where on earth have you heard that saying, Lovesick Puppy?"

"From Amelia —"

"She heard me saying that phrase a few days ago," replied Amelia, "When we befriended that stray dog."

Sofia's frown deepened as she tried to recall the incident Amelia was referring to. "Wait, you mean that scruffy little mutt we found?" she asked, her curiosity piqued.

Amelia nodded enthusiastically. "Yes, exactly! Remember how he followed us around, wagging his tail and looking at us with those big, sad eyes? He was so lovesick for attention and affection."

"He was also sad when Amelia wouldn't let him sleep with us," said Sarian.

"And you, Amelia, made him run away," Sofia half laughed. "Now, that wasn't very nice, was it? That poor dog is probably out there somewhere, all lovesick and alone," Sofia finished her sentence with a hint of sadness.

Amelia's face turned slightly red as she realized the consequences of her actions. "I didn't mean for him to run away," she admitted sheepishly. "I just thought it would be better for him to find his own place, you know? A place where he could truly belong."

Sarian nodded in understanding. "I get what you mean, Amelia. But sometimes, we must consider the feelings of others, even if they are animals. That dog had found comfort and companionship with us, and suddenly being rejected must have been hard for him."

Sofia sighed downheartedly. "I guess we should have thought about that before letting him get attached to us."

A castle guard suddenly stopped their words with his own. "My ladies, he is very near now, so we need full attention, please, unless you want to be his next meal."

Sofia, Sarian, and Amelia glanced behind themselves to the guard who had just spoken; he was pointing ahead.

"The famous Treelun is just around this corner."

Sarian's face cracked a smile. Amelia showed a slight look of worry. Sofia looked petrified.

"We must proceed with caution," the guard continued, his voice filled with urgency.

Sarian, always the brave one, stepped forward and spoke with determination. "Ah, stop it. We have faced countless dangers together, and this will be no different."

The castle guard shook his head. "Very well, but remember, Treelun is cunning and unpredictable."

Treelun has a long and distinguished history in the area. For centuries, he had lived in a quiet wooded grove, towering over the landscape with his massive size. Many generations of locals who believed he had special powers even worshipped him. With his flower-baring branches, he was considered a protector of the woods and its creatures. But to those who knew better, Treelun was a force to be reckoned with and one to be feared. He watched quietly and didn't make a sound, but with one shake of his trunk, his enemies would meet their fate amidst a shower of his potent and deadly death flowers. The victim would be immediately paralyzed and slowly suffocated to death, leaving behind a twisted husk of their former body. Those who found themselves in Treelun's forest were wise to remember the stories and not disturb this slumbering giant. Those who did were sure to hear the shaking of his trunk, which was a sign for them to run and never look back.

"Oh, Valar!" Sarian tilted her head up. "Look at him. He's beautiful!" Sarian stood in awe, her eyes fixed on the majestic sight before her. Treelun, the ancient forest giant, towered above them, his massive trunk reaching the heavens. The sunlight filtered through his branches, casting a mesmerizing pattern of shadows on the forest floor.

"Look at the size of his flowers!" Sofia's voice was filled with wonder but also fear.

"Don't get too close," Amelia whispered to them both.

"He looks so harmless, though," Sarian stepped closer. "Perhaps they said the tales of him being a monstrous creature were because the people of Entree Lea's Forest didn't want anyone seeing him."

"What are you on about?"

"I mean the people here in this forest."

"I didn't know any did," said Sofia. "I thought no one lived here apart from Treelun and the other trees."

"They've been here for thousands of years," replied a guard next to them, "Living in the heart of this forest, we call them the *Invisible ones*," he explained. "Legend has it that they possess an innate ability to blend seamlessly with their surroundings, making them virtually invisible to the naked eye."

"Why on earth would they want to reside here," Sofia asked him, "Knowing he was also here?"

"That's why I said maybe the tales of him are incorrect," replied Sarian, "Would you live here if the tales were true?"

"Are you mad? Of course, I wouldn't."

"Quiet!" another guard ordered stillness. "You'll wake him up."

"Don't be daft; it's all tales; that's what it is. I bet Treelun is not as dangerous as everyone makes out." Sarian stepped closer. "See, I knew it, harmless as a pussy cat," Sarian smiled. "We should make a detour to Froyen when this is over."

"Why?" asked Sofia.

"So, she can see her betrothed," laughed Amelia.

"Yes, that's right," Sarian turned to look at her. "So, I can tell him face to face I've been in Treelun's company."

"I don't think that's wise," spoken by Sofia. "This one trip is meant to be secreted, as in we tell no one we're seeing Treelun, remember?"

Sarian furrowed her brows, contemplating Sofia's cautionary advice. She understood the importance of discretion but couldn't help feeling a powerful desire to reveal her presence to her betrothed. It had been weeks since they last saw each other, and Sarian longed for a moment of connection. "But Sofia," Sarian began hesitantly, "I miss him so much. I yearn for his touch and his comforting presence. It feels unbearable to keep Treelun's meeting hidden from everyone."

"This time," replied Amelia. "Sofia's got a point there, Sarian; it's one thing to tell our partners we are going away on an adventure; it's another to say we are deliberately putting ourselves in harm's way."

"It's all fairytales," said Sarian, slowly walking forward. "As you will soon find out for yourselves."

"Well, I'm not going any closer," that had come from one of the guards behind them. "If he wakes, you will not want to see what happens next, and I do not want to see that happening either."

"Stay back if you want," Sarian replied, looking up at the highest point of Treelun's figure. "I'm not scared of any trees."

While Sarian walked forward, Sofia noticed something. "Oh god! Sarian, get back." She tried to grab Sarian's arm. "He's waking up."

The sound of Treelun waking up was a slight rustle of his vines, a low moan as if he were yawning, and a little shiver of the flowers attached to his enormous trunk. His branches, which spread out like a canopy, began to stir as the sun's rays began to peek through. His leaves started to move in the gentle breeze, and his trunk shifted a little in the evening light.

"Oh Valar, get back!" whispered one guard beside Amelia. "Walk away!"

"Don't be ridiculous!" said Sarian. "If a pack of people can live in this forest, surely he's no threat!"

"Stop trying to be a courageous female!" uttered Sofia through gritted teeth. "Get your backside here now!"

"You've no sense of excitement," said Sarian, turning around to face them. "Or brains to think any different." Sarian's words hung in the air, their sharpness cutting through the silence. The group stood there, stunned by the sudden accusation. They exchanged glances, their expressions a mix of surprise and anger.

Sofia stepped forward, her voice trembling with frustration. "Excitement? We've been on this journey for weeks, facing countless dangers and challenges. How can you say we lack excitement?"

Sarian scoffed dismissively. "You mistake danger for excitement, Sofia. Anyone can face difficult situations without truly experiencing the thrill of it all. You merely go through the motions."

Sofia's eyes narrowed as she retorted, "And what about brains? Are you implying that we're incapable of thinking differently?"

Sarian smirked condescendingly. "Oh please, spare me your feeble attempts at intellect. You follow the same predictable patterns, never daring to question or challenge the status quo."

"Sarian, for god's sake, look to the ground!"

"Don't be daft, Amelia—" When Sarian turned back, she saw the moving vines of Treelun touching her feet. The sight of the vines writhing, undulating like an angry ocean, made her panic--but only for a moment. As the others around her watched in terror, Sarian raised her head, her eyes bright, and her lips pulled into a massive smile. She knew the vines were harmless; they were just a natural part of the forest, only moving out of curiosity. "See what I told you!" she uttered while Treelun's vines softly caressed the exposed skin of her ankles. "He just wants to show us he's harmless."

"For Valar's sake!" one guard quickly walked towards her. "That's what he uses to deceive you, you idiot!" The guard's voice was filled with urgency and frustration as he reached out to grab Sarian's arm, attempting to pull her away from Treelun's enchanting presence. But she stood her ground, a defiant look in her eyes.

"I've seen enough," she declared, shaking off the guard's grip. "Treelun is not like the others. Can't you see? Look at how gently his vines touch me. He means no harm."

The other guards exchanged worried glances, unsure what to make of the situation. Treelun, a mystical creature believed to possess dangerous powers, had always been feared and avoided by most people. But Sarian seemed convinced otherwise. "He's just trying to gain your trust," another guard argued, his voice laced with scepticism. "Remember what happened to those who fell for his tricks before? We can't afford to let our guard down." As if in response, Treelun's vines retreated slowly, as if respecting the boundaries. "I've seen what he's capable of," he continued, his voice filled with caution. "Those vines may seem harmless now, but they could easily ensnare us if we let our guard down."

Sarian felt like her heart had been ripped from her chest as a guard dragged her away. She had never felt so helpless before. Tears streamed down her cheeks, and her body trembled with fear. Treelun's flowers seemed to shake in sadness, and his voice moaned in anguish as if he were mourning his prey's loss.

"I suggest we run!" a guard shouted, "We should run very fast!"

They did. Everyone ran along the paths they used to get there without turning their heads to see if Treelun's flowers were coming after them. When the travellers reached the bridge, the first guard leading the way abruptly stopped, causing all the entourage members to collide.

"The bridge," a guard shouted, "We can't run across it!" The bridge was composed of simple planks of wood laid down by the ancient builders. Sadly, the planks couldn't bear much weight. "It's too dangerous."

"I don't care! Just move across it," Sofia shouted now, "We don't want to become the next victims of Treelun!"

Chapter 8

Proof You're A Human

A guard would open the living room door at any moment, and Celahir must listen to Princess Amelia's fate. He knew there would be an argument about her and what to do with her. It would not be pretty. He had heard his mother discussing the various scenarios and potential outcomes: send her away, keep her in the castle, or even wholly disown her from the family. Celahir had always been close to Amelia, even when she seemed to be making potentially reckless decisions, so the prospect of her punished seemed almost too much to bear. As Celahir sat silently, he struggled to come to terms with how things had gotten to this point, and he hoped, somehow, he would be able to make the situation better.

"Remember," his brother Elensar had whispered to him. "You're only a witness here, so let us handle this."

Celahir nodded silently, his heart pounding in his chest, "Don't be rough on her," he whispered back. "It's not her fault."

"Pah," their mother, Queen Catreen, seated on the same settee as they cursed. "Not her fault! Of course, it's her fault."

Celahir glanced at his mother, her face contorted with anger and disdain. He understood her frustration but couldn't help feeling sympathy for the one this meeting was meant for. As the kingdom's youngest prince, Celahir had witnessed countless proceedings, but this one felt different. "Mother," he asked, "How do you know it's her fault?"

Celahir's mother, Queen Elensar, sighed heavily and fixed her son with a stern gaze. "Celahir, this is not the time nor the place for questions," she replied through gritted teeth.

"And I told you to stay out of it!" Elensar said crossly. "Remember what we told you to do when this starts."

"And what was that?" he answered sarcastically, but he knew already. *Stupid idiots,* he thought. *Why can't you just let me handle this?* "Yeah, stay silent, don't be a do good."

"I mean it. Don't mess this up, or I might interfere with your life!"

"Don't you dare!" Celahir clenched his fists, his anger simmering beneath the surface. He despised being treated like a kin, constantly overshadowed by his older brother's protective nature.

"Don't dare me, Celahir, because I just might, and it won't end well for Wendy if I do!"

"But she's got nothing to do with this!" Celahir took a deep breath, trying to calm himself before responding. "I mean it, Elensar, stay away from her!"

"Keep your mouth shut, or it won't go right for you either!"

"Go right!" said their mother, "I don't expect this to go right. I expect it to end how I wish it to end." Their mother, Catreen, had always been known for her mysterious and often unpredictable nature, but her words carried an unsettling weight this time.

Now he was getting concerned, and his sister-in-law wasn't even in the room yet! "What do you mean?"

"You'll find out soon enough."

"The same goes for you lot; say nothing." His brother had spoken to someone else; his four kin, Lathlorn, Alexander, Etheryn, and Lenith, stood in an orderly line next to a tall, glassed dresser, heads bowed. Elensar's words sounded heavy with a sense of secrecy and caution. The room fell into an eerie silence as his four kin exchanged glances, their expressions mirroring a mixture of curiosity and apprehension.

"Have you made sure Serria is well away from this room?" their mother asked one of the guards standing near the closed door.

"I have your Highness," one guard replied. "She's staying in the west wing tonight."

Their mother nodded, a sense of relief washing over her. Serria, their youngest sister, was always curious and had a knack for finding trouble. Keeping her away from the room was crucial to ensure the secrecy of what lay behind those closed doors. "Good. She may be old enough to court," her voice said. "But the last thing I need is my daughter hearing any of this when Amelia arrives."

"She won't, your Highness."

Before anyone else could say anything, the door to the chamber swung open – and there, standing in the doorway, was the human called William, flanked by a castle guard. The sight of him struck Celahir– he was a short figure, his frame perfectly dripping with confidence. His gaze seemed to be everywhere at once, piercing eyes, yet gentle in presence. There was something almost majestic about him, as though he was the answer to a question Celahir had been searching for a long time. The guard beside him, stern and silent, stood unmoving. Then he noticed someone else there, Princess Amelia. Amelia was short, standing around five-foot-seven-ish compared to those around her. She had long dark black hair cascading down her back, framing her mid-tone complexion that hinted at a Latin background and curves in all the right places, ample bosoms, full hips, and round, plump buttocks.

"At last, the impostors are here," said their mother.
Amelia looked stunned; stepping further into the room, she could probably see their mother's eyes blazing, her voice full of demanding power. Amelia had never seen the Queen like this, and it probably shook her to the core. And one more thing, Amelia wouldn't have expected any of this on returning home from her adventurous vacation.
"Excuse me!" there was a frown on Amelia's face. Behind her were her two friends, Sarian and Sofia.
"That's nice," said Sarian, coming further into the room. "They must have known we were coming back earlier."
"They don't look cheerful to see her," whispered Sofia.
"Bringing your friends into our family drama," the Queen said, her tone dripping with sarcasm. "Just what I needed."
Sarian and Sofia exchanged nervous glances, unsure how to react to the tense atmosphere filling the room. They had only heard stories about the Queen's strictness, never experiencing it firsthand.
Amelia took a deep breath, trying to remain calm despite the tension in the room. She knew the Queen's sarcastic remark was meant to provoke her, but she refused to let it get to her. "We didn't come here to cause any trouble," Amelia said, her voice steady. "We've just got back."
The Queen rolled her eyes and crossed her arms, clearly unconvinced by Amelia's words. "Well, you have a funny way of showing it," she retorted. "Bringing your friends into our personal matters is hardly a peaceful gathering, human."
"What are you on about?"
Celahir watched as Amelia's vision fell upon her four offspring. He saw the love and pride beaming in her eyes but was aghast as he saw the unconcerned gazes her kin's gave in return. He watched as her smile dimmed, his heart breaking as he saw the disappointment on her face. For a moment, he wished that her four kin could see what he saw - the motherly love radiating from her soul - and feel what he felt - the unconditional love between a mother and her offspring. However, he knew this was impossible since the world's ever-growing cynicism had clouded her kin's hearts and minds.
Confused by their reactions, Amelia's gaze drifted to his brother, "Elensar," his eyes were looking at the floor, "Elensar?"
"He won't speak to a human that's deceived him," uttered the Queen in her unsympathetic tone.
"Amelia, what's happened?" Sarian asked. "Has something happened while we were away?"
"You could say that," whispered Sofia.
"You're so call friend," the Queen was now talking to Sarian and Sofia, "Isn't as Shalimar as she'd like you to believe she is. More human, I think, is what stands before us."

Sarian and Sofia exchanged puzzled glances, unsure of what the Queen meant by her cryptic statement. The atmosphere in the chamber grew tense as they awaited an explanation.

Amelia scoffed dismissively, her eyes narrowing with defiance. "Your Majesty, I assure you that I am as Shalimar as they come. There is nothing human about me."

"You may have convinced yourself that you are, but I have seen enough to know otherwise," the Queen replied calmly, her gaze unwavering. "There is a depth in your eyes that betrays your claim, a flicker of emotions that only a human could possess."

"I assure you, Your Majesty, my loyalty lies solely with Shalimar," Amelia insisted, regaining her composure. "I have dedicated my life to serving this kingdom, its people, your son, and our children."

"Children! See, you even use a name spoken only in the realm of humans," the Queen interrupted, her voice tinged with suspicion. "Tell me, Amelia, how did you come to possess such knowledge? How did you acquire these emotions that are foreign to our kind?"

Amelia took a deep breath, her heart pounding in her chest. She knew that her response would determine the course of her future. With unwavering determination, she met the Queen's gaze and began to speak.

"Your Majesty," Amelia started, her voice steady yet filled with sincerity, "I understand your concerns and appreciate your curiosity. But please allow me to explain." She paused for a moment, gathering her thoughts before continuing. "I was not always aware of the realm of humans or their emotions," Amelia explained. "It was during my travels as a young girl that I stumbled upon a hidden library deep within the enchanted forest. Within its ancient pages, I discovered tales of love, compassion, and sacrifice that were foreign to our kind."

"Stop this facade of lies! It is I you speak to, Queen of the land you now stand in," the Queen's voice dripped with scepticism and authority, challenging Amelia's words.

Amelia stood tall, her eyes filled with determination as she faced the imposing figure before her. Undeterred by the Queen's interruption, Amelia took a deep breath and continued her tale. "Your Majesty," she began respectfully, "I understand your doubts, but I assure you that what I speak is the truth. The hidden library in the enchanted forest holds secrets lost to our kind for centuries." The Queen's piercing gaze bore into Amelia, searching for any sign of deception. But Amelia remained steadfast, her voice unwavering as she recounted her extraordinary discovery. "As I delved deeper into those ancient pages," Amelia continued, "I found stories of love from the humans that transcended boundaries and compassion that knew no limits. These tales spoke of sacrifices made for the greater good, selflessness that could heal even the deepest wounds."

The Queen's expression suddenly grew with more rage. "Enough! Unless you wish me to end your life here and now," she hissed, her voice dripping with venom, "And I would happily do it myself, human!"

Amelia's somewhat calm nature now showed an outward appearance of fear, words reflecting the same emotion. "I have already stated I am no such thing," Amelia's heart pounded as she desperately tried to maintain her composure in the face of the Queen's wrath. Taking a deep breath, she continued, her voice trembling slightly. "I am but a simple low Shalimar, Your Majesty," Amelia replied, her voice quivering with fear. "Born and bred like every other person here in your lands."

The Queen's eyes narrowed, scepticism etched across her face. "A low Shalimar? You expect me to believe that?" she suddenly raised an eyebrow, still unbelieving her words, "Tell me," the Queen signaled a guard to approach. "If you think you are a Shalimar," she signaled the guard with a nod of her head, "Why," with swift action from the guard, the top part of Amelia's two-piece dress ripped open, revealing just her stomach, "Do you have a hole in your stomach?"

Amelia, looking embarrassed, scrambled to cover her exposed midriff with her hands." That doesn't mean anything," she cried out. "I'm a Shalimar; I was born Shalimar!"

Then Elensar said, "Amelia!" her name was uttered in a mean way, causing Amelia to tremble with fear. "You know full well we're different!"

"Elensar," she said in such a heartrending way that he thought she would cry tears. "Elensar, why are you doing this!"

"The proof your human."

"I don't understand what you're saying!"

"Shalimars don't have holes in their stomachs." With a nod from Elensar's head, the guard pushed the human forward until they stood near Amelia. The human tensed, his eyes filled with fear.

Amelia glanced around, her gaze taking in all the people around her. Her gaze then settled back on the human. She could sense the palpable tension in the air as she observed the human standing before her. The fear emanating from their eyes was unmistakable, tugging at her heartstrings. She knew the weight of being thrust into unfamiliar territory, surrounded by strangers who held power over your fate. Amelia took a step closer to the trembling human with a gentle yet determined expression and saw a flicker of surprise mixed with apprehension. Clearly, they had expected hostility or disdain from someone of her stature. But instead, they found curiosity and empathy reflected in her eyes.

"This one before you have the same?" A guard rudely yanked the jumper the human wore upwards. "See, it's the same."

Celahir saw the human push the guard's hand away, pull his garments back down, and give an evil look to the guard before turning his sight to Amelia, now standing near him.

"Who are you?" she asked the human.

"William Defer from—"

"William, I don't know what you've said to my people or even if what you said was true; please, tell them it was a mistake, that you wouldn't inform anyone about these lands."

"I wish I could say that, but I have proof," William tried to explain. "I think a friend of mine, Tim, will tell someone about your lands. I don't know who, but I had to tell your people because I thought they should know." He paused, unsure how to proceed. "If I could, I'd take this back, but I can't undo it. I'm sorry if it jeopardizes your people; I had no intention of putting them in danger."

William tried to make his apology sincere, but he could tell by the look on the faces around him it wasn't enough for them. They had been protective of their land and its secrets, content to keep it hidden from outsiders. And now William had revealed it to someone else without consent. It was a mistake he wished he could take back, but he was resigned to whatever consequences awaited him. All he could do now was offer his sincere apology and earnestly ask for their forgiveness.

"What is this proof?" asked Amelia.

"Papers," he whispered. "Proof you're a human, as I am."

Amelia quickly looked around before turning to run out of the room. With lightning-fast reflexes, Celahir reacted and yelled, 'Wait!' But his brother Elensar had already dashed out after Amelia, reaching out and grabbing her arm to pull her back into the room.

Elensar sternly said, "Oh no, you're not!" With one hand pulling her back towards the room, he furiously replied to her fleeing movements, "You're going to stay to hear this young lady!"

Amelia's heart raced as Elensar's grip tightened around her arm. She struggled against his hold, desperately trying to break free and escape. Tears welled up in Amelia's eyes as she pleaded, "Please, just let me go! I can't stay here any longer." Her voice trembled with frustration and desperation, but Elensar remained resolute.

"No," he said firmly, his voice laced with determination. "You need to hear this, Amelia. It's important." Amelia's resistance only seemed to fuel Elensar's anger. With a sudden surge of strength, he forcefully pushed her back into the room, causing her to stumble and fall onto the floor. For a second, it looked as if Elensar was about to apologize but then took it back. "Lock that door," Elensar ordered a guard as they passed him.

Amelia was left lying in the middle of the room, rubbing her arm, as the guard reached for the key to the door and locked it shut with a loud click, the sound of the bolt being rammed into place afterward, no doubt the guard had fastened it closed, ensuring she would not escape again.

He saw Amelia cast her gaze towards Elensar, beginning to sit by his side, looking at him with an apologetic and frightened expression.

Amelia's heart raced with confusion and fear, so she mustered the courage to speak up. "Elensar, what is happening?" Her voice trembled, revealing her vulnerability.

Elensar remained silent, his eyes fixed on a distant point as if lost in his thoughts. The room seemed to grow colder, the silence suffocating. Celahir watched the scene unfold, torn between supporting his brother and comforting his sister-in-law.

Finally, Elensar's voice broke through the heavy atmosphere. "Amelia," he began, his tone laced with bitterness and disappointment. "We have discovered something that has shattered our trust in you."

Amelia's eyes widened in disbelief. She had always been faithful and devoted to their marriage to his family. What could have possibly caused such a drastic change in their demeanour?

"This human comes with letters from your old world," Elensar continued, his voice filled with anguish. "Letters from someone called Loryen—"

Chapter 9

Prince Celahir

During that meeting, Celahir was yelled at and accused of wrongdoing when he felt he had done nothing wrong in sticking up for his sister-in-law, Amelia. He was frustrated that he couldn't make the others see the sense of his argument or even understand what he was trying to explain. He had never thought he'd be involved in such a heated argument with his mother and brother, and the experience was exhausting and frightening for him. As the meeting ended, Celahir's mind was still reeling from the intense exchange of words. He couldn't shake off the lingering feeling of betrayal that hung in the air. Witnessing his family turning against him was disheartening, especially when he only wanted to defend his sister-in-law's honour. His frustration grew as he replayed the heated discussion in his mind. Each time he attempted to present his case, his family drowned his words with overpowering anger. They seemed determined to silence him, dismissing his perspective without considering it. Celahir had always believed that his family would stand united, supporting one another through thick and thin. But this confrontation shattered that illusion, leaving him feeling isolated and misunderstood.

William! Staying here on mother's orders, why?

Celahir's body was light as a feather, the warmth of his bath allowing him to drift away from the world. He let himself float away, gently descending on the bed and slowly shifting his arms under his head, using it as a makeshift pillow. He had a gentle gaze; his bright blue eyes momentarily looked up at the white ceiling, counting the tiny bumps that lined it like distant stars, ponderously thinking of all that had just gone on.

A frown appeared but quickly vanished; eyelids blinked, lower lip bit and a word escaped his lips. "Mother." The frown appeared again. *Hang on a minute! Why would the one who detests humans permit one to live under the same roof? What could be her motive?*

As he pondered these questions, a sense of unease settled within him. His mother had always been firm in her beliefs, unwavering in her disdain for humans. Her sudden change of heart was perplexing. It made him question everything he thought he knew about her. There may have been more to this situation than met the eye. Could it be that his mother had discovered something about humans they were unaware of? Or was she playing a dangerous game, using William as a pawn in some elaborate scheme? He couldn't shake off the feeling that there was an ulterior motive behind his mother's decision. It seemed unlikely that she would suddenly embrace a human without any reservations. After all, she had raised Elensar, Serria, and him with cautionary tales about their treachery and deceit. But what if this change of heart was indeed a test? A way for their mother to gauge their loyalty and determination to uphold her teachings?

This news of Amelia's falseness of breed was enough to send anyone over the edging of insanity. Still, he knew his brother wouldn't let their mother's hatred of humans cast any thoughts into his mind of disowning Amelia, hating her. Whereas himself, well, he'd probably crack so easily under the pressure of their mother's persistence of removing her from their world, he'd do just that, take her out of the castle, but not their world. Instead, he'd conceal her where Shalimar human helpers lived, a place called Andrathlion, but this forest would also be his brother's future home.

"Celahir, are you still awake?"

Andrathlion Forest was to be Elensar's new place of dwelling. The ancient woods were sacred, silent in the darkness, and old in the days. Elensar told him he saw a grand opportunity there. He'd envisioned a new castle, built on the patterns of ancient ruins, surrounding him in the wild. A new place of refuge, an escape, a place Elensar thought of as the residence of freedom, the liberation from the ties of Volarie. He'd imagined the freedom of this new home, all the tranquillity and rest, far away from the hustle and bustle of the busy city of Volarie. In this space, he told him he could be safe and prepare a sanctuary, a perfect dwelling for himself and his wife, Amelia.

"Celahir, are you awake?"

He did think Elensar had lost the plot in suggesting he move to the forest and live ruling there. His brother was always overconfident in himself, no matter what the matter, and his dream of playing King in a wooded kingdom was just too much for him to envision him doing it.

He had heard tales of others living in the forests, of strange events and bizarre happenings, and he was sure Elensar's suggestion was nothing more than a daydream fuelled by that fantasy of his. Yet Elensar was a Shalimar who always got what he wanted, whether with their mother or other means. He was a master manipulator, and he knew that soon Elensar would get his way, and the two of them, Elensar and

Amelia, would be making their way to the forest, whether she wanted to or not.

Gentle taps knocked on the door of his bedroom. "Celahir, I need to talk."

The bedroom door opened, and he remained unaware of its movement, nor did he hear the steps of someone entering his room. He was deep in thought, lost in his world, utterly oblivious to the presence of an intruder. *Mother, how many times have you cast a loving glance at my brother? How often have you run to his aid, helped him out in his hour of need? It seems all the time*, he thought as he looked back up to the ceiling and sighed; simultaneously, a hand reached out and touched him on his arm. "What in the stars!" his head turned to the side, he grasped a hand against his chest, "Amelia, you frightened—"

"I'm sorry," brown eyes blinked repeatedly. "I did call, knock; you can't have heard me. I need to talk to someone."

He smiled at the figure dressed in a long flowing floral gown, "My mind is always open for you," his body shifted into an upright position, and a hand covered hers. "What's wrong?"

"Where do I start?"

"Wherever the most worrying part is," he recalled his hand from hers. "That's the best place to start."

He heard her sigh. "But what if I don't even know where to begin? What if I can't put my worries into words?"

He reached across again and gently took her hand. "Sometimes, speaking out loud can help clarify your thoughts. Start with whatever comes to mind, even if it feels cluttered or unclear."

She nodded slowly, absorbing his advice. "But what if my worries seem trivial compared to others? What if they don't matter?"

He squeezed her hand reassuringly. "Every worry is valid and deserves attention. Don't compare your concerns to others."

"What if there are lots of them?"

"Start at the most worrying one."

"It could take some time."

"You do not need to mention time in this room." He saw her frown and tilt her head at his odd words. He smiled. "Listen. As long as you say all you need, that's all the time you need."

She shook her head and smiled. "You sound just like Elensar."

He chuckled softly, a hint of nostalgia in his eyes. "Ah, Elensar—We were quite the pair growing up. Always getting into mischief together." His voice trailed off as he reminisced about their shared adventures. "But you know," he continued, his smile widening, "Despite our mischievous nature, Elensar was always the one with the grand ideas. He had this way of dreaming big and making things happen. I guess some of that rubbed off on me."

She tilted her head curiously, intrigued by his words. "So, you're saying that being brothers influenced your outlook on life?"

He nodded thoughtfully. "Absolutely. Growing side by side, we learned from each other's strengths and weaknesses. So, as you said, maybe I am just like Elensar in that sense."

Amelia sat down on the bed and turned to face him. "Can I ask you something?"

"Yes."

"If all you heard in that room today was for Wendy, would you react with no words to her after hearing all that?" Amelia's voice trembled with concern as she awaited Celahir's response.

The room fell silent for a moment as Celahir contemplated his answer. Finally, breaking the silence, Celahir sighed deeply. "Would I react with no words to it? Of course, I wouldn't."

"I wish Elensar would give words, but I've no Elensar now. He won't speak to me. I tried to say something, speak to him downstairs, and he reacted as if I wasn't there."

"Are you sure?"

"Of course, I'm sure!" her words sounded angry, and tears began falling down her cheeks. "I saw the look of hate in Elensar's eyes."

"Elensar would never hate you," he wiped her falling tears.

"Once I thought that," she sniffled. "Now, I'm not so sure." Amelia wiped away her tears, her eyes filled with sadness and frustration. "I don't understand what went wrong," she confessed, trembling. "We used to share our hopes, dreams, and fears. But now it's like he's built a wall around himself, shutting me out completely."

"Then you don't know your companion well."

"I know he hates me right now!"

"Amelia, sometimes, the show of hate can cloak something else, like you were hiding true feelings that someone can't express."

"Don't be daft, Celahir; hate is hate."

"Sometimes, the only way to conceal things is to act indifferent to your feelings. Like getting their attention, just in a different way."

"Elensar didn't get my attention," she turned away. "He didn't allow me to give it to him."

Celahir moved even closer; he turned her head back to him. "Perhaps you should give him another try," watching brown eyes overfill with tears. "After all, is he not worth it?"

"I used to think so," Amelia sniffled. "I used to think I was worth a second chance, too."

"You are, sweetheart," he wiped a tear from her cheek.

"Well, I'm not," she cried out. "Otherwise, Elensar would've given me that chance I needed. But he didn't, and now it's too late." Her voice cracked with a mix of frustration and sadness.

"Don't say that," his fingers wiped another rolling tear away, and a hand came from her face. "You're worth a second chance."

Amelia's shoulders started to tremble; her head lowered, her eyes closed, and she sobbed aloud. "I'm frightened, Celahir; oh god, I'm so frightened!"

"What are you frightened of?"

"Of being alone, of never going back to how it used to be before all this happened!"

"I understand your fear, Amelia," Celahir whispered, his voice filled with empathy. "But you're not alone. I'm here for you, and together we'll find a way to navigate this darkness."

Amelia's sobs began to subside as she clung to Celahir's words of support. She slowly lifted her head, tears still glistening on her cheeks, and looked into his eyes with a mixture of vulnerability and hope. "But it's all my fault. I should never have come here or thought I was safe here."

"You are safe."

"No, I'm not!"

"Why would you think that?"

"I'm not safe from your mother now, not safe even from Elensar or his anger now, either."

"He might use anger on others; he wouldn't dare lay a hand on you," Celahir interrupted, his voice filled with conviction. "You must understand, Amelia, that none of this is your fault. You couldn't have known what would happen when you came here."

Amelia's eyes searched his face for any sign of doubt or hesitation. She desperately wanted to believe him, to find solace in his words. But the fear that had taken hold of her heart was not quickly dispelled. "But I should have known, Celahir," she whispered, her voice trembling. "Elensar's used rage before on me, not physically, but words he has; who's to say he won't again."

"I understand your fear, and I can't promise Elensar won't hurt you again with his words. But please believe me when I say I will do everything possible to protect you from harm."

"You don't know Elensar like I do." There was silence for a few moments as if Amelia were thinking something, and then she gasped, "Oh god, Celahir, what have I done!"

"You haven't done anything."

"I have," she despondently said, sighing again. "Your mother was right in saying I was born out of a lie; now, oh god! What punishment will I receive for this?"

"Punishment! When did she say this?"

"Downstairs after you left."

"She said this!"

"Yes," Amelia replied, her voice trembling with fear. "She said I would face punishment for my actions, for being born out of a lie."

Celahir's mind raced, trying to comprehend the gravity of the situation. He had always known that his family held secrets, but he never imagined it would lead to such consequences for Amelia. He took a deep breath, trying to steady himself before responding. "Amelia, you mustn't blame yourself for something beyond your control," Celahir said gently, his voice filled with empathy. "You are not responsible for the circumstances of your birth. It is unfair for anyone to hold you accountable."

Amelia's eyes welled up with tears as she looked into Celahir's comforting gaze. "But what if they're right? What if I deserve punishment?" she whispered, her voice barely audible. "God, she even said I was passing my falseness on to my sons. Falseness of breed," the tears were starting to well up again. "Your mother even said I was not worthy to be a mother to her grandchildren, not worthy to be her son's wife, to be the next Queen."

"Well, I can say you are worthy, worthy as a mother, valuable to this family's needs, as a Queen, you would bring back to the throne of Volarie a ray of brightness that's been missing for far too long," Celahir replied, his voice filled with sincerity. "Don't let her words define you. You are so much more than what she sees or says. Your strength, compassion, and unwavering love for your kin's make you the perfect mother and wife."

"I wish I were, could be all that. I wish time could slip back again, take this wretchedness I'm feeling, sink it to the depths of not ever having to remember it again."

"I'd do that for you eagerly, if possible, but I can't; it's something you have to do with Elensar's help."

"Elensar!" Amelia cried out. "How can I when he won't talk to me? Look at me. No, it's too late; I've lost him for good."

Celahir watched as Amelia set forth those sorrowful and pain-filled emotions through tears. His fingertips brushed against her face, the air between them heavy and tense yet comforting. For that fleeting moment, the weight of the gravity between them became overthrown by an indescribable pull, and he kissed her. As their lips met, time seemed to stand still. The world around him faded into insignificance, leaving only the intensity of their connection. In that stolen moment, Celahir could feel Amelia's vulnerability and longing, her heartache pouring into him like a torrential storm. But as quickly as it had begun, reality crashed back in. He pulled away from her, their eyes locked in a mixture of confusion and desire for a single second until Amelia leaned in for another kiss.

As if he'd lost control, Celahir suddenly yanked off her dressing gown and threw the garment over his shoulder. His movements were almost careless as if he had desired this moment for some time. He then swiftly opened his dressing gown with help from Amelia, revealing his naked flesh. Their desire was undeniable. Without considering the consequences, they surrendered themselves to one another in the most intimate ways. Their breaths mingled as he quickly pushed their lovemaking to the limits soon after his hasty entrance inside her body, generating pleasure for him and discomfort for her with each thrust he forced deep inside, creating a symphony of pleasure and pain sounds that sounded loud in his bedroom, however, halfway through, a voice outside in the hallway brought them back to reality.

"Can you believe that woman!" a voice shouted from afar.

Celahir's heart was pounding as his hand swiftly darted over Amelia's mouth, effectively muting her moans from being overheard by anyone in the adjacent hallway. His body was tense as someone was coming closer. He knew that the stakes were high and the consequences of being caught in such a compromising situation were far too significant to consider. As his heart raced, Celahir could feel Amelia's body beneath his own, her warm breath against his hand, her ample bosoms crushed against his chest, the soft, warm silkiness of her insides wrapped tightly around his fully erected shaft. He was fully aware of the danger they were both in. Celahir's heart raced with fear as he glanced around the room for a hiding spot. They heard the voice again.

"Can you believe that woman!"

The next minute, Celahir and Amelia were in a frenzy. Their hearts pounding and their minds racing, they grabbed their dressing gowns to cover their nakedness. Amelia gave looks to Celahir as if she didn't know what to do next. Suddenly, they heard noises almost outside his bedroom. Celahir knew they needed to hide, so he quickly suggested something. "If he sees you here with me, he'll misplace his grip on normality, so you must conceal yourself."

"Where?"

"Hide in that closet," pointing to the corner. Celahir saw her head turn in the same direction, seeing the tall oak closet, its doors partly closed. "Go swiftly; his steps march to my room in a rage." He saw her walk quickly to the cabinet; her sudden movement spurred him to follow her just as fast. He watched her open the doors, a flicker of fear on her face, and then she disappeared inside. "Whatever you hear," he said before he closed the doors. "Whatever you think of the words about to be set loose in this room, you must stay concealed, stay silent. Can you do this?"

"Yes."

He turned, closed the doors, and saw a nightie on his bed. He dashed over and pushed it under a pillow when he heard footsteps approaching.

"That woman!" his brother now stormed into the room, "Our mother suggesting such a thing of me!"

Celahir's heart raced as he tried desperately to calm himself down. He knew his brother had a fiery temper, and any wrong move could set him on a rampage. "Elensar," he tried to sound startled. "What did she say?"

"You should've stayed," Elensar's face was flushed with anger as he paced back and forth in the room. "You'd have found out!"

"I didn't because I was tired. So, tell me, what did happen," Celahir saw him stop, frown, and sniff the air, "Elensar?"

"Has Amelia been in here recently?"

"I don't believe so," Celahir replied, lying, knowing she was hiding in the room.

Elensar's eyes narrowed, suspicion flickering across his face. "Are you sure? I can smell her perfume lingering in the air."

"I expect it's the perfumed soap I used for my bath," he nodded to the adjoining bathroom, its door still open.

He saw Elensar furrow his brow, contemplating his explanation. He saw him step closer to the open bathroom door, inhaling deeply. The faint aroma of perfumed soap lingered in the air, intertwining with the natural scent of the room.

"I suppose you're right," he heard Elensar admit reluctantly, his concern easing slightly. "But it was so reminiscent of Amelia's fragrance that it caught me off guard."

Celahir nodded understandingly, a small smile playing on his lips. "Amelia has a unique scent that is hard to forget. Perhaps your mind played tricks on you."

He heard Elensar sigh and saw him run a hand through his hair. "I suppose you're right again," he conceded, though his eyes betrayed lingering doubt.

Celahir changed the subject, "So what happened after I left?"

Elensar's shoulders slumped as he recounted the events after Celahir's departure. "Well, after you left, things took a turn for the worse," he began, his voice tinged with a hint of regret. "After Amelia left the room, Mother set about belittling her, mocking, scorning in such a foul voice, I had to use words I wouldn't normally use in front of my kin's."

Celahir's mind raced as he tried to make sense of his mother's outburst. Why would she suddenly break her usual calm demeanour before Elensar's kin? "Your kin were there hearing it all!"

Elensar nodded solemnly, his eyes clouded with sadness and frustration. "Yes, they were," he replied, his voice heavy with disappointment. "I had hoped they would intervene or defend Amelia, but they remained silent. It was as if Mother's words paralyzed them, unable or unwilling to challenge her."

Celahir's brows furrowed in disbelief. "But why? How could they just let Mother treat Amelia that way?"

He heard Elensar sigh deeply, his gaze fixed on the ground. "I think fear played a significant role," he confessed. "Mother has always been domineering and manipulative; she knows how to control those around her. My kin's have grown accustomed to her ways over the years, and challenging her authority is something they rarely dare to do. But only the twins were there when this happened," he saw Elensar walk by the bed, look at the crumpled sheets, look at him, sniff the air again, then frown, "You know I can smell her perfume in here—"

"Elensar stop stalling."

"Okay, okay, okay," he heard him sigh, "Normally, I wouldn't let them hear such pollution from her lips or my own; this was different."

"That's unlike you," Celahir saw Elensar walk towards the closed closet. "But if you utter such words, you must have a good reason."

"Oh, I did," he heard him half-laugh. "Believe me, I did."

"What's the reason for your foulness?"

"Mother suggested I have nothing to do with Amelia."

Celahir raised an eyebrow, his curiosity piqued. "And you said?"

"I said, forget it," he watched him take a deep breath in, exhale it, "Valar, the smells even stronger over here; you sure you're not keeping her in that closet."

"No," Celahir replied, his voice wavering as he attempted to conceal the truth. He shifted uncomfortably, avoiding eye contact with Elensar. "So, what happened next?"

"Well," he saw Elensar turn around, "That's when it all started to be let loose, the foulness, the vulgarity of her words." he saw him walk forward. "She stated if she caught me uttering a single word to Amelia in her presence, she'd cast me as one of the humans."

"You're joking!" he glanced at the closet and followed quickly behind Elensar's steps. "Surely you must have heard wrong, Mother wouldn't cast you as a human."

He saw Elensar turn around and face him. "Then you don't remember the tale of long ago."

"What tale?"

"The tale of the wizard that lived in the Rokey Mountains, Dorthean. Do you not remember?"

"Dorthean! I have, but what tale are you speaking about."

"Long ago, there was talk of a certain happening upon that Mountain. A happening that uttered mother's name involved a human. A human that lost his life."

"And you're saying Mother had something to do with it?"

"Yes."

"That can't be right."

"She is a human hater, so I won't speak to Amelia. Instead, I'll obey Mother's words to ignore Amelia from now on."

"A human hater, yes mother is, a murderer, surely not!"

Unfortunately, his brother's following words were unheard by Amelia. "Come on, Celahir! How many times has she been there with us when we've been with those huma—"

"That's different!"

"Well, I wouldn't put anything past her to get someone else to do the same to Amelia," his brother turned around and headed for the door. "So, as I said, I'll obey Mother's words and not speak to Amelia."

"What do you mean?" he uttered as they reached the door. "You won't speak to Amelia, obey Mother's words?"

"I mean exactly that," his brother replied, "The only way I can protect Amelia, keep her alive, is by not uttering to her while in Mother's hearing range."

"But you'll speak in private? Why only in private, and why like that?"

"You need not interrupt people when they're speaking; you might learn more," his brother walked through the door and sighed. "I was going to say, that way, Amelia won't have the sentence we use on humans cast upon her."

"The killing one!"

"Yes—"

"But she's a Shal—"

"We don't know that now; just like those papers said, she's not a full Shalimar or Newton; in truth, we don't even know her true identity anymore," he heard Elensar sigh heavily, "I just need to do all this, do all mothers request for the next few days, it will give me time to inform our kins of the move. It also means Amelia isn't to be placed into the dungeons if I do this."

"The move, dungeon? Is Mother going to place her in it?"

"She won't be placed into it. Instead, I will take her and the kin's to our new home."

"You're new home in Andrathlion forest?"

"Yes," Elensar replied with a nod. "It's a secluded and protected place, far away from prying eyes and potential threats."

"But it's not ready yet, is it?"

"Not yet," he saw him turn away. "But that won't bother me. We can stay with Zenith until it is."

"But surely Mother will find her there!"

"Zenith says they've got more protection for Amelia there than I can provide here, so if I get her there, she'll be in safer hands," he turned away from him as if he was leaving, "But I've got to explain all this to Amelia, but I can't find her. Do you know where she is?"

"Elensar, wait," Celahir grabbed him by the arm, making him turn, frowning at him. "Don't go yet." For a fleeting few moments, Celahir had thought about telling Elensar his wife was hiding in his closet, the feeling of guilt at knowing Elensar was trying to help Amelia and he was stopping it from happening, "Elensar, I understand your concern for Amelia's safety," Celahir began, his voice filled with urgency. "But there's something you need to know before you leave."

Elensar's brows furrowed in confusion as he looked at Celahir intently. "What is it? Why are you stopping me?"

Taking a moment to gather his thoughts, Celahir continued, "Amelia—" But as quickly as the idea entered his mind, Celahir pushed it away. He couldn't bear to see the disappointment in Elensar's eyes, nor could he fathom the consequences that would follow such a revelation. "I think she went for a walk around the castle."

"At this time of the night!"

"I know it seems odd," Celahir replied hesitantly, trying to sound nonchalant. "Amelia always found solace in wandering during restless nights when you didn't return after the war."

"It was a bitter time for both of us," he heard Elensar sigh sadly. "Five years of torturous hell spent apart when we could have been together in each other's arms."

"I know, brother, I know," Celahir looked at Elensar, his eyes filled with understanding and guilt at something else he'd kept hidden from him and everyone else.

Amelia and his brother had endured unimaginable pain and loss, believing the other to be gone forever. Celahir even thought it, too, to the point he started caring for Amelia in a way a brother-in-law shouldn't while Elensar was presumed dead. Celahir saw a side to Amelia during this grief period that made him fall heavily in love with her, making him desperate to have her as his own. For a while, she rebuffed his advances, but in the end, he got his way, but it was a short-lived secret affair. Celahir had begun to see changes with Amelia during that time. He started to notice subtle signs of discontentment in Amelia. She would often withdraw emotionally and seem distant; in the end, she called it off two years before Elensar returned home, but that all happened long ago.

"Yes, but that's in the past, brother," Celahir smiled up at Elensar, "What matters is that you came home." He saw Elensar's eyes soften as he looked down; the weight of the earlier events seemed to momentarily lift from his shoulders, replaced by a glimmer of hope for the future.

"I'll speak later with you," he saw Elensar start to descend the passageway steps. "Hopefully, by then, this will be made better."

Celahir didn't wait to hear the bottom door opening-closing after his brother disappeared. Instead, he rushed back into his room and flung open the closet doors. "You've got to go quickly!" he dragged Amelia out of the closet. "Go back to your room!"

"After what he's just said! You've got to be kidding, *'I won't speak to Amelia now,'* Yeah, right, well, we'll see about that!" Amelia shrugged his hand away. "I'm going nowhere near him now."

Celahir's heart pounded as he watched Amelia defiantly reject his plea. He knew she was stubborn, but he hoped she would understand the situation's urgency. His brother's words echoed in his mind, filling him with dread. He grabbed Amelia's arm again, this time with more force. "Amelia, please! We don't have time for this. If you stay here, you'll be in danger," he pleaded desperately.

Amelia's eyes narrowed as she stared at him, her expression filled with determination. "I don't care about the danger anymore," she retorted fiercely. "Your brother can't just say those things and expect me to return to my room like nothing happened."

"Listen, if you don't go back to your room," his hand shoved her towards the door. "Elensar is going to know something's up."

"I don't give a rat's tail!" she turned around. "Let Elensar think it; let him see I've found another lover to fill his big shoes, his brother."

"Amelia, come one, see sense!"

Amelia's eyes blazed with anger as she glared at him, her voice dripping with defiance. "Sense? You want me to see sense? Well, maybe it's time you see the truth, too! Elensar has taken me for granted for far too long. He thinks he can control me, manipulate me like some puppet on a string."

Celahir took a step closer, his voice softer now, laced with concern. "Amelia, I understand your frustration, but this isn't how to handle things. Elensar may have made mistakes, but he loves you deeply. Don't let your anger blind you to that; now, please return to your room."

"My room! That's the last place I want to be in right now!" Amelia's voice quivered with anger and hurt as she retorted, her eyes welling up with tears. "How can you defend him, Celahir, after everything Elensar has done, said to me! Even saying it all in front of my children! I thought you would understand, but now everyone is against me, even you."

Celahir sighed, his gaze filled with empathy. He knew Amelia was hurting, but he also knew that Elensar's intentions were not malicious. "Amelia, I'm not defending his actions or excusing his mistakes. But love is complicated, and people make errors in judgment. Elensar is flawed, just like the rest of us; now, please."

"Fine, I'll go," he saw her stomp off toward the bedroom door, "But I won't go back to him, not after what I heard."

"Just be careful, Amelia, okay?" Celahir watched Amelia storm off towards the bedroom door, her face etched with pain and anger. He knew her wounds ran deep, and he couldn't blame her for wanting to distance herself from Elensar.

Amelia paused at the doorway, turning slightly to meet Celahir's gaze. "I will," Amelia replied softly, her voice laced with uncertainty. "I won't let him hurt me anymore."

Celahir nodded, "Remember, you're not alone in this," Celahir said gently, his voice filled with sincerity. "You have friends who care about you and will stand by your side."

"I hope so because they're all I have now." That said, he saw Amelia turn around and slip away.

Chapter 10

Shalimar Dorthean

Friends are an essential part of life. They are the people who stick by us through thick and thin, who make us laugh when times are tough, and who are always there to lend an ear when we need it. Friends understand us in ways that family can't and offer us a level of support and companionship that we can't find anywhere else. They are the people who celebrate our successes and help us through our failures. They stay with us through the good and bad times and remind us of the importance of having someone to lean on. Friends are the people who make us feel less alone and remind us that we're never truly alone. They make us feel seen and heard and remind us that we matter. Friends are the people who make life a little brighter and remind us that no matter what happens, we always have someone who cares.

Amelia needed her friends, so she went to meet them. You see, to Amelia, that feeling of loneliness would be happening all over again soon, the stares, whispers, and scowls from people in the public. The same reactions repeated as if playing back a memory of Amelia's entrance into Volarie all those many centuries ago. She didn't need the people, the Queen, or Elensar. She had Sarian, Sofia, and Anlease as her friends who would see she would be welcomed when they saw her. So, just a few months after the terrible meeting in the drawing room, she went to see Anlease but took Sofia and Sarian with her. The journey from Volarie to Anlease's house would've taken three, if not more, hours; they made that journey in under two hours.

"I can't believe it!" Amelia heard Anlease's surprised expression clearly after she told her everything. "Why? I mean, how?"

"I don't know," she slumped against the chair's back. "But this William seems to have turned them all against me." Amelia sighed, her heart heavy with the weight of betrayal. She had never expected a stranger to manipulate others to turn against her. Her voice trembled with frustration and confusion as she recounted the events to Anlease, Sarian, and Sofia.

Anlease leaned forward, concern etched on her face. "But why would William do such a thing? What does he gain from turning everyone against you?"

Amelia shook her head, trying to make sense of it all. "I wish I knew, Anlease. Maybe he has some hidden agenda or a grudge against me that I'm unaware of. But what hurts the most is that people I considered family are doubting me because of his influence."

Sarian's eyes narrowed as she pondered the situation. "We need to find out more about this William character. There must be something we're missing. Does he still have the papers?"

"Elensar's mother has them now," Amelia sighed heavily.

"If Queen Catreen has them, then nobody else will know."

Amelia answered with a second sigh, "I'm sure everyone already knows about me."

"How?" Sofia asked, frowning at Amelia.

"The looks, the stares I—"

"I doubt it," said Sarian. "It's just your mind playing tricks."

"Not this time," Sofia replied. "Amelia made the trip haste to get here because of the human haters."

Sarian bit her lip. She knew what Sofia was on about because she'd heard something that happened long ago; it made her shudder with fear even now. Sarian's mind wandered back to that fateful day, a dark chapter in her history. It was when a few humans and magical beings coexisted peacefully until a group of extremists emerged, fuelled by hatred and prejudice. They called themselves the '*Human Haters*,' whose sole purpose was to eradicate any trace of humanity from their world.

"Human haters!"

"Haven't you heard of them, Amelia?" voiced Sarian. "I can't—"

"No, I haven't, so tell me."

Sarian began.

Many years ago, when Sarian had been barely a kin of fewer than ten years, she'd sometimes go with her mother and brother to visit an aunt who lived in Bridton. During those visits, her mother and aunts would sit, talking of olden times, speaking of many things, like what had gone on since their last visits, all the usual mundane things that bore any young kin. However, when the talk became about a Shalimar called Dorthean, Sarian's mother told her and her younger brother to play outside in the garden. But Sarian wanted to hear what her mother was talking about, for this person her mother was about to speak about was well known to the older inhabitants of her village.

Dorthean was a wizard of old times, a relic of an era long forgotten, a master of arcane magics and unfathomable mysteries. His powers were a thing of legends, stories spoken in hushed tones around the fire while kin's listened wide-eyed and captivated. He could control the elements, bend the land to his will, and even break time, accessing powers beyond most people's scope. Yet despite these extraordinary abilities, he was a solitary figure who had chosen to retreat from society to study in the wilds. Despite his reclusive ways, his knowledge of arcane arts was unsurpassed, meaning many sought to learn from him. He inspired both horror and admiration in those brave or foolish enough to venture to meet him.

Sarian's journey took her past the sitting room with a slightly ajar door. Sarian's curiosity piqued as she strained to hear the conversation inside the sitting room. The voices were hushed, filled with a mixture of fear and intrigue. She couldn't resist the urge to inch closer, her heart pounding in anticipation. As she approached the door, Sarian caught a glimpse of her mother's face, etched with concern. Her mother was engrossed in conversation with an older woman whose voice conveyed wisdom and experience. Sarian recognized her as Mrs. Everly, the village's renowned storyteller.

"It's all fairy tales," Mrs. Everly repeated, her voice tinged with scepticism. "They say, but Dorthean's well known for such evilness."

Sarian's mind raced with questions. Who was this Dorthean? And what evilness was Mrs. Everly referring to? She strained her ears further, eager to uncover the secrets that seemed to hang in the air.

"They say he cut the flow from his neck," said Mrs. Everly, carrying on with her story, "To seep so slowly the poor human would die days later."

"How did they find this poor man?"

"He was left," Mrs. Everly said matter of fact-like, "Upon the peak of Rokey Mountains."

"How was he found so far up?"

"They say," Mrs. Everly leaned forward in her chair, "Someone found one of the goats upon the Mountain with a piece of the human's shirt, all bloodied in his teeth."

"If someone found a goat with the human's clothing, how come they blamed Dorthean for the human's death?"

"Would you live upon a Mountain in coldness all the time?"

"I suppose not," Sarian's mother replied, her brow furrowing with concern. "But blaming Dorthean seems unfair. He has always been kind to us and the other villagers."

Mrs. Everly sighed, her eyes filled with sadness and frustration. "People tend to fear what they don't understand. Dorthean has always been an outsider in our community, living alone on that mountain. It's easy for them to point fingers at him."

Sarian's mother nodded thoughtfully, her mind racing with questions. "But what if it wasn't him? What if there's something else up there on the Rokey Mountains that we don't know about?"

Mrs. Everly leaned in closer again, her voice dropping to a hushed tone. "There have always been rumours of strange creatures lurking in those mountains; tales passed down from generation to generation.

Some say they are ancient beings protecting hidden treasures or cursed souls doomed to wander. But there could be another explanation why the goat had the clothing."

"True," agreed Sarian's mother. "Maybe someone else planted the clothing there to frame Dorthean."

"Or maybe it was just a coincidence," suggested Mrs. Everly. "After all, goats are known to scavenge and chew on anything they find. It's possible that the goat stumbled upon the clothing and started chewing on it."

"But what about the blood on the shirt?" questioned Sarian's mother. "That seems like a significant piece of evidence."

"Blood could have come from anywhere," replied Mrs. Everly. "It doesn't necessarily mean it came from a human. Animals get injured constantly, and perhaps this goat had encountered some prey or predator before finding the shirt."

"If it was Dorthean, how did they find evidence to cast him as the killer?"

"By searching his dwellings," replied Mrs. Everly, "Looking for a clue pointing to the killer. The funny thing I don't get is that once they finished searching, they found the human had been living with Dorthean for some time."

"Living with him!"

"If you can call it that. More like treating the human with kindness, leading him to his death when they reached the top of the Mountain."

"I hope they made him pay for what he did," Sarian's mother said heatedly.

"They did," Mrs. Everly nodded, "Yet they let him return home again once he served his time."

"Surely, he didn't repeat his crime."

"Repeat, recruit."

"Recruit!" Sarian's mother

Mrs. Everly nodded solemnly, her expression mirroring Sarian's mother's concern. "He somehow managed to transform many minds about the humans, yet I don't know how he did it, but it worked enough for someone to write a song about them."

"Please," Sarian's mother asked, "Sing it to me."

"You don't want to hear an old voice like mine sing, my dear," Mrs. Everly replied with a gentle smile.

Sarian's mother reached out and grasped Mrs. Everly's frail hand. "But your voice has always been like a soothing melody to my ears," she insisted, trembling with emotion. "Please, just this once."

Mrs. Everly's eyes twinkled with nostalgia and sadness as she reminisced about the days when her voice resonated through grand concert halls, captivating audiences from all walks of life. The memories flooded back, bringing both joy and sorrow to her heart.

With a sigh, Mrs. Everly finally relented, realizing that this was not just a simple request but an opportunity to create a history memory for Sarian's mother and Sarian herself, whom Mrs. Everly knew had been listening to their conversation all along. "All right," she whispered, her voice carrying the weight of years gone by. "But promise me you won't judge this old voice too harshly," she saw Sarian's mother shake her, so she began.

"Long ago, there were silver moons and golden suns, clearest air and hushed sighs, blue crystal seas and grass so green, but the song of earth is no more. Not whispered in the wind, nor carried by mouth, for you, the breed without knowledge, chose land to cut, dig, drill, with no thought of care, but your desire to choose which land you'll next kill. Now you'll look back in regret; you had our help, had the time, but you choose to ignore and forget."

"I'm glad it's nothing like that here," said Sarian's mother once the song ended.

"Maybe that's why the human came here," Mrs. Everly replied, "Maybe he knew of this land."

"He might have, but I doubt it."

"Wouldn't you want to get away from that land?"

Sarian's mother paused for a moment, contemplating Mrs. Everly's question. She looked out at the peaceful landscape surrounding them outside the window, the vibrant greenery, and clear blue skies. It starkly contrasted with the land they had just witnessed in the song, a place filled with chaos and destruction. "I suppose it depends on what one seeks," Sarian's mother replied. "Some may yearn for adventure and excitement, even in danger. Others might prefer this land's tranquillity and safety, but how did he come to walk here? Is the portal not sealed from them?"

"They say," Mrs. Everly leaned forward, "He crept through another way, but I don't know if this tale is even true."

"Perhaps it was all someone's revenge against us," Sarian's mother suggested, "Someone who wanted to cause a problem in our world. What about King Tarron? He could've done such a thing. He could've given Dorthean the human to begin our hatred."

"Don't be daft!" Mrs. Everly shook her head, "He's been dead for many years, so how could it be him?"

"His body went missing, but his footsteps people still talk about; who's to say he is dead?"

"I don't know," Mrs. Everly shrugged her shoulders. "But it's been years since anyone has seen or heard from him," Mrs. Everly continued, her voice tinged with uncertainty. "People say he vanished into thin air, but I can't help but wonder if there's more to the story."

"There are words spoken of another involved."

"Another?" Mrs. Everly's eyes widened with intrigue as she leaned in closer, her curiosity piqued. "Who could this *'another'* possibly be? And why haven't I heard about them before?"

"Because it was someone with power, strength to veil such a happening and from informing others about it."

"Stop it, Leana; now you're making things up."

"I'm not," Sarian's mother protested, "People say the person held a throne of power used against this human."

"Who was it?"

"Queen Catreen of Volarie."

"Queen Catreen of Volarie? Are you serious?" Mrs. Everly asked, unable to hide the disbelief in her voice.

Sarian's mother nodded earnestly. "I know it sounds unbelievable, but I've heard it from multiple sources. There are whispers among the people that Queen Catreen possessed some supernatural power that she used against humans who opposed her rule."

And that's all the conversation Sarian heard, for her brother came along and gave a look that embarrassed her. "You know it's not right to listen in on other people's conversations, especially when private."

Chapter 11

Secrets Revealed

"And that's," said Sarian, "Where the story of the human haters comes from."

"Well, now you've cheered me up with that story," Amelia placed her glass on the table. "I thought you were trying to help me."

"Forget her story, Amelia," Sofia looked at her, next angrily at Sarian. "I'm sure she didn't mean to upset you."

Sarian sighed, realizing her attempt to share the history behind the human haters had backfired. She hadn't intended to upset Amelia; she wanted to shed some light on the origins of the hatred. Sofia's protective nature towards Amelia was understandable, but Sarian knew it was vital for them to understand the whole picture. "I apologize if my story upset you, Amelia," Sarian said sincerely, her voice filled with regret. "I didn't mean to dampen your spirits. But sometimes, understanding the past can help us navigate the present and build a better future."

Amelia looked at Sarian, her expression softening as she realized Sarian's intentions were not malicious. "I know you meant well," she replied, a hint of sadness still lingering. "It's just disheartening to think that such hatred exists."

"But what do you think?" Sarian asked this question of Anlease, "Can a race be so bitter?"

Anlease paused momentarily, her brows furrowing as she considered Sarian's question. "Can a race be so bitter? I wouldn't be able to judge a race I barely know."

"But humans have been known for thousands of years!"

"She hasn't seen them," said Sofia, "Probably doesn't even know what they look like."

"They look like us," voiced Sarian. "But with rounded ears and rounded bodies."

"There's nothing wrong with rounded bodies," Anlease sharply answered. "It's not about their physical appearance but their actions and beliefs. Just because they may look different from you doesn't mean they should be judged or labelled as bitter."

"There is when they run," Sofia laughed, "Wobble, wobble—"

"Oh, stop it; my sides will split apart with all the laughter," said Sarian. "The image is just too revolting to see." Sarian continued, "Wibble, wobble—And then they crash into each other, bam! Bam! Bam!" Sarian added, clapping her hands together, barely able to contain her amusement.

Sofia couldn't help but join in the laughter, her voice echoing through the room. "Can you imagine the chaos? It would be like a scene from a slapstick comedy!"

As their laughter subsided, Sarian wiped tears of joy from her eyes. "But seriously, Sofia, can you picture it? A group of wobbling creatures stumbling and crashing into one another? It's both hilarious and horrifying at the same time."

Anlease stomped her foot and shouted, "Stop it!"

"Wibble, wobble—"

"Enough!" Anlease interrupted, her voice filled with frustration. She crossed her arms and glared at Sarian and Sofia, who were still chuckling at the mental image. "I don't understand how you two find amusement in such things."

Sofia looked over at Sarian, then burst out laughing, soon followed by Sarian doing the same, uncontainable giggles echoing through the room, bouncing off walls and filling every corner.

"That's it. Anlease, come," Amelia walked over to her and wrapped an arm around her shoulder, leading her away from the giggling duo, "There's no point in trying to reason with them when they're like this."

"It's a joke, Amelia," laughed Sarian. "We didn't mean anything."

Amelia sighed, her grip on Anlease's shoulder tightening slightly. She glanced back at Sarian, her expression mixed with frustration and disappointment. "I understand it's a joke, Sarian," she replied, her voice tinged with annoyance. "But sometimes jokes can cross a line and hurt people unintentionally."

"Wibble, wobble," had been Sofia's remark, making Sarian giggle again.

Amelia's frustration grew as Sarian laughed, seemingly oblivious to the impact of their words. It made her drag Anlease out of the room into the kitchen to escape their ridiculous behaviour. "I know they're my friends," she said, her voice tinged with exasperation. "But sometimes, I just can't understand how they can be so thoughtless and insensitive. Are you okay? I'm sorry about that, about them."

Anlease, caught off guard by the sudden exit from the room, looked at Amelia with confusion and concern. "Yeah, I'm fine," she replied, her voice tinged with a hint of sadness. "It's just—Sometimes their jokes can be a bit much, you know?" She knew all too well how much Amelia valued her friendship with Sarian and Sofia, but she also understood that there were moments when their behaviour could be overwhelming.

"I understand," Amelia said softly. "They can sometimes be insensitive but try not to let it get to you. They don't mean any harm."

Anlease sighed again, her eyes searching Amelia's for understanding. "I know they don't mean any harm, but it still hurts sometimes," she admitted. "Being different is never easy."

Amelia squeezed her friend's shoulder gently. "I know it's tough, Anlease," she said empathetically. "But remember, you're unique and special in your way. Don't let their words define you."

Anlease smiled as they entered the bustling kitchen filled with delicious aromas. "It's alright," she replied. "I know they don't mean it. It's just that sometimes it feels like that's all they ever talk about with me." She looked away for a moment, then back up to Amelia. "Do you think they ever see me as anything more than a joke?"

"I don't think they always see you for who you are. But I do. You're strong, resilient, and can handle anything they throw at you."

"I appreciate that, Amelia." Anlease glanced around the kitchen, her gaze softening. "Thank you for being here with me. I know it's not easy dealing with them sometimes."

"No problem. That's what friends are for, right?"

"True, anyway, it's not like I remember much of that land, our old world; it just annoyed me slightly that they see us all as they described."

"That's right; you entered this land a child, didn't you."

Anlease nodded. "Yes, I was just a young girl when I arrived here; that must be six hundred years ago. Everything was so different, so unfamiliar. But over time, I've embraced this new realm as my own."

Amelia sighed and leaned against the kitchen counter. "I wish I could say the same. Sometimes, I can't help but feel like an outsider in this land. It's as if they see us as mere curiosities, relics from a forgotten past."

"You must have been living in a terrible time when you arrived."

"I was for my early years in Volarie castle," Amelia continued, her voice tinged with a hint of sadness. "But not as a prisoner, I must hasten to add. Elensar believed it was for my safety, sheltered from the chaos and dangers that lurked beyond those walls."

"Now times have changed; we're walking on our tiptoes."

"How right you are," Amelia nodded. "Yet you must find it harder to keep our secret here."

"It's not so bad as long as I keep myself to myself."

Amelia nodded again. "I wish I could do that; it's too late."

"Surely you can't mean that. You have a fine husband that loves you for what you are. Children that worship the very ground you—"

"My husband doesn't know she deceives him with a life that should've died long ago."

"I was going to ask you about the aging side of things. I took medicine because age was creeping up on me—"

"When did you do that?"

"Early thirties," replied Anlease replied. "I think, you?"

"Forties plus," Amelia said with a hint of regret.

Anlease leaned in closer, her curiosity piqued. "How did you discover this secret, the potion that helps us keep young? I mean for myself, Rotherkin gave it to me, but what about you?"

Amelia hesitated momentarily before continuing, her voice barely above a whisper. "It was a chance encounter with an old friend who had seemingly defied the laws of aging. I couldn't help but be intrigued and desperate to uncover their secret."

"Who was this person? Do I know them?" Anlease asked eagerly.

"You've heard of twins Borthron and Elysium, yes?"

"Yes, I have."

"The twins are old friends of my husband," said Amelia. "They knew a few humans living in our realm, and because they knew my true identity by having a steady viewing of me over the years, they led me to someone who could help my aging stop. That was Rotherkin."

"Ah, the wizard," Anlease smiled.

"Yes, the very same," Amelia confirmed with a nod. "Rotherkin was, is still, a powerful wizard who mastered the art of immortality. He possessed ancient knowledge and had discovered a way to halt the effects of time on his own body."

Anlease's eyes widened in fascination. "So, he could stop aging? That's incredible!"

Amelia chuckled softly. "Indeed, it is quite remarkable. When Borthron and Elysium introduced me to Rotherkin, I was initially sceptical. But after witnessing his abilities firsthand, I knew he held the key to youth."

Anlease frowned at her, then asked, "So, did you age in front of Elensar before medicine?"

"Yes," Amelia laughed a little, "You should have seen me hiding mine from him; it would have made you laugh mad. I did it with loads of makeup, hiding in the dark when undressed, and then I had Rotherkin's medicine. Mind you, it still doesn't help out with other matters that Elensar has a wife that deceives him by not allowing him to father as many children as he wishes."

"Ah," Anlease nodded, "That'll be the medicine doing that."

"It's still my fault."

"Why do you say that?" Anlease asked, her curiosity piqued.

Amelia sighed; her voice tinged with regret. "I should have been honest with Elensar from the beginning about why my periods have decreased so much over the years," she confessed. "I knew about his desire to have a large family, but I couldn't bring myself to tell him the truth."

Anlease looked shocked, then laughed, "Large! You already have four; how many does he want!"

Amelia chuckled softly, her eyes filled with amusement and sadness. "Five; I had Star as well," she sighed heavily, then smiled, "I know, they may seem like a lot to some people, but Elensar has always dreamed of having a big, bustling family of around ten at least."

Anlease's eyebrows arched in surprise. "Wow, ten, I had no idea. But Amelia, you can't blame yourself for not fulfilling his dream. You've given him five beautiful children; that's no small feat!"

Amelia nodded appreciatively at her friend's comforting words, "True; now, knowing Elensar right now, he'd flip out if he knew I was staying infertile, so it's best kept secret from all."

"What about your children? They'd understand, wouldn't they?"

"My children!" Amelia half laughed, "What would they say to a mother always telling them not to keep secrets?"

"Even ones like ours!"

Amelia paused momentarily, her eyes searching Anlease's face before she finally nodded. "Yes, even secrets like ours," Amelia replied softly, her voice tinged with vulnerability. "Especially secrets like ours."

"Perhaps your right," Anlease sighed. "It would only cause more problems. Yet your family, they would understand, wouldn't they, if you did tell them your secret, our secret?"

Amelia shook her head sadly. "I don't think so. Elensar wouldn't take too kindly to someone who's been keeping a secret from him for a few days, let alone over a thousand years, even if it were me."

"He must have mellowed with age to handle this secret!"

"Have you ever seen Elensar losing his rag?"

Anlease shook her head. "No, I can't say that I have. But that doesn't mean he wouldn't be furious if he found out about this secret."

Amelia's eyes grew distant as she reminisced about the centuries, she had spent with Elensar. "He's a wise and patient man, but there are certain things even time cannot soften. My secrets—Are against everything he believes in, and believe me, his waves of anger are not a pretty sight to see."

"Is it that bad?"

Amelia sadly nodded and looked around, fiddling with the jewelled bracelet around her wrist for a moment, her eyes filled with sadness and fear. "I've seen him in moments of great disappointment before," she whispered, her voice barely audible. "But nothing compares to the wrath he unleashes when he feels deceived." The weight of her secrets seemed to grow heavier with each passing moment. "If I tell Elensar my secret when his rage is released, bad isn't the word I'd use to describe it; horrendous probably fits better."

"Then I'll make sure I've no cause to let him use it in front of me."

Amelia half-laughed, "You'll be safe, Anlease; you've no cause for Elensar to release it, but for me, I'll probably vanish."

"Vanish!"

"Yes, and I'd like to do it now, vanish. Perhaps even slip back through the portal."

Anlease looked at Amelia with concern, her brows furrowing. "I understand your fear, but running away is not the solution."

"You're right; I'd wonder when I'd get caught."

"Since we're on the subject of the phrase, *getting caught*," Anlease started to walk away, "It's that time again."

Amelia frowned until she gave her a hint by taking a swig from an imaginary bottle. Amelia's eyes widened as she finally understood what Anlease was referring to. "Oh, the Carnoon Potion!" Amelia exclaimed, realizing it was the life medicine she was hinting at, then started following in her footsteps. "You've Carnoon, here, now!"

"Of course, I have Amelia," Anlease now started to walk back into a quiet living room; the previous laughter from Sofia and Sarian gone. "Don't you have some at home too?"

Once Sarian saw them enter the room, she stopped them, saying, "I thought you two got lost or something."

Anlease sighed, her shoulders slumping slightly. "No, we didn't get lost," she replied. "We were just—Caught up in something."

She saw Sofia and Sarian exchange curious glances. Anlease chuckled and replied, "Nah, just got caught up in a little adventure on the way here. But we're back now, ready for some fun!"

Sarian raised an eyebrow, intrigued by their mysterious behaviour. "Adventure? Do tell," she urged, her curiosity piqued.

Anlease glanced at Sarian mischievously before turning to retrieve a small vial from a dresser. "Well, you see, we stumbled upon this hidden potion shop while exploring the outskirts of town a few days ago. It's like a secret haven for all things magical."

Sarian's eyes widened with excitement as she took in Anlease's words. "A potion shop? That sounds incredible! How did you find it?"

Anlease smirked and leaned closer, whispering conspiratorially, "Let's just say we followed a trail of enchanted fireflies that led us straight to its entrance. It was like something out of a fairy tale."

Sarian couldn't help but be captivated, but Amelia said something to burst her excitement bubble. "Nah, she's just kidding."

"That's not nice, Amelia! I thought we were your friends," Sarian replied, her disappointment evident in her voice.

"You are."

"And me too," replied Sofia, fluttering her eyelids at her, "Am I?"

"Of course, Sofia, but only when you're normal."

"She," Sarian laughed, "Is never normal."

"And you are! You two are never normal," Amelia turned her gaze to Anlease, heading out the other living room door. "Anlease," she called when she realized she was leaving. "Perhaps if you've spare, coul—"

"I'm sorry, I've only a little left for myself. Have you tried Borthron and Elysium in Hildernbyth? Perhaps they have some."

Sarian frowned. "A little of what is left."

"Perfume," Amelia said quickly, not wanting to divulge her secret to them. "My favourite perfume."

"What!" Sofia said, all surprised. "You've used the big bottle Elensar brought you already?"

Amelia nodded sheepishly, her cheeks flushing with embarrassment. "Yes, I couldn't resist. It's so exquisite, and I've been using it sparingly, but it seems to have run out faster than I anticipated."

Sofia's eyes widened in disbelief. "But you told us that perfume is incredibly rare and expensive! How did you manage to go through it so quickly?"

"What did you do with it? Drink it!" asked Sarian.

Amelia's eyes darted nervously between Sofia and Sarian, her embarrassment growing. "No, of course not!" she exclaimed, her voice tinged with a mix of defensiveness and amusement. "I didn't drink it; that would be absurd!"

"Did you break it?" Sofia asked, frowning at her.

Amelia shook her head vigorously, her cheeks flushing with embarrassment. "No, I didn't break it either," she replied, her voice filled with a hint of exasperation. Now, if you'd stop asking, I'll tell."

"Oops," uttered Sofia. "Someone got out of bed on the wrong side."

"By her state," Sarian said with a childish giggle. "I'd say she fell out of the bed."

Amelia shot a glare at Sarian, her frustration mounting. "I did not fall!" she retorted; her voice laced with irritation.

"Don't be mean to her, you guys!" Anlease came to Amelia's rescue after entering back into the room. "I think she's got beautiful hair," Anlease walked up to Amelia and caressed her long black hair. "Now," she walked away from her. "Who's for a glass of weatherlin's?"

That question made Sofia and Sarian look at each other, smile, and nod their responses. Anlease's kind words not only diffused the tension in the room but also reminded them of the importance of empathy and acceptance. Amelia, touched by Anlease's gesture, felt a surge of gratitude towards her friend. It was moments like these that made her appreciate the bond they shared. Anlease had always been there to support her, especially during times when others were quick to judge or criticize. As they gathered around the table, pouring themselves glasses of Weatherlin's - a refreshing drink known for its vibrant colours and unique flavours - the atmosphere became lighter. The room filled with laughter and chatter as they settled into a comfortable conversation.

The rest of the day, evening, was spent as females in a gathering always do, chat, drink, laugh, eat, and talk about memories, fears, love, hopes, and dreams. The conversation deepened as the sun set, casting a warm golden glow over the group. They delved into their pasts, sharing stories of kin/childhood adventures and mischievous escapades that brought tears of laughter to their eyes. Each tale sparked another memory, igniting a sense of nostalgia that enveloped them like a comforting blanket. As the night wore on, the conversation took a more introspective turn. They began discussing dreams and aspirations, reflecting on how far they had come since those mischievous kin/childhood days. Encouragement flowed freely between them, like a gentle breeze carrying whispers of support.

Chapter 12

A Dream Of Better Times

Dreams are an essential part of our lives. They are mysterious, beautiful, and sometimes even frightening. They can be wild and full of surreal imagery, or they can be mundane and repetitive. Dreams can be an outlet for creativity, a window into the subconscious, or a source of insight and inspiration. They can offer a glimpse into the future or reflect the past. Dreams can transport us to other worlds, explore our desires, and help us process difficult emotions. They can provide comfort and guidance, providing a safe space to work through anxieties and insecurities. Dreams can help us understand our lives, relationships, and our place in the world. Whether or not we remember them, our dreams are vital to who we are, but we should return to the story.

Amelia's sleeping hours would now differ from Sofia's, Anlease's, and Sarian's dream worlds when nighttime came. Inside Amelia's dreamland that night, she wore a blue dress buttoned up to the neck, a white apron tied around her waist, and her long black hair tied loosely back away from her face. She was leaning over a stove in a small cottage kitchen in Weath. She held a pinch of mixed herbs over a pan in her fingers. These she dropped into the water, then walked to the far end of the kitchen where she'd previously been cutting vegetables and started to chop an onion with many tears falling.

When she finished this, she wiped a hand across her forehead, wiping a little sweat away, but some of it dripped into her eyebrows and eyes. "Shit! Oh no! Shit!"

Amelia was suddenly jumping up and down, rubbing her eyes. She ran over to the sink, grabbed a small glass from the draining board, and ran a little water into it. Next, Amelia tilted her head back, the glass sloping slightly over her eyes, letting it wash out slowly. Once she'd done this, her half-sighted, still stinging eyesight peered from the window above the sink.

Amelia smiled, heard someone coming up behind her, and felt a hand on her shoulder; she was supposed to be the only one in the house! She screamed in fright.

"Shh, Mycorm," whispered a male voice into her ear.

Only one person called her by that pet name. "Elensar!" Amelia's heart raced as she half turned to face Elensar, her husband. Relief washed over her as she recognized his familiar face, but the shock of his unexpected arrival still lingered. "Elensar, you scared me half to death!" Amelia exclaimed, trying to steady her breathing. "What are you doing here?"

Elensar grinned mischievously, his eyes sparkling with excitement. "I couldn't wait any longer. I missed you too much," he confessed, pulling her closer into a warm embrace.

Amelia couldn't help but melt back into him, feeling the tension dissipate. His touch was comforting and familiar, instantly calming her racing thoughts. She nestled her head against his chest and let out a soft sigh. "I missed you too, Melo," she whispered, using her pet's name for him, feeling a sense of warmth and security. She felt the hand slide away from her shoulder and go around her waist, a nose nuzzling in her hair. "But what on earth are you doing?"

"You look," Elensar breathed against her neck while still standing behind her, "Smell so good."

"I look sweaty," Amelia answered, laughing. "I've been pushing myself hard today."

Elensar chuckled softly, his eyes sparkling with admiration. "Sweaty or not, you radiate this incredible energy when you're in your element. It's captivating."

Amelia felt him kiss her neck, another hand fumbling around her waist. "Where are the twins?" she asked.

"Alexander and Etheryn?"

"Yes," she felt her apron go slack, felt it removed.

Elensar's chuckle deepened. "The twins are with their nanny in the garden," he replied, his voice filled with warmth.

Amelia's heart skipped a beat as Elensar's other hand gently caressed her neck, sending shivers down her spine. She leaned back into his touch, feeling a surge of desire coursing through her veins. His other hand fumbled around her waist, pulling her closer to him. Amelia felt a sense of liberation wash over her as the apron disappeared. The familiar weight lifted off her shoulders, allowing her to embrace the moment with Elensar fully.

With a mischievous smile, Elensar whispered into Amelia's ear, "You deserve to let go and indulge in your desires occasionally."

"Very true, but is that wise," the sound of cloth ripping made her frown, "To leave them unattended?"

"The guards are with them too."

"But what if something goes wrong?" she questioned, her voice tinged with concern."

Elensar chuckled, "Fear not," he reassured her, his confidence unwavering. "The guards are watching over them diligently. Besides, isn't it thrilling to let go of control for a little while?"

"I know, but I worry if you or—"

She heard Elensar sigh deeply. "I understand your fears, but sometimes, my love, you worry too much," he said with compassion and frustration. "Every last detail of this retreat has been meticulously planned and double-checked. I've considered all the possible risks and ensured everything will go smoothly."

"I just thought—"

"Well, don't think," Elensar interrupted abruptly, his tone laced with impatience. "Overthinking will only lead to unnecessary worry."

"It's the not thinking first that got me into coming here," she admitted quietly, feeling Elensar's presence close behind her. His words resonated within her, reminding her of the countless times she had let fear and overthinking hold her back from experiencing new adventures. This time was different; she had vowed to step out of her comfort zone and embrace the unknown.

"You told me you were enjoying this retreat."

"I am. I didn't think I'd be washing up all this," Amelia felt him kiss her shoulder while she was staring at a sink full of dishes and cutlery. "All the cooking, cleaning."

"You offered to do it, even when I suggested we'd bring someone along to do it all, but no, you said—"

"Sometimes it's nice to take care of things ourselves," she interrupted, her voice tinged with frustration. "But I didn't expect it to be this overwhelming. I thought we would have more time to relax and enjoy each other's company."

"Well, I can easily fix that for you," Elensar replied with a mischievous laugh, then kissed an exposed area on Amelia's neck, "Why don't you take a break from all this chaos."

"Then who's going to cook the rest of the dinner?" Amelia's voice held concern as she glanced at the other pots and pans scattered across the kitchen counter.

Elensar chuckled softly, his eyes twinkling with mischief. "Not you, that's for sure," Elensar replied, a mischievous grin spreading across his face.

"I can't just leave all this; besides, I haven't even started laying the table, and then there's the glasses they need—"

"Are you nervous or something?"

"Nervous? Me? No, why?"

Elensar raised an eyebrow, clearly unconvinced by Amelia's response. "Why? Because you're babbling is getting in my way."

"What!"

"I want to romance you, not talk about housework—"

Amelia's eyes widened in surprise. She had not expected such a bold statement from him, especially considering their casual and light-hearted conversation moments ago. "Elensar—"

"Stop talking!" Elensar had used a sterner voice. "I'm not here to engage in idle chatter."

Amelia's heart skipped a beat as Elensar's commanding tone cut through the air. She felt a rush of adrenaline course through her veins, unsure how to respond to his sudden change in demeanour. Her mind raced, trying to process the implications of his words. Was he serious? Only one way to find out. She took a deep breath, summoning every ounce of courage within her. With a determined look, Amelia met Elensar's gaze and replied with a slight tremor, "Really, then what do you want?"

"You Mycorm," Elensar's voice dropped to a low, intense whisper. "Naked," he growled without breaking his stare on her, "And willing," he whispered, his voice dripping with seduction.

Amelia's heart raced, captivated by the raw intensity that emanated from him. Something about Elensar's presence in this state terrified and enticed her, making her lure him to say more. "Really, and what about our dinner?" It was like she was playing with fire, teasing the flames that danced between them.

"Who cares about the damn dinner!" Elensar's eyes narrowed, his voice low, husky, and sensual, "I want you."

Amelia felt his arms suddenly go over her head. She should've been angry, but she liked it when he used that authoritative voice. She smiled and abruptly frowned, seeing a pair of hands in front of her, holding a long white cloth. "Elensar!" Amelia exclaimed, her hands reaching out to touch the fabric. "What are you doing?"

"Just blinding love to you for a while," Elensar replied mischievously, his voice filled with playful anticipation.

Confusion mixed with excitement coursed through Amelia's veins as she allowed herself to be blindfolded. "But what if someone comes into the kitchen and sees us?"

"Oh, I'm not planning on keeping us in here," Elensar whispered, his warm breath tickling Amelia's ear. "Do you trust me?"

With a soft smile playing on her lips, Amelia whispered back, "Yes." She felt his hands come around her waist when her words ended, his entire length pressing into her from behind. She felt lips delicately kissing her neck, hands moving erotically upon her figure, and then a hand suddenly interlocked with one of hers. Amelia felt her blindfolded figure move from the sink to the top of a table, and now she heard a door open. Elensar steered her down a long hallway and a flight of small stairs. Amelia heard a door open, a click behind, then locked when she entered another room. She felt a slight breeze of air circle around her. Was Elensar moving to be in front of her?

"Don't peep."

Amelia laughed. "I can't, I'm blindfolded, remember."

Elensar chuckled softly. "True, but I wouldn't put it past you to find a way," he teased playfully.

"You know me too well," she laughed back. Amelia felt a surge of excitement mixed with a hint of nervousness. She trusted Elensar implicitly, but there was always an element of surprise in these games that kept her on her toes, and this one he was playing was the first one for her. Elensar's mischievous chuckle at hearing her words caused Amelia to tilt her head in his direction. "All right, I won't peep," she said playfully, trying to hide her curiosity. "But I can't promise I won't try to figure out what you have up your sleeve."

"Who says I'm wearing sleeves," Elensar replied, laughing, and raising an eyebrow in amusement.

"Well, then, I guess I'll have to search elsewhere for your secrets," she teased. "Perhaps they're hidden in the mysterious smile you're showing now."

"You are peeping!" he laughed.

"No, I just know you too well," she replied, "But don't worry, I won't give up that easily. I'll find those secrets of yours, one way or another."

"Oh, you're determined, aren't you? Well then, let the search begin. But be warned, my secrets are well-guarded."

"Hmm, well, we'll see—" She suddenly felt Elensar's hand take one of her own, and it guided her on a marvellous tour. With her arm slightly raised, her fingers traced his forearms and touched his bare chest. "You are sleeveless and topless," she laughed.

"Well," his voice carried a hint of teasing, "I like to keep cool in this scorching heat."

"What scorching heat," she giggled, "We're still inside."

Elensar chuckled softly, "Ah, Mycorm, you have yet to discover the secrets. Step closer and feel the warmth that surrounds us."

Amelia took the hint, making her fingertips begin their journey again, roaming over the tight muscles of Elensar's midriff and then moving down to tease the tops of his thighs. Amelia paused there for a moment before forging onto his buttocks. She felt the warm sensation the smooth skin produced as she caressed them with her fingertips, and then she squeezed hard.

"Gently, Mycorm, gently," he whispered, his voice filled with caution and desire.

Amelia released her tight grip, allowing her fingertips to glide over the smooth skin again. The warmth of their touch sent shivers down her spine, igniting a fire within her. In the background, she could hear Elensar breathing heavily and knew she was giving him as much pleasure as she was taking from it, but it didn't stop there. She moved her hands around the front and felt an item- a warm shaft.

"Hmm," Amelia suddenly laughed, "I think I've just found your secret, Melo?"

"I think you might be right, Mycrom," Elensar gasped as if struggling to breathe.

Amelia could feel its solid length with her fingertips as she ran them along its side. His pelvis rocked forward with every movement she made, and she wondered if her touch delighted him as much as it did her.

If this had been Amelia's first time with a Shalimar, curiosity would have gotten the better of her. She would have slowly trailed her hands down the pole between the slender legs. But as she reached down further, she may have been surprised, as her hands came to a point where Amelia was sure she should have encountered something else, yet there was nothing there; you see, Shalimar's don't have testicles.

"That's enough, Mycorm," Elensar gasped, his voice laced with a hint of playfulness. "Now it's my turn—"

Amelia didn't have a chance to finish what she was doing as Elensar abruptly picked her up and threw her onto a bed. Elensar swiftly removed her blindfold. A bit of fear entered her thoughts for a second as he pinned her hands above her head. Amelia stared back at Elensar, frozen in fear, uncertain of what he would do next. Then, the corner of his mouth crooked up, and she noticed his eyes shining mischievously. As Elensar held her hands firmly above her head, Amelia was captivated by the intensity in his eyes. Something was alluring about how he looked at her as if he could see right through her defences.

"Don't worry, Mycorm," Elensar leaned closer and whispered huskily, a voice laced with seduction. "I won't do anything you don't want me to," he gently brushed his lips against hers, "But don't be expecting much sleep tonight or tomorrow morning—"

"I gathered that the moment the blindfold came out," Amelia laughed. "Oh, heaven help me, I forgot my crutches."

"It's okay," he responded, chuckling softly, "I'm sure I can whisk up a wheelbarrow for you to use, and I'll even do you the honour of pushing you around in it until your fully capable of walking on your own again," he replied with a wicked grin.

With a mischievous glint in her eyes, Amelia decided to take the teasing up a notch. "Well, if you're going to push me around in a wheelbarrow, I demand a crown and a sceptre too! After all, I will be the Queen of that makeshift chariot," she declared dramatically, pretending to be offended by his words.

He chuckled and played along. "Of course, Your Majesty," he replied with mock seriousness. "I shall be your loyal servant and fulfil all your royal commands. But I must warn you, Your Majesty, that with great power comes great responsibility," he added with a mischievous grin.

Amelia raised an eyebrow, her playful demeanour shifting into a more regal one. "Oh, I am well aware of the weight that comes with the crown," she said, her voice dripping with mock authority. "But fear not, loyal servant, for I shall rule gracefully and benevolently."

"Good to hear," Elensar smiled down at her," But for now, my beautiful Queen, I sense a desire raging through your veins that only I can fulfil."

"Pray, servant," Amelia smirked, "How do you know this desire you speak about courses through my veins?"

Elensar chuckled softly, his eyes twinkling mischievously. "Oh, my Queen, your desires are not hidden from me; even if stood miles away from my side, I could still smell it oozing from your pores, the drizzle of perspiration that drips down between your ample bosoms, between your legs," he kissed the tip of her nose, "Your desires are like a fragrance that lingers in the air, impossible to ignore," Elensar continued, his voice filled with a playful tone. "They dance around you, whispering secrets only I can decipher."

Amelia's cheeks flushed with a mixture of embarrassment and intrigue. She had always prided herself on her ability to conceal her deepest longings, but Elensar seemed to possess an uncanny understanding of her innermost desires.

"But how?" Amelia asked, her curiosity piqued. "How can you possibly know what lies within the depths of my heart?"

Elensar's gaze softened. "My Queen," he began, his voice gentle yet confident. "It is not just your words or actions that reveal your desires to me. It is the way your eyes sparkle when you speak of them, the subtle tremor in your voice when they consume your thoughts, but enough speak of desires and Queens, I must bed my wife before I lose more hours here."

Amelia blushed at Elensar's bold statement, feeling a mixture of surprise and amusement. She couldn't help but be captivated by his charm and straightforwardness. "Elensar," she said, her voice tinged with laughter, "You never fail to surprise me with your audacity." She playfully rolled her eyes before continuing, "But I suppose you're right."

"I'm always right," he replied with a laugh.

Chapter 13

Return Home

The next day, Anlease kissed each of her friends, Amelia, Sarian, and Sofia, goodbye as they parted ways. Two of them, Sofia, and Sarian, were fortunate enough to escape the night relatively unscathed, while Amelia looked far worse for wear with a sore head and vows never again to drink so heavily. Three hours later, the three travellers rode on horseback with castle guards in tow through Volarie's city. They passed by arched buildings and domes lining a boulevard and delicate alabaster fountains on the street corners. If the travellers looked up, they would have seen the intricate and shining architecture of the rooftops, reflecting the sun in glittering diamonds. The streets were alive with thriving markets and merchants of all kinds, with the people of Volaries City smiling and welcoming each other with open arms. Everywhere, there were lanterns, from the tiny to the grand, all sparkling with serene beauty. The travellers followed the street to the city's centre and found another large marketplace bustling with life. The scent of fresh fruits and vegetables filled the air, and craftsmen hocked their wares on the sides of the roads.

Everywhere they looked, something was intriguing to see or buy. Then they passed over cobbled streets lined with streams, willow trees, and stunning, brightly coloured flowers. Curved roofs of the city's grand buildings, adorned with delicate shutters, arched over the roads. Then came Sofia's home, where the horse and riders stopped and tied horses to a rail outside her home.

Inside Sofia's home, upon entering the living room, both Amelia and Sarian stepped back in surprise. The walls were magnolia, and in the middle were three settees, all blue and each a different size. Adding to their surprise was the set of four huge paintings, each strategically placed in the four corners of the room. The first painting they noticed hung on the north wall and was of Sofia and her kin Dinendal standing together in a field of wildflowers. On the south wall was a picture of a small town named Lurth, where Sofia once lived with her beloved companion Etheryn before the latter had tragically passed away. To the west hung a painting of Volarie, and on the east wall hung a portrait of a tall, blonde-haired figure seated on a wooden chair. Though the two had come to Sofia's house for a casual visit, Amelia set her sights on the painting on the east wall. Slightly intoxicated, Amelia viewed the picture with great interest.

Amelia couldn't help but feel drawn to it as if the figure in the painting had something to say to her. "This picture," Amelia's figure swayed slightly. "I like it." Even Amelia, still a bit unsteady from the night before, couldn't help but admire Armur's talent. Dinendal, Sofia's son, asked about the story behind the portrait of Etheryn, his father, to which Amelia responded. "After Armur painted it, Elensar and I decided to give it to your mother as a gift and did a great job with his likeness," Amelia reached out and touched it. "Did you see the painting he did of my family?"

"Yes," replied Sofia. "He uses great detail in all his paintings."

"But the way he does it," Amelia moved away from the painting. "It seems as if he's caught the very spirit of his subjects in the canvases," her slurry words finished by the time she half walked, half stumbled away from it.

"Hey, perhaps he's caught their spirits," Sarian's words slurred. "They always say a painting of a dead figure can see, watch, and listen to everything around it."

Dinendal, Sofia's kin in the same room, swayed slightly in his single chair, his blue eyes watching, a haze blurring his view of them all.

While she got up from her seat to get another drink, Amelia turned around and stood in front of Sarian's seated figure. "See-through a painting," she asked. "See us here?" She saw Sarian nod.

"Haven't you heard of it before?"

"Nope," Sarian watched as Amelia sat beside her, picked up a glass of wine, and went to drink; the glass was empty. She raised her gaze to find her pouring a drink. "If you're offering Sofia, I'll have another, please."

"Do you think you should?" Sofia replied, frowning at Amelia. "This one's not like the drink we had at Anlease's."

"Nah," Sarian laughed. "It's stronger, just what we need."

"Mother," said Dinendal. "Aunt Amelia and Aunt Sarian can handle it."

"That's right," Amelia laughed loudly. "You tell her."

"Amelia! He's only a thousand years old—"

Dinendal chuckled softly, "I understand your concern, Mother. But trust me, I've had my fair share of wild nights and survived them all. This drink will be no different."

"Ah, come on, Sofia," laughed Sarian, "He's not a little kin."

Sofia sighed, giving in to their persuasive arguments. "Alright then, but just one glass Din."

Amelia settled back into her chair. "Okay, Sofia, let's have another."

Sarian had been watching Amelia from across the room. She had noticed she had developed a slight habit of spilling drink wherever she went. She watched as she noticed a drop of red liquid but failed to see what had caused it. She slowly walked over and tried to think of something to say to avoid embarrassing her. As Sarian approached the couch, she carefully chose her words to strike a balance between acknowledging the incident and reassuring Amelia. "Accidents happen," she said, joining Amelia on the couch. Her voice carried a gentle tone laced with empathy.

Amelia looked up, surprise flickering across her face as she realized Sarian had witnessed another clumsy moment. A faint blush coloured her cheeks as she attempted to explain herself. "I don't know what's wrong with me today," she admitted sheepishly. "I seem full of accidents recently."

"Don't worry about it."

"What accidents?" asked Sofia, looking over at them both.

"I never mentioned an accident," replied Sarian.

"Accident," was Amelia's reply while trying to hide a red stain on the sofa with her hand. She was feeling embarrassed and awkward. "There's been no accident."

"Why are you trying to hide that mark then, Amelia," Sofia said, half laughing at her.

"I haven't done anything, Sofia; I haven't!"

"It's all that drunk she's been drinking," laughed Sarian.

"You're as bad as her," Sofia shook her head. "Both intoxicated, getting words wrong."

"Isn't that always the way when you've been drinking?" Din said, tilting his head to the side. "Olla and espy words."

"Oh my god, Din," laughed Amelia hysterically. "You're so funny. Do you even know what you're saying?"

He tilted his head and frowned. "I think so, but I'm as bad as you two if I don't."

"Then you're as bad as we are, Din," laughed Sarian.

"I don't think I'm like you unless I've just turned into a female."

Sarian turned to Amelia, winked, then turned her gaze back to Din. "Okay, try this question out for size. What's craved but is never again?"

For a second, Din thought hard, then laughed. "An Apple. Did you know it, Aunt Amelia?"

Amelia chuckled and shook her head. "No, I didn't know the answer either. But it makes sense now that you say it, Din."

Sarian grinned mischievously, enjoying the playful banter between her friends. "Well, sometimes the simplest questions have the trickiest answers. Let me try one." She paused for a moment, contemplating her next riddle.

Din leaned in closer, intrigued by Sarian's quest to have a go. "Alright, hit us with your best shot."

Sarian's eyes sparkled with excitement as she posed her next question. "What has keys but can't open locks?"

Amelia furrowed her brow, deep in thought. After a few moments of silence, she shrugged and admitted defeat. "I have no idea."

Din scratched his head, pondering over the riddle. Suddenly, a light bulb appeared above his head, and he exclaimed, "A piano!"

Sarian clapped her hands in delight, impressed by Din's quick thinking. "That's correct!" she exclaimed, her eyes shining with admiration. "A piano has keys, but they can't open locks. Well done, Din! Now it's your turn."

"Okay," Din rose from his chair and placed his drink on the table, "Here's one for you." He slowly walked to the centre of the room, sniffing at the air, walking as if prowling around for something.

"Get on with it," said Amelia, laughing at his odd behaviour.

Din suddenly pounced upon the table and crouched there momentarily. Seconds later, he stood up with a puffed-out chest, screaming his challenge. "I roar like a lion; I eat like a lion; I'm the only lion; what am I?"

There was a collective silence in the room for a moment, then a gasp, then words. "'You, Din, are the King."

At this, Din let out a triumphant roar that echoed off the room's walls. He bared his teeth and flexed his mighty muscles, then let out a puff of smoke with a satisfied smile. "That's right," Din declared proudly. "No matter how many other people come and go, I will always be the King of this family," Din began strolling back to his chair, bowing to everyone and even to invisible people as if to say '*Thank you for watching*' then he tripped over a rug, stumbled into his chair. That little episode of his had Sarian and Amelia rolling around on the sofa in tears of laughter.

"That's quite enough, Din! You're showing yourself up!"

"Ah, Mother, it's only a joke," laughed Din. He straightened his dishevelled clothes and flashed a sheepish grin at Sarian and Amelia, who were still in fits of laughter on the sofa.

Amelia wiped away tears of joy from her eyes and managed to gasp between giggles, "Oh, Din! You never fail to entertain us with your antics."

"I have another one for you that isn't so active."

Curiosity piqued, and Amelia eagerly urged him to continue. "Well, go on then! Don't keep us waiting," she exclaimed, her anticipation growing.

Din started making high-pitched squeaks as if he were a chicken, flapping his arms like wings simultaneously.

"Oh Valar, stop it, Din," Sofia cuffed him around his head, making him abruptly stop. "You, you should know better."

"What should I know better?"
She cuffed him around the head again. "Don't encourage your aunts when they're intoxicated like this."
Din rubbed his head, looking slightly sheepish. "Sorry, Aunts. I didn't mean to make things worse."
Sofia sighed, her frustration melting into concern. "I know you didn't mean any harm, Din. But sometimes, it's important to be mindful of the situation. You Aunts may be in high spirits now, but we've seen how quickly things can escalate."
Amelia replied with a giggle, "Oi you, I'm not intoxicated; I'm in high spirits."
"I like that," Sarian wrapped her arms around Amelia. "Oh, I like that. Let's be in high spirits together." Amelia's giggle grew louder as Sarian embraced her.
"Oh, for Valar's sake! Pack it in, you two."
"What's the matter, Sofia? You can join in." Sarian separated herself from Amelia and opened her arms. "A friendly hug always makes things better."
Sofia rolled her eyes, unable to hide her annoyance. "No thanks, I'll pass on the lovey-dovey fest," she retorted, crossing her arms over her chest.
"Don't be a stinger," Amelia laughed. "Come on."
"I think maybe we should sober you up," Sofia walked into the hallway. "Get you home."
"But it's not even late yet!" Amelia shouted. "Come back here!"
"I'm getting you something to get you back to normal."
"She's normal, well nearly," laughed Sarian hysterically.
As Sofia descended the hallway, she racked her brain for a solution. She needed something practical yet gentle enough to ease Amelia's intoxication without causing any harm. Suddenly, an idea struck her. She hurriedly entered the kitchen and rummaged through the cabinets, searching for a specific herbal remedy she had used in the past. After a few moments of frantic searching, she found what she was looking for—a small bottle of ginger extract. With the bottle in hand, Sofia quickly mixed it thoroughly with a few drops and herbs into a glass of water.
Returning to the living room, Sofia extended the glass toward Amelia, "Some of this medicine is for you as well." She handed them all an odd-looking mixture of liquid and herbs, slurping around in three small glasses.
"I'm not drinking this!" Amelia eyed her glass. "It looks disgusting!"
"Neither am I. What's in it anyway?"
"It's Mother's secret remedy for drinking. Not very useful," Din said, sipping from his glass. "Always makes me feel sick."

"What's in this thing?" said Amelia, sniffing her glass contents. "It isn't going to make us sick as well, is it?"

"Stop asking questions. Just drink it down in one go."

Sarian took a sip and abruptly spat it out. "That's revolting!"

"That's it!" Amelia gagged. "I'm so not drinking it now!"

"You want Elensar to see you like this!"

"I told you, Sofia," she placed her glass on the small wooden table before her. "I don't care what he'll see; besides, he'll be busy running after his darling mummy anyway."

"At least he'll be able to catch her."

Sarian's words made Amelia break into a laugh that sounded out of control. Sofia tried to get Amelia up from the settee, "I want to get you back."

"You want to take me back! Back to where!" she stood up and wobbled about so severely that she had to lean against Sofia.

"Home," Sarian got up. "You know where home is, surely."

"Home," Amelia echoed softly, carrying both longing and uncertainty. "Yes, I should go home."

"Aunt Amelia!" shouted Din as they led her into the hallway. "Can you tell Lathlorn I'll see him later than planned today? Something urgent crept up; it needs my full attention."

"What's that," Amelia called back, "Need more of mummy's secret remedy?"

"No, it's not that," he replied gently. "It's something else entirely. But don't worry, I'll take care of it."

"Amelia," Sofia pulled Amelia further down the hallway. "You're impossible," she walked to the front door.

"I'm not impossible, Sofia, just hard to live with sometimes."

"Yes, don't we know it!" Sofia opened the door; Amelia wobbled through it to her horse tied up outside the house. "I think I better come with you," Sofia replied, watching Amelia half stumble, trying to climb up upon her horse, "Just to make sure you get home in one piece." The next minute, they were seated on Amelia's horse. Before they left, she spoke in a warning tone to Sarian, "Stay here, okay."

"Look you, Sofia," Sarian waved a finger at her and began turning around to go back into the house, "I know how to handle my drink," in a state of blindness, she fell against the door, then straightened herself up. Sarian blinked rapidly, trying to clear her vision. "I'm fine, I'm fine," she slurred, attempting to sound composed despite her apparent intoxication. "Just a little stumble, that's all."

"For goodness' sake, Sarian! I can only deal with one drunkard at a time," Sofia wrapped her arms around a still-intoxicated Amelia, the horse's rein already in her hands, "Now get inside before you give my house a bad name!"

"Oops, sorry," Sarian was saying before the door shut.

Sofia and Amelia returned to Volarie Castle, home of the royal family. Sofia didn't want anyone to see just how bad Amelia was still drunk - especially her mother-in-law, Queen Catreen, who Sofia was sure would be highly disapproving. Therefore, Sofia quickly directed Amelia to the back door, praying that nobody would be there to witness her inebriated state. But the universe had other plans. Just as they stepped onto the stone steps leading into the castle, Amelia tripped and stumbled forward. And there, standing right before them, was the one person they had been trying to avoid, Queen Catreen. Sofia froze, her heart pounding as she waited for the Queen's reaction.

Queen Catreen had always been known for her temper, and no one was sure what to expect. After a few uncomfortable moments, the Queen finally spoke. "You cheap drunken little whore!"

The words, '*You cheap drunken little whore,*' were screamed at Amelia, followed by bouts of rage and fury. Amelia's face had gone white with shock as she flinched at the first verbal assault, but then she started laughing, making the Queen even more mad. Again, more angry words came forward, directed at a now stumbling around Amelia with Sofia trying to keep her upright.

Chapter 14

A Dilemma

Etheryn, the eldest of the four, spoke first. He had seen the whole ordeal and told them how their parents had been arguing like wild animals and how the argument had escalated. Lenith, the third sibling who had chosen to stay out of the fray, frowned. Alexander, Etheryn's twin brother, was staring off into the distance. Lastly, Lathlorn knew that he had to be strong for his younger brothers to make sure this would not happen again, and the only way to do that was to suggest something in private to them all. So that's what Lathlorn did; he called a secret meeting where they were all standing now, in the garden of Volarie, discussing the situation and trying to make sense of what had happened. The four siblings stood silently, united in a joint agreement.

Lenith, the youngest, spoke first. "You can't speak of such things," he said solemnly. "It can't be said."

Alexander turned to his twin Etheryn. "Grandmother's mind has faded," he said with sadness. "It isn't wise to suggest that our mother took those papers into her thoughts. We mustn't make it known that we are aware of it."

Lathlorn tried to reassure his brothers. "We worry for nothing," he said. "Grandmother will be okay with the news."

Alexander took a deep breath and looked at his siblings. "We must act to prevent Grandmother from discovering what we know," he said. "We must keep silent on this matter, no matter the cost. The safety of our mother depends on it."

Lathlorn, the eldest, turned to him. "But if we say nothing, we're just as much to blame if the human dies."

Alexander turned to his twin Etheryn. "The sharpness in grandmother's mind has faded. It may not be wise to suggest that our mother took those papers into her thoughts.

Lenith shook his head; this was wrong. He wanted to grab his brothers, turn them around and flee. How would they tell their grandmother that their mother took the papers without harming her? He knew she would be appalled, shocked, and angry; the thought of it worried him. But he had to trust that his brothers were sure of their actions and had thought it through properly. "This is wrong," Lenith shook his head. "This will end wrong."

"Oh, for goodness' sake!" Etheryn's words made Lenith shake his head and look at him, "Stop fretting; you'll make Alexander tremble in his boots before we've even gone to see Grandmother!"

"That's not funny," Alexander slapped Etheryn on the back.

"It wasn't meant to be."

"So, we're all agreed," Lathlorn looked at his three brothers. "We tell grandmother today."

"I don't wish to be there," voiced Lenith. "I don't want to be the one who has to answer to Father once he hears about this."

"Father won't know it was us."

As if Etheryn heard something, he suddenly turned around and walked to the far end of the garden while his brothers watched him with surprise. Seconds later, he returned to them. "It's okay. It's only one of the castle guards."

"Make good use of the gift you have; keep your ears peeled for any more noise," Lathlorn stepped closer to him. "We don't want anyone listening to this conversation."

"I suppose you'll be asking me to keep my eyesight peeled as well," said Lenith mockingly.

"Only if you wish, but as you offered, maybe you should."

"Lathlorn," said Alexander. "What does it matter? Our minds will be heard the minute we enter the castle."

"Use your gift to block anyone who crosses our path."

"Are you crazy!" Lenith stepped up to Lathlorn. "You'll send Alexander's mind into chaos."

"It will do him no harm," Lathlorn replied angrily; seconds later, they argued.

"What is it with you!" shouted Lenith. "You're always doing this, causing arguments."

"Stop being so immature," replied Lathlorn angrily. "Mama's do-gooder, that's what you are!"

"You'll take those words back, or else!"

"Or else what, you're go running to mother, hide behind her back! Grow up, Lenith, smell the roses!"

"Mister Perfection!" Lenith said mockingly to Lathlorn. "Isn't it about time you smelt the roses!" Lenith's hand reached out.

Just as Lenith shoved Lathlorn in the chest, Lathlorn grasped him around the neck with his arm. "If anyone thinks he's the perfectionist here, it's you!" his grip tightened. "Now grow up, or I'll give you a hiding!"

"Stop it, both of you!" Etheryn pulled Lathlorn away and stepped between them. "You're acting like maddened animals!" Lathlorn's eyes blazed with fury. His chest heaved with each ragged breath, his anger threatening to consume him. But Etheryn stood firm, his voice filled with frustration and concern. "Enough!" Etheryn exclaimed, his tone commanding yet tinged with sadness. "We are better than this." His words hung in the air, momentarily silencing the heated tension between Lathlorn and Lenith. Etheryn's gaze shifted from Lathlorn to Lenith. "We are brothers," Etheryn continued, his voice softer now but still filled with determination. The two brothers stared at each other for seconds, then stepped back when Alexander's words of sadness slipped out.

"If we tell grandmother, do you think the silent fighting will end between mother and father?"

"You heard what grandmother said. If father speaks his words to mother in front of grandmother," uttered Etheryn sadly. "Then grandmother will punish him."

"How do you know this?" a shocked Lenith asked.

"Go on, Alexander," Etheryn looked at his twin. "Tell them."

"She did utter something along those lines."

"What do you mean?" asked Lathlorn.

"If father speaks to mother, he's just as human as she is, will even be treated as such."

Lenith's face held a frown. "You must have heard wrong!"

"He didn't," voiced Etheryn. "I was there when it was said."

"Then maybe we should go," Lathlorn nodded towards the castle. "Maybe we can sort out this thing between them once and for all."

"You are right there!" Lenith voiced sadly. "It'll probably finish them."

"Or make them stronger," Lathlorn smiled at Lenith and walked to him. "I'm sorry."

"If you weren't my brother, I wouldn't forgive you, but you are, so you shall have my forgiveness."

"How would it make them stronger?" asked Alexander.

"I've seen this before," said Lathlorn. "This same unhappiness they now carry around with them many centuries ago. Back then, I thought they would never survive another day with each other. They proved both Star and me wrong. They came out of that sadness with joy, the news of two new brothers," Lathlorn looked at Alexander and Etheryn, "You two."

"Oh, Valar!" Etheryn rolled his eyes. "Don't say our mother will be carrying another two by the end of this."

"Two, no," laughed Lathlorn. "Possibly three or even more."

"Now you're speaking downright ridiculous rubbish," Lenith laughed. "She doesn't want anymore; she still thinks I'm the kin of the family."

"No, she doesn't think you're the kin of the family," laughed Alexander. "She thinks you're the baby."

"Oh, stop it!" said Lenith while his brothers took the mickey from him. "This baby kin isn't a baby; he's a thousand years old!"

Lathlorn placed his arm around his shoulder and led him away. "Then let's get this thousand-year-old into the castle with his brothers to tell grandmother a grown-up suggestion."

"I still don't think this is wise," protested Lenith as they left the gardens. "This isn't going to turn out right."

"What!" Alexander ran up behind them. "You see the future as well!"

"Nope, would you want to?"

"No, you're probably right," Etheryn reached the back door. "Better not to see something that's in the future."

Alexander's eyes widened in surprise as he processed Etheryn's words. The idea of seeing the future had always intrigued him, but now, standing at the precipice of such a possibility, he couldn't help but feel a twinge of uncertainty. He glanced at Etheryn, who was already opening the back door with a sense of urgency. Perhaps there was truth in his words - it was better not to know what lay ahead. As they stepped into a corridor, Alexander couldn't shake off the nagging curiosity that tugged at his mind. He turned to Etheryn, his voice filled with apprehension and intrigue. "But imagine all the possibilities," he said, his tone laced with wonder. "Knowing what awaits us could help us make better decisions, avoid pitfalls—It could change everything."

Etheryn glanced at Alexander, his expression thoughtful. He understood the weight of his brother's words, for he, too, had been plagued by the same curiosity many times. The corridor they found themselves in seemed to stretch endlessly, its walls adorned with ancient symbols and mysterious carvings done by their ancestors. "I can't help but wonder," Etheryn replied, his voice tinged with a hint of excitement. "What if we could glimpse into the future? What if we possessed the knowledge to navigate through life's uncertainties with certainty?"

Alexander nodded; his eyes fixed on a particularly intriguing symbol etched into the stone wall as they passed it. "Imagine the power it would grant us," he mused. "We could avoid heartache and disappointment, seize opportunities before they slip away."

As they continued down the corridor, their footsteps echoing softly against the cold floor, Etheryn's mind wandered deeper into this realm of possibilities. He couldn't help but be captivated by Alexander's words, his imagination taking flight. The idea of possessing such power, the ability to shape their destinies, was both exhilarating and terrifying. Etheryn's thoughts danced with visions of a life free from uncertainty and regret. As they ventured further into the maze of corridors, Etheryn became drawn to the enigmatic symbols adorning the walls. Each seemed to hold a story, a secret waiting for someone to unravel them. He reached out tentatively, tracing his fingers along the ancient carvings as if trying to decipher their hidden meaning, but he knew what they were, what they meant.

Thousands of years ago, someone had craved them to protect those inside from evil forces that had infiltrated their castle. The symbols were a form of ancient magic designed to ward off any future intruders and ensure the safety of the castle's inhabitants. As Etheryn continued with his brothers toward a stone stairwell, he couldn't help but feel a strange connection to these symbols. It was as if they were calling out to him, whispering forgotten tales of power and danger.

"Right here we go," Lathlorn started leading his three brothers to the first stone step of the stairwell. "Nobody backs out," his brothers shook their heads. "We'll get this sorted for our mother now, this day." Lathlorn took a deep breath, his heart pounding with determination. The four brothers stood at the entrance of the ancient stairwell, its stone steps worn with age and mystery.

As they ascended the first step, anticipation filled the air. Lathlorn glanced back at his brothers, their eyes reflecting fear and unwavering loyalty. They had always been there for each other through thick and thin, and today was no exception. With every step they climbed, their mother's plight grew heavier on their shoulders. At the top of the stairs was a thick oak door with a round handle. Lathlorn used this to open the door. Three brothers followed him into another corridor fitted with a deep blue carpet. Alexander, being the last to enter, closed the door behind himself.

As they ventured further into the corridor, the air grew colder, and a sense of foreboding settled upon them. The deep blue carpet beneath their feet muffled their footsteps, creating an eerie silence that amplified the weight of their mother's plight. Lathlorn, the eldest brother, led the way with determination etched on his face. His broad shoulders bore the burden of their mother's troubles and the responsibility to protect and guide his younger siblings. With each step, he could feel the weight growing heavier, as if fate was testing his resolve. The corridor seemed endless, its walls adorned with faded tapestries depicting long-forgotten battles and ancient legends—the flickering torches lining the passage cast dancing shadows that played tricks on their minds. Yet, fuelled by love and determination, they pressed on.

A soft glow emanated from an archway ahead as they reached a bend in the corridor. Curiosity piqued, they quickened their pace, drawn towards the ethereal light like moths to a flame. The glow intensified as they approached the archway, bathing the corridor in a warm and inviting radiance. The air seemed to hum with an otherworldly energy, whispering secrets of untold wonders that lay beyond. With each step closer, their hearts beat faster in anticipation. The tapestries on the walls seemed to come alive, their faded colours regaining vibrancy as if infused with new life. The battles depicted in the ancient threads appeared more vivid than ever, telling tales of bravery and sacrifice resonating deep within their souls.

As they crossed the threshold of the archway, a breathtaking sight unfolded before them. They found themselves standing in a vast chamber bathed in an iridescent glow, with intricate carvings of celestial beings and celestial bodies in a dance of cosmic harmony on the walls. In the centre stood their grandmother, Queen Catreen. As if she had already sensed their presence, she was already facing them, standing as if waiting for her four grandkins to come closer.

As they approached their grandmother, a sense of awe and reverence washed over them. Queen Catreen's regal presence commanded attention, her hair cascading down her back like a shimmering waterfall. Her eyes, the colour of a bright sky, sparkled with wisdom and love as she gazed upon her grandkins. "My dear ones," Queen Catreen spoke softly but with an air of authority. "I'm guessing this isn't a social call this time."

"I'm afraid not," replied Lathlorn.

"Then be seated," she pointed to a long sofa in the corner.

"If you don't mind," this was Alexander speaking. "Comfort should be our last thought today."

"Indeed," their grandmother suddenly frowned. "I sense you've all come to tell me something of dire importance?"

"Correct," answered Etheryn.

"Then continue." Her words hung in the air, anticipation building within each grandkins heart.

The room fell into a heavy silence as the four siblings exchanged nervous glances. They knew that what they were about to reveal would change everything, and the weight of their secret seemed almost unbearable.

Lathlorn took a deep breath, gathering his thoughts before he began. "Grandmother," he started, his voice steady but filled with an underlying tremor, "We have discovered something—Something that threatens not only our kingdom but the entire realm."

Queen Catreen's eyes widened with concern, her regal composure momentarily faltering. "What is it?" she asked, her voice barely above a whisper.

Alexander stepped forward, his usually confident replaced by a sombre expression. "We have uncovered evidence of a plot against you," he revealed, his words hanging heavily in the air. "There are whispers of treason within our court."

"Alexander, stop, let me speak, say the words," Lathlorn's voice sounded worried. "He spoke wrong, used the wrong expression," he'd directed his words to their grandmother.

Alexander's eyes darted towards Lathlorn; confusion etched across his face. He had always been the one to speak with conviction and clarity, but now his words seemed to falter. Lathlorn's interruption only added to the tension in the room, and their grandmother's piercing gaze intensified. Taking a deep breath, Alexander composed himself and continued, "I apologize for my choice of words, but the gravity of the situation cannot be understated. There are indeed murmurs of disloyalty within our court." His voice trembled slightly, betraying his inner turmoil.

Lathlorn's worry transformed into a mix of concern and frustration. "But Alexander," he interjected again, "We must be cautious with our words. We don't want to create unnecessary panic or suspicion."

"Tell me," their grandmother's words directed toward Lathlorn, "What you want me to hear."

Lathlorn's concern deepened as he observed his grandmother's piercing gaze. He understood the weight of her words and the importance of choosing them wisely. Taking a deep breath, he composed himself before responding. "Grandmother," Lathlorn began, his voice steady yet filled with earnestness, "My brothers and I stumbled upon something that could disrupt our world's delicate balance." He paused for a moment, gathering his thoughts before continuing. "But us exposing this news will also put an innocent life at risk."

"Whose life?" Their grandmother had asked.

"Our mothers," the four brothers said together.

Their grandmother raised an eyebrow and then scowled at them all. "You come here to speak of her! That traitor! Then I'm not surprised; has she been poisoning my grandsons against me?"

The so-called traitors' four sons looked at their grandmother in shock. The room fell silent, the weight of their grandmother's words hanging heavily in the air. The four sons exchanged bewildered glances, their eyes reflecting a mix of confusion and hurt. How could their beloved grandmother accuse their mother of such treachery?

One by one, they mustered the courage to speak up, their voices trembling with a blend of concern and disbelief. "Grandmother," Lathlorn began cautiously, "We would never conspire against you or allow anyone to poison our minds. Our mother loves you deeply; she has always respected and cherished your role in our lives."

Etheryn stepped forward, his voice filled with genuine sincerity. "We understand that there may be disagreements between you and mother sometimes, but we have always strived to maintain peace and unity within our family. We would never betray your trust."

Alexander's eyes glistened with unshed tears as he spoke softly but firmly. "My thoughts repeat what my brothers have spoken; our mother has always stood by your side, grandmother."

Lenith, the youngest brother, spoke next. "Yes, grandmother, Alexander is right," his voice filled with determination. "Throughout the years, we have witnessed countless times how our mother has been your unwavering support, confidante, and pillar of strength. She has sacrificed her dreams and aspirations to ensure your happiness and well-being." As Lenith spoke, his gaze shifted toward his older brother,

Lathlorn, who nodded to continue. "We have seen the countless sleepless nights she spent by your side when you were ill," Lenith continued passionately. "We have watched her tirelessly tend to your needs without hesitation or complaint. And even during the darkest moments when life seemed unbearable, she never wavered in her love and devotion for you."

The room fell silent as the weight of his words hung in the air, and then their grandmother broke the silence with her own words. First, she sighed loudly as if slightly annoyed; then comments followed. "Then you better tell me what it is that you are so desperate to tell me." Her voice was curious and concerned, causing everyone's attention to shift towards him. Lenith hesitated momentarily, feeling the weight of their secret pressing against his chest. The room seemed to hold its breath, waiting for him to reveal what had been troubling them. Taking a deep breath, he began to speak, his voice trembling with emotion.

Chapter 15

A Bittersweet History

Elensar looked out of the spire window, watching the faraway people harvesting in the fields; he sighed, turned away, and another sigh escaped between his lips—*my sweet Amelia.* Elensar was thinking of the private meeting he'd just had about a past event that happened over a thousand years ago. It was an incident involving his wife, Amelia, and now he was reliving that meeting again, repeating it inside his head as if to make sense of it. Elensar had quietly repeated a second knock on the door of a partially decayed house in the middle of a forest near Kental Bay.

"Maybe he's not here," Elensar's brother Celahir had spoken, then stepped back to look around a little. "Look at this place, been deserted for centuries by the looks of it."

"That's the whole point in meeting here," replied Elensar. "So, no one can see or hear us."

"Aren't you curious why he chose this place to tell us something?"

"The meeting wasn't meant to include you," Elensar rolled his eyes. "You've come along because your nosy."

"No, I've come along to give you support."

"Why do you think I need support?"

"Who arranges meetings in a dark forest, in a destroyed house miles from any signs of civilization? Someone who wants to give someone very secreted news and perhaps even has a terrible impact on the one it's told to. That, my dear brother, is why I'm here, in case you need a shoulder to weep against."

"Oh, for Valar's sake—"

"There isn't a Valar, remember?"

"Celahir, no," Elensar shook his head and whispered more words quickly. "Remember our terms when we left the dead city. Everything we learned had to stay in that place."

"I know, I know, it was just a sl—"

The door opened.

"Come, don't dally out there," a brown-bearded person dressed in a long black cloak said those words. "Forest have ears too."

"Rotherkin," Celahir answered, nodding his head, and passing him to go into a hallway behind him. "Nice to see you again."

"Likewise. Are you joined at your brother's hip?"

"No, he's not," Elensar said, following in his brother's footsteps. The pungent smell of mildew and a flurry of dust gathered around their feet as they treaded further away from the entrance. "But it appears he thinks I need protection."

"I never said that," Celahir replied as the door was closed. "But if he needs a shoulder, I'm here."

"I can assure you," Rotherkin replied, wavering them into the rest of the hallway towards a small living room. "He'll not need a shoulder; it's not that sort of meeting."

"Well, either way, I'm here," Celahir then looked around himself and asked, "Who on earth left this place so ruined?" asked Celahir as Rotherkin slowly guided them into a small living room.

"Once upon a time, a wizard called Jetso lived in the deep, dark woods, these woods. He was small and elegant, with a long, pointy nose and bright, sparkling eyes."

"A bit like you, minus the elegant side of things."

"I'm all those things and more, I'll have you know," replied Rotherkin, tapping him on the shoulder. "Jetso was a kind and gentle wizard, always looking out for the little creatures of the woods and always offering a helping hand to those in need. He was always cheerful and had a way of making those around him feel at ease. He often wandered around these woods, exploring the many secret paths and hidden glades, gathering wild berries and mushrooms, and collecting firewood for the cold winter nights that would be gone for centuries."

"Yes, don't remind me," laughed Elensar. "I'm just glad it's back."

"So am I," said Celahir. "So, about this Jetso, tell more."

"He had many friends among the birds and animals of the forest, and they would often join him on his adventures. The wizard enjoyed singing as he did his daily tasks, and his voice was as sweet as the nightingale's song."

Celahir laughed, "It sounds as if you weren't the only one with a singing gist then, brother."

"I never said I was the only one."

"Well," carried on Rotherkin. "Jetso had a special way of communicating with the trees and plants and could often be heard murmuring secrets to them as he passed by. One day, Jetso decided to build a small cabin in the middle of these woods."

"Ah, right; now we're getting to my earlier question about the ownership of this house."

"Indeed," replied Rotherkin. "He worked hard, gathering logs and stones and crafting the house with two hands. He filled the place with furniture he had made himself and kept it warm with a cozy fire. Soon, Jetso's cabin became a haven for all the forest's creatures. He welcomed them into his home, and they gathered around the fire, sharing stories and singing songs late into the night."

"Animals, singing?" chuckled Celahir. "Now that's a new one."

"I hear people say trees can speak," replied Elensar, looking around the living room they'd entered. "Who's to say animals can't."

"Elensar is correct," said Rotherkin, following behind Celahir. "Jetso's cabin became a place of peace and harmony, and the forest's creatures looked forward to visiting him and spending time in his company. Jetso eventually passed away, but his cabin remains in the woods as a reminder of his kindness and friendship. The cabin you are both standing in right now."

"It would have been quicker if you just told us Jetso used to own this house," laughed Celahir. "Instead of giving us a full rundown of his history."

Elensar rolled his eyes and sighed heavily. "Now, Rotherkin," his eyesight went to him. "What is so important you call a meeting in secret for me?"

"Sit down," he pointed to a dusty yellow sofa. "Both of you." They did after wrapping their purple cloaks around themselves. Rotherkin took a seat in a single yellow dust-covered chair near them. "

"I'm just going to come out and say all this because there's no better way of starting this conversation."

"Okay," said Elensar, frowning at the same time. "Begin then."

Rotherkin sighed heavily, then began. "Now I'm going to take you back in time, to be precise, to when Tilleryn returned from the old dark lands."

"Elensar's Tilleryn," asked Celahir. "You mean Elensar's, Tilleryn?"

"He means no other," Elensar bluntly answered. "Go on, Rotherkin."

"When Tilleryn returned to Volarie, she was pregnant; a forced union with the now deceased Prince Lucian caused this; you remember that Elensar?"

"I do," he said in a slightly heated tone.

"But what you do not know is that kin were alive when born, taken away from her straight after birth—"

"Alive?" Elensar sounded like he didn't believe the words he had just heard. "But I saw the kin after it was born?"

"You were not there the day the kin were born; you were away at the time, am I correct?"

"Well, yes, I was, but I was back mere hours after the—"

"And yet you were still not there to witness the birthing—"

"I only missed a few hours of the kins entry and held that kin as if it were my own upon my arrival."

"You held a deceased kin that day when you arrived, correct?"

"Yes," Elensar bowed his head. "And Tilleryn as well."

"I am sorry for your loss," Rotherkin gave comforting words. "For that kins loss too, but Tilleryn's kin lived, was taken away for its protection."

"Protection," asked Celahir. "From whom?"

"From Prince Lucian."

"Why?"

"Why, you ask why?" Rotherkin looked over at him. "Tell me something; would you not hide an object if you knew it would cause problems?"

"Of course, I would."

"And if that cause could make things better for one but not the other, you'd still hide it, yes?"

"Yes," answered Elensar this time. "What does this have to do with the deceased kin?"

"Why else would you hide something from someone," said Rotherkin. "Who only uses something to gain more power?"

"But the deceased kin had no power over anyone."

"You are correct, but the living one did; Lucian's kin did. That's also why we hid her away, so Lucian couldn't use her to gain more power over us back then. We had to conceal her somewhere safe."

"So, I was lied to," said Elensar, confused. "You all lied to me, made me grieve over a kin that wasn't Tilleryn's?" Now, he sounded angry. "And you let me live with that grief for thousands of years!"

"We did not just hide Tilleryn's kin for Lucian's sake; we also hid her for your sake."

"My sake," he'd suddenly shouted. "What did you think I would do? Use that kin for my purposes? I had no purpose other than to see Tilleryn happy!"

"Elensar," Celahir had touched his sleeve. "Calm down."

He shrugged it off angrily. "Don't tell me to calm down!"

"Listen," Rotherkin's voice spoke. "I haven't brought you here to witness your rage let loose. I brought you here to tell you the truth."

"Bit late for that now," he angrily replied, then gave him a stern glance. "Where did you hide the kin? With that Newton in the forest, I'm guessing."

"We did; well, Etheryn and a company of five guards did."

"Etheryn!"

"Etheryn!" They'd both said that at the same time.

"Yes. Etheryn and a company of five guards delivered the few days-old kin to somewhere she'd be safe from Prince Lucian's dark hunter warriors. They took her to the human world."

"I already know that part," had been Elensar's sarcastic reply. "But I'd like to know how they knew she would be safe with a stranger."

"We didn't know at first. We had to find someone who could look after the kin, someone with knowledge of our ways, like a Newton—" A loud sigh from Elensar's direction interrupted him for a moment. "I can stop if you want?"

"Nope, carry on."

"Etheryn and his company found a red-roofed building surrounded by trees, and living there was a young widow in good health. She was everything they were looking for, but people can be deceiving, so they were curious if this woman could keep the kin secret. But to make sure she did, one of the guards with a gift of seeing into the mind went to her door and knocked upon it. Ten minutes later, he returned, saying she was the chosen one—"

"And next?"

"Next, Etheryn visited this same person, which gave him insight into the innards of her home, to every room. It also gave him an excellent chance to speak with the woman to determine if she was everything they sought. She was."

"I can't believe Etheryn never told you any of this?" Those words came from Celahir, directed at his brother. "Never mentioned it!"

"Neither can I!"

"I'm sure he would have been sitting here telling you himself if he were here now."

"I'm sure he would," said Elensar. "But he's in Seaport Southern Shores, so you are telling me; now speak more."

Rotherkin sighed, then carried on. "They placed the kin on a porch by the front door just before dawn. Etheryn scribbled words onto a piece of paper, slipped it under the kin's arm, and knocked loudly on the front door; Etheryn and the others retreated quickly into the shadows of a large nearby bush to watch the front door opening. Their secret waiting only required minutes of worrying, for the door opened quickly, and a widow took the kin into her new home, and that's about all I can say now."

"Apart from deceased kin," Elensar spoke heatedly. "What you've just told me is already known, so you have wasted my time here."

"Elensar, don't be so harsh," his brother said. "It wasn't Rotherkin's doing that caused this story to be spoken to you."

"So, what is the point in this secret meeting then? For me to relive the heartache I carried for over two thousand years. To mourn Tilleryn's passing again?"

"No," replied Rotherkin. "It is to make you see that your wife Amelia is not the course of any issues here in this world or any world; she is innocent in all of this, for she is not the Heart kin."

"Rotherkin," replied Elensar. "I already know that."

"Then why do you speak," asked Rotherkin. "In the manner as if you loath her very spirit?"

"I have spoken nothing of my wife in this meeting to warrant those words from you."

"I speak of words outside of this room."

"Rotherkin, what are you talking about?"

"I hear words, gossip floating around that your hatred of your wife has reached new levels of such that I had to intervene—"

"Oh Rotherkin," this was Celahir speaking. "You've heard wrong."

He looked at him, "When my birds speak of it, the truth comes first."

Elensar's voice came next. "Fortunately, they are wrong this time, and I have played my part well if it reached your ears."

"If what reached my ears?"

Elensar shook his head. "I'm not going into it with you."

"Do you not care for Amelia now? Do you not care I try to fix it for you?"

"You need not fix anything because nothing's broken."

"That's not what I hear from within the castle walls or grounds."

"Look," Elensar suddenly stood up. "I will tell you this to at least put your worrying thoughts away. Amelia is my heart, and she's treated as such."

"Treated with cruel words?"

"No," sighed Elensar. "With hidden agenda."

"Then perhaps you should cross-exam that agenda and make it into a kinder one."

"I have, believe me, I have."

Yet things about her made him cross-examine his thoughts this evening, like her rounded ears and hairs upon her body. They bore no hair except on their heads; then, her figure was more rounded than the average female's. Her long labours were filled with pain, screams, and cursing, whereas a female Shalimar's labour was short, silent, and peaceful.

However, this wasn't the only time he had had doubts about her. He'd had them many years ago, too. Back then, the list of her pains worried him, ones that contained teeth aching and her stomach hurting. The monthly bleeding between her legs that used to happen nearly always dwindled to less than three in twelve years. Then there were her bones aching; if not her aching bones, she'd say it was the hot air in the room causing her pain. Then, one year later, he returned from a council meeting in another province and found her coughing, sneezing, vomiting, and glowing with sweat for five whole days. Illness? It's something they never experience. Those painful illness times she shared, he did think odd, but after his chat with Pern, the physician, he just put it down to her being different, unique.

Then Elensar had flashbacks to their first encounter in Lurth, their first kiss on the bridge. It made him smile. Elensar remembered the first time he saw Amelia in a green laced dress, wearing a full-faced masquerade mask with a drink in her hand, and he remembered how he'd tried desperately to see her again during that Marchdon ball Etheryn and Sofia had organized. He did. Elensar then remembered their courting days and weeks. It all came together perfectly. For the love part, she'd set this alight the moment he set his eyes upon her, making him realize she was everything he wanted in a lifelong mate, so Elensar gave her something; Elensar gave her half of a royal courting leaf pendant that two lovers could wear, this was something he'd never done to any of his lovers before, yet this wasn't to be his only surprise.

Barely a day after Amelia arrived in his homelands, inside his home and bedroom, someone cloned themself to look like him and raped Amelia, forcing her to carry a seed. However, this was no ordinary seed. This seed planted was no seed of Elensar's loins. No, that seed belonged to Lord Elrohir from Seaport Southern Shores. How did he know this? Lord Elrohir did all this? These questions were answered when this same Lord took their daughter Star two hundred years later, and Amelia, for some unknown reason, just accepted it. But that wasn't the end. Since Amelia was used in this way, sharing a union with another ending in a new life, she was to be bonded to Lord Elrohir in Seaport Southern Shores, but he told her this news. He also said she would be free if she denied him, but Amelia hadn't denied it yet; it was as if Amelia thought she didn't need to.

I might have to remind you again, present-day Elensar thought crossly. But it wasn't up to him to remind her; Amelia was the one who had to remember, not him. Maybe his constant reminders in the early years had put her off saying it; perhaps she still saw no wrong in what this lord Elrohir had done to her, to them.

The present-day Elensar sighed again and frowned. *What did I hear long ago about myths about committing to half-breeds or even humans? Was it that they'd be filled with disappointments for both parties if done? Yes, that's it, but that's a load of rubbish*! But then he started to think of things that made him sadder. He experienced grief when the kin daughter he would've named Sarath was born dead just two years after Lenith was born. *I never wish to experience that sort of sadness again; I don't want to have any sorrow anymore.*

He looked as if thinking to himself for a minute, then angrily answered himself aloud. "Yeah, right! Well, let's see if that little dream shenanigan worked, shall we," he was talking about his dream visit inside Amelia's dream world while at Anlease's home, "If not, perhaps Sofia and Sarian can make her change her mind. Make her see sense, and come back to me with open arms, a warm kiss for my lips." He sighed again and said, "Yes, Sarian and Sofia." They were always good at making her come back to him after they'd argued, but what they told her to make it happen, he didn't know, didn't care. Just as long as Amelia knew this was her home, where her family, her lover, was waiting for her to return home. And perhaps tonight, they would be lying entwined in each other's arms, whispering their love for each other, instead of Amelia's arms pushing him away as she had done since her return.

He heavily sighed this time and strolled to the door; his trembling hand reached for the handle and opened it. He walked down a flight of stone steps, down the long corridor towards his bedroom. His head tilted towards the winding stairway as if listening to something that sounded far away. A loud sound made him rush towards the stairway and take the steps swiftly until he reached the bottom. His next strides ran down a long hallway, flinging open a door at the end so quickly it bashed against the wall. Arriving in another long corridor, he ran halfway down it and abruptly stopped in front of his mother, Catreen, Amelia, and Sofia.

"Let me explain!" Sofia pleaded with Catreen, "She drinks to numb the pain of a personal secret, and it wasn't my intention to bring her here in this state."

"Look at your wife!" shouted Catreen. "She can't even stand up!"

He couldn't deny that what he was seeing didn't make him angry because it did, but because Amelia smiled in a way that made him think everything was back to normal, he smiled back. *Thank you*, he thought happily to himself.

"Don't you dare take her side!" his mother read his mind and stepped up to him. "She's intoxicated!"

"Mother," he uttered calmly. "Intoxicated or not," a hand slid under Amelia's arm. "She's still part of my family."

"Then she'll infect you. Elensar," now she was using a softer voice, "My wise son, she's drunk; that's why she looks at you. Tomorrow, it shall be wordless words, lonely nights again."

"And?"

"Elensar, listen to me; I know these things."

"Mother, you know nothing of love."

"I know, love; I had love from your father before he left me."

"And he died. Why mother? Why did our father, Rolzulern, die? Shall I tell you why?"

"Stop it! You don't know why Rolzulern died!"

"He died because of your moods that wouldn't adjust for him," he let go of Amelia's arm and walked up to her, "He died because he had to find love in another's arms."

"He never died because of that; he died of old age."

"I may have been young, but I remember everything," Elensar retorted bitterly. "I remember the nights he spent away from home, searching for solace in someone else's arms. I remember the arguments and the tears that plagued our household."

"Stop it!"

Trembling with emotion, Elensar continued, his voice filled with resentment and sorrow. "You can't deny it, Mother, I saw everything. I saw how his absence tore our family apart piece by piece. And now you want to rewrite history and pretend that he died peacefully? No, he died burdened by the weight of your mistakes."

"Stop it!"

"Why? Does the truth hurt Mother? It should. Now leave us to stride away from you, for Sofia to go back home, for you to take these words you've said, dwell on them until you get the right mood into your mind about us." With those words said by him, he turned his back on her, took Amelia by the arm, and walked down the hallway.

Just before Elensar's hand reached the handle, his mother spat spiteful words. "You think you can just walk away from this? You're making a big mistake, son," his mother sneered, her voice dripping with venom. "Have your night of passion; by sunrise, you'll be weeping on my shoulder when she wakes from this slumber; you wait and see!"

He turned back to face her. "If this night of passion happens, so be it, but let it be known, this day, you're no longer my mother," a hand grabbed a door handle. Amelia's unsteady figure was guided through the doorway swiftly while his mother screamed at him.

"Then see if I care that you'll be a sufferer too!"

Elensar didn't bother answering back to those heated words; he did slam the door shut. As the door slammed shut behind him, a wave of conflicting emotions washed over him. Part of him felt guilt for leaving his mother in such distress, but another part knew that he had to break free from the toxic cycle that trapped them both. He couldn't bear to witness her destructive behaviour any longer.

"Sufferer?" asked Amelia. "Who will be a sufferer?"

Elensar's arm circled her shoulders. "Don't fret words about it." He kept her stumbling, falling, tripping figure close to his own to their bedroom, not a single angry word uttered about the state of the condition she'd arrived home in from his lips.

Elensar paused at the bedroom entrance before raising his hand to the knob. He could still hear his mother's echoing words in the back of his mind, warning of sorrow in the morning, yet he also could feel the warmth of Amelia's body against his and the calming effect it had on him. He twisted the door handle and went inside, guiding the still-unsteady woman to the centre of the room.

Elensar slowly pulled away from her embrace, standing there momentarily before turning to look at her. "Whatever happens by sunrise, promise me you won't forget today," he said, a slight hope in his words.

Amelia smiled slightly before reaching out and grabbing his hand. 'I won't forget,' she said quietly.

After he locked the door in that room, Amelia turned around, stepped up, stood on tiptoes, slipped a hand behind his head, and began pulling him gently closer to her. For the next few moments, she reacted as if she was a different person, kissing him fiercely, making him pucker his brow at her peculiar behaviour; however, for those few moments of doubt, he didn't stop her kisses. Amelia pulled him further into the room when those kisses ended, heading towards their bed. It was moving a little too fast for his liking, "Amelia, stop for a moment, think what you're doing," for some reason, she looked hurt he'd said that.

"Why do you speak to me now when you couldn't be bothered? I wish I'd stayed talking to William," she pulled away.

Elensar pulled her back, "When did you speak with him!"

"I just spoke to him outside."

She'd just lied to Elensar; how did he know? William was in the dungeon and had been for the last few days. He played the ignorant game of not knowing that piece of information. "You speak to him, but don't speak to me; why?"

"You don't want to speak to me."

"I've been trying since that argument in the living room," he heard her sigh deeply and saw her give him a sorrowful look that made him feel very protective over her.

"I know you have," she whispered. "And I feel terrible for ignoring you, but you deserved silence after what you said."

"Yes, your right; I did deserve your silence, but if we don't talk, how can we sort it out?"

"Sometimes, you don't need to use words to sort things out."

"What would you use?"

"Silence."

"Silence! That wouldn't work."

"It worked enough to be noticed, didn't it?"

Elensar thought about her words and nodded his agreement. "But has it worked enough to get us back together as husband and wife or just friends?"

She smiled. "What do you think?"

"If I say what I desire," Elensar's voice trembled with vulnerability as he continued, "You might throw it back in my face."

"Then I'll say comfort to you."

He was confused by her words; then he realized she'd used his tactical game of hiding words within words. He played along as if he didn't know she was using it. "That's your answer, comfort?"

"Yes."

"You want to forget everything I've said and done?" Elensar couldn't help but feel a mix of emotions swirling within him. Confusion battled with a glimmer of hope that they could salvage their fractured relationship. "But why?" he asked, his voice laced with vulnerability. "After everything I've put you through, how can you still want to forget it all?"

He heard Amelia take a deep breath before answering, her voice steady yet filled with sincerity. "Because I know that people make mistakes, Elensar. We all say things we don't mean in moments of anger or frustration. And while your words hurt me deeply, I also understand you said those words while in pain and confusion."

Elensar slid his arms around her waist and pulled her up against himself, feeling the warmth of her body against his. They stood there, wrapped in each other's embrace, as the tension dissipated. "I promise I'll never do anything like that again," he whispered, his voice filled with sincerity. "You mean everything to me, and I never want to jeopardize our trust ever again."

"Okay," she'd replied softly, her fingers tracing circles on his back. "I believe you. But remember, trust is fragile. It takes time to rebuild."

Elensar nodded compassionately, grateful for her forgiveness. "I understand."

"Good," she kissed him, "Why do you have to be so damn good-looking?"

Elensar chuckled softly, his cheeks turning a faint shade of pink. "Well, I suppose it's just a lucky combination of genetics," he replied modestly, his eyes twinkling with amusement. "But really, it's your kind heart and forgiving nature that makes me feel truly attractive."

Her smile widened as she playfully nudged him. "Oh please, don't try to sweet-talk your way out of this one," she teased. "You know very well the effect you have on people."

Elensar shrugged with a bashful grin. "I've paid little attention to it. It's always been your inner beauty that captivated me from the start."

She leaned in closer, her voice barely above a whisper. "Well, I can't deny that your outer beauty is captivating too." Her lips brushed against his cheek gently before she pulled away, leaving him momentarily breathless.

Elensar's heart skipped a beat as he looked into her eyes, his voice trembling with vulnerability, "Would it make a difference to you if I were ugly?" he asked, his insecurities laid bare.

"Oh yes," she replied without hesitation, her gaze unwavering.

Elensar's heart sank for a moment, fearing her response. "How?" he managed to utter, desperately needing to understand the depth of her feelings.

A gentle smile graced her lips as she stepped closer, closing the physical distance between them. "I wouldn't be standing in your arms if you were ugly," she whispered, her words carrying an undeniable sincerity.

"You wouldn't!"

"No, I'd be with someone much prettier."

"Ooh, you're such a romantic," Elensar had laughed at her words.

Amelia grinned mischievously, her eyes sparkling with playful delight. "Well, Elensar, what can I say? I have high standards for beauty," she teased, gently poking his side.

Elensar feigned offense, placing a hand dramatically over his heart. "Oh, so you're saying I'm not beautiful enough for you?" he exclaimed in mock disbelief.

Amelia's laughter filled the air as she wrapped her arms tighter around him. "Oh no, my dear Elensar. You are more than enough for me," she replied sweetly, kissing his cheek softly. "But it's always fun to keep you on your toes; now, where's my homecoming present?"

"Homecoming present!"

"Hmm," she kissed him and gazed around the room, "Where's my food and drink?"

"Food and—" he laughed, whispered, "You'd have seen this room filled with fruit, water, cured meats," he lowered his head, looked directly into her eyes, "It would have sustained us for days, only you didn't come to our chambers on that night, did you?"

"Which night?"

"The night of your homecoming."

"We shouldn't talk about that now."

Elensar sighed softly, a hint of disappointment in his voice. "I understand if it's still too painful for you to discuss. But I want you to know that I had prepared everything for your arrival. I wanted to make it special."

"I know you would have done it, and if I had returned to our chambers, I would have loved it," Amelia smiled at him sweetly.

Elensar's disappointment lifted as he saw Amelia's genuine smile. He returned her smile, his heart swelling with affection for the woman standing before him. "I'm glad you understand, my love," he said softly, gently brushing a strand of hair behind her ear. "I just wanted everything to be perfect for our reunion."

Amelia leaned into his touch. "And it would have been perfect," she replied, her voice filled with sincerity. "But what truly matters is that we're together again."

Elensar nodded, feeling gratitude for Amelia's understanding and unconditional love. They had spent weeks apart, and now that they were finally reunited, he didn't want to waste a single moment.

"Now," he heard Amelia whisper to him. "Are we going to bed, or will we spend the whole night talking?"

Elensar laughed, "As much as I desire you in our bed right now, the bedding side of things can wait a little longer," he pulled her closer, "Something more pressing needs our attention, my beautiful little wif—"

"Little—"

"Well, you are," Elensar laughed, "Compared to the other adult females living here—"

"I'm not that small; I'm five foot—"

"I like, love your adult smallness in height," he kissed her again, "Especially when in my bed—"

She playfully swatted Elensar's arm. "Oh, stop it," she giggled, her eyes sparkling affectionately. "You always know how to make me feel special."

Elensar grinned mischievously, his voice filled with adoration. "Well, my love, it's hard not to appreciate everything about you. Your petite stature adds to your charm and beauty."

"You charmer you," she pressed against him. "Want to go to our secret little place? A room full of history, a room used not often. A room, a wooden chair we used on special occasions."

"Amelia!" inside his head, a vision of them making love on the throne had Elensar now laughing at her, "You saucy little minx!"

"Well, it has been ages—"

He laughed. "Well, not really; we did have—" Oops, he nearly let slip about the night he'd invaded her dream. He quickly rectified his words. "Some interesting encounters," he said, skilfully avoiding any mention of the night he'd invaded Amelia's dream. He knew it was a secret he couldn't reveal, especially now that their relationship was back on track, blossoming into bloom again. "Don't get me started on that yet," he nuzzled his nose against hers and drew back a little. "Now, I wanted to say this a while ago, our wedding anniversary—"

"Wedding anniversary!"

"Yes. It's in a few weeks, remember?"

"Ah, yes," she smiled. "And what are you planning to give me? Not anything too extravagant, I hope."

Elensar laughed and held her firmly against himself, saying to her while he did this, "I want to give you something that belongs to me. A kin."

"A child," her voice barely above a whisper; one of her hands went to her belly.

Elensar nodded, his gaze filled with tenderness as he brushed a strand of hair away from her face. "Yes, my love," he replied softly. "I want us to bring another new life into this world, a kin that will reflect our love and the bond we share." He gently caressed her cheek, his eyes shining with anticipation. "Imagine the joy that will fill our hearts when we hold our new kin for the first time," Elensar murmured, his voice filled with excitement and awe. "We will watch them grow, guiding them through life's journey—"

Amelia smiled. "You've been asking me for ages, haven't you? Perhaps even mentioned it to Sarian and Sofia?"

"I might have uttered something like that in passing."

"You," shaking her head. "I thought so." She laughed. "So, if they did as you asked, what would you like for the answer, Elensar?"

Elensar paused for a moment, his eyes fixed on Amelia's face. He had been waiting for this moment, carefully planning his words, and hoping she would finally see how much he wanted another kin. With her question hanging in the air, he took a deep breath and gathered his thoughts. "Mycrom, I'd like the answer to be yes."

"Then I agree with you this time."

Elensar's heart skipped a beat as he heard Amelia's response. A smile tugged at the corners of Elensar's lips. His arms around her waist tightened, crushing her up against his own. "I should get you to write it down, so I have proof. *My wife agreed to have another kin*," he whispered, his voice laced with excitement and anticipation.

"You don't need proof."

"But what if you forget?"

"Forget, forget what?" A soft chuckle escaped Amelia's lips. "Forget the joy that fills my heart every time I see you? Forget how your laughter echoes in my mind even when we're apart. Melo, those are memories etched into my soul. Now, if you don't mind, we'll get back to our discussion; something popped up while I was away, which got me thinking. Something to do with Martha, Andrin's sister."

Elensar's arms around her waist came away. "Martha!"

"Just something that came up in a conversation with Sarian and Sofia while we were away about you two."

"Now you're confusing me."

"You know, you two, a couple."

For a second, he thought she was accusing Martha and him of something, so he dug around in old memories to find something, and soon after, he did. She was correct; they'd been a couple for a very short time; it all happened long ago.

"Elensar?"

He took a deep breath, his gaze shifting away momentarily before returning to meet hers. "I understand that it's been bothering you, Amelia," he admitted, his voice laced with regret. "But dwelling on the past won't change anything now."

"You said we could talk about anything."

"Yes, but I didn't mean absolutely everything."

"But you don't like it when I do it."

Elensar's frustration grew as the conversation continued to escalate. He could feel his patience wearing thin, but he knew he had to choose his words carefully. "I understand that you want to know, but there are certain things that I believe should remain private," Elensar replied, trying to maintain a calm tone.

Amelia suddenly crossed her arms and narrowed her eyes. "Why should it be off-limits? We've always been open with each other."

Elensar sighed again, feeling the weight of their disagreement pressing upon him. "Yes, we have been open, but there are boundaries within that openness. Some things are better left unsaid."

"I thought we promised to share everything. Now you're telling me that's not true?"

He paused for a moment, searching for the right words. "It's not about breaking promises or going back on my word. It's about protecting our relationship and respecting each other's boundaries."

"But this has something to do with us."

Elensar started to worry. It looked as if this night might end with an argument, so now he tried to sway the uneasy subject his way by saying his following words softer. "What does?"

"Martha and you."

"Amelia," he kissed her, "Please don't start an argument between us about something that happened so long ago."

"I'm not trying to start an argument," her voice tinged with frustration. "I just need you to listen," she pleaded softly, her voice tinged with vulnerability. "I've been carrying this weight on my shoulders for weeks, and I can't bear it alone anymore."

Elensar reached out and gently held her hand, silently urging her to continue. "Make it short."

"All right. Sofia said something to me about when you two were a couple."

"What did she say?" Elensar's voice was calm, but his eyes betrayed a hint of concern.

"I know what he's like, always playing the teaser; even with Martha, he was the same. What did she mean when she said she knew what you were like, that you always played the teaser? Did you do that with Martha?"

Elensar could feel his heart rate quicken, his mind racing to find the right words to explain himself. Memories of his past relationship with Martha flooded back, and he couldn't help but feel a pang of guilt. Taking a deep breath, Elensar mustered up the courage to respond honestly. "Amelia, I won't deny that I used to have a playful side when I was with Martha. We had our fair share of teasing and banter, but it was all good fun."

"But why did Sofia say that you were always playing the teaser? Is there something more to it?"

Elensar sighed, "This is about teasing!"

"At the moment, yes, it is. So, you played jokes on Martha?"

"Yes, I did." He laughed, "But never to hurt her," Elensar continued. "Martha and I had a strong bond, built on trust and understanding. Our teasing was just a way to connect and keep the spark alive in our relationship."

"Did you know her well? You know, like we know each other."

"What on earth are you on about now?" Elensar's frown deepened as he struggled to comprehend Amelia's cryptic words.

His mind raced, trying to piece together the puzzle she had presented him. What did she mean by '*know her well?*' And why was she suddenly bringing up their shared experiences in a suggestive manner? Confusion clouded Elensar's face as he searched for answers. He had always considered himself wise, but Amelia's enigmatic behaviour left him utterly lost. He couldn't shake off the nagging feeling that there was something important he was missing. Taking a deep breath, Elensar decided to confront Amelia directly. "Amelia," he said firmly, his voice tinged with frustration, "I need you to be clear. What exactly are you trying to say?"

"You know, us, the bed, it—"

"Oh, that!" Elensar interrupted Amelia, his eyebrows furrowing in confusion. He had expected a serious conversation, but her response caught him off guard. "Did I know her well?" he said. "No, I know you better," he replied quickly, "Why did you ask me that?"

"Do you like me, Elensar?"

"Do I like you?" *What a stupid question!* "No, I love you."

"Did you love her? Martha."

"I did," he finally answered, his voice tinged with a hint of sadness. "But it was different. I cared for Martha deeply, but it wasn't the same as what I feel for you," he continued softly, "Martha was a part of my past, and yes, we shared beautiful moments but had our fair share of struggles, too."

"Did you bed her?"

His face tightened with discomfort. "Amelia!" he exclaimed, taken aback by her blunt question.

"It's a simple question."

"It's also a personal question that doesn't need answering."

"I thought we could discuss anything."

Elensar's gaze softened before he looked away, his voice barely above a whisper. "Some things are better left unsaid, Amelia. They're buried deep within me for a reason."

"Why?"

"Amelia, please understand that this is not a conversation I am comfortable having with you," he replied, his voice tinged with frustration. "It's not about trust or our relationship; it's about respecting Martha's privacy and boundaries."

"So, you're saying you won't be honest with me? We're supposed to be partners in everything! How can we truly be if there are secrets between us?"

Elensar gently took her hand, trying to convey his sincerity. "Amelia, being partners doesn't mean we must know every detail of each other's lives. It means trusting and supporting one another unconditionally."

"Then I'd have to say, Elensar, by the way, you're reacting, you did bed her."

"Then leave it at that."

"Then that also means you loved her too if you bedded her."

"No, I didn't."

"Okay, so if it wasn't love, what was it?"

"Lust."

"And lust doesn't count as love?"

"No, lust doesn't count as love," Elensar replied firmly. "Love is a deep connection, an emotional bond that goes beyond physical desires. Lust is merely a fleeting attraction, driven by primal instincts."

"Do you lust me?"

Elensar laughed jokingly, "I lust after every single inch of you all the time," his laughter subsided as he looked into Amelia's eyes, his expression turning serious for a moment before he spoke, "No, I don't lust you," he said softly. "What I feel for you goes far beyond that. It's a profound affection, a genuine care that transcends physical desires," he said softly. "But lust and love are not mutually exclusive. They can coexist beautifully and passionately as they do with us, but when I was younger, I was naïve to those words, what they meant."

Amelia furrowed her brow, trying to comprehend his words. "I don't understand what you're saying."

"In a nutshell, I said differently when younger, for I was naïve to understand what lust and love meant. Now I am older, wiser to say what I feel—"

"Naive! I can't see you ever being naive."

"I was, but I was also intelligent enough to deny I ever loved Martha."

"Intelligent enough to deny love?" Amelia repeated, her voice tinged with scepticism. "But why would you deny it? Love is a beautiful thing, isn't it?"

Elensar sighed, his eyes clouded with memories. "Love can be beautiful, yes. But it can also be complicated and messy. Back then, I was afraid of the vulnerability that came with it. I didn't want to expose myself to the pain and heartache accompanying love."

"And Martha was fine with that, with you denying you loved her."

Elensar sighed, running a hand through his hair. "I think you are reading more into this than necessary."

"You're probably right, but then again, you did—"

"You aren't jealous of the past, are you?"

"No, it's just—"

Elensar pulled her against himself. "Then you need to stop asking me about it, okay," he saw Amelia nod; he released her, and she stepped back one pace from him. He kept his arms around her waist. "Now, as I was going to say before, there's another matter."

"Which is?"

Elensar gazed into Amelia's eyes, his grip on her waist tightening slightly. He could feel her warmth against his, sending a shiver down his spine. He took a deep breath, trying to gather his thoughts. "It's difficult to put into words."

"Just go ahead with it."

He sighed. "I've been doing something that goes against my beliefs as a husband," Elensar swallowed hard, his voice trembling as he spoke. "I'm protecting you, but I can't tell you why."

"Why can't you tell?" Amelia's voice quivered with a hint of hurt.

"Amelia," he began softly, "I wish I could explain everything to you, but all I can tell you, for now, is that we are leaving for Andrathlion next week."

"I thought we were leaving in the summer?"

Elensar sighed, his eyes filled with a mixture of sadness and determination. "Plans have changed, Amelia," he replied, his voice tinged with regret. "There are certain circumstances that require us to rush our departure."

"But why can't you just tell me what's going on?" she pleaded, her voice laced with frustration.

"Believe me, Amelia, I wish I could share everything with you," he said earnestly. "But there are forces at play that I cannot fully disclose yet. It is for your safety and those we care about, so please, say yes."

"I understand your concern for our safety," Amelia replied softly, her voice tinged with uncertainty. "But how can I say yes without knowing what we're getting into? I need more than just vague explanations."

Elensar sighed, his gaze never wavering from hers. "I know it's difficult to trust blindly," he admitted, his voice filled with empathy. "But sometimes, Amelia, you have to take a leap of faith in what I say, ask of you," he heard her sigh heavily, "Then it's a yes?"

"I suppose we could go."

Elensar saw her figure start to sway. It made him pull her against himself and hold her tighter. Elensar felt warmth and affection as he had her in his arms. The world around them seemed to fade away, leaving only them locked in an intimate embrace. He couldn't help but be captivated by her presence, her every movement sending ripples of desire through his veins. As their lips met once more, time stood still.

"Are we going to spend all night talking?"

Amelia's playful interruption brought him back to reality, and he chuckled softly against her lips. "No," Elensar whispered. "We don't have to talk all night if you don't want to."

Amelia leaned back slightly and looked up at him with a mischievous glint, her fingers tracing delicate patterns on his chest as she teased, "Well then, I don't want to."

"You want comfort now," he kissed her again. "Then kiss me back, make us contented in each other's arms."

Leaning closer, she whispered against his lips, "Comforting sounds nice, but I have a better idea."

"You do, pray tell me?" With a flicker of anticipation in his eyes, Elensar eagerly awaited her suggestion.

Amelia's fingers continued their delicate dance on his chest as she said, "Let's forget about talking for now and let our bodies do the talking instead."

Elensar got the hint straight away. He quickly picked her up and began carrying her to their bed. As they reached the softness of the bed, Elensar gently laid Amelia down, his eyes never leaving hers. Their gazes locked in a fiery connection, conveying a deep understanding that words could never capture. Without hesitation, Elensar lowered himself onto the bed beside her.

"Elensar," Amelia slurred that out, "You not taking me to our special place?"

"Amelia," Elensar whispered, his voice filled with tenderness and understanding. "You've had quite a bit to drink tonight. I think it would be best if we stayed here and rest."

"Rest!" Amelia mumbled, "That's the last thing I want to do. I order you to take me to the throne room now!"

Elensar chuckled softly, his eyes sparkling with mischief as he looked at her. "No, Mycorm, our special place will have to wait for another time," he replied, his voice filled with a teasing tone.

"Oh, you're so horrible," she laughed, "And so damn sexy."

"Well, I don't know about the sexy side of things," he gently kissed her lips, "Do you have any idea how happy you make me?"

She grasped his face in her hands. "No more words are needed."

"But Amelia—"

"Shut up and lust me!"

"I'm not going to lust you; I'm going to make love to you," he leaned over and smiled at her. She released her hands from his face. He kissed her, and his tongue slipped between her lips; inside, it went, searching delicately and softly, then retreated. His kisses lowered over her chin and neck; hands began searching upon her dress, tracing curves and bumps with his fingertips.

"Elensar," Amelia murmured, her voice filled with vulnerability and desire.

Elensar raised his head and leaned closer, his lips brushing against her earlobe as he whispered, "Yes, Mycrom?"

"Were you like this for Martha?"

"You know how to turn someone off, don't you?" Elensar sat up and turned away. He felt Amelia sit beside him and felt a hand on his shoulder. He turned to face her.

"I'm sorry," he saw her biting her lip. "It's just, well—"

"You've nothing to worry about," Elensar smiled at her and moved closer, "She was just like a leaf from a tree that floated by, whereas you, my little rose petal," he gently pushed her to lie down again. "Well, that rose petal looked so good, I couldn't let it slip by. So, I trapped it," he kissed her, "A rose I've trapped for my use to devour it slowly over thousands of years—"

"And what use is that?" she asked, her voice trembling slightly.

Elensar's smile widened, his eyes gleaming with excitement and anticipation. "My dear, imagine the power that lies within a rose," he whispered, his voice filled with an otherworldly charm. "Its delicate beauty holds secrets untold, its essence brimming with life and energy." As he spoke, Elensar's fingertips traced the contours of her face, "For thousands of years, I have sought the rarest and most exquisite roses, their petals to sustain me," he continued, his voice laced with a hint of longing. "Each petal grants me vitality beyond measure, granting me immortality and strength, and you, Mycrom, you are my rose."

"But why me?" Amelia whispered to him.

"The roses I encountered throughout the centuries," Elensar said with tenderness, "Lacked the essence of a soul that could ignite my own, but enough talk of roses and meanings; I desire to get this infernal dress off you."

"And how do you plan on doing that?"

"Oh, don't worry," he chuckled, his fingers already skilfully tracing the delicate buttons on the front of her dress, "I've had enough practice in figuring that out," each button was released with a soft click, revealing glimpses of Amelia's bare skin beneath.

"Really," Amelia replied, her voice laced with anticipation. "How much practice did you need?"

"Not much, if I'm honest; I'm a fast learner." As the final button came undone, the dress fell open to the sides, revealing a pair of ample bosoms, a belly button, underwear, and legs closed together to Elensar's sight, bathed in the dim light from the room. "Valar," Elensar breathed heavily, taking in the full view of her nakedness in his sight, "I love it when you wear this dress!" his hands gently slid down Amelia's arms, leaving a trail of goosebumps in their wake.

"Yes, well, I didn't intentionally put it on, knowing you would remove it later."

"I know you didn't, but I'm thankful for your foresight," his touch was tender, filled with a mixture of desire and reverence. "You always have a way of surprising me, even after all this time we've been together, Mycorm."

"And you never cease to amaze me either, Melo," she whispered, their eyes locked in an intimate gaze, their connection deepening with each passing moment. "Don't look at me like that, it'll only make me—"

"It'll only make me want to open those legs of yours so I can take you sooner," he finished her sentence with his thoughts aloud, his voice barely above a whisper. "Unless you want me to?"

"I don't know," she giggled at him, "You tell me."

"Are you sure you want me to answer that?" He saw her nod; her legs twitch out of the corner of his eyes; he saw her swollen-looking breasts, their nipples erect, crying out for attention. "I would say yes, am I correct?" He had seductively asked, hoping she'd say yes because he was quickly losing control over himself to stop taking what he desired the most from her, the answer for him to go ahead and take her.

"Maybe," Amelia smiled at him, "You can find out for yourself?"

He leaned in closer, his eyes filled with anticipation. "And how exactly should I find out, Mycorm?" he whispered, his voice dripping with desire. He felt her fingers trace along one of his legs to the inner thigh, sending shivers down his spine.

"Well," she purred, her voice laced with mischief, "Maybe you could start by getting out of your clothes."

"Really?" With a mischievous smile playing on his lips, he slowly unbuttoned his shirt, revealing glimpses of his toned physique underneath. "Is this what you mean?" As each button gave way, he felt her gaze intensify, her eyes devouring him hungrily. He stood up next to the bed, facing her. As the shirt slipped off his shoulders and fell to the floor, he stood before Amelia in nothing but his trousers. "Want me to carry on?"

Amelia nodded with a soft gasp escaping her lips, unable to find a voice amidst the overwhelming desire coursing through her veins.

Elensar could feel her eyes tracing every contour of his body, igniting a fire within him that threatened to consume them both. A surge of confidence surged through him as he took a step closer. Elensar reached for the belt of his trousers, unbuckled it, and then threw it away from himself. Three buttons became unfastened next, making his trousers loose. With his head risen to stare seductively at Amelia, Elensar let those trousers glide over his hips to land in a pool around his feet, watching a mix of terror and excitement grow upon Amelia's face as he did it. "Amelia," he asked seductively, "Still want me to carry on?"

Amelia's voice quivered with anticipation and nervousness as she stammered out her response. "Yes, I do," she managed to say, her eyes locked onto his every move.

Elensar couldn't help but feel a surge of power coursing through him, knowing that he held Amelia's undivided attention. With a mischievous smile playing on his lips, his voice dropped to a low whisper, filled with desire and mischief. "Are you sure you can handle me today because I won't be letting you off easy?" he asked, his words dripping with seduction.

"Won't be—Won't—Won't be let off—"

"We haven't been properly intermate in weeks, so I'm forewarning you, don't expect much sleep for the next few weeks."

"I'm sure—I'm sure I can handle—"

"Eyes up, Mycorm," he chuckled, seeing her staring gaze quickly go from his erect shaft to his eyes. "Is that so?" he continued, his voice dropping to a husky murmur as he continued their tantalizing exchange. "Because I have a feeling these next few weeks will be unlike anything you've ever experienced," he started to walk toward the bed, and as he approached it, a mischievous glint danced in his eyes, reflecting the dim light of the room. "Tonight, I'm going to show you that I—"

"Stop bragging about it," Amelia interrupted, a playful smirk, "I've already given you permission."

"Well, in that case," Elensar suddenly laughed, "I'm not wasting any more time in words here," his eyes sparkled with excitement as he crept onto the bed, his voice seductively saying as he did, "Now let it begin—"

Chapter 16

Reality Kicks In

The night was over; afternoon had arrived, and rays of daylight entered their room through the bay window. That bright sunlight revealed a vision of two lovers covered loosely by a sheet, entwined in each other's legs, arms, and faces so close they were almost touching. That same sunlight also caused Amelia's eyes to open, see his blue eyes staring back at her.

"Amelia?"

"Why am I unclothed and feeling like you've made love to me?"

"Well, that did happen—"

"Oh my god," she began, moving away from him.

Now Elensar was watching Amelia's legs swiftly clamber off the bed; he saw how her feet hit the ground and fell upon the floor, then got up again. For a moment, Elensar had a terrible urge to strike out his hands, drag her onto the bed, and tie her up in his arms and legs so she couldn't leave him. How could it have come to this? Barely less than two hours ago, they finally fell asleep together after a marathon lovemaking session. As Elensar's mind raced with confusion and desperation, he tried to grasp the sudden shift in their relationship. It felt like a whirlwind of emotions had engulfed them both overnight.

Elensar needed answers, and he needed them now. "Hang on a minute," he moved to the end of the bed, swung his long legs over the edge, grabbed his dressing gown, and quickly put it on; he walked forward. "If you let me explain—"

"You're pathetic; what did you do? Use a spell on me so you could rape me all night! It explains why I'm so fucking sore that I can barely walk now!"

"You think I used a spell to catch you, to make love to you!" he strolled forward. "I used nothing but what's in my heart!"

"Yeah, right!" Amelia lunged forward, grabbed her dress, turned around, and dressed quickly. "You are unbelievable," she said, walking toward the bedroom door and standing there momentarily, "Why do you always force what you can't have?"

"I don't force anything that won't come to me of its own accord."

"What did you just say!"

Elensar couldn't understand what had triggered her sudden mood change. One moment, Amelia had been talking to him with an emotionless expression, and the next, her mouth had dropped open in surprise. Her strides towards him were quick and determined, and the hand she raised in a single swift motion told him that the coming slap was unavoidable. It only took a blink of an eye for her hand to connect with his cheek and sharp pain to shoot through his face. He found himself raising his hand to hit her back, but he stopped at the sound of her scream.

"Take that back!" The words were angry and demanding. She screamed again with the same intensity. "Take back those words!"

Elensar could only stare at her in surprise, his mind scrambling to recall what he had said that had been so wrong.

"You know what I'm talking about," her tone of voice was full of hurt.

Realization suddenly dawned on him. Had he said something cruel about Amelia in someone else's earshot, and those words had gotten back to her? His other hand went to his face, covering a throbbing, stinging cheek. But why did she hit him? That was his next question. "Why did you strike me?" Elensar's voice trembled as he asked, "I don't understand."

"Because you lied."

"I lied!" Elensar's voice quivered with disbelief as he stared at Amelia standing before him. "When have I ever lied?"

"Then, just then, you did it with words to me," said Amelia angrily. "Take back those words again," she commanded, her eyes blazing with determination.

"My words of, *I don't understand*?"

"No, you idiot! The other words, you said. *'You don't force anything that won't come to you of its own accord.'*"

"But I've never forced anything!" Elensar's voice quivered with frustration as he vehemently defended himself.

"Okay, let's make it simpler. Remember what happened when I was pregnant, the one after Lenith? We named her Sarath, remember?"

"Sarath," that name was played on his tongue as if trying to remember its use in memory, then it hit him like a ton of bricks.

Elensar suddenly felt a chill run down his spine, one night filled with such regret and shame. Elensar remembered how the evening had started full of love and devotion, then came rage as Amelia withdrew her affection, saying she was playing along, teasing him to see how far he'd go. Elensar went too far after hearing those words! How demanding he had been and the rage that had erupted within him as he hadn't gotten his way. Elensar hadn't known his actions would hurt his beloved and their precious unborn kin, Sarath. His rough hands had ripped through Amelia's fragile body like nothing but a piece of cloth. In his blind rage, he had taken Amelia in ways that immediately and painfully caused her to miscarry their kin, Sarath.

For Amelia's part, unknown to Elensar, she hid her role away from memory, her blame for allowing him to do this to her, even enjoying, encouraging Elensar to step further. Amelia buried the truth deep within her, locking it away in a dark corner of her mind. The pain of losing their unborn child was unbearable, but the shame and guilt that consumed her were even more suffocating. Amelia couldn't fathom how she had reached a point where she found pleasure in his violent actions, where she had become an accomplice to her destruction.

The present-day Elensar looked down at his hands, now quivering at the painful memory. He wished he could turn back time and make it all disappear, but he knew it was too late for that to happen. He felt a wave of guilt and grief and desperately wished to apologize and make amends for his actions. But words could never make things right again. Elensar now swallowed a lump of guilt down his throat.

His eyesight went to a tall clothes dresser in the room. Hidden inside it, in a wooden box, was something from that night. His vision went back to Amelia. "It breaks my heart to think I have done that, forgotten such a time in our lives when everything turned black for you—"

"Me! It wasn't anything to do with me! You dragged me onto the bed, then raped me; you caused me to miscarry—You know what, fuck this!" She opened the door and went through it.

As Amelia stormed out of the room, Elensar couldn't help but feel a pang of guilt. Deep down, he knew she was right - he had avoided the topic for far too long. The incident they were referring to was a dark chapter in their shared history, one that had caused a rift between them.

Elensar stood momentarily, contemplating whether to chase after her or let her have some space. But his love for her compelled him to follow, to confront the unresolved emotions that lingered between them. Elensar found Amelia standing on the stairwell to their bedroom, her back turned towards him as tears streamed down her face.

Elensar approached cautiously; his voice filled with remorse. "Amelia, please—Let's talk about it. I know it's painful, but we can't keep burying our memories of that fateful night. Your words lay the blame solely on me, but someone else was also involved."

Amelia turned around abruptly, her eyes red and swollen from crying. "I know. What do you want me to say that I was also to blame?" Her voice trembled with a hint of anger. "Yes, I, too, was to blame; are you happy now I have admitted it out loud to you?"

Elensar stood there, stunned by her sudden outburst. He had never seen her like this before—So vulnerable, yet so defiant. A wave of guilt washed over him as he looked into her tear-filled eyes. He had always prided himself on being rational and level-headed, but now he realized how blind he had been to his mistakes.

It was true; they were both at fault for that fateful night. "No," he whispered, his voice laced with remorse. "I don't want you to say anything just to appease me. I want you to know I understand my part in this, too."

Elensar's admission caught her off guard. Her anger momentarily wavered as she searched his face for any signs of insincerity. Seeing none, she took a deep breath and composed herself. "I hear you loud and clear; now I need to go, get away from here before my head explodes with all this stuff!"

Elensar watched Amelia turn away, her steps heavy with the weight of their conversation. The air between them was thick with unresolved emotions, and he knew their healing journey would not be easy. But Elensar was determined to make amends, to mend the fractures in their relationship. As Amelia walked further away, he couldn't help but feel a pang of regret. He wanted to reach out, hold her back, and tell her everything would be alright. But he knew that actions spoke louder than words, and his actions needed to reflect his remorse.

With a heavy heart, Elensar let her go, knowing that this separation was necessary for both, but he also knew what he needed to do next, something he should have done long ago. Elensar went back up the stairwell, back into their room, and retrieved a small wooden box from the tall clothes dresser in the room; he covered it with a bedsheet, then carried it out of the castle, down winding stairs, and into the garden, seeking the rose bush he'd seen a few weeks ago.

Carefully, Elensar created a small hole at the base and placed the box mid-way before pushing dirt around and above it again. After this, Elensar went to see if he could talk to Amelia again, but she'd gone out, probably gone to see her friends again. Instead of looking for Amelia, Elensar went up to the spire tower and watched Amelia walk slowly down to the city's courtyard towards Sofia's home, occasionally stopping as if the walk were causing her pain, or she was out of breath. After watching Amelia knock on Sofia's door, Elensar saw her enter, and that's where Elensar stayed for a good three hours, watching, spying, if you want to call it that, his eyes filled with adoration and possessiveness. Elensar had always fiercely protected Amelia, unwilling to let anyone or anything threaten their bond, their marriage. The intensity of his love for Amelia bordered on obsession, consuming his every thought and action. To him, she was his everything, the centre of his universe, and she was his property, or at least that's what he thought.

Chapter 17

Lenith Plays Matchmaker

From the moment he learned to read, Lenith had always found solace in the pages of books, in the author's words and the stories they told. The castle library was his sanctuary, where he could forget the world's troubles and lose himself in the pages of a book. Today, he arrived to find that he shared the library with his mother. Her head hung heavy, and her pale hands lay idle in her lap, holding a book. Lenith's heart sank as he took in the sight of his mother, her usually vibrant and lively spirit now replaced by a veil of sadness.

Lenith approached her cautiously, unsure of what had caused this sudden change in her demeanour. "Mother," he said softly, his voice filled with concern. "What troubles you? Is there something I can do to help?"

"Lenith!"

He noticed her eyes were red as if she'd been crying; he went on his knees before her, "Mother, you cried tears!"

"Tears of reading."

"Should I destroy it for you?" he glanced over to the small-lit fire.

"Lenith, if you burnt this book, you'd have to burn nearly all of these here," Mother looked around. "No, you mustn't burn them."

"What are you reading?"

"The Tales of a Dead Winter's Dream."

Lenith studied the thick open book in her hands with a heavy heart. His mother had been so quick to start reading again. He had heard of it, a cautionary tale of dreams gone wrong. He knew he had to step in. "Mother," he began, gently taking away the book and taking her hands in his own. "This isn't a book meant for us to read. This book holds great sorrow and darkness that we ought not to bear. I don't want you to read it and add to the sorrow that's already been with us for so long." Lenith gazed into her eyes, trying to make her understand the gravity of the situation.

After a moment, she gave a slight nod, and Lenith tucked the book away, quoting a line from the same book as he did. "'*Better not to wander through this land of death lest you become a part of it.'* Mother," he began gently, "Why do you insist on delving into stories with unhappy endings? There is enough sorrow in the world already."

"I was only reading it to discover what happens in the end."

"Mother, have you read it before?" Lenith's voice carried a hint of sadness as he spoke those words.

"No."

"I have, and the ending isn't happy; after writing her last letters, she casts her life away, fearing there's no other way out."

"That's sad."

"That's why this book isn't for you." Lenith stood up and walked away, only to fetch another book. "If you must read," offering a discoloured brown book. "This one you'll find more suitable."

His mother glanced at the book sceptically, raising an eyebrow. "Are you sure this one will be more suitable?" she asked, her voice laced with curiosity. "This one says, '*Trust a stranger.*' Surely, that's not good!"

"What if you didn't? How would you know if you discarded their help when you most needed it? Strangers can become friends if you trust them," Lenith saw her nod in agreement. "Perhaps strangers that are companions can also help each other if they speak."

"Perhaps," his mother looked at him angrily, "One of those strangers doesn't want to talk to the other," she mumbled.

"Then you won't find out unless you speak first."

"Lenith!" she'd scolded him, her voice filled with frustration.

"I'm only trying to help."

"I know, but sometimes things must run a course before it's changed."

"If you wait that long, you will end the course but cross the line without a winner." Lenith sighed, his eyes filled with concern. He understood her desire to let things unfold naturally, but he couldn't bear to see her suffer any longer. "But what if waiting prolongs the pain? What if speaking up is the only way to find a resolution?"

She looked at him, torn between her beliefs and his valid point. "I don't want to make things worse by rushing into it," she said softly. "Sometimes, patience is the key to understanding."

Lenith nodded, acknowledging her perspective. "I get that, but there's a fine line between patience and complacency. We can't let fear hold us back from seeking the truth."

"Lenith, that's enough preaching! You may be my child, but that doesn't give you the right to lecture me, God! You're just like your father."

"No, Father doesn't call me a child; he calls me kin."

"You are rebellious and stubborn," her angry stare changed into a half-smile, "Right down to the kin bit. Now find a book, sit with me for a while."

"Only if you promise not to get angry anymore."

"If you stop lecturing me, I won't."

"That doesn't mean," walking away to get a book. "Just with me, with father too."

"Lenith!"

"I know, I know," Lenith sighed, flipping through the pages of a book absentmindedly. "But it's not just about me and Father. It's about all of us learning to communicate better, and anger isn't a good way out of a problem," he walked back over, "Speaking is."

"God, you don't give up, do you."

"For my mother, never," Lenith sat next to her. "I don't give up," he replied firmly. "Because giving up means accepting that things will never change, and I refuse to believe that. Now, shall we carry on speaking or reading?"

"Read; it's quieter."

Lenith didn't get to open his book; the library door opened, and Father walked with a long clay pipe clenched between his lips. Lenith winked at him; to that, Father frowned. Lenith nodded to the empty chair next to Mother, "Come join us, Father."

"If he's going to join us," that was said by Mother, "I'm leaving!"

"No, you'll stay," Lenith placed a hand on her raising lap; she now gave him an angry look. "Remember what I said," he stood up, walked over to Father, "Father, take a book, read with Mother. She gets upset easily and will need comfort from you."

"Lenith!" Mother and Father synchronized their words.

Lenith ignored their synchronized protest and continued his voice firm. "I mean it. Both of you need to spend some quality time together. Mother needs your support right now, Father."

Lenith knew he'd stepped over the line, but nobody else would utter it if he hadn't told the truth. Lenith went to the far end of the room. He pretended to look for another book, watching Father take his empty seat beside Mother. Lenith stayed by the bookcase for twenty minutes, listening to the occasional puffs upon Father's clay pipe, turning pages, and sighs from Mother's lips. Then, at some point during silence, the room's quiet atmosphere abruptly changed into a hostile one.

"What's the matter?" Mother rudely said to Father. "I get your silence now?"

Lenith turned his gaze to Father. He thought his eye might have gone to Mother, but he didn't look up from the book he read. Father puffed the pipe he smoked on hard.

"That's right, just act as if I'm not here; I can do that as well."

Father looked up and gave her an almighty stare; the pipe almost fell from his lips.

"What, can't you speak through your lips!" she sarcastically answered. "Your mother gives better death stares without trying."

Father took the clay pipe from his mouth, his voice tinged with weariness." Do you wish me to answer your words?" Lenith saw her nod; Father placed his book on his lap, leaning a little nearer to her, "These lips of mine don't want to utter words, for even you wouldn't believe whatever I wish to say."

"Try your words; I'll see if I can do that."

"What do you see before you?"

"I see someone who used to love me; now his mother's mind has poisoned him against me; now he wishes me gone from his life."

"Have I said such a thing to you?"

"You don't need to; it's written on your face."

"Then you read wrong," father's voice trembled with confusion and hurt as he responded, "Amelia, never have I wished for you to be gone from my life. How could you think such a thing?"

"How do you expect me to imagine anything else? It's plain—"

"Maybe you should've tried harder, Amelia."

"If I tried any harder, Elensar, I'd have gotten the same answer."

"The answers are easy to see. Am I not still here in this room—"

"And it's the longest time you've spoken to me since—"

"That's not true!" Father's voice rose. "I've given you ample chances to talk to me after what you told me a few months ago! I persistently await your arrival, yet you never do come. All I can do is anticipate when I can speak to you, share my feelings, and erase the chill between us. And it bothers me when you don't come back to your chamber with me at night or in the mornings anymore since that disagreement. Despite all I've tried, you'd prefer to keep animosity lingering between us and persist in shutting me out. I'm left alone in the dark, with no one to turn to, with only my thoughts to accompany me as I wait for a sign that you may want to soothe the icy veil that now divides us. I thought that would only take us apart, yet we seem to be drifting further away from one another."

"No, you're wrong," his mother replied in a heated tone, "I can't perform in an act with you always ending in sadness."

The argument was getting heated between his parents, and it made Lenith sigh quietly and even made him think of stopping them, but nothing would get sorted if he got in the way. So Lenith decided to stay quiet and let them carry on.

"How do you know it'll end in sadness? Are you there to predict the future?" his father interrupted. "We've been through tough times before, but we always find a way to make it work."

Lenith watched as his parent's locked eyes, their expressions mixed with anger and hurt. He had seen them argue countless times, but this time felt different. The tension in the room was palpable, and he couldn't help but feel a sense of unease.

His mother took a deep breath, her voice trembling as she responded, "Yes, we have, but this is different, Elensar; since those damn papers came into our world, everything has turned my life upside down, and I can't handle that."

His father's face softened for a moment before he retorted, "I understand your frustration," Father replied, his voice filled with empathy. "I've seen how these papers have affected you, and I've felt the weight of it, too. But remember, you're not alone."

"But that's just it; I have been alone! You don't talk to me; everyone else either gives me a side eye or—"

"But I've been trying to talk to you," Father shook his head in dismay. "How long have you felt this way?" he asked, his voice filled with concern.

"Since that meeting with your mother," Mother admitted, her voice barely above a whisper. "It's like an invisible barrier separates me from everyone else."

"But you had your friends, Sofia, Sarian, and Anlease—"

"Yes, they helped me through it by getting me drunk!"

Father's face fell, his concern deepening. "I had no idea," he said softly. "Why didn't you tell me when it first happened?"

"I didn't say anything because I overheard you say something while I was—" A deadly silence followed Mother's words. Lenith's heart raced as he listened to the tense exchange between his parents. He had never heard his mother speak with such seriousness before, and it sent a chill down his spine.

"Amelia," Lenith heard his father's voice speak with concern in the tone after a few moments. "What's the matter?"

Lenith's mind raced with questions and worry. What could his mother have overheard? And why was it causing such tension between his parents? He strained his ears, desperate to catch any further snippets of their conversation. He longed to burst into the middle of the room and demand answers, but something held him back. Perhaps it was fear of what he might discover or a lingering respect for his parents' privacy. Finally, after what felt like an eternity, his father spoke again.

Father's voice was softer this time, filled with genuine concern. "Amelia," Father said gently, "Please tell me what's troubling you. We've always shared everything; don't shut me out now."

Lenith saw his mother raise her head, her eyes filled with tears; a hand went over her mouth, then fell away. Lenith's heart sank as he watched his mother struggle to find the words. He had never seen her so vulnerable, and it pained him to witness her pain. Lenith saw his mother take a deep breath as if trying to steady herself before finally speaking.

Mother's voice trembled as she uttered words next, "Oh god, I can't tell you, I can't—"

"What can't you tell me," Father's voice was filled with concern and a hint of urgency as he reached over and gently grabbed Mother's hand. Lenith watched their interaction, his heart pounding, sensing that something serious was about to be revealed.

Mother hesitated for a moment, her eyes welling up with tears. She took another deep breath, trying to compose herself before finally finding the strength to speak. "Elensar," she began, her voice quivering, "There's something I've been keeping from you—Something I never wanted you to know."

"It's okay," Father interrupted gently, his eyes filled with concern. "Whatever it is, you can trust me. We've always been honest with each other."

"I can't, I can't," Mother suddenly rushed up from her seat and started pacing back and forth, her hands trembling with anxiety.

Father rose from his chair, reached out to her, and gently grasped Mother's shoulders, trying to steady her. "Amelia, please," Father pleaded softly, "You don't have to tell me if you're not ready. I won't push you."

Mother looked into his eyes, searching for any sign of judgment or disappointment. But all she found was unwavering support and love. She took a deep breath, trying to calm the storm of emotions within her. "No, Elensar," she finally said, her voice barely above a whisper. "I can't; it will kill you, kill me too; I have to go—"

Father reached out and gently grasped Mother's trembling hands, his touch providing a grounding force amidst the chaos. His voice remained steady, filled with understanding and compassion. "Amelia, Mycorm," he said, his words laced with tenderness. "You don't have to face this alone. We are in this together, always."

Mother's eyes welled up with tears as she looked at Father, her heart torn between the desire to protect him and the overwhelming need to escape the suffocating darkness that consumed her. With a mixture of fear and determination etched on her face, Mother took another deep breath, gathering strength from Father's unwavering support. "Elensar," she whispered again, her voice quivering but resolute. "I can't stay here any longer; I'm leaving at least for a few days to clear my head."

"Leaving, where to!"

"Hildernbyth to see the twins."

"Why do you want to see the twins?" Father's brows furrowed as he tried to comprehend her words. "But why now? Why this sudden urgency?"

"I just do—"

"Then I'll come with you," Father replied softly, stroking her arm. "We'll leave together later today."

"No, I want to go alone," Mother interrupted, her voice firm. "I need some time to myself to figure things out."

Father's face fell, a mix of confusion and concern etched across his features. "But Amelia, we've always faced everything together. Why do you want to go alone now?"

Mother took a deep breath, gathering her thoughts before responding. "I love you, Elensar, and I appreciate your support. But this is something I need to do on my own."

"Then, if you won't let me come," Father insisted firmly. His voice was concerned and determined: "I'll have my guards escort you to Hildernbyth."

"Please, Elensar," tears start to well in Mother's eyes, "You don't understand I need to go alone!"

"I do, my love, I do," Father stepped closer, "I know what you did; I don't care that you did it, that you took—"

"You know!" Mother had looked stunned, "You know I've—"

"The papers, yes, I know you took them, but I don't care—"

"The papers! You think I was spea—Oh god!" Lenith saw a hand go over her mouth; she started crying more. "No, no, you don't understand! Oh god, I must go; I must go now!" She turned on her heel and was about to flee, but Father caught her by the arm.

Father's grip tightened around Mother's arm, preventing her from escaping. His face was etched with concern and confusion as he tried to make sense of her panicked state. "Amelia, what's going on? Why are you so terrified?" he asked urgently.

"You don't, can't understand!"

"Amelia, please calm down," Father pleaded gently, trying to soothe her trembling form. "You need to tell me what's happening. I can't help you if I don't understand. Stay here; we can mend this, whatever it is, Amelia, please, you must listen to me. An hour, that's all I'm asking for!"

"I don't have an hour spare. I don't even have minutes to spare."

"Amelia, please," Father's voice trembled with desperation as he pleaded with Mother to stay.

"Elensar, please let me go!" Mother started to pull away from him.

"Amelia, I beg you to reconsider," Father pleaded, his voice cracking with emotion. "We've been through so much together. Remember the love we shared? The dreams we had. We can't just throw it all away."

"I'm not throwing anything away; I just need to go now," Mother twisted her arm out of Father's grip and ran for the library door.

Desperate fuelling Father's actions made him chase after her, his voice trembling with a mix of fear and longing. "Amelia, please! Don't leave like this," Father called out, desperately hoping she would stop and reconsider.

Lenith saw his mother open the library door and slammed it shut. Then he saw Father halt his running steps and stand silently in the middle of the room, looking dumbfounded and confused. So, he stepped away from the bookshelf, walked over, and touched his shoulder. "Father, you need to go after her; sort this out."

"I don't think it'll work this time, Lenith."

"But Father," Lenith pleaded, "You can't just let her walk away like this. You always find a way to make things right."

His father sighed heavily, his shoulders slumping under the weight of the situation. "I've tried, Lenith. I've tried countless times to mend the cracks in our relationship, but they seem to have turned into irreparable chasms."

"But Father," Lenith insisted, his voice trembling with desperation, "You can't give up now. You've always found a way to overcome obstacles together. Remember when you rebuilt the old jewellery box for her? Or when you fixed the broken vase, she used to love in the living room, the one everyone said was beyond repair?"

His father's eyes met Lenith's, filled with sadness and resignation. "I remember, son," he replied softly. "Those were different times, simpler problems. This—This is something deeper."

"Father, you are wrong; those tears in her eyes were of wanting help, not sadness. Now take her away from here, from all this madness, to somewhere she can't run away from when you speak with her," Father gave him a confused look. "It's the only way you can do it."

"Perhaps you're right," Father turned away from him. "But I don't know where."

"Take her somewhere calming, where there'll be no interference, where you know it will turn out all right, somewhere she has good memories from."

"There is one place, a place we had a lot of good times in."

"And?"

"I could fetch her from the twin's house, take her there."

"Yes, you should go swiftly, for Mother has already taken your horse and gone," Father looked at him, eyes saying, '*How would you know this?*' "Then perhaps you'll come back home with even happier news to tell us," Lenith smiled, "Perhaps the news of another brother or sister?"

"Lenith," Father laughed, "You're impossible."

"I know, but it helps. Now get going before Mothers' feelings change." Lenith watched as Father turned away, laughing, sprinting out of the room hurriedly in his footsteps. Lenith shook his head and smiled as he walked to the window. Outside that window, Lenith saw Mother seated upon a horse galloping into the forest behind the castle. *Go, Mother, but he's coming to help you*, he mouthed silently to her, then turned his gaze back into the room.

Chapter 18

Amelia Seeks The Twins Company

Now, barely less than an hour later, after that meeting in the library and after leaving Volarie, Amelia was riding her horse with full swiftness until finally reaching the destination of Hildernbyth, where her horse walked past some Shalimars exchanging goods. Still, she didn't stop until a good few moments passed. But if Amelia had placed her footsteps in a different direction, she'd have visited the shoreline line and walked on sun-drenched sand that afternoon. She'd have walked along the shore of a lonely beach. Nothing stirred in the seaside's surreal stillness until a distant sound of waves slowly broke through. The soft crunch of the white sand would have been her next step, the sea soothingly hushing and whispering as it surged over the rocks cut into the seafloor. Amelia's heart would have swelled as she reached the shore's end, amazed by this place's beauty. Amelia would have been astonished by the sounds and sensations surrounding her when she stepped onto the rocks. The air was cold and salty; a fresh breeze would have blown on her face while the sun baked the rock slices. Amelia would have taken a deep breath and immersed herself in the serenity and grandeur of the beach and its surroundings. Her eyes would've wandered along the coast's edge, feeling a natural balance and peace of this perfect place, a beach out of this world, but Amelia didn't take this path.

When Amelia stopped, she dismounted and looked around. Seconds later, she walked up a little pebbled path and knocked upon a wooden door of an oak-beamed house with a newly thatched roof. "Amelia, what in the stars!" said a tall male with golden hair dressed in a long, graceful robe after opening the door.

"Amelia!" came a voice from behind the door. "Amelia is here!"

Amelia had entered a cottage with a thatched roof, which immediately made her feel so cozy and warm. It was surrounded by tall oak trees and felt homey, with its fireplace crackling cheerfully away. The furniture was all comfortable and inviting, making her want to sit down immediately, but she didn't. There was a small kitchen off the side, where you could find the ingredients to bake something delicious. Every item had its place.

The walls of the living room were filled with wooden shelves, each groaning with books, knick-knacks, and treasures. The bright floral curtains and comfortable quilts made the cottage stand out in her memories. For a moment, everything seemed perfect. The birds sang sweetly outside the living room window, and the sun shone through the trees, creating a fabulous light show. It was the most peaceful and beautiful place she had ever been to, but Amelia wasn't here to carry on admiring the twin's home; she was here only for one purpose: to give them something.

"You've come alone?"

"I can't speak to an invisible person; where is he?"

"Here." Borthron half-shuffled out from behind the couch, revealing himself as a tall, slim male with messy hair and a mischievous grin when standing upright.

"What were you doing down there?" asked Amelia, seeing a person on their hands and knees, rummaging around behind a sofa a moment before. "What is it that you were searching for?" Amelia asked gently, her voice laced with genuine concern.

"I've lost Cinders," Borthron whispered, his voice trembling with fear and desperation.

"Who's Cinders?" Amelia asked, her curiosity piqued as she glanced at Elysium and then Borthron.

"His spider," confirmed Elysium, shaking his head, "I told him not to leave him unattended, but he never listens," Elysium sighed, frustration evident in his voice.

"Spider?" Amelia's voice trembled with a mix of curiosity and fear.

Elysium walked to the sofa. "He'll show up when he's hungry."

"Yeah, or when someone steps on him," Borthron looked around, sweeping the floor with his sight. "Then he'll certainly show up."

Amelia raised an eyebrow, her curiosity piqued. "So, you're telling me an invisible spider is roaming around here?"

Borthron nodded solemnly. "Yes, Cinders can turn invisible whenever he wants. It's a handy trick, especially when he doesn't want to be found."

Amelia couldn't help but feel a mix of fascination and unease at the thought of an invisible spider lurking in their midst. "But why would you have an invisible spider as a pet? Isn't that a bit— Unusual?"

Borthron chuckled, scratching his head. "Well, Cinders isn't exactly a pet per se. He just sort of—Adopted me. I found him one day while exploring an ancient cave deep in the forest. Ever since then, we've been inseparable."

Elysium chimed in with a mischievous grin. "And let me tell you, Cinders is quite mischievous himself!"

Amelia stepped forward, her eyes narrowing as she tried to hide her curiosity. "Mischievous? How so?" she asked, her voice laced with intrigue.

"Amelia, be careful!" Borthron swept the wooden floor with his eyesight. "Watch where you put your feet."

"Oh, for goodness's sake!" she shook her head. "So, what else have you both been up to lately."

"Oh, Amelia," sounded Borthron, all excited. "We've so much to tell you since your last visit with Elensar. That reminds me, where is he?"

"He couldn't come," Amelia answered with an uneasy tone.

"Couldn't come?" Borthron replied, his brows furrowing in concern. "But he never misses a chance to see us,"

"Oh," had been Borthron's reply, turning away as if he hadn't heard what Amelia had said and went through an open doorway.

"Come on!" Elysium gripped him by his arm and pulled him back into the room, "Something's not right."

"What isn't right?" asked Borthron as he was led back into the living room.

"Oh, for goodness's sake!" Elysium shook his head in distress, "Why would Amelia arrive unannounced? Something's not right."

Borthron glanced at Amelia, his brow furrowing in confusion. "What do you mean? Why wouldn't she drop by without informing us beforehand?"

Elysium sighed, "It's not like her. She's always been meticulous about planning and scheduling. This sudden visit feels off."

"He's right," Amelia replied, "I apologize for the surprise visit," Amelia said, her voice tinged with concern. "But I had no other choice. It's urgent."

Elysium furrowed his brows, studying Amelia's face for any signs of deception. They had known each other for years, and he trusted her implicitly. However, something about her demeanour now made him question the gravity of the situation. "What's going on, Amelia? Why are you so worried?" Elysium asked, his voice laced with a mix of curiosity and apprehension.

"I've done something; if Elensar finds out what I've done, I'm dead. My life will be in danger," Amelia whispered, her eyes darting around the room as if expecting someone to appear at any moment.

"What have you done?" Elysium asked, his voice barely audible.

Amelia's heart raced as she looked at the concerned faces of her friends. She knew she had to explain herself, but her actions weighed heavily on her conscience. "I didn't mean for any harm to come from it," Amelia whispered, her voice trembling. "I was desperate and thought if I took them, it would better my situation."

Elysium's eyes softened with understanding, but Borthron remained sceptical. "Desperation can cloud one's judgment," he said sternly. "But secrets have consequences, Amelia. You must understand that."

Amelia nodded, tears welling up in her eyes. "I do understand now," she replied, barely audible. "And that's why I'm here, seeking your help. Elensar must never find out what I've done."

Elysium placed a comforting hand on Amelia's shoulder. "We will do everything we can to protect you," he assured her. "After all, my brother speaks a few truths in his last words; Elensar has a few secrets hidden."

"Yes, like keeping monkey skulls in a locked closet."

Elysium sighed then replied, "No, he doesn't, that's just talk."

Borthron frowned, then cast a glance over to Amelia. "You haven't done anything with your kin's, have you!"

"Borthron," shouted Elysium, "That's enough!"

Borthron crossed his arms and huffed, clearly annoyed by Elysium's reprimand. "Fine, I'll stop," he muttered under his breath.

"Go find your spider." Elysium turned back to Amelia. "I'm so sorry."

Amelia looked at Elysium with a mix of confusion and concern. She had never seen her friend so agitated before. Elysium's words were sharp, cutting through the air like a double-edged sword. It was clear that his twin had deeply unsettled him. "Hey, it's okay," Amelia said softly, touching Elysium's shoulder. "You don't have to apologize for anything. But what just happened? Why did you react like that?"

Elysium took a deep breath, trying to calm himself down. His eyes wandered for a moment before meeting Amelia's gaze again. "It's just—Sometimes I forget how long I've been alive, how much I've seen and experienced," he replied, his voice tinged with sadness. "And when someone questions my actions or treats me like a kin, even my twin, it stirs up emotions I thought I had long buried."

Amelia nodded understandingly, "You sounded like Lathlorn just then; he tends to let his emotions go astray, too, when triggered, but I haven't come to speak about him."

"So why did you come?"

"I need you to look after something," out of her dress pocket, she pulled a bundle of old, discoloured papers that William had brought into their world. "No one else must see them, you understand," she said. "I need some more medicine as well."

Elysium nodded; his curiosity piqued by the mysterious papers. He carefully took hold of the bundle, feeling the weight of history in his hands. The pieces were fragile, their edges frayed and yellowed with age. As he unfolded them, Elysium discovered a collection of handwritten letters, each bearing a different date. Intrigued by the contents, Elysium glanced up at Amelia, whose eyes held a mixture of desperation and trust. "What are these?" Elysium asked softly, his voice filled with both concern and fascination.

"These letters," Amelia began hesitantly, "Hold secrets from long ago. Secrets that could change everything if they fell into the wrong hands."

Borthron swung open the door swiftly to reveal a figure standing on their doorstep. "Oh, I wasn't expecting another visitor today from Volarie's—City."

"Amelia," they heard Elensar's stern voice asking. "Is she here?"

Borthron looked back and saw her shake her head at Elensar's question. He turned his gaze back to Elensar and spoke to him. "No, Your Highness. She's not here yet."

Elensar's eyes darted behind him, searching for signs of Amelia's presence. His left hand rolled into a fist, a clear indication of unease. "Where else could she be?" he muttered under his breath.

"If you give me a few minutes, I'll explain how I know she should arrive soon." He saw Elensar nod, his stern gaze still fixed upon him. Borthron sighed and took a deep breath before beginning to explain. "Well, this morning, we received a message from one of Volarie's messengers that Amelia had requested to see us. It was addressed to '*The Hands of Borthron and Elysium'* and wanted us to meet her here at our house."

"Do you think me unintelligent!" Elensar sounded impolite words. "My horse from Volarie is here, tied up right outside your house!"

"She Isn't—Here. Perhaps she went to see someone else and just—Maybe she'll come here later," Borthron finished his sentence, trying to calm Elensar down.

Elensar's frustration was evident as he rolled and unrolled his fist. "But why would she send a message specifically to you if she had no intention of meeting you? And why is my horse here," he questioned, his voice filled with concern.

Borthron understood Elensar's confusion and shared his sentiments. "I don't know, my friend," he replied honestly. "Perhaps there was a change of plans or an unforeseen circumstance that forced her to alter her course."

Elensar suddenly froze, sniffed the air, and then returned his gaze to him; this time, he held a vivid look on his face. "You lie. Only one person wears that perfume, my wife, and it's a fresh scent left."

Borthron's heart skipped a beat as Elensar's accusation hung in the air. He had hoped to conceal the truth, but his friend's acute senses had betrayed him. "I—We didn't mean to deceive you, Elensar," Borthron stammered, his voice filled with remorse. "We thought it best not to burden you with the truth until we knew more. But yes, you're right. It was your wife's perfume that you sensed." He saw Elensar's eyes narrow, his expression full of anger. Taking a deep breath, Borthron began recounting what he had discovered earlier that day but used it as a decoy to hide Amelia's presence at their house. "I followed her trail of bare footsteps left through the forest," he started cautiously. "It led me to a secluded clearing where I found signs—" He saw Elensar listening to his words, his eyebrows puckering occasionally. He carried on. "Signs of a struggle," Borthron continued, his voice trembling slightly. "There were broken branches, trampled grass, and bloodstains on the ground." He paused for a moment, glancing at Elensar to gauge his reaction. A flicker of concern in his friend's eyes reassured him that his decoy was working. "I followed her footstep trail further," Borthron continued, trying to maintain an air of urgency. "It led me to a hidden cave deep within the forest's heart. Inside, I found remnants of a campfire and some torn fabric." He emphasized these details, hoping they would divert Elensar's attention from Amelia's actual whereabouts.

Elensar leaned forward, his curiosity piqued. "Did you find anything else?"

Borthron hesitated for a moment before replying. He knew he had to tread carefully with his words. "I discovered her bare footprints leading away from the cave—"

"Footprints?" Elensar repeated, his voice filled with intrigue. "Are you certain they were hers, perhaps fresh ones?"

Borthron nodded, his gaze fixed on Elensar's face. "Yes, they appeared to be quite recent. The ground was still damp from the morning dew, and her toe imprints were distinct."

"Were other footprints with hers? Perhaps shoed ones," he heard Elensar ask, his voice sounding with curiosity and caution.

Borthron shrugged, his brows furrowing in deep thought. "It's hard to say," he replied, his voice tinged with uncertainty. "This part of the forest is rarely visited by anyone other than us. But there have been rumours of strange happenings lately." He saw Elensar's interest piqued at the mention of rumours.

"What kind of rumours?" He felt Elensar prodding, sounding eager for more information.

"Well, there have been whispers of eerie sounds echoing through the trees at night," Borthron continued, his eyes darting around as if searching for unseen words. "Some say they've seen flickering lights dancing among the branches, like mischievous spirits playing tricks on unsuspecting travellers."

Elensar's curiosity had grown with this false tale, making him seem to lean in closer, his eyes widening with anticipation. "And what about those who ventured into this part of the forest? Have they encountered anything—Unusual?"

Borthron hesitated, his gaze shifting towards the floor. "A few brave souls have claimed to witness shadowy figures lurking in the shadows," his voice barely above a whisper. "They speak of an overwhelming dread that washes over them as if something ancient and malevolent is watching their every move."

"You're quite the storyteller, aren't you."

Borthron frowned at him, his sudden change of demeanour. "Storyteller? Well, I'm only telling you what happened."

"Really?" He saw Elensar raise an eyebrow as if disbelieving his words. "You don't smell like you've been in a forest or a cave."

Borthron felt frustrated at Elensar's scepticism but knew he had to convince him somehow. "Yes, really," Borthron replied, his voice tinged with annoyance. "I understand that it may sound like a mere tale to you, but I assure you, these accounts are not to be taken lightly."

He witnessed Elensar cross his arms over his chest. His eyes narrowed as he studied him intently. "And what evidence do you have to support these claims?" he asked sceptically.

Borthron sighed deeply, feeling the weight of the burden of Amelia hiding in their house, of him trying to make an excuse for Elensar to leave, on his shoulders. He knew that convincing Elensar would be an uphill battle without solid evidence. "I admit, the evidence is scarce," Borthron admitted reluctantly. "But there have been reports of unexplained disappearances in the—"

"Borthron, just stop it now."

He gave Elensar a confused expression, his voice sounding the same. "Stop it?"

"You don't have to make up a story to hide the truth from me."

"But I'm not making it up."

"Really? Why didn't you mention Amelia's perfume scent in the forest, the cave? You mentioned it at the doorstep of this house?"

"Elensar, I'm not lying."

"Look down at your feet, Borthron; what do you see?"

His sight went to do just that; then his eyes grew larger. He was looking at shoe imprints, those of a female shoe with a crest of Volarie imprinted in the mud leading up to the door, none leaving from that area. The game was up. Borthron's heart sank as he realized the gravity of the situation. The evidence was right in front of him, undeniable and damning. He had been caught in his web of deception, and there was no way out. His mind raced, desperately searching for an explanation that could salvage the remnants of his credibility. But deep down, he knew that any attempt to justify his actions would only further tarnish his fragile reputation. Elensar's piercing gaze bore into Borthron, silently demanding an explanation.

The silence hung heavy in the air, suffocating Borthron with its weight. Finally, he mustered up the courage to speak. "I—We didn't think it was relevant," Borthron stammered, his voice betraying his unease. "I mean, we were focused on finding Amelia and bringing her back safely. Her perfume scent seemed insignificant compared to the urgency of the situation." Borthron's unease grew, and he shifted uncomfortably under Elensar's unwavering gaze. He knew he had made a grave mistake by dismissing something that now seemed crucial. "I apologize," Borthron managed to say, his voice barely above a whisper. "I underestimated the significance of her perfume scent. I thought we needed to focus solely on finding Amelia quickly."

"Borthron, enough, please," Elensar put a hand up to stop any more of his words. "Just let me inside; I know she's in there; I can smell her perfume moving around there."

He was half right; Amelia wasn't moving around much, but she was moving around slightly, trying to hide her sight from the front door where Elensar and Borthron were.

Amelia's heart raced as she heard Elensar's voice outside. She knew she couldn't let him find her, not now. Not when she was so close to walking away. With every passing second, her anxiety grew, and she desperately thought about searching for a hiding spot that would keep her concealed.

Standing beside her, Elysium suddenly put his hand on her arm as if he knew what she was thinking. "Don't, he'll hear your footsteps."

He was right, Elensar would, for the floor was wooden, and any steps would create a distinct creaking sound that would give away her location. Amelia's mind raced, trying to devise a plan to avoid detection. She glanced around the room, desperately searching for any hiding spot to conceal herself from Elensar's prying eyes.

"Try a little harder next time," Elensar's voice again. "Now, will you let this visitor inside politely or barge by?"

"Elensar, you don't have—"

"Borthron, just get out of my way," they saw Elensar step forward and push him back into the hallway against the wall; Amelia darted back into the living room and hid behind a sofa, "You have no right to hide my property from me."

"Amelia is your wife, not your property—"

"She is my property, and you will give her to me if you know what's good for you!" Elensar grabbed him by the throat, "I'll kill you if I have to—"

Borthron gasped for air, his eyes widening in fear as Elensar's grip tightened around his throat. He struggled to break free, desperately clawing at Elensar's hand, but Elensar's strength was overpowering. Gasping for breath, Borthron managed to choke out a few words. "You—You can't—Treat her like this," he gasped, barely audible.

Elensar's eyes burned with fury as he squeezed harder, his face contorted with rage. "She belongs to me! I won't let anyone take her away from me!"

Amelia watched in horror from her hiding spot behind the sofa. Fear gripped her heart as she realized the dangerous situation unfolding before her.

"Elysium, help me!"

Within seconds of Elysium's name being spoken, he was by his brother's side; his hand already removed Elensar's own from his brother's neck. "You don't ever use force in my home—"

"I just want Amelia back, okay—"
"She's not here—"
"Oh, for goodness' sake, she is!" Elensar rolled his eyes, "Just let me sort this out."
Amelia's heart raced as she watched Elysium intervene, his presence bringing a glimmer of hope amidst the chaos. She peeked out from behind the sofa, her eyes filled with gratitude for his timely intervention. Elysium's calm demeanour contrasted sharply with Elensar's aggression, and she couldn't help but feel a sense of relief wash over her.
Elysium gently pulled Elensar away from his brother, his voice firm but composed. "Violence is never the answer, especially within these walls," he stated firmly, his eyes locked with Elensar's. The tension in the room dissipated slightly as Elysium's words hung in the air.
Elensar huffed in frustration, his anger momentarily subdued by Elysium's presence. "I just want Amelia back," he pleaded, desperate. His eyes darted around the room, searching for any sign of her.
"Rudeness won't achieve anything."
"Rudeness! Who's talking about rudeness!"
"You are."
"I just want to see her."
"Then calm down."
"I am!"
"You're not."
A downhearted sigh slipped out of Elensar's mouth. "Elysium, is it that hard to welcome an old friend?"
"You know I would with open arms. But today, I have to decline your entrance into my home."
"Then I'll repay your words with bitterness," Elensar lost his tolerant look. "You've been an old friend of mine for many fallen years; maybe it's time for us to part ways."
Elysium's eyes softened, a hint of sadness flickering in them. "Elensar, you know that's not what I want. But there are things you don't understand."
Elensar clenched his fists, frustration bubbling within him. "Then explain it to me! Why can't I come in? What has changed between us?"
Elysium took a deep breath, trying to find the right words. "It's not about us, Elensar. It's about protecting what you hold dear, your wife, and you being in this state isn't helping you, us, or her. I fully understand your situation but walk away for a moment."
"No, you don't. You've no idea of my situation."
"What's she done for you to act this way?"
"That's no concern to you or your brother."
"I don't want your presence here if it causes problems."
"I cause problems! She's the one causing the problems."
"It doesn't look like that to me."

"I cause problems. Is that what you think of me?" Elensar's voice trembled with a mix of anger and hurt. "You have no idea what I've been through, what she's put me through." His eyes were filled with pain, reflecting the weight of something he was hiding.

Elysium's expression softened, realizing the depth of Elensar's emotions. "I may not fully understand your situation, but I can see how much it has affected you. I don't want to dismiss your feelings, but I don't want to see you suffer anymore."

Elensar scoffed bitterly. "Suffering is all I've known for weeks now. And it's all because of her." He clenched his fists tightly, struggling to contain his anger, "So Elysium, old friend, please, I'll ask once more. Will you let me sort this out with her?"

"Then my answer isn't what you want to hear."

"Then I've no choice." With those bitter words ended, Elensar lunged himself at Elysium.

For moments, the sound of shuffling in the hallway terrified Amelia. Whenever the door slammed shut, she would cautiously peek around the couch and look toward the entrance. Amelia's heart raced as she watched Borthron, a tall and imposing figure, exerting his strength against the door. As the shuffling sounds grew louder, Amelia's anxiety intensified. She knew that Elensar wouldn't give up easily; he was known for his stubbornness and refusal to accept defeat. Borthron, however, was equally determined to protect her from any harm. With each slam of the door, Amelia's grip on reality tightened. She felt trapped in their home, a sanctuary now becoming a battleground. The fear of what might happen next consumed her thoughts, and then it went silent. That silence made her braver, for it meant only one thing: hopefully, Elensar had gone. With that thought, she tiptoed to one of the windows and peeped out.

She saw Elysium leading Elensar away calmly. Amelia's heart raced with fear and excitement as she watched them move further away. The sight filled her with hope, knowing this might be her chance to break free. Without wasting another moment, Amelia quietly slipped out of the room towards the back door, careful not to make any noise that could alert anyone to her escape—every step she took felt like a victory, each breath filled with newfound determination.

Amelia's mind raced with thoughts of what lay ahead as she moved through the dimly lit corridors of the twin's house. She knew that escaping would not be easy; numerous obstacles were likely awaiting her outside these walls. But she refused to let fear hold her back any longer. Amelia opened the back door and stealthily walked on the path around the house to the front. Tied up in the same place where she'd left her horse, she now tip-toed to that area. As Amelia reached her horse's side, the majestic creature nuzzled against her hand, sensing her unease. Amelia whispered soothing words into his ear, silently reassuring him that everything would be alright; then she mounted him, ready to start an escape journey, but she wouldn't be sitting there long. Amelia immediately felt someone grab her from the saddle. Startled and disoriented, she felt the firm grip tighten around her waist. Panic surged within her as she realized someone had forcefully snatched her from the back of the horse. Her heart pounded in her chest, and a scream escaped.

Frantically, Amelia fought against the unknown assailant's hold, desperately trying to break free. Her mind raced with questions - who was this person? What did they want? Fear mingled with anger as she refused to succumb to their control. With every ounce of strength Amelia could muster, she twisted and writhed in their grasp. Her body strained against their iron grip, but it seemed futile. During the chaos, adrenaline coursed through Amelia's veins, sharpening her senses. She noticed a glimmer of something familiar in the assailant's eyes, a fleeting recognition that sparked a flicker of hope within her. Could it be someone she knew? Or was it merely a trick of the mind?

Pushing aside the fear that threatened to consume her, Amelia mustered all her courage and called upon every ounce of resourcefulness she possessed. With a sudden burst of energy, she aimed a swift kick toward the assailant's vulnerable knee. A sharp cry escaped their lips as they momentarily faltered, allowing Amelia to break free. She turned to face her opponent.

Chapter 19

The Retrieval

A sharp cry escaped Elensar's lips when Amelia attacked him. One of his hands covered the knee she'd kicked. Elensar's eyes widened in pain as he struggled to regain his balance. Despite the agony coursing through his body, Elensar's instinct for self-preservation kicked in. He knew he had to defend himself and find a way to better this dangerous situation. With gritted teeth and determination etched on his face, he mustered every ounce of strength. Summoning all his willpower, Elensar managed to steady himself and take a step back from Amelia.

With his hand still clutching his injured knee, he said, "Amelia, I know this looks bad, but you wouldn't have stayed and listened to what I have to say if I let you go." Elensar knew he had to choose his following words carefully. He needed to convince Amelia that he meant no harm and that there was a reason behind his actions. With a deep breath, he continued, "I understand that you're scared and confused right now, but I promise you, Amelia, I never wanted any of this to happen." His voice wavered as he spoke, hoping his vulnerability would resonate with her. He slowly released his grip on his injured knee and extended his hand toward her in peace. "Please, let me explain everything. There's so much more going on than you realize."

"Like what?"

He'd heard her voice tremble with curiosity and scepticism when she said those words. He knew she had been through so much already, and the last thing he wanted was for her to be dragged deeper into a world she barely understood. He saw her take a step forward towards him. She was now studying his face, perhaps searching for any signs of deception.

He saw her look at his outstretched hand; she finally spoke up. "Like what?" he heard her say again, her voice softer this time. "I've been kept in the dark for far too long. I deserve to know if there's more to this mess than meets the eye." Her words hung in the air, heavy with expectation.

Elensar gathered his thoughts, realizing that this moment could determine their future together. "I'll tell you things you'll probably hate me for, but honesty is the best policy. So, I'll start at the beginning."

"Go on."

"I haven't been speaking to you in public or Mother's sight because I'm trying to keep you alive. But I'm sick of lying, trying to appease my mother's orders."

"What orders?"

"She wants me to have nothing to do with you because she believes you have poisoned our royal line."

"I have not!"

"I know that," Elensar replied softly, his eyes filled with sadness and frustration. "But my mother is convinced that your presence in our lives will bring destruction and chaos. She believes you are the reason behind all the misfortunes that have befallen our family."

"Really! So, she is at the bottom of our troubles, causing all this between us?"

"I'm afraid she is."

"Then why don't you stand up for yourself against her!"

"I have tried," he sighed, his voice tinged with resignation. "But no matter what I say or do, Mother remains steadfast in her beliefs. It's like she has built a wall around herself, shutting out any possibility of understanding or reconciliation."

"I always had a feeling in the back of my mind that she wasn't who everyone thought she was. I even remember a story Sarian told me a while ago. About someone with royal blood connected to a human's demise. It wouldn't surprise me if it were her!"

Elensar nodded, a look of realization dawning on his face. "You think she's the one Sarian was talking about? The one with royal connections and a dark past?"

"Yes."

He paused for a moment, deep in thought. "It would explain a lot," he finally replied. "Her unwavering beliefs, her refusal to listen to reason. Perhaps she's hiding something she fears will be exposed if she lets down her guard."

"But why would she go to such lengths? What could be so terrible that she'd build walls around herself?"

"I'm not sure," he admitted, furrowing his brow. "But sometimes people do things out of fear or desperation. Maybe something in her past haunts her, something she can't escape."

"It's possible."

He nodded in agreement, his gaze fixed on her face as he contemplated her words. "Maybe she's been hurt before, betrayed by someone she loved or deeply trusted. That pain can make it difficult for anyone to let their guard down again."

"Or maybe she's just born like that, hating those she thinks are better than her. I still hate her."

"You have every right to."

"And I refuse to believe such baseless accusations," he heard her declare, her voice filled with determination. "I have done nothing but love and support you over the many years I have been with you and your family, and I will not let your mother's unfounded fears dictate our future."

He reached out and gently took her hand, his touch comforting yet tinged with a hint of resignation. "I appreciate your unwavering faith in me," he whispered, his eyes searching hers for understanding. "But my mother's beliefs run deep, ingrained by years of superstition and paranoia. It will take more than just our love to change her mind."

"Then we shall prove her wrong," she used an asserted tone, a fire igniting within her.

He smiled weakly, grateful for her unwavering support.

"And now I understand why you've been distant," she said, her voice filled with empathy.

He sighed heavily, running a hand through his hair in frustration. "I've tried reasoning with Mother countless times, but she refuses to listen. Her mind's clouded by prejudice and fear, so that's why I mentioned to you that we leave Volarie and start a new life with our kin's in Andrathlion forest. But I already told you this, but you weren't in a fit state to remember me saying it."

"Fit state?"

"The night Sofia brought you home."

"Oh, that night."

Elensar took a deep breath, gathering his thoughts before he began to speak again. "Amelia," he started softly, "I know I've kept you in the dark for far too long. But believe me when I say that my intentions never meant to hurt you or anyone else."

"I know," he saw her smile at him. "Let's not go there anymore."

"Agreed. Now, how about we get going from here?"

"Where to?"

"Somewhere far away from here."

"If that's what you wish, we can," he saw her turn away from him. "I've got to return to Borthron and Elysium's first before we go."

"Why?"

"I forgot something."

"Something, like what?"

"Just papers."

"Papers? I'll go, get them for you." He saw her look at him oddly for a second, so he asked, "Is there a problem?"

"No," that was said rather quickly.

"Then let me go get them for you."

He heard her sigh heavily, then almost whispered, "Okay, go."
"Okay," he stepped away a little, "Stay here, okay?"
He saw her nod her response; he turned to leave then noticed Elysium was inches away from them, probably been there the whole time. "Elysium!"
"Elensar," he replied. "What did you think I'd allow you to go unchecked in Amelia's presence?"
"No, I just didn't realize you were here; I mean here right by my side."
"I noticed," he half laughed. "But it's understandable, Elensar. Amelia has a way of captivating one's attention." Elysium's eyes twinkled as he spoke.
Elensar couldn't help but feel a pang of guilt for being so absorbed in his conversation with Amelia that he hadn't even noticed his loyal friend standing beside him. "I apologize, Elysium," Elensar said sincerely. "I didn't mean to disregard your presence. You know how much Amelia means to me."
Elysium nodded understandingly, his expression softening. "Of course, Elensar. I've always known how important she is to you. That's why I'm here—to ensure her safety and your happiness."
"Well, I thank you for that," he put an arm around Amelia's shoulder. "We need, or should I say, to get something from your house. You've something that belongs to us?"
"We do?" said Elysium, full of surprise in his voice.
"Yes," replied Amelia. "Those papers I gave you."
"But I thought you gave them to me to hide?"
"I did but know I don't want any more secrets to cause problems, at least not with my marriage," she lifted her head and looked up at Elensar, "I meant our marriage," she gave a small smile, saw Elensar returned the smile, understanding the unspoken message behind her words. Amelia turned her attention back to Elysium, her expression softening. "I trust you, Elysium. But those papers hold important information that could help us in our current situation. We need them back."
Elysium nodded, his surprise slowly fading away. "Of course, I understand. I'll retrieve them for you right away." He turned and started to head towards the house.
"I'll come with you," replied Elensar, following behind him slowly. "Amelia, can you stay with our horses?"
"You're going to leave me with the horses alone?"
"Yes."
"How do you know I won't just get on one and ride away?"
"Because," Elysium smirked, "He trusts you, Amelia. Besides, these horses are far too loyal to abandon you. They know they have to protect and serve."

Elensar watched the exchange between his friend and lover with a knowing smile. "That I do, trust her with all my heart," Elensar replied. "So, do you mind staying with them?"

Amelia nodded; eyes fixed on the majestic creatures grazing peacefully nearby. "Of course," she replied, her voice gentle yet determined. "I'll ensure they're well taken care of while you two retrieve the papers."

Elysium and Elensar exchanged a grateful glance before continuing their journey towards the house. The path leading to it was adorned with vibrant flowers and towering trees, casting a comforting shade over them. As they walked side by side, Elysium couldn't help but feel a sense of relief knowing that Elensar was by his side in a now more pleasant mood. Silence enveloped them momentarily until Elysium broke it with a soft sigh. "So, is this what that outburst outside our home was about, the papers?"

"Not quite, but most of it."

"You wish them now?"

"Yes, quicker would be good, and some medicine for my knee if you have any."

"Of course. Follow me."

Elensar went inside Borthron and Elysium's house using the back door, following Elysium into a study. Elysium gave Elensar a bottle to drink from to heal his wounded knee. Elensar gingerly accepted the bottle, his eyes filled with gratitude. As he took a sip, a soothing warmth spread through his body, alleviating the pain in his wounded knee. Curiosity sparked as he glanced around the study room—the walls adorned with intricate tapestries depicting mythical creatures and far-off lands. Shelves lined with ancient books and artifacts whispered tales of forgotten civilizations.

Elensar couldn't help but feel a sense of wonder in this enchanting space, and then he remembered why he'd returned to the house. "The papers, I need them as well, if you don't mind," he said.

"Ah yes," Elysium walked to a painting on the wall near them then gently lifted it off the wall, revealing a hidden safe behind it. The safe door swung open with a soft click, revealing a stack of old papers neatly arranged inside. Elysium carefully handed the documents to Elensar, who eagerly examined them. The pages had been filled with faded ink and delicate handwriting, each holding fragments of Amelia's family history. It was as if time had stood still within those pages, preserving stories and knowledge passed down through generations.

Elensar carefully rolled them up and placed them inside his shirt into a hidden pocket, then looked at Elysium and said, "I'll make sure I hide them well."

"They would have been safe here, but I fully understand you wanting them in your possession."

"Thank you, Elysium," Elensar smiled at him. "Well, I guess it's time we left."

"I heard you're going elsewhere," Elysium said, now starting to leave his study. "Not back to Volarie."

"That's correct. I've planned a small getaway for us."

"An excellent idea, quite romantic. Have you told Amelia where you're taking her or is it a surprise?" asked Elysium.

Elensar smiled, his eyes twinkling with excitement. "Oh, it's a surprise," he replied, his voice filled with anticipation. "I wanted to create a magical experience for Amelia, something she would never forget."

Elysium chuckled softly; his curiosity piqued. "Well, you certainly have my attention now. Care to share any hints about this mysterious getaway?"

"All right, but you must promise not to tell anyone as I want us not interrupted," he whispered playfully. "I've planned an escape to Sturn's establishment."

Elysium's eyes widened in delight as he imagined the beauty and tranquillity of such a place. "Oh, I know his place well; I can only imagine how much Amelia will adore it."

"Exactly!" Elensar exclaimed, his excitement contagious. "But I'll add a few things to make it even better."

"Like what?" Elysium asked, his curiosity piqued about Elensar's plans for enhancing his escape to Sturn's establishment.

Elensar grinned mischievously, his eyes sparkling with anticipation. "Well," he began, "I've heard that Sturn has recently acquired a rare collection of exotic plants from distant lands. I thought it would be a delightful surprise for Amelia, as she has always been fascinated with botany."

Elysium's eyes lit up at the mention of the exotic plants. He imagined Amelia's face lighting up joyfully as she explored the vibrant and unique flora. "That sounds enchanting! But what else do you have in mind?"

By now, Elensar and Elysium were out in the living room, walking past the sofa Amelia had hidden behind over an hour ago, and saw Borthron walking in through the front door.

Borthron looked at them, his eyes widening in surprise, walking toward them both. "Where have you two been all this time?" he asked, his voice tinged with concern and annoyance. "I went in search for Amelia because she slipped away, only to find her outside standing near the horses." His mind raced with questions, but his twin spoke up before he could voice them.

"It's okay, Borthron," Elysium reassured him, a warm smile spreading across his face. "Everything's been cleared up now."

Borthron couldn't help but feel a mixture of relief and frustration. Relief that Amelia was safe, and everything resolved, but frustration at not being informed about it sooner. He took a moment to compose himself before responding. "I'm glad you found her," Borthron said, his voice still tinged with concern. "But why didn't either of you let me know? I was worried sick."

"We're telling you now; it's only just happened."

Borthron sighed, his worry turning into frustration. "I understand that, but you both know how important it is for us to communicate."

"Borthron, it's fine, really, and now Elensar and Amelia will be leaving us on good terms, even going away to a romantic place."

"Oh, that's nice; whose idea was that?"

"It was Elensar's idea," replied Elysium with a smile. "He wanted to make sure they left on a positive note and create some beautiful memories together."

Borthron nodded in agreement. "Ah that's nice." By now, they were all making their way back to the open front door, making their way outside. "He's such a romantic," Borthron now said as they stood in the open doorway. "You always were, even in your dream shift—"

"Borthron, he doesn't need to be reminded about his gift," Elysium slapped his brother gently on the shoulder. "I'm sure he knows it."

"But just watch it; I might slip into yours," Elensar chuckled, his eyes gleaming mischievously. The group laughed; spirits lifted by the light-hearted banter. A cool breeze brushed against their faces as they stepped outside, carrying the scent of blooming flowers and freshly cut grass.

"Okay, that's it! Get out, get out quickly!" Borthron laughed and pushed him out onto the path. "I'll no longer have you lingering; Amelia looks impatient to see you." As Borthron's gaze lingered on Amelia, he couldn't help but notice the slight furrow in her brow and the way her eyes darted around. He assumed she had been lost in thought or preoccupied with something else.

Little did he know, Amelia's apparent distraction had nothing to do with their conversation or anything happening now. Unbeknownst to Borthron, Amelia's mind was holding a nagging worry about the small blue bottle she had accidentally dropped behind the second couch while seeking refuge behind it earlier. It had slipped from her grasp during a moment of panic when they were unexpectedly interrupted by Elensar.

Elensar turned his head towards Amelia. "That she does, that she does," he smiled. "Now, my good friends, today shall be forgotten?"

"Of course," Elysium nodded. "Forgotten, forgiven, now go, rectify the problem."

"Oh, I will. Oh, I forgot to ask, are you going to the renewal vow?" said Elensar, smiling at the twins Elysium and Borthron.

"Ah, Prince Andrin and Sarian," Elysium returned the smile. "That's tomorrow, isn't it?"

"It is," replied Amelia as they had all reached her standing by the horses. "And we should get going soon."

"Well, I'm ready if you are," Elensar lovingly gazed at her and turned away from the twins. "Are you ready, my love?"

"Did you get the—"

"I've got the papers, don't worry, I'll not tell."

"Is that all? Didn't you retrieve anything else?"

"No, did you leave anything else there?"

"No, just my scarf; I could go—"

"We'll get it next time," an arm circled her back, giving a long stroke down her spine. "We must get back to normal again."

He heard Amelia sigh and saw her eyes filled with relief and anticipation. "Yes, you're right," she replied, leaning into Elensar's comforting touch. "We've been through so much lately; it's time to find our way back to the life we had before all this chaos."

Elensar nodded in agreement, his voice filled with determination. "Exactly. We've overcome countless obstacles together, and now it's time to focus on rebuilding what we had lost."

"I miss those lazy mornings when we would stay in bed until noon," Amelia confessed with a wistful smile. "And our impromptu picnics in the forest around our home—I long for those carefree moments again."

"As do I, but first, we both need to retrace my earlier footsteps."

"Earlier footsteps?"

"Before I came here—"

Chapter 20

Stur's Inn

Before all this commotion at the twin's house started, Elensar had been in a different region. He'd taken Lenith's advice and had travelled to Weath's only inn before he went after Amelia. He spent half an hour looking inside each room until he found the right one, he wanted. Once he ensured the room was free, he booked it for two nights. Then, he spent an hour preparing the room's layout for their arrival, adding a few extra details to the room, hoping they would add more luck to the outcome of their stay.

From there, Elensar flew to Hildernbyth in the quickest time he'd ever done to get to the twin's house. Now the reason he went there to that inn, did all this, was many years ago, a Shalimar had cast a spell over this inn, and it seemed whoever entered it would leave with lighter hearts, but this was just rumours that'd been flying around for thousands of years. Those who didn't believe in the tales said the food cooked there caused lighter hearts to appear, for you see, the owner, Stur, was also renowned for his cooking.

Well, this was where both Amelia and he were now. Stur's had cooked them a delicious meal of fresh salmon with salad for their starter. The main meal, pork, covered with a cheese topping, boiled potatoes, carrots, peas, and the pudding, was fresh stewed peach, covered with a lemon sauce. For drinks, he selected Lurth's mineral water for them both. When they finished the meal, he congratulated Stur, but as Stur guided them to their rooms, he said his portions could've been smaller. Stur laughed and said customers told him the quantities were small, so he made them bigger. He replied that he hoped the breakfast wouldn't be so big either, to that Stur laughed then walked away.

Once alone in the room, Amelia asked him why they hadn't returned to Volarie. This question started a three-hour discussion about why they hadn't; by the end of the conversation, he had achieved everything he'd set out to do. He'd won his wife back, he was happy, and by the time the moon started rising in the sky, they'd retired to sleep, but he awoke to a gentle breeze across his naked skin. Now, instead of expecting to see his wife sleeping in his arms, his sight found her standing by the window looking out, wrapped up in a top sheet.

Confusion washed over Elensar as he blinked away the remnants of sleep, trying to make sense of the scene before him. The soft light filtered through the window, glowing gently on his wife's silhouette. Her usually tousled hair cascaded down her shoulders, framing her face with an ethereal grace. As Elensar's gaze travelled from her dishevelled appearance to the view outside, he noticed a peculiar stillness. The vibrant hues of dawn painted the sky, blending shades of pink and orange with streaks of gold. It was a breathtaking sight that often captivated them both.

"My love, why do you stand there?" Elensar asked, sitting upright in the bed, head resting against a headboard.

Amelia turned slightly and smiled, "I couldn't sleep."

"Are you worried about something?" Elensar raised his hand, beckoning her, "Come here, my love," he said softly.

"I'm just taking the view. But why do you ask if I was worried?"

"You don't usually wake unless you're worried about something," she turned to look out the window again; he removed himself from the bed and felt a slight chill in the air upon his naked figure but didn't mention it as he walked over to her. "Are you?" he slipped his arms around her waist, "Amelia, you're freezing!"

Amelia sighed, her breath fogging up the windowpane. She leaned into his embrace, seeking warmth and comfort. "I guess I am a little worried," she admitted softly, her voice tinged with vulnerability.

Elensar tightened his grip around her waist, pulling her closer. "Tell me what's bothering you," he whispered, concern evident. "Damn, you feel so cold to touch, why is that?"

"It must be the wind slipping through the windowpane."

He tightened his arms around her. "I don't think it's that; there's no wind outside."

"Perhaps it's just cold in here."

He cuddled more into her, "The coldness you wear, it feels as if you've been standing outside."

Amelia looked at him and laughed. "The only thing I'm wearing now is this top sheet and you."

"You know what I mean," he laughed, tightening his grip. "Well, instead of you standing here feeling cold, why don't you return to bed and warm yourself up, Mycorm?"

Amelia playfully pushed him away, pretending to be offended. "Are you suggesting I'm not warm enough for you?" she teased, raising an eyebrow.

He chuckled and pulled her closer, kissing her forehead softly. "No, Mycorm, you're always warm enough for me," he whispered. "But I can't help but worry about you feeling cold."

Amelia's expression softened. "I appreciate your concern, but I promise I'm perfectly fine," she reassured him. "It's just one of those nights where the chill seeps into your bones, and anyway, this sheet and you are keeping me warm," her eyesight moved back to looking out the window.

"But you still feel cold to me," a hand moved to her hair, moved it away from her neck, while whispering, "Well, perhaps not as cold; you could still do with warming up, Mycorm," he lowered his head, kissed the soft skin he'd exposed.

"I'm not that cold."

"You are to me," his kisses slipped further down her neck, pressing the entire length of his naked skin into her back, "Valar, you smell delicious tonight."

"Look at that!" she exclaimed, her voice filled with surprise and amusement. She pointed towards the sky through the window.

"Mycorm," speaking as if he hadn't heard her, his hands now cupping, gently squeezing hidden breasts, "Let's go back to bed."

"Elensar, look—"

"I'll warm you up, Mycorm—" Elensar was gently moving his fully aroused state against her, wanting her to know he craved her in his bed again, "Taste you, make love to you again—"

"Elensar, look!"

"At what?" he sighed; movements stopped; hands fell away.

She raised a hand and pointed to the sky. "There! Look! It was a shooting star, a purple one!"

Elensar let out a frustrated sigh, torn between his desire to continue their intimate moment and Amelia's insistence on diverting his attention. He reluctantly tore his gaze away from her, following the direction of her pointed finger toward the night sky. As he looked up, his eyes widened in awe. There it was, a streak of vibrant purple cutting through the darkness, leaving a trail of shimmering stardust in its wake. It was a sight that took his breath away, momentarily making him forget about their interrupted passion.

Amelia's face lit up with excitement as she turned to Elensar, her eyes sparkling joyfully. "Did you see it?" she asked eagerly.

A smile tugged at the corners of Elensar's lips as he nodded, captivated by the rare beauty they had just witnessed. "Yes," he replied softly, his voice filled with wonder. "It was magnificent."

"I've never seen a star that colour before. It was enchanting,"

"Not as enchanting as you are," he whispered, his arms squeezed around her waist. "Come back to bed; let me warm you."

"I want to savour this a little longer."

Elensar watched her intently, his eyes filled with adoration and longing. He understood her desire to savour this moment; it was rare to witness such ethereal beauty. But he also yearned for her warmth beside him, craving the intimacy they shared beneath their cozy blankets. "You can watch this sight another time." he turned her around and cupped her face with his hands, "I'm sorry I was such a coward not to sort this out earlier."

"It doesn't matter." She kissed him. "It's sorted, isn't it?"

"It is," he released her face, "But I'd still like us to move away from Volarie as soon as possible."

"Do we stay at Zeniths until it's ready?" Amelia asked, her voice filled with uncertainty.

Elensar paused for a moment before responding, "Yes, best to. For tonight, you'll stay with me."

"I hardly expect I'll be staying with anyone else tonight."

"I should hope not!" Elensar chuckled softly, his eyes twinkling with amusement. "Now, I must ask you something. If we're to start over again, as in a fresh start, what better way than with a new existence? I know we said we'd wait until our wedding anniversary to conceive a kin again, but—"

"I don't remember saying anything of the sort!" Amelia's voice rose in frustration as she vehemently denied the accusation.

"Well, we did," replied Elensar, "But why wait till then? Why put off what can happen now, this hour, this night."

Amelia's eyes narrowed, her frustration giving way to confusion. "Wait, what are you talking about? What needs to happen now?"

Elensar leaned forward, his voice filled with urgency. "You know exactly what I'm talking about, Amelia," a hand went to her covered stomach, "You know how much I like to see this belly swelling."

Amelia laughed, "I know you do," she kissed him, "And you treat me with delicate hands during it, and for that, I would consider it happening again, but I think I'm too old for that kind of thing to happen anymore."

"Old!" Elensar laughed. "You're still in your prime to give me hundreds more if I wanted Amelia. Look at my aunt Sarathion; she was twenty-five thousand years old when she gave birth to my youngest cousin, Serion."

"But isn't that quite unusual? I mean, to have a child at such an advanced age?" Amelia raised an eyebrow, her curiosity piqued.

Elensar's eyes sparkled with a mix of amusement and pride. "No, not at all; our family possesses a unique lineage, blessed with longevity beyond the comprehension of most immortals."

Amelia couldn't help but be intrigued by such extraordinary lifespans. "So, what happened to Serion?" she asked, her voice filled with genuine concern.

Elensar sighed. "I don't want to be saddened with talk of despair tonight; this is our night, not the past."

Amelia persisted, her curiosity getting the better of her. "But understanding what happened to Serion might—"

"Shh," Elensar's head bent toward her, lips gently kissed hers before he continued, "Let's focus on us tonight, not the past."

"Us," Amelia smiled at him, "Then tonight you can give me what you've desired for some time."

"Desired?" Elensar raised an eyebrow, a mischievous glint in his eyes. "Oh, do tell me, Mycorm. What is it that you think I desire?"

"A baby, Melo, and a night filled with passion and pleasure," Amelia whispered, her voice laced with anticipation. She leaned in closer, her breath warm against Elensar's ear. "I've seen the longing in your eyes, felt the intensity of your touch. Tonight, I want to explore every hidden desire within you; when you've done that, I'll grant you to give me a baby."

Elensar's lips curled into a seductive smile as he traced his fingers along the curve of Amelia's cheek. "Ah, Mycorm," he murmured huskily, "You have always known how to awaken the deepest desires within me." His hand slid down her neck, "But I think you mean you mean a kin—"

"No, baby," Amelia laughed, interrupting his words.

"Kin or baby," Elensar smiled down at her, "I'm just happy you've granted it to take place tonight, but first, I want to make love to you again, and I know normally it takes—"

"Bloody days if you had your way!"

Elensar laughed at Amelia's playful protest, knowing all too well the aftermath of their previous sexual encounter caused her to struggle in walking for a few days; he'd witnessed it for himself, "I know," his eyes gleamed with excitement, "But tonight we'll keep it to a minim of a few hours, but for now, I want to kiss you—" his hand cupped her chin, lifting it slightly. "Then I'll make love to you." Elensar's grip on her chin tightened ever so slightly, his touch both gentle and commanding. His eyes locked onto hers, filled with determination and vulnerability. "Will you allow me to kiss you first?"

"Yes, Melo," Amelia whispered, her voice barely audible as she succumbed to the intensity of Elensar's gaze.

Elensar's fingers traced a delicate path along her jawline; he poised his lips to kiss hers; a loud, downhearted sigh interrupted him. Elensar looked around, also looking to see if Amelia had made that sound, but she had her brown eyes closed, lips partially open, waiting for his kiss; perhaps he had just imagined it. He shook his head and tried to focus on the moment. The soft glow of the candlelight danced across their faces, casting a warm and intimate ambiance in the room. His heart raced with anticipation as he leaned in again, closing his eyes and letting his lips brush against hers. But just as their connection was about to deepen, another sigh echoed through the room, louder this time. Startled, he pulled away and glanced around, searching for the source of the interruption.

Amelia's eyes fluttered open; confusion etched across her face. "Elensar," she whispered to him. "What's up?"

Elensar's mind raced with possibilities - perhaps it was an unwelcome guest lurking in the shadows or a sign that fate had other plans for them, or maybe he overreacted. Elensar took a deep breath, trying to calm his racing heart. He couldn't shake off the feeling that something wasn't right. The sigh felt too close and intimate to be dismissed as mere background noise. It carried a weight of familiarity that sent shivers down his spine. "I'm not sure," Elensar replied cautiously, his voice barely above a whisper. "I thought I heard something."

"You're as bad as me," Amelia laughed at him. "Did it have a female voice this time?"

"A male voice speaking to you inside your head?" Elensar asked, his curiosity piqued. "What does it say?"

Amelia shrugged, her expression turning serious. "It's hard to explain. It's like whispers in my mind, sometimes guiding or warning me about things."

Elensar's eyes narrowed with intrigue. "Whispers guiding and warning you? That sounds both fascinating and unnerving. Have you ever tried to decipher the source of these messages?"

Amelia sighed, her brows furrowing as she contemplated Elensar's question. "I've tried," she admitted, her voice tinged with frustration. "But it's like trying to catch smoke with your bare hands. But yours, what voice was it, a female one?"

Elensar laughed, "No words were spoken; it was more a sigh."

"Perhaps it was the wind slipping in under the door."

"Maybe," perhaps he was overreacting.

Drawing Amelia closer, he kissed her and began moving her back toward the bed, the soft mattress he would be making love to her again. As their lips locked in a passionate embrace, Elensar could feel the intensity of their connection growing stronger. The weight of their shared desires and dreams seemed to hang in the air, fuelling their passion for each other. With every step towards the bed, he couldn't help but imagine the new future they were about to create together, the one in Andrathlion, in their new home with their four kins and possibly a fifth kin if everything went well tonight.

The softness of the mattress welcomed them, cradling their bodies as they intertwined in a dance of love and intimacy. They shared countless moments of tenderness and vulnerability on this bed when they arrived at Stur's. But tonight, was different; tonight, held a deeper significance. Their love was about to manifest itself in a way that would forever change their lives again. As his hands caressed her body, his mind wandered to the union that caused this blessed event, for you see, a parenting union is not like an ordinary love-making session. A parenting union was a procedure that required stillness while he delivered the seed, an understanding that any sudden movement could jeopardize the fragile seed's chances of survival. In his mind's eye, he envisioned the delicate dance of conception - Elensar's seed seeking out Amelia's waiting womb. It was a profound act of trust and vulnerability between them, an intimate exchange that symbolized their commitment to each other.

Five hours later, that very same night, Elensar's wish had come true; cuddled up together in the warmth of a large double bed in a dimly lit room, Elensar trailed kisses upon Amelia's belly where his newly planted seed now lay sleeping, waiting for the day to be born.

Elensar gently caressed Amelia's belly, feeling the gentle stirrings of life beneath his fingertips. It was as if their unborn child could sense his touch, responding with tiny imaginative flutters that brought tears of happiness to his eyes.

He spoke as if the kin could hear his voice through the wall of Amelia's belly. "My little one, I cannot wait to hold you in my arms and shower you with all the love and warmth that fills my heart," Elensar whispered, his voice filled with awe and anticipation. "I promise to protect you, guide you, and be there for you every step of the way." As he continued to caress Amelia's belly, Elensar imagined all the adventures they would embark on as a family. He pictured teaching their kin how to ride a horse through vast meadows, exploring enchanted forests together, and sharing stories under the starry night sky. "You will grow up surrounded by love and laughter," Elensar murmured, his voice filled with unwavering devotion.

"We," Amelia's voice sounded more tired than Elensar's. "And your brothers will create memories that will last a lifetime, our precious one."

"Until then," Elensar's voice spoke with love. "I will watch you grow in your mother's care in her belly daily. I will hasten the days away until I see you delivered and fixed to feed on your mother's ample breasts for the first time." Feeling overwhelmed with emotions, Elensar gently pressed his lips against Amelia's belly again, feeling an indescribable connection forming between him and their unborn kin. "But for now, your mother needs sleep, so I will hush words till she's rested well."

Gently pulling away from Amelia's belly, Elensar gently kissed her forehead and drew her into his arms, naked flesh against naked flesh, warmth against warmth. In this intimate moment, time seemed to stand still. Their bodies pressed against each other, creating a cocoon of safety and love. Elensar could feel the steady rhythm of Amelia's heartbeat against his chest, synchronizing with his own. It was as if their souls were dancing together, entwined in an unbreakable bond. With every breath they took, their connection grew more assertive. Elensar marvelled at the miracle growing within Amelia's womb, a tiny life with so much promise and hope. He imagined all the adventures they would embark on as a family, the laughter and tears they would share with their siblings, and these thoughts helped him fall into a peaceful sleep.

The next day arrived, a new day at Stur’s Inn; the smell of food cooking filled the air as Elensar and Amelia made their way down to the inn's bustling dining area. The aroma of freshly baked bread and sizzling bacon greeted them, instantly awakening their appetites. They found a cozy corner table near a large window, allowing the warm sunlight to stream in and bathe them in its golden glow.

Elensar couldn't help but admire the picturesque view outside as they settled into their seats. The window overlooked a serene garden adorned with vibrant flowers and a small fountain that glistened under the morning sun. It was as if nature had conspired to create the perfect setting for their breakfast. Amelia's eyes sparkled with excitement as she perused the menu, her fingers tracing the enticing descriptions of each dish. The inn's renowned chef and owner, Stur, was known for his culinary prowess and ability to transform simple ingredients into extraordinary creations. Today's menu promised an array of delectable options that made it difficult for them to choose. It wasn't long before Stur entered the dining room holding two large plates filled with breakfast items. Elensar's eyes widened with anticipation as Stur approached their table, carefully balancing the plates filled with mouthwatering breakfast items. The aroma of freshly brewed coffee and sizzling bacon filled the air, making their stomachs growl in response.

Amelia couldn't help but giggle at Elensar's childlike excitement. "I can see that you're looking forward to this," she teased, her eyes sparkling with amusement.

Elensar grinned sheepishly, his cheeks turning slightly pink. "Well, who wouldn't be excited about a delicious breakfast after a long night of activities?" he replied, winking at her but also trying to hide his enthusiasm but failing miserably.

Stur placed the plates in front of them with a flourish, revealing a delectable spread that could rival any royal feast. Fluffy pancakes were drizzled with maple syrup, perfectly scrambled eggs sprinkled with herbs, crispy bacon strips glistening with grease, and a colourful assortment of fresh fruits.

The burst of flavours instantly awakened their taste buds as they dug into their food. The pancakes were light and fluffy, melting in their mouths with a hint of sweetness from the syrup. The scrambled eggs were creamy and infused with aromatic herbs, adding a delightful, savoury touch. Each bite of the crispy bacon brought a satisfying crunch and a burst of smoky goodness. The fresh fruits provided a refreshing contrast, bursting with juiciness and vibrant colours. It was a breakfast fit for royalty, and they savoured every mouthful, relishing in the culinary masterpiece before them.

Stur appeared when they'd finished, noticing Elensar's empty breakfast plate, but Amelia's wasn't. "Was the food not to your liking, Your Royal Highness?"

"It was lovely," Amelia said, smiling at him. "But it was rather a lot."

He next looked at Elensar, who had a satisfied grin. Stur couldn't help but chuckle at the contrast between the two. "I see you have quite the appetite, Prince Elensar," he remarked.

Elensar shrugged nonchalantly. "Well, I have to keep up my strength for all the royal duties," he replied with a mischievous twinkle.

Amelia rolled her eyes playfully. "Or maybe it's just because you can't resist indulging in every delicious dish that comes your way," she teased.

Stur joined in their banter, enjoying the light-hearted moment. "It seems like you both have different approaches to breakfast," he observed. "But I must say, seeing such contrasting personalities in the royal family is refreshing."

Elensar grinned while Amelia chuckled softly. "Yes, they are as different as night and day," Amelia agreed. "But now we should prepare ourselves for the rest of the day."

"Indeed, important matters require your attention," Stur replied. "Shall I assist you in preparing for the day ahead?"

Amelia and Elensar exchanged a glance before Amelia spoke up. "That would be most helpful, Stur," she said gratefully. "We have a busy schedule today, and your assistance would be greatly appreciated. Perhaps some sandwiches to accompany our journey if that's not too much trouble."

Stur nodded, his mechanical eyes gleaming with a hint of excitement. "Of course, Princess Amelia," he replied with a slight bow. "I shall prepare a selection of sandwiches for your journey. Is there any preference you have in mind?"

Amelia exchanged another glance with Elensar, contemplating their options. "Something light and refreshing would be ideal," she suggested, her mind racing through the possibilities. "Perhaps a combination of fresh vegetables and herbs, with a tangy sauce to add some zest."

Elensar chimed in, his voice filled with enthusiasm. "And let's not forget some thinly sliced roasted turkey or chicken breast," he added. "It will provide us with the necessary protein for our busy day ahead."

Stur listened attentively, processing their requests in his advanced memory banks. "Understood," he acknowledged. "I shall gather the ingredients and prepare the sandwiches promptly."

"Thank you, Stur," Amelia nodded, watching as he nodded, then turned to leave. "Well," she smiled at Elensar. "I guess it's time we make ready to leave."

"Leave?"

"Yes. We have Andrin and Sarian's secret wedding vow ceremony later today," she whispered to him. "So, better get ourselves organized."

"Ah yes, I nearly forgot," Elensar returned her smile, his eyes sparkling with anticipation. "You're right, my love," he replied, his voice filled with excitement. "Although I will be sad to leave this place." Elensar looked at Amelia with excitement and sadness in his eyes. They had been enjoying Stur's Inn's peacefulness and warm hospitality, but now, it was time to move on to the next chapter of their journey.

Amelia couldn't help but feel a pang of nostalgia for the cozy inn that had become their temporary home as they packed their belongings. The crackling fireplace, the friendly staff, and the delicious meals they had shared would forever hold a special place in her heart. Elensar sensed her melancholy and gently squeezed her hand. "I know how much you loved it here, my dear," he whispered. "But remember, our adventure is far from over."

Amelia nodded in agreement.

Two hours later, Elensar and Amelia were now outside at Stur's Inn, with Stur, the owner, standing in front of them, a massive smile on his lips, "Out already?"

"I'm afraid so," Amelia smiled.

Stur noticed they had all their belongings on the ground next to them. "I thought you were staying longer," he looked at them with puzzlement. "The room not fitting for you?"

"The room was lovely, but I'm afraid—"

"We could," Elensar smiled at Amelia. "Stay here; forget about going to the wedding if you want."

"I like it here, don't get me wrong, but I think we should go."

He whispered, "We don't have to rush there yet."

"Why not?"

"The rooms have already been booked for today as well."

"When did you do that!"

"Before I brought you here," he saw Amelia give him a confused look. "We could stay—"

"I know what you're saying," she whispered back, "But I need to go to the wedding first; then we can come back here, all right?"

Elensar sighed, nodded, and turned back to Stur, "We'll see you later, then we can properly celebrate the expectant of my future kin."

Stur looked at them and smiled, "Ah, I see," he laughed. "Such good news, such a happy occasion to look forward to, a birth," he said, clasping his hands together.

"Not for me," whispered Amelia as she approached their belongings.

"Your Highness, let me sort your luggage out," Stur turned and called out, "Kenton,"

A tall, lanky person dressed in brown trousers and a short-sleeved shirt with a friendly smile emerged from the inn and approached them all. "Yes, Stur?" he asked, his voice filled with warmth.

"Please assist the Highness with their luggage by taking it to the stables," Stur instructed, gesturing towards the bags and suitcases near Amelia and Elensar.

Kenton nodded and swiftly moved to help them. As Kenton approached the pile of bags and suitcases, he couldn't help but feel a sense of awe. The luggage was exquisitely crafted, adorned with intricate patterns, and made from the finest materials. It was evident that these belonged to individuals of great importance. Amelia and Elensar, the Highnesses in question, stood patiently beside their belongings. Amelia, with her regal poise and elegant attire, exuded an air of grace and sophistication. Elensar, on the other hand, appeared more reserved but carried himself with an undeniable aura of authority. Kenton knew this task was not just about carrying luggage but an opportunity to serve those holding significant societal positions.

With a deep breath to steady his nerves, Kenton approached Amelia first. "Your Highnesses," Kenton said as he extended his arm towards their luggage. "May I have the honour of assisting you both?"

Amelia smiled warmly at him and nodded graciously.

"Thank you," said Elensar. "Your name is Kenton, right?"

"Yes, Your Highness," he bowed slightly. "I'll take these to the stable for you both."

As Kenton carefully picked up the luggage, Amelia couldn't help but notice his solid and confident demeanour, a perfect balance of humility and authority.

Elensar watched as Kenton effortlessly lifted the heavy bags, impressed by his strength. "You seem quite capable, Kenton," he remarked with genuine curiosity.

Kenton smiled modestly, grateful for the compliment from the prince. "Thank you, Your Highness," he replied humbly. "I have been serving here for many years, and it has taught me to be efficient and attentive to every detail."

Amelia's eyes sparkled with admiration as she listened to Kenton speak. "Stur is truly fortunate to have you by his side," she said sincerely.

"Thank you, Your Highness, I appreciate your words." With that, he moved their belongings to the stables.

Chapter 21

The Wedding Vows Of Andrin And Sarian

Sarian had been dreaming of her forest wedding vow for years. She had imagined the night sky filled with twinkling stars, the intoxicating scent of the trees, and the enchanting beauty of the forest that seemed to come alive with the moon's soft light. She had envisioned her beloved prince Andrin standing beside her, pledging their love and commitment to one another and their lives together. She had imagined the sweet melodies of the birds, the gentle rustle of the leaves, and the mystical music that seemed to carry the couple away in the moment. Sarian was determined to make it a reality, and she did. The venue she had chosen was covered in towering trees, surrounded by lush foliage and wildflower blooms. There was even a path lined with hanging lanterns that led to an archway covered in twinkling fairy lights. Sarian was determined to make her forest wedding vow unique, so she set about decorating the venue with wood accents, ferns, and greenery to bring her nature-inspired décor to life.

The massive pale brown marquee Sofia had arranged was like something out of a fairytale. A breathtaking sight greeted guests. The interior was adorned with cascading vines and delicate ivy, intertwining with twinkling lights that cast a warm and intimate glow. The lanterns and wildflowers styled to look like garlands hanging from its wooden beams. It was the perfect setting for the night, with a magical and inviting atmosphere. Soft music filled the air, creating an atmosphere of elegance and sophistication. The flickering candlelight danced across the marquee, casting a warm glow on the faces of the arriving guests. The champagne flutes clinked together, their effervescent bubbles symbolizing celebration and joy. Each guest was handed a glass by impeccably dressed servers, who moved gracefully through the crowd with trays adorned with delicate hors d'oeuvres.

As guests settled into their seats, their eyes drew to see the tables adorned with meticulously arranged centrepieces of wildflowers. Each bouquet was a masterpiece, showcasing a harmonious blend of colours and textures. The vibrant blooms spilled over rustic wooden vases, intertwining with lush greenery to create a natural yet refined ambiance. The wedding cake was the centrepiece of the festivities, five stories high, fashioned to look like a forest, with intricate details that showcased the beauty of the Shalimar realm.

Sarian gazed at her reflection in the mirror of a makeshift cloth hut, with her blonde hair intricately curled and piled high atop her head, with feathers adorning each side. Her delicate ivory gown had its skirt dappled with layers of lace. She felt every bit a princess. Her maids stood behind her, wearing similar dresses in natural shades of green, blue, and brown. Sarian turned, admiring each exquisite design with a smile. Her maids had seamlessly blended the fabrics and silks at her request to create a beautiful ombre of colours that subtly shifted from one shade into the next.

Once ready, Sarian and her maids ventured out into the forest surrounding the hut. The sun was beginning to set, making the tall grasses glimmer with dew, and adding an ethereal charm to the scene. The air was sweet with the smell of flowers as the group made their way toward an area of the forest. Sarian saw a cart loaded with fragrant posies. She plucked out large daisies and bright poppies, crafting her bouquet with carefree joy. When Sarian had chosen all the flowers, the maids tied the grouping with a ribbon of pale brown. The wildflowers blended in a fragrant mix as the party continued towards a different forest area.

Andrin, too, felt like the luckiest person alive. Sarian made him feel complete in every way, and though life had thrown them each a few curveballs, he was never more certain about anything than he was about being with her. Andrin stood in front of the mirror in his wedding outfit, a bright green tunic with gold embroidery and a golden cape, a stunning outfit that fit his slim frame perfectly. He smiled as he saw his reflection; he had never felt more confident or excited about his future. As he admired himself, his best friend Elensar stood behind him.

Andrin had known Elensar after his mother and Elensar's father had perished in a shipwreck that Elensar's sister Serria had caused when she was only three years old. But that information was kept secret to only the Orian royal family members, never to be spoken outside their castle walls, and Andrin didn't know this bit of information, for if he did, I'm not so sure he'd have been friends with Elensar, or his brother Celahir.

This terrible shipwreck incident caused an instant connection as they both grieved their parents and found support in one another. Centuries had passed since then, and Elensar and Andrin remained excellent friends. Whenever a hurdle threatened to trip either of them up, they were swift to be there for each other, and getting through their teenage years was undoubtedly a lot easier for having the comfort of a kindred spirit. But he was the only friend in Elensar's life back then; there was Etheryn as well.

Etheryn had been a passionate, old-fashioned warrior with a spirit for adventure that led him to his untimely end in the dark and treacherous tunnels of Droven. It was here that he encountered a fire snake and was not able to escape its wrath. Etheryn's demise devastated everyone who knew him, but none more so than his long-time friend Elensar and Etheryn's wife Sofia, who had been expecting his kin.

"If you need my opinion," Andrin heard Elensar say, "I'd say you're ready now,"

He turned around and saw Elensar smiling at him. "Well, now is as good a time as any," he replied, smiling. "Let's go, shall we."

"Lead the way."

Andrin walked to the hut's door, opened it, stepped outside, and was met with a slight breeze hitting his face, the scent of pine trees and birds singing, and stars twinkling in the night sky. Further out, he saw lights in the distance and heard murmurs of whispers, whispering from the wedding guests waiting for his and Sarian's appearance to begin their wedding vows before them. There weren't many people in that wedding forest, around fifty invented people they knew. Andrin took a deep breath and turned to look at Elensar, who was still standing by the door, eyes twinkling with a gleam of anticipation. The two walked from the hut, crossing the grass to the lighted ceremony area. As Andrin strolled, his heart thumping, he couldn't help but think of Sarian, his soulmate, who would be standing at the altar with him.

Everything was leading up to this moment, and nothing would stop him from getting there. Andrin stepped onto the makeshift outdoor altar and flinched when he felt Sarian's hand's warmth. Andrin turned and saw her beautiful face lit with happiness and love, making his heart swell with emotion. He took her hands in his, and they faced each other, ready to renew their vows in front of their guests. "Will you step by my side, walk by my side for eternity?

Sarian could barely contain her joy hearing him ask that question, but she replied, "I will."

Andrin nodded and smiled at her, "As I look upon us," Andrin recited his words. "I see fire, ice, and wind combined in these two souls I wish to join."

"I am yours to tame—" they both said together.

"I see love; I see tears; I see sadness."

"I am yours to fix—" Again, spoken together.

"I see all the colours of our world revolving around us."

Voices joined again, "I am yours to combine all—"

"You are my sun," Andrin's voice spoke alone. "And I will always love you."

"You are my moon," Sofia lovingly uttered those words. "And I love you—"

"Together with the sun and moon, we are whole." And that was the end of the vows.

When Andrin's words spoke of the fire and ice in both of their souls, of the love and tears they shared, and of the colours of the world revolving around them. Andrin promised to be her confidant, companion, friend, and lover. He'd vowed to honour and cherish her and their life together for eternity. The wedding vow was a beautiful reminder of their commitment to each other. It reminded them of the joys and sorrows they would face together and the strength they would draw from their love. It reminded them that they were in it together, for better or worse, and that their love was strong enough to withstand any challenges they faced.

The forest the vows had taken place in seemed to come alive as the night air filled with singing birds. Everywhere Sarian and Andrin looked, they could feel the moment's magic. Fireflies danced around them, adding a magical touch to the romantic scene. The sun had set, but the stars were bright in the night sky, and the moon shined down on the ceremony, adding a soft, ethereal light to the surroundings.

The meal started with roasted wild mushrooms, followed by a salad of freshly harvested greens and flowers from the forest; next came a steaming stew of seasonal vegetables and potatoes with a hint of smoked bacon added for flavour. The main course was a progression of local specialties, including roast rabbit, pan-fried trout, and the area's famous blackberry cobbler.

Sofia, Sarian's friend, had arrived at the evening event with her son, Din, both carrying an object with them; Sofia's was a brooch that dimmed to a pale blue light when they reached the party. Din's was a ring that did the same. The two looked around at the beautiful flower arrangements, the romantic music playing in the background, and the happy guests. They soon found themselves joining in the revelry of the after-party.

As the reception wore on, Din got closer to a beautiful, raven-haired woman on the other side of the marquee. He eventually built up the courage to ask her to dance, and by the end of the night, he had somehow convinced her to accompany him for a romantic stroll in the moonlight. As they stood looking out over the stars, Din finally realized what a special night this was- not just for the vow ceremony but the start of his adventure in love. He thanked his mom for letting him come and wished her the best as they parted ways.

Sofia watched her son walk away, feeling love and sadness. She knew that Din was now ready to leave the nest and would soon embark on a thrilling new journey. Sofia smiled and watched as her son's silhouette slowly blended in with the shadows of the night, then felt a tap on her shoulder. She turned around to see Martha standing before her.

"Hay there, you came," Martha said with a big smile.

Martha had arrived earlier at her twin brother's vow ceremony wearing a beautiful pale green dress, something tucked under her arm, and a pale blue glowing glass flower in her left hand. She felt a stirring of joy and sadness, as this was the last time, she and her brother would be together as twins. As Martha watched Andrin and Sofia join hands earlier at the altar, all her memories of them as diminutive kin, playing together and laughing, rushed to the surface. Martha knew that Andrin was blessed to have found someone who loved him the same way she did, and she couldn't be happier for him.

At the reception, Martha's eye was drawn to her brother, dancing on the floor with Sarian, surrounded by friends. Martha smiled, tears stinging her eyes. Later in the night, Andrin caught Martha's eye and whispered something to his wife before he walked over to her.

Andrin hugged her, and Martha knew he was feeling the same bittersweet sensation. "You know I love you, right?" he murmured.

"Yes, I know. I love you too." Martha hugged her brother one last time before he returned to the dance floor. As she watched him embrace Sarian, she felt a fondness and admiration. She looked down at the glass flower in her hand and smiled, knowing that no matter what, her bond with Andrin was unbreakable, then looked up and saw Celahir, Elensar's brother, walking towards her.

Celahir made the journey to this secret ceremony with magic in tow; a mysterious gift had appeared in his room: a long staff carved with runes of light and marked with a moon and stars, but he wasn't the only one to receive a gift, all the guests had received gifts, all different from one person to the next, all used to get to the secret location. With a prayer for guidance, Celahir picked up the staff and embarked on a journey into a forest somewhere in their lands. The trees soon closed around him in a protective embrace, and at times, Celahir felt he was going round and round in circles. But whenever he hesitated, the staff seemed to shine a more brilliant blue light, encouraging him to go until it was supposed to dim to a paler colour. At last, the trees parted, and he emerged into a clearing filled with joyous music and laughter, Sarian and Andrin's ceremony. The celebration went off without a hitch until a loud shout was heard near the end, freezing everyone in fear.

Volarie castle guards rushed out of the nearby forest, torches blazing. They commanded the musicians to stop playing and the crowd to remain silent. Scanning the area with their eyes, they ran around searching for something or someone. The tension in the air was palpable as the guards scoured every nook and cranny of the celebration grounds. Whispers of confusion and concern spread through the crowd like wildfire, each person desperately trying to glimpse what had caused this sudden intrusion. As the guards continued their frantic search, their expressions grew increasingly grave. They were not merely on a routine patrol; something serious had transpired. The musicians stood frozen, their instruments hanging limply by their sides, unable to comprehend the abrupt halt to their joyous melodies. Suddenly, a calm conversation ensued among the guards, their urgent voices barely audible over the anxious murmurs of the crowd. Their eyes darted toward a distant corner of the celebration grounds, where a group of females was standing.

Everyone stood in complete silence, watching the guards until one of them finally made an announcement. "There she is!"

At first, Amelia thought they were talking about Sofia or Martha, but she was corrected when hearing the following sentence loud enough for others to hear.

"Princess Amelia, you are to come with us."

Amelia stood still, her eyes wide in shock and confusion. They had come looking for her, and they meant business. "What have I done," she said, watching them almost come to her in quick footsteps. Amelia's heart sank as she noticed Elensar was also walking towards her, running frantically with a look of fear on his face. She knew he had seen what happened to her—being arrested by the castle guards for her supposed *'crimes.'* She couldn't believe that she was put in this situation, especially when all she wanted to do was help keep the human William alive.

"On whose orders," Elensar had shouted as he ran toward her.

"The Queen's," they'd already reached her side, hands grasping at her arms, keeping her from fleeing.

"Elensar," she cried out in fear. "What's happening?"

Elensar was by her side now, standing in front of them all. "A misunderstanding," he turned a worried look at the guards. "I think they must have heard the order wrong."

The guards exchanged glances; expressions filled with scepticism. One of them stepped forward, his hand resting on the hilt of his sword. "Your Highness," he said sternly, "We have explicit orders from the Queen herself. Princess Amelia is to be taken into custody immediately."

"Then we'll speak with my mother about this first," Elensar went to take her by the arm. Elensar's eyes widened in shock as the guard forcefully grabbed his hand, preventing him from touching the sleeve.

"Your Highness, if that's what you wish, you may; she must come with us," the guard declared coldly, his voice devoid of sympathy or understanding.

"No!" Elensar protested vehemently, his voice filled with frustration and desperation. His free hand clenched into a fist as he struggled against the guard's grip. "You can't take her! She has done nothing wrong!"

"Your Highness," one guard uttered, "She is to come with us."

"Please, Your Highness, just let us take her peacefully—"

Elensar's mind raced as he tried to come up with a plan. He couldn't let them take her away, not now, not when she needed him the most. Taking a step back, Elensar composed himself and looked directly into the guard's eyes. "Listen to me," he pleaded, his voice filled with desperation. "I understand you have your orders, but can't you see? She is carrying our kin. She needs my support!"

The guard's stern expression softened briefly but then hardened again as he shook his head. "I sympathize with you, Your Highness," he said with a hint of regret. "But I cannot disobey the Queen's direct command."

Elensar felt a surge of anger rise within him. "I am ordering you to let her come with me!"

"I'm afraid the Queen's order outranks you, your Highness."

"Does it! Well, we'll see about that!" he went to grab her by the arm but was pushed away.

"Your Highness, please! You can see her when she's settled," they moved Amelia away from him.

Elensar's face contorted with anger as he watched Amelia escorted away. "I want to see her settled first," he ran up behind them, trying to stop them from taking her away.

"Your Highness!" one guard stopped before him, and another walked to his side, "We will use force if we have to!"

Elensar's eyes locked with the guard who had threatened force, and Elensar could see the unwavering loyalty in his gaze. It was a loyalty born out of duty, but Elensar knew he needed to appeal to their humanity if he could convince them. "Please," he pleaded, his voice filled with desperation and sincerity. "I understand your duty, but I implore you to consider what is at stake here!" he tried to peer over the guard's shoulder, but the guard remained stoic, unmoved by Elensar's plea. The guard shifted slightly, blocking Elensar's view of Amelia and their tightening grip on her arm. "I must go with her!" Elensar pleaded, straining to peer over the guard's shoulder. "You must let me—"

"Elensar!" he heard Amelia sound worried as they started to escort her further away from him, "Elensar, what's happening!"

A surge of adrenaline surged through Elensar's body as he formulated a plan in his mind. Without hesitation, he lunged forward, attempting to break free from the guard's grip. But the guard was strong and held him firmly in place. "Please!" Elensar pleaded once more, his voice filled with anguish. "Amelia needs me! I can't just stand here while you all take her away!"

"Your Highness, please listen; you can come with us, but you need to calm down," one of the other guards standing next to him spoke sternly yet compassionately, trying to reason with Elensar amidst the chaos.

Elensar's voice trembled with a mix of anger and despair. "I understand you're just doing your duty, but can't you see? Amelia is innocent! She doesn't deserve this!"

The guard's expression softened slightly, his gaze flickering between Elensar and the commotion around them. "Your Highness," the guard began cautiously, "I believe you. But we need more information before intervening, but you can follow behind her."

With a deep breath, Elensar nodded in understanding. "I will follow behind her," he replied, determination lacing his words. Elensar anxiously set off, two guards walking by his side, all three walking a good twenty feet behind the rest, "I'll see to this wrongdoing if it's the last thing I ever do."

"Your Highness, this is no wrongdoing," said the guard, walking beside him, "Amelia has to be escorted to the dungeons to remain until the Queen decides what she wants to do with her."

Amelia had reached the forest edge and was now being led deeper into the forest by the guards who maintained a tight grip on her arms, their expressions stoic and unreadable. Suddenly, a rustling sound echoed behind them, causing the guards to halt abruptly. Their heads swivelled around as they instinctively reached for their weapons; their expressions transformed from stern determination to utter disbelief. Amelia followed their gaze and gasped in awe at the sight before her. Emerging from the dense undergrowth was a majestic creature unlike anything she had ever seen. It was a wolf, but not an ordinary one. Its fur shimmered with an ethereal glow, reflecting silver and midnight blue hues. Its eyes glowed with an otherworldly intensity, radiating wisdom and power.

The guards released their grip on Amelia's arms, momentarily forgetting their duty as they watched in astonishment. The wolf approached them cautiously, its movements graceful yet purposeful. It emitted a low growl that resonated through the forest, commanding attention, and respect.

Amelia felt an inexplicable connection as the wolf drew nearer, its piercing eyes locked onto hers, revealing a depth of wisdom and understanding beyond mere animal instinct. At that moment, she sensed an unspoken bond forming between them, as if they were two souls intertwined by some ancient force.

Still captivated by the wolf's commanding presence, the guards stood frozen in awe. They had never witnessed such a display of power and grace before. It was as if the forest itself had come alive through this magnificent creature.

Amelia took a tentative step forward, her instincts guiding her towards the enigmatic being. The wolf's growl softened into a gentle rumble, its message now one of reassurance rather than intimidation. Amelia felt an invisible thread pulling her closer to this extraordinary creature with each step she took. As she reached out her hand hesitantly, the wolf lowered its head ever so slightly, inviting her touch, but it never happened.

A sudden rustling noise behind them caused the wolf to prick its ears to look where the noise was coming from. Through the dense underbrush, Elensar and the remaining guards suddenly emerged.

The wolf's growl became a low warning rumble, its protective instincts kicking in. It backed away slightly, its eyes fixed on Elensar and the guards, its hackles raised as it maintained a defensive stance between Amelia and the guards, then it turned on its heels and ran.

"We need to get her to the castle now!" The guard's urgency was palpable as they quickly grabbed Amelia by the arms again, forming a protective circle around her. They began to march towards the castle, their steps quick and purposeful.

Amelia was placed deep into the dungeon of Volarie's castle, a punishment feared above all else. As the heavy door slammed shut, Amelia's heart sank. The sound reverberated through the damp, cold air, sending shivers down her spine. She stood there momentarily, her eyes adjusting to the darkness that enveloped her. The stench of mildew and decay assaulted her senses, making breathing difficult.

Amelia's first night was in complete and utter isolation, with a rugged, bare floor as her bed.

Chapter 22

Princess Serria

On this day, Serria walked towards a private garden that belonged to her late father, decorated with white and blue roses and ivy adorned atop her head. Her white dress trailing behind her gave her an angelic look as she was meandering her way to the grave garden. A gentle breeze rustled through the leaves as Serria approached the private garden entrance, carrying a faint scent of nostalgia. The garden had always been her sanctuary, where she could find solace and connect with her father's memory. With each step she took, memories flooded her mind like an old film reel playing in slow motion. She recalled the countless afternoons spent here, hand in hand with her father, as he shared his wisdom and love for nature.

Princess Serria was a beautiful, tall, blonde-haired being from Volarie with an ethereal appearance complemented by her piercing blue eyes and flawless porcelain skin. Serria epitomized grace, emanating an aura of elegance and serenity wherever she went, commanding attention and admiration from all who looked at her. However, Serria's beauty went far beyond her physical attributes. She possessed a gentle and kind-hearted nature that endeared her to fellow Shalimars and other creatures of their realm. Serria often spent hours caring for the injured woodland creatures, comforting, and healing them with her soothing touch. Despite her immense beauty and noble birth, Princess Serria was not one to rely solely on her external advantages. She possessed a sharp intellect and a keen sense of justice. Serria constantly sought knowledge, devouring ancient texts and manuscripts to understand her world's intricacies and challenges better.

In conclusion, Serria was not solely defined by her physical beauty but by her inner qualities that shone just as brightly. Her altruism, intelligence, and regal presence made her a beloved person among the Shalimars and a respected figure among all magical beings. Serria's ability to embody grace, empathy, and wisdom made her a true beacon of hope and inspiration in the enchanted realm of Volarie, but Serria wasn't always like this. Around her left wrist was a single solid gold ring with a tiny white stone on top, an enchanted bracelet worn to keep specific thoughts out of Serria's mind from being passed onto anyone else.

Sierra stopped in her tracks as her gaze fell upon a large white marble slab adorned with an intricately engraved V-shaped tree in black, with a dove perched above it in flight leaning against a tall hedge. She leaned forward, studying the design details, the way the branches supported the dove, suspended in the air as if it were about to ascend further. Then her gaze went to the left; a wooden door caught her sight. She sighed loudly, then went to open it.

Serria had gifts bestowed upon her at birth, just like any other Shalimar. Some had one gift, and some had two gifts bestowed upon them. Skills like long vision, sight, hearing, running, mind reading, dream shifting, foresight, and many more. Her mother's gifts could make people say what she wanted. Her older brother Elensar's were dream-shifting and an emotional song enhancer. Her brother Celahir's was mind-reading. Serria's was speed, running as fast as the wind, and her second one could get someone to do what she asked. The gift of getting people to do what she wanted was why she wore the gold bracelet.

Serria's hand moved the leaves of a huge rose leaf out of the way, opening to see an enclosure behind it. The sight before her was nothing short of breathtaking. Tall rose bushes loomed around the perimeter of the enclosure, their brilliant colours and fragrant scent filling the air with their beauty. Directly in front of her was an ethereal white cement platform, rising from the ground and stretching up to the walls of the enclosure. The walls were entirely covered in ivy, its lush tendrils reaching up to paint an exquisite tapestry of green along the section.

In the centre of the platform was a mesmerizing hologram of a towering, handsome man with long, blonde hair that cascaded down his back, dressed in a deep purple tunic and dark trousers. He held a glowing orange ball in his right hand and an open book in his left. His presence was both commanding and inviting. His face was gentle yet stern, and his eyes looked into your soul. He radiated a sense of wisdom and power as if he had been alive for centuries and knew the universe's secrets. He stood there as if to say, '*Come, learn from me*.'

Serria moved towards the platform and the figure standing in the middle. A hologram of her father, Rolzulern Oronra, husband to Queen Catreen, father to Elensar, Celahir, and herself, now stood before Serria as a nostalgic reminder of the past. The holographic projection captured the commanding presence and regal grace that her father had exuded during his reign. Each time Serria encountered the hologram, it felt as if she was transported back to her childhood, watching her father lead their kingdom with wisdom and compassion. The hologram served as more than just a reminder; it became a symbol of her father's legacy and a source of inspiration for Serria.

As Serria gazed upon the hologram, memories flooded her mind. She remembered how her father would gather the courtiers and advisers for counsel, his booming voice echoing through the castle's grand halls. He was a leader who valued humility and progress, always seeking the welfare of his people above all else. Serria admired the stories of his ability to connect with individuals from all walks of life - he had the rare gift of making each person feel heard and understood.

Rolzulern, the hologram, smiled down at her. Words were then softly spoken, "Serria, you grow more beautiful each time I see you."

"Hello, Papa," Serria smiled back at him. "I know it's a bit later than normal, but everyone has gone out, and I feel alone."

"I'm always here for you, my love," Rolzulern, the hologram, smiled again. "After all, isn't it a father's duty to always be around?"

"Thank you, Papa," Serria said, running up to hug him.

Rolzulern smiled his sweetest smile before quickly enveloping his daughter warmly. The two stayed in each other's embrace for a while, enjoying each other's warmth and companionship. Even with everyone else away, Serria was content knowing she had her papa by her side.

As they slowly broke apart, Rolzulern looked deep into his daughter's eyes and said with strong affirmation, "I am always here for you no matter what; I will never leave you."

His reassuring words comforted her, and Serria couldn't help but smile again, feeling the love radiating from her papa.

"I'm so proud of you and all you've accomplished," he said with a fondness in his voice.

She blushed, touched by his words. He was always encouraging and kind, and she was thankful for his love. "Thank you, Papa," she said, hugging him. "I wouldn't be here without you." He had been with her through thick and thin, and she was grateful for his presence. Serria sat down on the platform, her bracelet twinkling in the sunlight. "I wish you were here in the flesh."

Rolzulern knelt in front of her. "As do I, but we have these moments together, do we not?"

"I'm sorry, Papa," she suddenly burst out sorrowfully. "I'm sorry I caused your death."

"Hush, hush, my love," a hand came out and stroked the top of her head. "Let's not let bitter memories creep in."

"I cannot help it; it's all I think about these days," she suddenly cried. "I wish they had never told me what I did; I wish they never told me I killed you."

"Sweetheart," her father lovingly replied. "You're hurting, but it's in the past, and we must move forward. I'm still here for you, and despite everything, I still love you," he whispered, gently wiping her tears with his thumb. "I understand you carry a heavy burden, but dwelling on the past will only consume you. You must find a way to forgive yourself."

Serria looked up at her father, her eyes filled with anguish. "But how can I forgive myself when I took your life? How can I move on knowing that I caused so much pain?"

Her father's voice remained calm and soothing as he spoke. "You must remember, my love, life is filled with unforeseen circumstances and tragic accidents. It was not your intention to harm me; it was a terrible twist of fate."

"But I should have been more careful," Serria sobbed. "If I had known sooner the consequences of my gift, none of this would have happened."

"My darling daughter, blaming yourself will not change what has already happened," her father gently interrupted. "Yes, perhaps we should have told you sooner, and it could have prevented the accident, but you were very young, not old enough to understand how a thought gift was supposed to work."

"You mean the dark side of my gift, my curse of making people do what I want," she said, now sniffling.

Her father sighed, his eyes filled with both sorrow and understanding. "Yes, my dear, that is what I mean," he replied softly. "But it's important to remember that your gift is not inherently evil. It's how you choose to use it that determines its nature."

"Well, it's under control now, secured by this," she rotated a bracelet, given to her a few days after their father's passing, around her tiny wrist for a moment, then gazed down upon the solid gold ring with a white stone on top.

As she stared at the delicate white stone on the ring, memories of the moment they told her about its purpose entered her memory. She'd been around twenty years of age at the time, still a tiny kin in a Shalimar life cycle, but old enough to understand the consequences of right and wrong. Serria was informed to go to the living room, and when she did, her mother, brothers, and even Lord Howden and Rotherkin, the wizard, were waiting for her arrival. Rotherkin cast a spell over her bracelet and made it loose; her mother then took it off and kept it upon herself. Next came words that told her about the dark side of her thought gift. Of course, she told them they were making it all up, that no one could make someone do something they don't want to do.

So, they made an experiment to show her their words were valid. They handed her a small box. Inside lay five pens and five blank pieces of paper. They explained that they wanted her to get someone in the room to write something down and that the words would only come from her thoughts. Each person then collected a pen and paper from the box and stood back, waiting for her to start.

At first, she laughed at them all, unbelieving her thoughts could make anyone do something she wanted. So, to see if she could do it, she changed their plans without them knowing. She instructed one person not to write but to make a paper flower, and they did. She watched in awe and confusion as Rotherkin followed her guidance, his chubby fingers meticulously folding and shaping the delicate paper material. Soon after this happened, her mother put the bracelet on her wrist, and Rotherkin again cast a spell to secure it, never to leave her wrist. Then her mother asked her to repeat what she had just done with Rotherkin, so Serria did, but it didn't work this time.

That's when Serria realized the power she held before she wore the bracelet could manipulate people into doing what she wanted, and that's also the time they told her what happened to her father and why a hologram of him was on their castle grounds. It was to keep Serria in check when she was younger and keep him in her memory.

"It's a beautiful bracelet," the hologram words of her father interrupted her thoughts. "As beautiful as the young lady's wrist it sits upon. A lady who has come so far to accept that sometimes life isn't always roses and candy."

Hearing those words spoken by her father, the sobbing slowly ceased, and she leaned against his broad chest. For a fleeting moment, a memory flooded her thoughts, an old memory related to why she had just acted as she had done in his presence. She'd been around four years of age, hiding behind a door listening to her mother complain that her father was always away, which annoyed Serria because she wanted him back home. Serria's young mind struggled to comprehend the complexities of her parents' relationship.

She couldn't understand why her father was always away, leaving her mother lonely and frustrated. As she continued to eavesdrop on their conversation, a sense of longing began to stir within her. In her innocent heart, Serria yearned for a complete family unit where both parents were always present and engaged. She longed for the warmth of her father's embrace and his laughter filling their home. The absence of his presence left an emptiness that even her mother's love couldn't fill, so she decided to do something about it. With childlike faith, she sent her thoughts out to him, unaware of her actions' consequences.

'Papa, come home; Mama needs you here, we all need you here, I want you here.'

A few seconds later, he replied, *'How do I come to you?'*

'Make them turn the ship around; if it fails, you must swim to us.'

'I'm coming, my love.'

Then she went into the room and told Mother, "I've asked Papa to come home; he's swimming here now." She hoped with all her heart that her father would return and be with her.

When she said all this, the look on her mother's face was not the expression Serria expected. Instead of the joy and excitement Serria had anticipated, her mother's face turned solemn and distant. It was as if a dark cloud had suddenly overshadowed the room, replacing the warmth and hope that Serria had been clinging to.

Her mother's following words were even more confusing to a young Serria. "What have you done!" Her voice trembled with a mix of sadness and resignation.

Serria's heart sank as she tried to comprehend her mother's reaction. What had she done wrong? All she did was muster up all her energy to deliver her father back home, but instead, she had disappointment and despair.

Tears rose in Serria's eyes as she struggled to find the right words. "I—I thought you would be happy for us all," she stammered, her voice barely audible. Confusion clouded her mind, making it difficult to understand why her mother reacted this way.

Her mother took a deep breath, steadying herself before speaking again. "Serria, it's not that I'm not proud of you or your thoughts," she began softly, her voice tinged with regret. "But life can be unpredictable, and sometimes our thoughts lead us down paths we never expected."

Little did she know that her innocent yearning for her father's return would set a series of events beyond her comprehension in motion. As Sarian and Rolzulern's thoughts travelled through the vast expanse of their universe, they encountered cosmic energies and ancient forces drawn to the purity of her kin like faith. Unbeknownst to her, these energies began to converge, intertwining with the threads of fate and weaving a tapestry of unforeseen consequences. The universe responded to her heartfelt plea, but not in the way she had anticipated. A ripple was felt in a distant realm by unknown beings, where time and space intertwined like an intricate dance. It started as a faint tremor, barely perceptible, but it grew stronger with each passing moment. The fabric of reality began to shift and twist as the universe responded to the young girl's call. Unknowingly, her wish had come true; only it came at a cost much greater than anyone could have imagined. It caused her father to drown hundreds of miles offshore trying to swim back home to them, but not only did Rolzulern die that day, but fifty-seven others lost their lives due to his actions of trying to get back home to his family.

Chapter 23

The History Of King Rolzulern Oronra

Throughout history, love stories have captivated audiences, whether fictitious or true. One iconic love story that stands above the rest is that of King Rolzulern and Queen Lana. This mighty King and secretive Queen from the land of Volarie and Hilderynbyth, respectively, kept their forbidden romance hidden away from public view for many years, even when married. Their story began many years before when he was a mere royal prince. During a royal vacation to the distant kingdom of Hilderynbyth, Rolzulern fell for the beautiful Princess Lana. Beauty struck him like a stone to his heart, and at once, he became enthralled by her presence.

King Rolzulern was an icon of kingship, a renowned ruler, and a sought-after bachelor when he was younger. He was born in the prosperous kingdom of Volarie and groomed from a young age for future kingship. Befitting a future King, Rolzulern mastered many skills during his formative years, from diplomacy and archery to astuteness and bravery. His skilled manoeuvres led to the flourishing of his kingdom and drew him admiration from all corners.

Rolzulern had pale skin and impeccable features of the Shalimar race, making him a sight to behold. His charisma, poise, and physical appeal earned him the nickname *'The Handsome Prince*' among the people of his kingdom. He was a much sought-after bachelor, with many suitors vying for his attention. Noble regional families sent their daughters to court him, hoping to become the prince's bride. Wealthy merchants gifted him exotic items and tried to prove their worthiness for him to choose as a potential bride. But he was only interested in one back then, Lana of Hilderynbyth.

Princess Lana of Hilderynbyth possessed an ethereal beauty that seemed to radiate from within, captivating the hearts of all who looked at her. Her porcelain skin glowed with a delicate flush, and her eyes sparkled like sapphires, reflecting the depths of her compassionate soul. But it was not just her physical appearance that endeared Princess Lana to the people of Hilderynbyth. Her kindness knew no bounds as she tirelessly worked to uplift those in need and bring solace to those suffering. Whether it was visiting orphanages or hospitals, Lana's gentle touch and warm smile brought hope and comfort to countless lives.

She was a young Shalimar with long blonde hair that shined in the sunlight, a slim figure admired by many, and a voice that spoke with a calming and soft-spoken tone. She was compassionate and generous towards people and animals, offering her help and kindness to those in need. But what truly set Lana apart was her singing voice. Her angelic voice soothed the people and wildlife around her as if her singing tranced them. Her talent was so extraordinary that it even stopped the warring armies of her father's kingdom from their conflicts—to listen to her sing. Princess Lana was said to be a woman of incredible beauty and wisdom. Leaders from the neighbouring kingdoms sought Lana's hand in marriage, but despite her shard beauty, she was unwilling to be tied down to any of them. That was until Prince Rolzulern of Volarie unlocked her heart with his charm and good looks. A great love was born between the two.

Rolzulern and Lana courted soon after they met; she saw him as a match for a husband, and he saw her as his Queen, but there was a problem. Though Rolzulern wanted nothing more than to join in union with her, his father had forbidden it due to a history of quarrels between their kingdoms. Despite his love for the Princess and his desire to be with her, Rolzulern had no choice but to accept his father's wishes. A year later, his father introduced him to his future wife, Lady Catreen.

Lady Catreen was a young girl of average means who had shown her dedication and commitment in his father's court, serving as his mother's lady in waiting. Rolzulern was initially hesitant about the idea of an arranged marriage, but his reservations began to fade as he got to know Lady Catreen. He found her intelligence and ambition captivating, and her unwavering dedication to her duties in the court impressed him greatly. As their courtship progressed, Rolzulern discovered that Lady Catreen's thirst for knowledge extended far beyond the confines of the castle walls. She would spend hours engrossed in books on various subjects, constantly seeking to expand her understanding of the world. Her curiosity was infectious, and Rolzulern became drawn to her intellectual conversations and debates.

Rolzulern and Lady Catreen wed one hundred and twenty-two years later. Their wedding was grand, filled with luxury and extravagance, befitting their royal status. The venue chosen for the ceremony was the magnificent chapel in Volarie's city centre, adorned with cascading flowers, shimmering chandeliers, and intricate tapestries that depicted the rich history of their ancestors.

During their marriage, Rolzulern was a dutiful and loving husband to his new consort, Lady Catreen, but the union lacked the passionate connection he had experienced with Princess Lana. He admired Catreen's intelligence and kindness and genuinely cared for her well-being. However, deep down, he knew that his heart belonged to another, but he knew that pursuing Princess Lana would not only betray Lady Catreen but also jeopardize the stability of their kingdom. Yet, the more he tried to resist his desires, the stronger they seemed to grow. As the years went by, Rolzulern found himself torn between his duty as a husband to Catreen and his still undying love for Princess Lana, who at that time was now a lady in waiting to Catreen. Princess Lana's presence in the castle became more frequent as she served Lady Catreen diligently. Her beauty and grace continued to captivate Rolzulern's heart, making it increasingly difficult for him to ignore his feelings. The stolen glances and fleeting moments of connection only fueled the fire within him. He tried desperately to free Lana from his thoughts, to push the regret and sadness out of his heart and mind, but that was about to change.

One evening, as Rolzulern sat alone in his study, he found himself lost in a sea of memories. The flickering candlelight cast shadows on the walls, mirroring the turmoil within his soul. He reminisced about the recent days when he and Lana had stolen glances between them, their eyes locking in brief moments that felt like an eternity. He could still feel the warmth of her gaze, making his heart skip a beat and his palms grow clammy. But now, as he sat in solitude in his study, Rolzulern couldn't help but wonder if he had made a mistake by pushing Lana away. The ache in his chest intensified daily, reminding him of the void she had left behind. He yearned for her presence, her laughter, and how she effortlessly brightened up even the darkest corners of his world, and he started to wonder if Lana still held a flame for him; well, Rolzulern got the answer to that same question the same evening and from then onwards a secret affair began with Lana behind Catreen's back.

The two would often escape to secluded places on the outskirts of Volarie or near her kingdom, for she was now married to King Mindos, a ruler whose kingdom was called Froyen. While this was not ideal, them having a secret love affair, to Rolzulern, she provided sanctuary and comfort from the constant demands and obligations of ruling the kingdom, and her wisdom, guidance, and unconditional love were gifts that Rolzulern cherished deeply. His soul found solace in her affections, so one day, as a thank-you for her love, he planned an extravagant trip to a secret destination for them, but tragedy struck them both.

The fateful day we will now speak about tells the story of a ship, the Tieanta. Tieanta was filled with grand people wearing elegant clothes and jewellery. She was one of the two merchant vessels of its time, owned by the illustrious shipping family of Sir Quarnelen and proudly captained by Yannik, a veteran of the Volarie navy. It was occupied mainly by general passengers seeking new lives in faraway places. The ship was operated by a highly experienced and loyal crew that had never left it in three hundred years since it was first built. They were also equipped with all the necessary provisions, including the legendary Tranquilly Pear, an edible yet powerful crystal that could cure any illness onboard. Every time the Tieanta set sail, it was the talk of the city. Cast with a spell that should make it unsinkable, the Tieanta was an ash wood ship with lofty silver sails, boasting sixty grandly designed cabins and five stately cabins fit for royalty. Even with no life rafts, the vessel seemed to sail away with impunity from the sea, air, and wind terrors. The Tieanta also had a strange habit of vanishing from sight - either disappearing altogether, leaving no trace of the ship or crew, or just falling out of sight for a few hours before suddenly reappearing again, and it was this happening that made the lovers want an adventure on this magical ship full of mysteries.

On a vibrant summer day, Tieanta departed from the grand port of Hildernbyth with the secret lovers on board. Passengers of grand in their finest clothes and most-priced jewellery, folks looked onward eagerly to the new lives awaiting them in faraway places, but they would never reach their destination. Twelve days into the journey, King Rolzulern and Queen Lana looked out the porthole of their cabin onto the deep-sea expanse surrounding them. A full sun hung in the sky. A light breeze filled the sails, and the ship softly rocked them in a rhythm gently from side to side. The twelve days had been a tumultuous adventure for the brave lovers who had disguised their identity, days spent traversing the high seas, providing ample opportunity for romance and adventure. The couple had seen distant lands, harrowing storms, and all kinds of sea creatures. But it would not be a sea creature that would end their journey. Later that night, after most had gone to their cabins or were working below the decks, Rolzulern, while holding a sleeping Lana in his arms, received a message via thoughts from his daughter, Princess Serria. '*Papa, come home; Mama needs you here; we all need you here; I want you here.*'

As if in a trance, he replied to her words with his thoughts. '*How do I come to you?*'

'*Make them turn the ship around; if it fails, you must swim to us.*'

'*I'm coming, my love.*'

When Rolzulern silently stepped out of the embrace of his beloved Lana, thoughts of home filled his feverish mind. He was determined to do whatever it took to return Tieanta to where it belonged so he could get home. On board the ship, the defiant captain Yannick refused to return the vessel to its rightful destination no matter how many pleas Rolzulern made. The captain was an immovable object, so Rolzulern had no choice but to take direct action to get the ship back home. Rolzulern began readying himself for a daring mission to scuttle the ship and send it to the bottom of the ocean. Though those awake on board tried their best to stop him, Rolzulern was relentless, and no one could stop him in his mission. Tieanta would be sent to the bottom of the ocean with all lives on board, except for Rolzulern, who chose to swim back to his home, hearing the wailing of those left to die, but all he wanted to do was to swim home to his daughter. He didn't know or realize the ship was hundreds of miles from shore. He drowned, not during the ship sinking; he drowned trying to swim back home to his family.

Chapter 24

Volarie Dungeon's

It must be morning now!

William saw a Shalimar enter his room with a bowl of food and a small mug of water spilling on his floor. He didn't raise his body from the straw mattress; instead, he saw him place his food and water onto a small table in the far corner, ignite a candle, then the guard walked back to the door, gave one last look at him, and then he was gone. William was in a dungeon cell, a prisoner to his grief and despair. The only light that pierced through the cell's darkness was from a small window near the ceiling, a glimmer of hope that he held on to. William thought of his loved ones and prayed to the Lord for guidance. He had been in this prison for an eternity, alone with his sorrow and no one to console him. William felt trapped, isolated from the world, and forgotten. He shouted and screamed until drained of energy, yet no one responded. William could hardly move; his muscles felt like bricks from the lack of exercise and proper nourishment. William had no idea how long he had been in there or how much longer he would remain. All he had was his thoughts and a faint glimmer of hope, a hope that kept him going.

William raised his body, walked over to the food, picked up the bowl, and looked inside. A small bread roll and fatty white meat in a light gravy sauce were in that bowl. Williams's stomach made a sound telling his mouth to eat the food. Seconds later, he was doing that, but it was gone within three mouthfuls. The mug was the next thing he picked up. The water was the next thing to hit his lips; this was better, cooler, and more refreshing. Then he heard a voice calling out from one of the other cells - a faint, barely audible whisper that seemed to be coming from the darkness.

"Is that you, William?"

The voice was steady and firm, seemingly not phased at all by the surrounding darkness, and it made William pause for a moment to take stock of the situation. Was someone else in his prison cell with him? Could it be that he wasn't alone after all? These questions raced through his mind, yet he didn't move - still feeling shocked, as if stuck in a long dream from which he could not wake.

"William? Over here."

He turned his head to the left.

"No, look the other way."

He turned the other way, strained his eyes, and frowned.

"Come closer."

William did slowly. As he reached the far wall of his cell, he noticed something unusual- a tiny hole carved out near the wall's bottom. William quickly crouched down, desperate to see into the gap. To his amazement, he could make out the faint voice of another person trapped inside. He asked curiously, "Who are you?"

"Do you not remember?"

"My mind stole my memories."

"It's I, Amelia. You met me a few months ago in the castle's upper drawing room," her face appeared at the hole.

"Amelia?" Williams's body slid down and sat on the cell floor. "Why are you down here?"

"No one's told me the answer but you; why are you here? I thought you went back through the portal."

William ran a hand through his messy hair, frustration evident in his eyes. "Papers," he sighed, "It's all to do with those damn papers they think I still have! I wish I'd never come here!"

"I'm so sorry. I knew I shouldn't have taken them—"

"You took them!"

"Yes."

"And all this time! God damn! Why did you take them?"

"I knew I should've taken them," Amelia's voice was filled with regret. "But I couldn't risk it. I had to escape with them. I thought you would be safe on the other side."

A wave of anger washed over William as he realized the gravity of his situation. "Do you know what I've been through? I'm here because of you!"

"I know, for that, I ask forgiveness."

William wasn't one to hate, not even for the woman that sent him here. He saw her hand, touched as if to forgive her. He withdrew, words said without any hint of annoyance. "I hope your family will be as forgiving."

"That's a joke!" Amelia half scoffed. "Three of my sons won't talk to me. My mother-in-law detests me, my husband; he doesn't even know of my dilemma."

"You have a problem?" asked William.

"If you could call it that."

"What would you call it?"

"A dangerous situation that I can't solve in here."

"It can't be that bad."

"Oh, believe me, it is," Amelia replied, her voice tinged with frustration. "We're trapped here with no way out, and time is running out," her face disappeared.

William didn't know this, but behind the wall, she'd gone to her wrist to touch her bracelet. But the bracelet Elensar had given as a present to her on their three-hundred wedding anniversary wasn't there. Queen Catreen had taken it away from her.

"Amelia?"

"I'm still here, but I'm feeling exhausted now."

"Why don't you rest your head down for a while?" his head peeped into the hole in his cell wall into hers.

He heard Amelia sigh, her tired eyes meeting his concerned gaze. "I wish I could, but they won't let me. They're watching my every move," she whispered, her voice filled with frustration.

"Fuck them, your health is more important." William's voice was filled with anger and determination as he spoke those words. He couldn't bear to see Amelia suffer any longer. Their living conditions were deplorable, with no privacy or freedom. But William refused to let their captors dictate their lives any further.

"I appreciate your concern, William," Amelia whispered, her voice barely audible. "But we have to be careful. Any sign of defiance could lead to severe consequences."

"To hell with consequences, they have us here now; what more can they do, take away our beds?" William's voice grew louder, filled with frustration and a hint of rebellion. "Amelia, we can't continue living in fear like this. We've already lost so much—our freedom. It's time we take a stand."

He saw Amelia glance around nervously, probably ensuring no one was within earshot. "I know it's hard to accept, but we mustn't underestimate their power," she replied, her eyes darting toward the guards outside their cells.

"But what about our dignity? Our right to live without constant surveillance and control?" William argued passionately. "We can't let them strip away our humanity any further."

"I don't disagree with you, William," Amelia whispered. "But I'm tired, tired of all this. I want to sleep."

William looked at Amelia, his heart heavy with understanding. He knew all too well the exhaustion from fighting against an oppressive system day in and day out. The constant surveillance and the lack of privacy wore him down, chipping away at his spirit. He offered her a small smile of solidarity. "I understand your weariness, Amelia," he said softly. "I'm sorry; go, lay down, and get some rest."

"Maybe you're right," William watched as she nodded gratefully, her eyes brimming with exhaustion. She mustered a weak smile in return and slowly made her way to the small bed in the corner of her cramped cell. "William," she called out, lying down. "Tell me of your Cutton Folly."

"Where do you want me to start?"

"Tell me about the house you lived in."

He closed his eyes momentarily, allowing himself to return to where he once called home. "That's right; you lived there, didn't you."

"Yes, I did."

"I expect it's changed since you saw it last. When I brought it, I had to renovate it before I could live in it."

"What did you do?"

William paused for a moment, reminiscing. "Well, when I first brought the house, it was in quite a state of disrepair," he began. "So, I embarked on an extensive renovation project and made a few modifications; I think the hardest bit was fixing the walls."

"The walls!"

"I thought I'd fixed them, cracks and all; they kept returning."

"What kept coming back?"

"The cracks. At first, I thought there were mice between the walls making the cracks; now I'm unsure."

"Why?"

"Well, don't laugh; I'd had a bit to drink this night, and at first, I thought I was imagining things, but a light kept flickering in and out of the wall despite my attempts to ignore it. It was too big to be a lightning bug, and it moved in a strange, undulating pattern, unlike any lamp I had seen before."

"You must have been scared?"

"I was scared, but curiosity got the better of my fear, and I decided to investigate further. I got up from my bed and got close to the wall. I thought I was hallucinating, but the light kept coming from a crack in the wall. I had no idea what it could be, and I was too scared to investigate further that night."

"You must've been quite drunk to see that happening."

"That's what I thought, only when it happened again, I hadn't had a drop; it was different. This time, it happened after I fell asleep."

"So, how come you saw it?"

William's voice trembled as he continued, his gaze fixed on some distant memory. "You're going to think I'm crazy when I tell you this."

"What?"

"Well, it wasn't the light that woke me up; it was the coldness in the room, whispering words and stuff."

"Spooky."

"I got freaked out," he saw Amelia sit up and look through the hole in the wall at him, "Those words freaked me out big time."

"What were they saying?"

"You don't want to know."

Amelia's curiosity piqued as she leaned in closer, her eyes widening with anticipation. "Come on, don't leave me hanging! What were the words?"

He hesitated for a moment, his gaze shifting nervously around his cell. The memory of those haunting whispers still sent shivers down his spine. "They were speaking in a language I couldn't understand at first," he finally confessed, his voice barely above a whisper.

"A language you couldn't understand. That's even creepier. Are you sure it wasn't just your imagination playing tricks on you?"

William shook his head vehemently, his eyes filled with fear and uncertainty. "No, I swear it was real. The words felt cold and sinister, like crawling under my skin."

"I think your mind must have been playing up, surely."

"I know what I heard," he insisted, his voice trembling. "It was as if the words were seeping into the depths of my mind. They were ancient, foreign, and filled with otherworldly power. Then it changed into words I could understand."

"So, what were the words spoken to you?"

"It'll give you nightmares, did me for weeks after."

"What could be any more of a nightmare than this?"

"You are right," said William. "This is worse; what I heard was even worse."

"Worse?"

William paused, his eyes darting around nervously before continuing. "Look, if I tell you, you promise not to freak out."

"I won't."

"When I first got to look at those papers, it mentioned your name. A name like that is unusual, but I remembered it as if I'd seen and heard it many times."

"And?"

"Well, it was only the other day while I was in here that I remembered where I'd heard it."

"Where did you hear it?"

"The first night of the coldness, the whispering words and all, that's when I heard it first."

"What did it say, this whispering voice?"

"You have a part to play in helping me get what I want, Amelia."

"What!"

"You have a part to play—"

"I know that! What do you mean you've—"

"It just kept repeating those words, many more, over and over again all night, stopping me from sleeping until I shouted no more."

"Did it say anymore after that?"

"No, it fell silent after I shouted. But the next night, as soon as I closed my eyes, it started again. The same voice, the same words." William's voice trembled with fear as he recounted his experience.

"This is getting creepy," Amelia said, concern evident in her voice. "Who or what could be behind this? And why you?"

William shrugged helplessly. "I have no idea. It felt like someone, or something was watching me, controlling me. It was like a nightmare that I couldn't wake up from. Then, the following day, it said something else."

"What?"

"It's hunting for you."

"What!"

"Hunting," said William. "It said its brothers were hunting for you."

"Jesus!" Amelia sounded worried, even frightened. "Now you're freaking me out."

"You wanted to know."

"I know; I didn't expect it to say something like that either," Amelia replied, her voice filled with curiosity and unease. "But why would it say that? What does it mean?" she asked, her voice trembling slightly. The thought of being hunted sent shivers down her spine.

"I'm not sure," William admitted, his brow furrowing in deep thought. "Maybe there's more to that house than we initially thought."

"Christ, this is one scary tale you're telling me."

"You asked me to tell you."

"I did, bloody hell; I didn't think you would be telling me this; I thought you'd be telling me a ghost story or something."

"If it were a ghost story that I could handle," said William, making a shiver go down his back. "This I can't."

"Jesus! Did it say anymore, the whispering voice?"

"I don't think I should carry on."

"I've been through worse."

"I'm telling you now; you won't like it."

"Well, I won't know until I hear, will I."

"Are you sure?"

"Yes, I'm sure," replied Amelia with a determined look in her eyes. "I can handle it."

William hesitated momentarily, contemplating whether to share the terrifying tale that had haunted him for weeks. He knew the consequences of revealing it could be dire, but he also trusted Amelia's strength and resilience. Taking a deep breath, he began recounting the spine-chilling encounter that had left him sleepless and filled with dread. "It showed me where the portal was via its bright light on the wall, how to get to it, and what I should do once I got through it."

"Anymore?"

"Only a few more words, then it stopped."

"What were its last words?"

"They were in here the other night."

"What did it say?"

"Thank you. Amelia's mine now."

The cells fell silent as his words hung in the air, filling the atmosphere with an eerie sense of foreboding. Amelia felt her heart skip a beat. She couldn't comprehend what she had just heard. The colour drained from her face as she struggled to process the implications of those haunting words. Her mind raced with questions, her thoughts consumed by fear and confusion.

Chapter 25

Another Time, Another Place

Volarie Castle drawing room was a spectacular sight to behold. Through its large, arched entrance, one could take in the incredible beauty of the room. Upon entering, your gaze would see a lush red and gold carpet stretching out beneath the many pieces of gilded furniture that filled the room. In the centre, a large chandelier lit up the room in a symphony of twinkling lights, exposing the intricately carved details of the mahogany and marble furniture. The windows, draped with heavy velvet curtains, adorned the walls, and offered a glimpse of the elegantly manicured gardens outside. The overall effect of the room was to establish a feeling of royal grandeur, from the glitz and glamour of the furniture to the comfort of the warm, inviting atmosphere. All in all, the castle drawing room was indeed a sight to behold. But on this day, this room was being used for something else: a private meeting.

"But I've been speaking to Mother!" Etheryn heard Lenith utter. "You even saw me when we were in the library a few months ago!"

"I'm not on about you!" their father shouted at Lenith. "Your older brothers seem to have forgotten how to speak." Lathlorn, Alexander, and Etheryn stood before their father and looked down.

Etheryn felt a lump forming in his throat as the weight of their father's words settled upon them. He exchanged a worried glance with his brothers, their eyes filled with guilt and confusion. How had they reached this point? How had their once-loving family become so fractured?

Lenith, always outspoken, took a step forward, his voice trembling with emotion. "Father, we haven't forgotten how to speak," he said earnestly. "We've just been trying to protect ourselves."

Their father's face contorted with anger as he interrupted Lenith. "Protect yourselves?" he spat out incredulously. "From what? Your mother?"

"What you've done is inexcusable!" their uncle Celahir joined the conversation. "She's your mother, yet you've thrown her away as if she were nothing!"

"And you, Lathlorn! At least—" their father's voice rose, "Look at me!"

Etheryn saw out of the corner of his eye Lathlorn raised his fair head, looking at their father. His ice-blue eyes looked their father in the face with a steady but vaguely pleading expression. He noticed the shadows under his brother's eyes, the dirt on his tunic from where he had been in the woods earlier, and the wild blond locks that framed his face. But most of all, he noticed the unbearable sadness in his gaze that seemed to break his heart with a glance.

"Of all my kin's, you! Does the word family mean nothing?"

"Grandmother is family," Etheryn heard Alexander whisper.

"What did you just say!" Uncle Celahir marched up to him and demanded he repeat what he had just said. He fiercely grabbed his face by the chin and pulled his gaze to meet his own, rage and intensity written across Uncle Celahir's face, and his voice boomed with anger. "Repeat it now!"

Alexander swallowed hard, feeling the weight of his uncle's grip on his chin. He knew speaking his mind could have dire consequences, but he couldn't back down now. Taking a deep breath, he mustered up the courage to repeat his earlier words. "Grandmother is family," Alexander said firmly, his voice quivering slightly. "She has always been there for us, guiding and supporting us when no one else would."

Uncle Celahir's grip tightened even more, causing Alexander to wince in pain. The room fell silent, waiting for Uncle Celahir's response. His eyes bore into Alexander's with an intensity that sent shivers down his spine. "You dare speak of her in such a manner?" Uncle Celahir growled through gritted teeth. "She is nothing but a traitor to our bloodline!"

"But she is family, is she not?"

For a flash of a second, Celahir gritted his teeth and raised his other hand to deliver the blow. At that moment, Alexander closed his eyes and waited for the impact. Every muscle in his body tightened as he tried to brace himself for the pain, he was sure was coming; time almost seemed to stand still as the anticipation ran through him.

"Celahir! What's the matter with you!" their father's voice boomed, cutting through the tense air like a thunderclap.

The sound echoed in the room, reverberating off the walls and shaking Celahir out of his rage-induced trance. His hand froze mid-air, inches from Alexander's face. Celahir's eyes darted toward their father, his expression mixed with anger and confusion. He slowly lowered his hand, releasing the tension in his body as he tried to regain control over his emotions. "What's wrong with me?"

"Yes, you've been in a right grumpy mood since you returned!"

"Well, what do you expect!"

"You got a happy answer from her, didn't you?"

"Yes."

"Then back off! Don't take your parting sadness out on my kin's!"

"I'm not!"

"You were; there's no point in being physical with my kin's; they'd still speak the same." The room fell into an uneasy silence as father and sons locked eyes, each searching for understanding in the other's gaze. Their father took a step forward, his voice softer this time but filled with authority. "What would your sister Star say," said their father, walking before them. "If here to witness this?"

"She would sign we were wrong," uttered Lathlorn. "That mother should've been given a chance to defend herself."

"And when she looks down from the sky," he stood before Alexander. "What would she see?"

"Traitors of her flesh, blood," was Alexander's quick reply in case he would say more unkind words.

"And Etheryn, you disgrace the namesake of a good friend."

"Father, we didn't know it would end like this."

"You will raise your head to look at me when you speak!" he angrily shouted at him.

Etheryn did; he saw the rage in his father's blue eyes. Etheryn's heart sank as he met his father's furious gaze. The disappointment etched on his father's face cut deep, reminding him of the immense burden they had brought upon their family name. He had always strived to live up to the legacy of his namesake, for his honour and integrity. But now, Etheryn stood at the precipice of disgrace, contrasting everything his father had taught him. He never intended for things to unravel like this, never expecting their actions to lead them down such a treacherous path. As silence hung heavy in the air, Etheryn mustered the courage to speak again. "Father, I, we beg your forgiveness," he pleaded, his voice trembling with remorse. "We never meant to disgrace our family or tarnish the memory of your dear friend."

His father's anger seemed to waver as he momentarily listened to Etheryn's heartfelt words. The weight of disappointment still lingered. "How did you think it would end then?" asked their father.

"Not like this."

"You should've thought harder before spilling such things into your grandmother's ears."

"We thought we were doing no wrong," replied Lathlorn.

Uncle Celahir answered his words. "Keeping some secrets hidden is wiser if you know they will cause problems. So," he turned his head back to the four kin. "Is there anything we can do about it?" he looked at each of them. "Well, is there?"

The drawing room door opened, but the four kin, Elensar and Celahir, didn't hear nor see who had entered. Amid their heated conversation, absorbed in the debate of their differences, they failed to notice the figure looming in the doorway. However, they carried on regardless, their voices echoing off the walls as they talked louder and faster. Emotions ran high as they pushed the limits of their comfort to make their points clear.

"Uncle Celahir," uttered Lenith. "There's something we could do about the portal."

"Which is?"

"We could ask Rotherkin to perform a spell at the gate."

"We could ask him to close the portal," said Alexander. "To make sure no one else comes through it."

"How would you ensure it was closed," their father asked.

Lenith paused, considering his father's question. "Well," he began, "Rotherkin is known for his magical seals and barriers expertise. If we ask him to perform a spell designed to close the portal, I believe he can ensure its complete closure."

Uncle Celahir nodded in agreement. "Indeed, Rotherkin's mastery of magic is unparalleled. If anyone can permanently seal off the portal on their side from our side, it would be him."

Alexander chimed in; a voice filled with determination. "And we could provide him with any necessary resources or assistance."

"But it still needs to be open for us to use," their father said.

"Agreed," replied Uncle Celahir.

Lathlorn furrowed his brow suddenly, deep in thought. "But what if closing the portal on one side has unintended consequences? What if it affects our ability to travel between realms?"

Alexander replied. "We could send someone through to ensure its closed but remains open to just our race, the Shalimar."

"Someone like who?" asked Uncle Celahir.

He shrugged his broad shoulders, "Anybody."

A stern voice came next, making everyone in the room stop and turn to the source. Queen Catreen, their grandmother, had entered the room earlier, listening quietly to their conversation before stepping in. She surveyed the room with a piercing gaze, her eyes radiating a strength that demanded respect. "You can't send one of us," she said, her voice strong and authoritative. "The situation is far too dangerous, and none of you have the training or the necessary skills, and that portal is for us to use, so it has to be someone of a different race."

"Mother!" Uncle Celahir walked over to her and placed a kiss on her hand as if giving a sign of respect and admiration. Elensar's kin then repeated their uncle's actions and went in line to give their grandmother a similarly respectful gesture. Elensar did not move from his position and instead cast a dark look full of evil hatred that spoke a million words as to what he thought of the elderly matriarch at that moment. It was clear to everyone that Elensar was not happy to be in the presence of his mother.

"We'll still go through it, spell or no spell," their grandmother said.

"What about William, he's not of our race?"

Their uncle Celahir frowned. "William! Do you think that's wise? He might be unsuccessful; he might even die goin—"

"Well, he is a different race to us," said Etheryn. "But how will the spell work?"

"I'll check through our library before we do anything," their Uncle Celahir replied. "I think I have seen something in there that somewhat relates to this same incident; I think that portal also only goes to the human world."

"How do you know that?" Their grandmother had asked him with suspicion in her voice.

"Same way I know about what I mentioned earlier, from the books in the library." He sighed heavily next. "It worries me that William still might die going through it," said their uncle Celahir, with concern on his face.

"Should that worry you?"

"No, but—"

"Don't concern yourself with one life that means nothing."

"No," uttered their father sarcastically. "That's just like you, Mother. Don't concern yourself with a life not worth living. Your answer would be to fling them into a dungeon, forget about them as you've done to my wife!"

"She's human!" her voice rose. "She deserves to be in a pit, the key thrown to the southern wind."

"Where is the fire-breathing dragon, the one that you'd use to burn her soul, the hungry wolf that would tear flesh from her bones!" said their father furiously to her. "You'd use all this on a traitor without a second thought. You even speak as if Amelia is one, yet you keep her alive in a dungeon; why?"

"So that you can see the foul creature for as long as she lives, for who she is," she replied angrily, "A human that's poisoned my line of descendants."

Their father walked away, mumbling words to himself as he did.

"What did you just say!" shouted their grandmother.

He turned around and gave her an evil glance. Their father's eyes narrowed as he locked gazes with their grandmother, a sinister smile on his lips. "Oh, nothing important," he sneered, his voice dripping with contempt. "Just that it's about time someone ended a family-cursed one." The room fell silent, the tension thickening in the air. The siblings exchanged bewildered glances, unsure of what was unfolding before them between their father and grandmother.

Their grandmother's face contorted with rage as she stepped toward their father, her voice trembling with fury. "You dare speak of curses? You are the one who brought this upon us!" she spat; a voice laced with venomous accusation. "You and that thing have tainted our bloodline for generations!"

Their father said out loud angrily, "Go lie on the ground, let the earthly feelers drag you down into their dark, damp land," he turned around and started to walk forward, "And stay there."

"I've taken your scowls, I've taken your moods, I'll not take those words. Amelia isn't a hero for you to worship."

"A hero!" his steps stopped, and he spun around. "If she were one, I'd lie at her feet eagerly, mount her statue high so everyone could see it, but heroes are rare and hard to find. No, she's no hero; she's something more. She's the life-giver to these lands."

"Don't you dare cast her like that!"

"Why?"

"I'll have no human given that title."

Uncle Celahir joined in. "It's too late, for that's what she is."

"Cast your words away, Celahir," she angrily replied. "I'll have no words from my son's lips but what she is, a human who isn't worthy of anyone looking upon her."

"And Star, what, who is she?" uttered Lathlorn. "Did mother not give birth to a lifesaver!"

"Lathlorn!" their grandmother said as if heartbroken by his words.

"But for now, I hope she brings the lightning down to punish you for your hateful words."

"Lathlorn!" she uttered again, hurt in her voice. "You, I thought you'd have understood more of what I was talking about!"

"I did! I do, but I'm not bitter about that or the humans."

"Then you should."

"Why should I!"

"Because the human realm kept your mother away from you. She left you. She gave you, your father, your sister, up."

Lathlorn's voice trembled with anger and pain as he vehemently defended his mother. "You don't understand; she didn't leave us willingly! There were circumstances beyond her control."

"But she still left, Lathlorn. She made a choice that affected all of you, and shall I tell you something you don't even know?" she hissed at him, "Do you want me to position a thought in your mind that'll give you a true picture of your mother?"

"Speak it; I'll not keep your words in my memory."

"The day before your mother left for that world, that hateful place, she was seated at the dining table—"

"So?"

"Listen well. That trip Amelia wanted to go on, she wanted to go alone, without any guards to watch over her."

"So?" questioned Lathlorn, his eyes narrowing with suspicion. He had always known her mother to be strong and independent but mentioning her venturing into a dangerous realm without protection seemed out of character.

"Lathlorn, you've heard the rumours about Tarron's silent bride, Speantal, haven't you."

"Yes," he hissed at her.

"Do you not think it stupid to say when we all at the table knew what could happen if she went unaccompanied?"

"No."

"Why?"

"Mother wouldn't do that to father; seek another lover in another world."

"Lathlorn, you don't know the human realm, as I, others know. You're not wise enough to give your mother excuses to better the arguments."

"I'm wise enough to stand up for Mother when she isn't here."

"Then a maddened family characteristic runs through this family," she directed her words to all of them in the room. "A family characteristic of failings."

"There are no failings in my family!" their father boomed across the room. "There are far too many for even me to utter in you!"

"You make me laugh," their grandmother turned an evil gaze toward their father. "I think it wasn't just our words she went against; she's been against your words plenty of times."

"She hasn't!"

"No? Tell me differently from what I hear from your bedroom when you argue."

"I can't tell different because there's no difference." Their father's voice trembled with a mix of frustration and sadness.

Their grandmother's eyes narrowed as she studied her son. "You've always been blind to her true nature, right? She may wear a mask of innocence, but I see through it. She challenges and undermines you, yet you defend her blindly."

Their father clenched his fists, his face turning red with anger. "You don't understand! She's my wife, the mother of my children. We have our disagreements like any couple does."

"Ok, Lathlorn," she cast her sight his way. "You're the nearest to their room after me; tell me, am I telling lies."

Lathlorn bit his lip. No, grandmother wasn't lying, but from what Etheryn could read from Lathlorn's mind, his brother wasn't about to get involved, so to avoid answering the question, he looked down to the ground and shuffled his feet uncomfortably.

"There you go!" their grandmother's angry voice again. "He's answered the question. Yes, he has."

"He's heard no such things, just as you haven't!"

"Oh, you're wrong, my dear son! You've forgotten the walls to the upper floor are not as thick as you think, so I hear plenty. I hear everything, I know about everything, even that little secret you're keeping from us all."

"I don't know what you're talking about."

"You want me to tell the secret in front of your kin's!"

"I have no secrets from my family. Whatever you think you know, it's all just a figment of your imagination," he retorted, his voice laced with frustration.

Their grandmother's piercing gaze bore into him, her eyes filled with anger and disappointment. "Don't play innocent with me, young man. I may be old, but I'm not blind." She leaned in closer, her voice dropping to whisper, sending shivers down his spine. "You think you can hide your secrets from me? From this family? We have always been there for each other through thick and thin. Secrets only breed mistrust and pain; it's a pity I'm not looking at more people in this room."

"What on earth are you on about!"

"Your little secret."

"Little secret?"

"Come, my dear son. You've forgotten already! Let me remind you. What was the name you chose for your last unborn kin?"

"What are you on about?"

"Her name Elensar; what was the name you chose?"

"I—I—"

"Ah yes, Sarath."

"But—But—"

"Then there was that little secret you hid under the rose bush; you want me to carry on, Elensar."

His mouth dropped open. "You knew what happened!"

"Yes, my dear son, I knew all along," their grandmother replied with a sinister smile. "You see, a mother always knows," she replied, a big smirk across her face. "It was right to do what you did back then to Amelia."

"It was the wrong thing to do!"

"It was the right thing to do."

"How can that be!"

"You were her husband; a husband should never be denied anything from his wife."

"Now you're saying us, husband and wife!"

"I said it in the past tense, you idiot," she turned her back to him. "You *were* her husband, get it!"

"You've become so bitter, twisted in these last few—"

"Father," Lathlorn had butted in before he had the chance to say anything more, "Grandmother—"

"Lathlorn the wise," said their grandmother sarcastically, "You're pathetic, both of you; even Star would've said the same," her voice said sharply. "She was the wise one, not you two," she was looking at both Lathlorn and Elensar when she said that.

"Wise or not," now Alexander joined in. "She was still our sister; she'd never have signed about Mother as you've talked about her."

"And how would you know?" She glanced at him; her irritation apparent in her rising tone. "You and Etheryn weren't even born when she was alive. What makes you so sure you know anything?"

He opened his mouth to speak, but she cut him off, her voice growing louder. "So, my grand kin's are turning against me now!" Her next annoyed stare turned back to their father standing by the door. "You, you've done this!" She angrily pointed at him, her temper flaring. "If you two think you know better, you're fooling yourselves. Step aside and let me do what needs to be done."

"I've done nothing, and you will do nothing either!"

"You're poisoning me with lies again."

"Perhaps you shouldn't have put Amelia into the dungeons!"

The room fell silent, the tension thickening with each passing second. Grandmother's eyes narrowed again, her anger boiling over. She took a step forward, her voice trembling with fury. "Amelia deserved to be in the dungeons! She betrayed our family; she disgraced us!" Her words echoed through the room, filled with resentment and justification.

"She made a mistake in taking those papers, just like any young person would. But locking her away is not the solution. It only fuelled the fire of rebellion within us all."

"Well, I wouldn't worry now."

"What shouldn't I worry about?"

"There's nothing in her cell related to you, so why care about her."

"What do you mean, there's nothing in there!"

"Just a little removal done, so she has no memories lingering."

"What?"

"Little memories," she laughed wickedly. "Little presents."

He angrily looked at her, "You've taken her bracelet!"

"Yes."

Father whispered, drawing in air, "And what else have you taken from her?"

"Everything," she replied with a chilling smile. "Every precious memory, every cherished moment, all erased from her mind."

Father's eyes widened in horror as he struggled to comprehend the magnitude of her actions. "How could you do such a thing?" he asked, his voice trembling with anger and despair.

Her laughter echoed through the cold, sterile room. "Oh, dear son, you always were too sentimental for your good. Memories are nothing but burdens that hold us back. I have liberated her from the shackles of her past."

His fists clenched tightly at his sides as he fought to control his rising rage. "You don't understand," he seethed through gritted teeth. "Memories shape who we are. They give us purpose and meaning."

She shrugged indifferently, dismissing his words as inconsequential. "Purpose and meaning are overrated," she sneered.

"What else have you taken from her?"

"Nothing else unless you've gifted her something else."

Father couldn't believe it, "You've taken things from her and put her in the dungeons? Amelia is my wife! How could you do this?"

Grandmother laughed wickedly, "Oh, I thought it would serve as a warning to the rest of you, a warning that says family secrets are not tolerated, even if it involves my kin hiding them."

Father looked at her with angry eyes, "You bitch! You have no right to imprison my wife! She is innocent and does not deserve this treatment. How could you betray your own family like this?"

Grandmother's laughter echoed through the room; her eyes gleaming with a twisted satisfaction. "Innocent? Oh, my dear son, you have no idea what secrets she has been hiding from us all these years. Secrets that could humiliate our name and tarnish our reputation."

"Again, I call you bitch!"

"That's not very nice," she'd said mockingly.

"You're by far," hissed their father, "The most vindictive person I'm connected to."

"Well, I've heard better threats made against me."

"Then hear this one. I'm glad Amelia and I joined your line of descendants to a race you despise, but to make it even more enjoyable to see you squirm, we added another to the family list."

"You what!"

"That's right, Mother, a kin seed planted just before you put her into the dungeon. A kin who will grow up knowing the truth about you and your wicked ways. You thought you could escape the consequences of your actions, but we have ensured that your legacy will forever be tainted."

"You bastard!" Their grandmother's face turned pale, shock and anger evident in her eyes. She struggled to find words, her voice trembling as she finally managed to speak, "You can't do this to me! I am your mother!"

Their father stepped forward, his voice filled with determination, "No, you were never a mother to me, to us. You were a tormentor, a manipulator. We endured years of your cruelty, but no more." Their father's words echoed through the room, resonating with liberation and empowerment.

"How could you, how could you," their grandmother sounded defeated. "Of all the things—"

"Well, you wanted a better threat; I just delivered it to you," he turned around, opened the door, and turned back to her. "I got it wrong; it's twins," he laughed, then slipped through the door and slammed it shut.

The four kin looked at each other in shock. Their father had just announced that their mother was pregnant with twins. Uncle Celahir was shaking his head, looking displeased. Grandmother was standing only a few feet away, scowling fiercely. The room went silent as the news sunk in. The twins would be the fifth and sixth kin in their family. Grandmother looked stern, her eyes showing disapproval and her lips pressed tight together. The four kin were at a loss for words; nobody knew what to do or say.

Chapter 26

The History Of The Shalimar And The Wizards

Down in the dungeons of Volarie castle, William heard a voice talking; it made him shake his head, turn himself to face the wall, curl himself up, and sigh, "Jesus Christ, not again!" For a split second, he thought they'd let Amelia's husband in her cell again so they could spend the night together. But her voice sounded different this time, so William called out to her. "Amelia?"

"Oh god!"

Inside William's mind, he debated whether to go over there and look through that hole in the wall, but he had second thoughts about doing it. The last time he'd made a mistake by thinking the noises he'd heard in Amelia's cell were telling him a guard was raping her. Instead, he saw Amelia and her husband, Elensar, going at it like a bull in a pottery shop. He felt embarrassed, foolish, and ashamed to have been wrong and caught peeking. Since that incident, fear and doubt have been growing inside him - fear of making a similar mistake and doubt about his judgmont. He wavered between two thoughts, seeing this new opportunity as an exchange to prove himself. Should he go and look or stay quiet? He couldn't decide what to do. Part of him wanted to take the risk, but the other part feared that he might again mess up and make a fool of himself. William sat there trembling between scared and brave, unsure if he should take the plunge, waiting for a sign to tell him what to do.

"I can't see!" he heard Amelia's voice again, "The light, it's gone!"

William dragged his aching body away from the edge of his bed and pulled himself across the cold, hard cell floor, making his way toward the small hole in the wall. He strained his eyes and peered through the small opening, hoping to glimpse Amelia. When his vision adjusted to the darkness of the other cell, William saw her lying on her bed. She was wearing the same prisoner's clothing he was, though hers looked more tattered and worn. He was immediately caught off guard by what he had seen; her beautiful black hair was now short and choppy just above her shoulders.

"Amelia!" she didn't answer; he called again, "Amelia!"

This time, she heard him, turned her head, and asked, "What's up?"

For a second, William could see faded marks of bruising on her face; it was probably the shadows of the cell. "I thought you called."

"No," she half sat up and brushed a strand of hair away from her eyes. "But you, how are you?"

"How am I?" His hand slowly crept up to his chin and stroked the coarse and domed facial hair covering it; the previous weeks blended in his mind like a big, jumbled mess. When had it all started? How long had he been in this cell? The confusion was evident in his empty gaze. Questions ran through his head like a loop, yet he could not find the answers. Was he in a dream? How did he lose his way in such a short amount of time? He felt so tired and helpless. "I don't understand," he said in a barely audible whisper. But, despite the confusion and fear, he felt a tiny spark of hope somewhere deep within him, hope that he would soon find the answers he was desperately searching for; Amelia answered one of his questions.

"You've been out of it for months."

"Months? But I don't understand?"

"Neither did the dungeon guard. He came to give you food; you were in such a slumber during the last few weeks he thought you were dead."

William remembered seeing the guard enter his room; it was as if he were out of his body, looking down; something now made him frown. A remembrance of something terrible happening inside Amelia's cell.

Oh god! Now William remembered someone had visited her a few weeks ago. His motionless body couldn't call for help as someone grabbed a handful of Amelia's long black hair and cut it with a small dagger. He couldn't scream for help or assistance when one of them stomped his foot down hard upon her stomach. But it wasn't just the two guards and Amelia in that cell. William also saw someone else in her cell, laughing at her screams of pain. Before unseen powers forced his eyes shut, he'd been looking at their Queen Catreen. The present-day William was shocked. "Oh god!" he said, "Amelia!"

"What's the matter?"

"Don't speak; you should be sleeping, resting."

"What's the matter?" Amelia rose from her bed and walked to the hole. He watched as she walked; her walking confused him, for she wasn't walking with a limp or crawling on the floor, crying with the pain of broken bones. He saw an average person walk slowly but certainly, as they did daily.

"Let me see your face," he asked as she reached the hole.

"Why?"

"Please, just show me your face." She placed herself so he could see; the next minute, she watched his eyes grow and his mouth drop open.

"What! Stop it; you're freaking me out!"

"You're—Old! You're—"

"Thanks! Weren't you born with manners?"

"I'm sorry; I didn't mean to offend you," he stammered, his shock becoming embarrassment. "It's just that—I expected someone younger."

She couldn't help but chuckle at his reaction. "Well, appearances can be deceiving, can't they?" she amusedly replied.

He quickly regained his composure and tried to salvage the situation. "No, no, it's not about your age. It's just that—You look so different from what I saw first."

Curiosity piqued; she leaned closer to the hole in the wall separating them. "Different? How so?"

He hesitated for a moment before finding the right words. "I guess I pictured someone more—Younger looking. But you still have an aura of wisdom and experience surrounding you."

A smile tugged at the corners of her lips as she listened to his explanation. "Well, thanks very much, but I'm not old."

"No! I mean, you're old!"

"Yes, I know."

"Amelia, I mean your skin; it looks old!" a frown replaced her smile, and a hand went to feel the skin upon her face, "Your hand!"

The next thing she did was back away from him, letting a shriek out while she did, "Oh my god!"

"What the hell is going on!" The old face before him seemed to have witnessed countless years of wear and tear. Deep wrinkles etched across its face, telling tales of a life well-lived. Once vibrant and full of life, her eyes reflected a dull sadness. "Amelia," he repeated, "What the hell is going on!"

"It can't be, it can't be!"

"Amelia, talk to me, speak, tell me what, why this has happened."

"I—I didn't think it would happen so soon!"

"But how?" he asked. "Why!" William saw her figure return to the hole in the wall dividing their cells and sank to the floor.

On the other side of the wall, Amelia found solace in twisting the bracelet around her wrist. It was a delicate piece of jewellery that Elensar had given her on their anniversary—a token of their love and commitment. Each twist brought back cherished moments they had shared—laughter-filled evenings, stolen kisses under moonlit skies, and whispered promises of a future they had envisioned. Her words softly spoke, "I can't understand it. Rotherkin told me the—"

"Rotherkin?" When a few moments passed, he asked again, "You were talking about Rotherkin?"

"Rotherkin?" Spoken as if Amelia had forgotten the name mentioned.

"Yes, you mentioned Rotherkin?"

"Yes, I did mention him," Amelia replied, her brow slightly furrowing as she tried to recall the context of their conversation. "But I can't quite remember why I brought it up," Amelia continued, frustration evident in her voice. She tapped her finger against her chin, deep in thought. "It must have been related to something we were discussing earlier." Her mind raced, desperately searching for the missing puzzle piece connecting Rotherkin to their conversation. She closed her eyes, attempting to visualize their shared previous moments. Flashes of images and snippets of dialogue flickered through her mind like an old film reel. Suddenly, a faint memory surfaced. It was a fleeting mention of Rotherkin during a discussion about life medicine. Amelia's face brightened as fragments of memory started to resurface. "Ah, yes! He's a kind wizard, an elder of Volarie everybody calls Rotherkin."

"What on earth is a wizard doing here in this realm?"

She sighed, fingers releasing the now severely twisted bracelet. "It's a bit complicated. Rotherkin's kind, the Etherole's, once walked these lands before the Shalimar people, but I think only a few are left."

"Did they live here in this place?"

"Yes, but they used to live elsewhere," she explained. "They lived in houses built underground around the same time the Shalimar became another inhabitant of their realm."

"Really?"

"Really," she replied, her eyes sparkling excitedly. "It's quite fascinating. These houses were not your typical above-ground structures like we have today; they cleverly designed them to hide beneath the earth's surface." Her hands moved as she spoke, painting an imaginary picture of the underground dwellings. "The ancient inhabitants of this place were incredibly resourceful. They dug deep into the ground, creating intricate networks of tunnels and chambers that served as their homes."

Her words piqued his curiosity further, and he couldn't help but ask, "But why would they choose to live underground? Was it for protection from the Shalimar?"

She smiled knowingly before answering, "No, the Shalimar moved underground with them, too. But protection for both kinds was certainly the main reason. Living below ground provided them with a natural shield against harsh weather conditions and potential threats from outsiders. It also helped them maintain a more stable temperature throughout the year."

He nodded, intrigued by the idea. "So, they were like pioneers, finding innovative ways to adapt to their environment?"

She laughed, then shifted closer to the hole in the wall so that he could see her sitting in full view of each other. "I guess. Then these borrow houses moved above ground."

"So, whatever threatened them must have gone for them to do that?"

"Most had. You see, before everyone went underground, creatures like wild goblins used to roam—"

"Wild goblins?"

"That's what they called them."

"Well, I don't think I'd want to live above ground, especially if wild goblins were waiting for a tasty meal to pop into their mouths."

"You're so funny," she half-laughed, "You'd be too tough."

Cheeky," laughed William, "Tell me more about these Goblins."

"They were stout creatures, rounded pot bellies, little chubby legs, and mischievous grins," Amelia continued. "They were known for their mischievous nature, always up to some trouble. They had long, pointy ears that twitched at the slightest sound, allowing them to navigate through the darkness easily."

"Tell me more."

"Legend had it that goblins possessed an uncanny ability to blend into their surroundings," she added, leaning closer as if sharing a secret. "Their skin would take on the colour and texture of their surroundings, making them nearly invisible to the untrained eye. They could hide in plain sight, lurking in forests or settlements without being detected."

More curiosity had sparked, so he asked, "So, were the Etherole and Shalimars killed by these wild goblins."

"No."

"The arrival of the wizards?"

She laughed, "No."

"How did the Shalimar appear here?"

"God, you ask many questions."

William shrugged. "I'm just trying to make sense of all this. It's not every day that we stumble upon a hidden realm filled with magical creatures and ancient prophecies, and I won't know unless I ask. Or do you not want me to ask?"

"You're just like Elensar, always ending with another question."

"I don't think I'm a Shalimar."

"Sorry."

"You're forgiven. Now, how did these Shalimars arrive here?"

"See, I told you, another question."

"Well, it's a valid question," replied William with a mischievous smile. "But I suppose we should start from the beginning."

Amelia leaned back against the cell wall, gazing up at the ceiling, recounting how the Shalimar had arrived in this land. "Legend has it that long ago when the universe was still young, there existed a hidden realm, this realm. The Shalimars arrived here through the portal. Where they came from before is a great secret: in normal times, if I told you, they'd kill me for it."

"I think maybe you shouldn't tell."

"What does it matter? We're as good as dead in here anyway."

"That's comforting to hear, not!"

"I'm sorry; sometimes things slip out of my mouth."

"You're forgiven," said William, "Now, please, I'd like to hear more about this tale."

"Look, can you do me a favour before I do this?"

"Like what?"

Amelia remarked, "I know I may be asking a lot of you. But I'm keeping a journal right here—Well, it's more about my life and the people around me," she said. "And I was wondering if you could write in it too?"

"Why?"

Amelia paused momentarily, considering how to explain her request, then replied, "I value your perspective and insights. You have a unique way of looking at things, and I believe your thoughts would add depth to my journal."

William raised an eyebrow sceptically. "But why do you need me to write in it? Can't you write about our conversations yourself?"

Amelia took a deep breath before responding. "Yes, I could certainly do that. But having your own words in the journal would make it more authentic and meaningful. It's not just about documenting what happened; it's about capturing the essence of our friendship and your impact on my life."

"I see," said William.

"It would mean the world to me if you could. That said, it would take up quite a lot of your time. So, are you up for it? Just your view, though."

"You want me to write what I see."

"Yes, what you see, feel, perhaps you could even sketch yourself."

"You're asking for a lot."

"I realize, but—"

"Okay," William groaned. "I'll do it all; I'll write my part in your journal only if you finish this story."

"Deal," Amelia replied with a smile he couldn't see, relieved William had agreed to her request. "I truly believe your contribution will make this story come alive."

William nodded, eyes scanning the room as if searching for the right words. "I'll do my best," he murmured, his voice tinged with uncertainty. "But I must warn you, my observations might not be what you expect."

"That's what I'm looking for," she assured him. "I want your unfiltered thoughts and emotions. Don't hold back."

"You're weird, you know."

"So, people tell me, but will you do it."

"Okay, but this story—" she disappeared from his view and popped back, pushing some paper through the gap in the cell wall. He pulled it all the way through and unravelled it. "Where did you get this from?" he asked, getting a pen out of the gap too.

"I asked for it."
"You asked for it!"
"Yes."
"Okay, that's just weird."
"Will you, do it?"
"What if someone finds what I've written?"
Amelia smirked mischievously, her eyes glinting with excitement. "That's the beauty of it, William," she replied, leaning closer to him through the gap in the cell wall. "No one will ever find what you've written."
William furrowed his brow, unsure of what Amelia was suggesting. "What do you mean? How can you be so sure?"
Amelia leaned back slightly, her voice dropping to a conspiratorial whisper. "I have a plan," she said cryptically. "You see, this paper is special. It's enchanted."
William's eyes widened in surprise and curiosity. Enchanted paper? He had never heard of such a thing before. His scepticism began to wane as he considered the possibilities.
Amelia continued; her voice filled with conviction. "Once you've finished writing your story, all you have to do is fold it up and say a specific magic word I'll teach you. The paper will transform into a portal, transporting you to the realm you've created within your story," Amelia explained, her eyes sparkling excitedly. "Imagine it, stepping into a realm of your own making, where your characters come to life and your wildest dreams become reality." Her words hung in the air, igniting a sense of wonder from William's side of his cell, who was believing every single word that came out of her mouth of her words. "But be warned, William," Amelia continued, her tone more serious. "Once you step through that portal, you become an integral part of your story. Every decision you make will shape the narrative and affect the lives of your characters. It's a responsibility not to be taken lightly."
"Really! Oh, wow," he scrutinized the paper as if trying to see the magic hidden inside. "This truly is magical."
"Well, it would be if it were true," Amelia said, laughing at him.
William gave her a confused look, "But you just said—"
"A load of lies," again a laughing sound made. "
He rolled his eyes at her, then threw the paper to the floor. "So, I'm guessing I won't be off the hook if they find my part in your journal."
"I wouldn't worry about that."
"Why?"
"They can't read our English language."
"That's all well and good, but what if you get into trouble having it?"
"I'm going to hide it."
William raised an eyebrow, intrigued by her confidence. "And where do you plan on hiding it?"

She smirked mischievously. "In plain sight, of course. No one would suspect it's right under their noses."

Curiosity piqued; William leaned in closer. "Tell me more. How do you plan on pulling that off?"

She leaned back, crossing her arms with a sly grin. "Well, I've been studying ancient encryption techniques—"

"You're doing it again, aren't you," he rolled his eyes again. "More lies. Just get to the point already, the main storyline." William's patience was thin, and he couldn't help but feel sceptical about her claims.

Amelia laughed at him, "Only because I wanted to bring some laughter into these cells of ours."

William crossed his arms, a hint of annoyance evident on his face. "Laughter? In these cells? Amelia, we're locked up here, facing imminent danger, and you think it's appropriate to crack jokes?"

Amelia's laughter subsided as she met William's gaze. "I know it seems strange, but sometimes humour is my only weapon against despair. It helps me cope with the darkness that surrounds me."

William then understood, and his mood quickly changed when he asked the following question. "I apologize then. Would you like to begin again? Start with the story?"

"I guess," she sighed loudly. "Well, it's written in one of Volarie's many history books that the Shalimars began life like us."

"Human!"

Amelia paused momentarily, her eyes flickering with curiosity and excitement. She continued, "Yes, human. The Shalimars were once just like us, living ordinary lives in a different realm. Then later, there were ones with special powers that went into the human realm, mixed with them, breed with them, so the Shalimar was born."

"That still doesn't explain why they came through the portal."

"The Wizards, or Etherole's, used to roam the human realm; while visiting, they saw how the humans treated these half-breeds. The Etherole invited these half-breeds to come through the portal because it was the only place the Etherole thought the half-breeds would feel safe in."

"Ah. So how did the Etherole's kind get extinct?"

"I didn't say extinct; I said there weren't many left."

"Then how did some of their kind die?"

"A plague from your realm."

"Our world," he reminded her.

She nodded. "The plague seeped through the portal."

"You mean the black plague."

"I don't know if this black plague."

"Back in 1348, still to this day, there's a fishing town by the sea called Weymouth; it's told this was the place the plague, a death-ridden disease, struck its first victims, from there it swept all over England."

"You had this plague there as well!"

"If it's the same, yes."

"I've heard the word *Plague* but never really knew what it was."

"Well, the Black Death was a bacterium-born disease carried in the blood of wild black rats, fleas living on them."

"I wonder if it was these rats, and what did you call them fleas?" she saw him nod. "These animals could've brought that plague through the portal. But if you said it happened in 1348, I don't know if it was that plague; the Etherole and Shalimars have been here a lot longer than that."

"Perhaps it was another plague, similar to the one that entered through the portal; it might have; what do you think?"

She nodded again. "It could have been since the portal at that time in history had always been opened, since the Etherole's had no threat from your world, I mean our world; perhaps they thought they were safe from anything. As I said, this infectious disease wiped out five million Etherole and Shalimars in just two years. Or put it this way, in Volarie, up to thirty thousand of these races lived here; out of that city's population, twenty-eight thousands of them succumbed to that disease."

"I expect the effect was worst because it was so overcrowded."

Amelia nodded. "The summer of that last year was abnormally wet. There was grain rotting in the fields due to the nearly constant rains. With the harvest so adversely affected, it seemed certain that there would be food shortages; however, their biggest problem once this plague was gone was not having enough people to harvest their food."

William shifted his weight, getting uncomfortable on the cold floor. "There was a song sung about that plague."

"The Etherole's had one too."

"They did; how odd!"

"Not if you heard it. I think it's quite sad."

"How did it go?"

"Cora tendon mentor lea, wren tare threnody, me ante pore. Sere lent hews mere kentia; sere lent manta flue hadean."

"What does it translate into?"

"Roughly translated, it went a bit like this: Loop a pouch full of remedies around your waist, a handkerchief to hold a sneeze, another to wipe a tear. If these remedies fail in your need, we all die on the grass."

"That's a bit like the one we have, except our kind believed holding a posy of flowers to the nose kept the plague away."

"That's sad."

"Hang on a minute!"

"What?"

"You said the portal at that time in history was open."

"And!"

"The portal must have been closed after that outbreak. How come I was able to get through it?"

"God, we could be here all night explaining the history of this land."

"Don't we have all night?"

Amelia sighed, "Do you want to know?"

"Yes."

She began again, this time right at the beginning. "In an age when the lands, sea, and air were newly developed in the human world—"

"I like the sound of this tale."

"Shh."

"Sorry."

"It's said there was a secret dwelling there, but none, save the open-minded knew its whereabouts. These open-minded beings called Etherole's were a race of many skills, restless in their roaming and of such kind-hearted that even a fallen leaf before reaching the ground would release a tear of wretchedness from their eyes, would cause their hearts to despair."

"Whose hearts, the Etherole?"

"Yes, be quiet, will you," he nodded. "Now, when man first appeared, it's said many a curious Etherole's would stroll about the human lands, listening, observing, but didn't interact with the humans for they were forbidden to do so by a rule set out by the firstborn Etherole called Gloryindeal."

"Gloryindeal! That's an odd name."

"I suppose so. Gloryindeal's rule forbids no contact, never changing an outcome, never stealing from man, killing any beast or being while visiting the human lands; it was complied with by all for nigh on three thousand years. But was promptly broken in the four thousand years by their leader Gloryindeal upon his first trip into the human lands."

"That sounds bad news."

"It could have been, but we are talking of the Etherole's, not humans. When Gloryindeal and his two servants saw a sight, that mournful viewing moved their hearts to despair. That sight cast in the twilight hour upon a dirt-ridden track leading to a vastly huge dwelling had Gloryindeal throwing hands out to two fallen figures broken with bones, bloodied with years of abuse from their owner. Now Gloryindeal's two servants, Heldrin and Meyern, that accompanied him on his first visit—"

"Heldrin and Meyern?"

"Yes, they were also astonished to see such a sight, for this was their first visit. So, when Gloryindeal heard the figures crying silent wretched words from their minds that only an Etherole could understand, he quickly told them they were taking them back home with them."

"Sounds like this Gloryindeal was a smart man."

"Smart Etherole," she laughed, "Now Heldrin and Meyern complied, rounding up their grey and white horses. However, not by foot did they walk to the secret invisible portal that Gloryindeal and they used to enter the world of man. It was by winged horses."

"They flew too!"

"Yes, they flew through the portal, only stopping in the first village of the Etherole's world called Lurth to heal the broken beings."

"I think I flew over that village when I arrived here."

"You probably did. Anyway, while there, the healer called Powlin noticed something about the two beings that had him mentioning their ancient tapestries in the great hall—"

"Ancient tapestries!"

"Stop interrupting me!"

"Sorry, go on."

"Now Gloryindeal listened intensely to Powlin's explanation that these beings might be similar to those in the tapestries. When Gloryindeal asked him why he thought this, Powlin showed the being's tall figures, long hair, and pointed ears. Gloryindeal agreed with Powlin, for only days ago, he'd been looking at those foreseeing tapestries, images not of humans. This news confused Gloryindeal, and he asked Powlin if they were not humans, then what race he should call them. But Powlin could not grant Gloryindeal's request, only able to say that when the two beings had time to heal, perhaps they would have the answer."

"Did he get his answer?"

"Shh."

"Sorry."

"So Gloryindeal, his two servants, and Powlin waited four days and nights while the two beings lay in deep slumber, muttering no human words every so often that they wondered what they were saying. Upon the fifth night's rising moon, one opened its eyes and gave Gloryindeal a chance to ask his question."

"Which was?"

"The first answer given to Gloryindeal was with fear in the eyes of the being, its head turning as if searching for its companion. Gloryindeal calmed the being with a small hand, directing the being's gaze to see its companion lying but a few feet away from it. This sight eased the being to tell its story to Gloryindeal, which consisted of them being born from light much brighter, hotter than the sun."

"Hotter than the sun!"

"Yes, now from there, the story moved to mingle with humans, of half breeds being born, forcefully used to exhale their magical powers of knowledge upon the humans, whenever, at whatever time they the humans called for it. Then, the story switched to even more terrible tales. The being told them of being cast out as rubbish when their powers no longer had service to the humans. The being had already talked of them having special powers of knowledge, but they had more than that in powers. They had the power to turn anything into gold, rock into food, and some powers they kept at bay for fear of the humans making them use these. This story made Gloryindeal sad that the race of humans could do such a thing of demanding such powers of wonder."

"If it were me, it would make me livid, not sad."

"That's not all, though. Gloryindeal was angry that the humans wanted to steal such knowledge. It made him mad that they did not want to find answers for themselves. So Gloryindeal told the being that as long as his blood ran in each of his descendants, he desired no power from them; he also decided that any Etherole's who came across this being would swiftly, with haste, take them back to their lands. Yet he still had no name to call the being."

"No name?"

"That was until its companion awoke and spoke its first words. For the next few hours, Gloryindeal understood some words spoken between both beings; other words were not, yet two words kept constantly arising above all, Elf and Race, so at first Gloryindeal thought he'd call their race *Elf*."

"So that's where that name *Elf* comes from!"

"No, listen first. Gloryindeal didn't know that the companions used abbreviated words to name each other. Elf, which meant Elfordin, and Race for Racenil, but they didn't correct Gloryindeal at the time with their real names because they felt no need to tell him."

"Ah, okay, I get it. Bit weird the Shalimar couldn't name their race themselves."

"Well, I was just getting to that part too."

"Go on."

"Many years later, these elf people used a different name for their race; they called themselves Shalimar."

"Shalimar, huh? That's an interesting choice," mused William. "I wonder why they decided to change their name."

Amelia nodded and continued, "Legend has it that the elves chose the name Shalimar to reclaim an identity and distance themselves from the negative connotations associated with their past names called *'Elf*."

"How would they have known, heard about Elf negativity? It only comes from the world of humans."

"That's correct; again, your words are ahead of this tale." Amelia continued, "Over time, some Shalimar would still visit the human realm secretly; they learned the term *'Elf'* had become synonymous with mischievousness and trickery in many human cultures."

"Intriguing," replied William. "So, by adopting the name Shalimar, they could redefine how others perceived them?"

"Exactly," confirmed Amelia. "The Shalimar people wanted to be recognized for their true nature—a mostly wise and noble race with a deep connection to nature and magic. They believed that by embracing this new name, they could shed any preconceived notions and forge a fresh path for themselves."

"Ah, right."

"And that's how the Shalimar came to dwell here, and because Gloryindeal was the first to bring these people into their lands, he was the one while alive to name everyone brought before his presence in the great hall of Weath. He named the two first beings Vorlearn and Vorwern—"

"Vorlearn and Vorwern!"

"Vorlearn for the female meant first of many; for Vorwern, his name meant the first speaker of the Elf or Shalimar, as we'll call them from now on. These two first Shalimars prospered in life and raised many kin's but never forgot their helper, taking them from a despairing world. So, when their firstborn was taken before Gloryindeal to be named, they requested to name him Gloryindeal too, which also meant, in Etherole tongue, son of the first. Gloryindeal granted them this with a smile upon his lips. And that's how it went on, century after century—"

"Century after century!"

"Yes, they're immortal. Anyway, the Shalimars taken from the human world were sent before Gloryindeal. With a voice that resonated like a gentle breeze through the trees, Gloryindeal began bestowing new names upon each Shalimar. Each name carried a weight of significance, representing their unique essence and purpose in the immortal realm. As Gloryindeal spoke each name, an ethereal glow enveloped each Shalimar, marking their transformation into beings of everlasting life. This all happened until the day of Gloryindeal's last breathing word that uttered, *'No more can I name you, for now, it is the turn of you to name your descendants.'*"

"So, it was the wizards, I mean the Etherole, who gave them everlasting life?"

"Yes," Amelia replied. "The Etherole wizards, masters of ancient magic and guardians of the Shalimar lineage, bestowed upon them the gift of everlasting life. It was a pact forged in the depths of time, a bond between mortal and ethereal realms."

"So how can they still live long lives if the Etherole stopped naming them?"

"Well," Amelia explained, her voice filled with mystery, "The bond between the Shalimar lineage and the Etherole wizards runs deeper than mere names. While naming was once a crucial part of bestowing everlasting life upon them, it is not the sole source of their longevity." She paused for a moment, gathering her thoughts before continuing. "You see when the Etherole ceased to name new members of the Shalimar lineage, it marked the end of an era. However, the ancient magic infused within each member continued to flow through their veins.

It became an inherent part of their being, sustaining their immortality even without further intervention from the wizards."

"So, what happened next?"

"From then on, each Shalimar name chosen was to describe a wide variety of feelings, right down to the meaning of despair they felt while living in the human world, but not many selected that name *Yolthorn*, for it was a name with a meaning that they wished to forget. Another century passed with Shalimars living alongside the Etherole, yet the Shalimar and Etherole were not alone in that land."

"Not alone?"

"There were roaming goblins; the Shalimar called them beasts, the Etherole's called them goblins. These creatures with swollen, long-haired bodies, long-running legs, and sharp teeth had tasted the flesh of roaming Shalimar and Etherole. So, by the time Vorlearn and Vorwern reached an age where silver hair grew from their once golden heads, the Etherole and Shalimars were being dwindled in numbers to such a degree that to remain alive was only possible by living underground."

"Underground?"

"That's how they all lived for a century, living, breathing, breeding underground like moles, until words from the last-born kin of Vorlearn and Vorwern uttered his plans of moving back above ground to slay the beasts that made them retreat underground like wounded prey. Alexander, meaning strong-minded, had reached an age of a thousand years; his strength was that of five beasts rolled into one, his mind sharp, alert, his eyes, bright and long seeing could see much in the dark and by day."

"Beasts!"

"Shh—Now these qualities Alexander held were seen as a gift of power to help them abolish the beasts for eternity. So many shouted their agreement with his plan. On the other hand, his parents feared their race's lack of knowledge about illness or open wounds would cause their son to die. So, Alexander's parents, Vorlearn and Vorwern, bid him no more to go above ground for fifty years. But Lethlorlin, one of Gloryindeal's descendants, assured that with help from his father's ancient spiritual amulets, Alexander would be safe."

"This just gets better!"

"Poor Vorlearn and Vorwern just shook their heads. When they could no longer hold back any of Alexander's words or preach to others of freedom waiting above ground for them, they gave him their blessing, but only if he agreed to take the amulets and a force of three thousand to aid him in the battle against the roaming beasts."

"So, did he go?"

"Alexander went forth above the ground on the night five days after his parents blessing with a roar of such it unsettled the birds sitting in the trees nearby. From there, Alexander took his three thousand strong armies dressed in iron body armour with small amulets of spiritual stones, silver, and gold embedded in its breastplate across plains, mountains, and waters of each land seeking out every beast night and day, through rain, snow, gales, sun, and droughts."

"So, it took quite a bit to get rid of them."

"Yes. That episode in time took two hundred years, two hundred years of many beasts maimed, killed, and devoured of their fatty flesh. It also consisted of Etherole and Shalimar dying on days when they lost all hope of freedom. Still, once they had accomplished the war between fierce beast Etherole and Shalimar, the army's arrival back to their underground homes was greeted with an abundance of cheers and merriment of a victory parade that would've lifted many a dampened heart. For Alexander himself, the Shalimar Lethlorlin, descendent of Gloryindeal, bestowed upon him the greatest gift a Shalimar could give."

"What was the gift?"

"The gift of granting good back to all that's evil, this he gave not as a spell, nor granted it through their magical potions, he gave it in the shape of a small stone amulet shaped like a heart."

"Ah."

"For the next eighty thousand rolling years, the peaceful life of freedom granted timber houses of Shalimar and Etherole rebuilt above grounds. Fields to be planted and harvested without the threat of a lurking fierce beast watching nearby, animals of lesser threat were bred to the full capability of feeding many hungry mouths if need be. Such was life for them that none thought any threat could ever linger with them anymore until the day a plague came to their realm."

"That must have been that plague we discussed earlier."

"I think this was an earlier one. This plague spread out its feelers like a spider's web, reaching into every crack and corner of each land. It spilled way down into caves that disappeared deep below mountains, into waters it swam briefly, but deadly it spilled poison into all drinking wells."

"That doesn't sound too good, does it?"

"No. With this disastrous disease gripping the land, many of Etherole's thoughts turned to the Shalimars, remembering their lack of knowledge in treating the illness that may finally end their existence. So, they herded the Shalimars from their homes, sent them to live by the sea, and ordered them to stay there until called to return."

"Did they have to wait long?"

"The Shalimars waited patiently by the sea for eight centuries. Still, no word came from the Etherole to return home, no sound from a horn blown to summon them when twenty centuries passed, no bird to cry its message from the Etherole in the ten more centuries that followed, so the Shalimar left upon their thought something bad had happened. They were right. The disease had struck down many of the land's first inhabitants, the Etherole, but not many of the Shalimars by the sea met the same ending for some unexplained reason."

"Weird."

"Many Shalimars thought perhaps the Etherole had cast a spell over them to keep them safe, for they knew they still had not conquered the skill to heal themselves from illness. Others said the sea winds kept the plague and death decay at bay. Others said the amulet around Alexander's neck given by Lethlorlin saved them from the disease."

"This tale is getting even odder!"

"Whatever it was that saved the Shalimars wasn't known or revealed to them, but from then on, the Shalimars of old took no chance in that disease coming back into their realm without any protection to defend their race against it. They learned how to heal wounds and mend broken bones, but many still believed that Alexander's amulet had a hand in their survival, so they decided to take it to the centre of gatherings, Mirnith."

"Mirnith!"

"Yes, it's a place surrounded by rocks. Now, once in Mirnith, they displayed the amulet not upon a cloth in an open house so that all could see it whenever they wished; they placed it into a giant pointed boulder located in the middle of a large black tower surrounded by five smaller ones—"

"Black towers!"

"That's where the amulet stayed for seventy-five centuries, watching silently as many Etherole passed from its world, watching many new Shalimars born into it. It also saw something else arrive. It saw the arrival of a beast, not in the shape of an animal, Shalimar, or man. Now, if the amulet could've talked, he would've said his name was *Heart of the lands*, but the beast's name was neither good nor wise; it was *Greed*."

"Greed!"

"Greed that no Shalimar or Etherole ever experienced before, yet merely two hundred years later, greed that'd spread out in the lands by foot came to his tower and seeped into his boulder, making him too weak to stop dying.

"Oh no—"

"Now, just as the black tower swallowed more greed, evilness, hate, and cruelty from every crack and cranny, the amulet was taken secretly, given as safekeeping to a fair maiden from Volarie heavy with an unborn child. At the same time, inside the tower, the illness spread even more of its evilness to a King called Tarron, son of Dreaydon, and the other was Prince Lucian, youngest son of Tarron. This illness would cast a shadow of blackness across half of the Shalimar lands, to the point the Shalimars who dwelled there, now called themselves 'Mintos,' meaning 'Shadow' in their Shalimar tongue. On the other side, the Shalimars referred to themselves as the same, 'Shalimar', where their realm was in complete daylight staying unchanged until a thousand years later, the amulet sited back in its rightful place made all anew again. This past is just the foundation of the story of this realm."

"The foundation! How much more is there to tell?"

"In recent years, not much; the only thing different now is instead of six royal domains being in this realm, there's only two now."

"Two royal domains?"

"Froyen and Volarie."

"What happened to the others?"

"The others got de-royal."

"De-royal, why?"

"They decided two castles were enough, I guess."

"So why was Volarie kept?"

"Volarie's the oldest city, so I expect that's why, but I haven't told you everything about the past yet."

"The past, how much more is there?"

"Loads."

"What about you?"

"What about me?"

"Well, you must have played a part in the history of this land."

"Some of it."

"And which some of it did you play a part in?"

"I suppose mine started when I was born."

"When was that then?"

"1968, but I thought you knew that?"

"I'm just testing you," he laughed a little, "Now tell me about yourself, why you came here, why you didn't return to our world."

"I was born in 1968; then I came here."

"I know that; what I want is more information."

"Why?"

"I like to know something about the person I'm talking to."

Amelia sighed, "Do you want me to start at my beginning?"

"Best place to start."

She did, and by the end of that meeting, he knew almost everything there was to know about the land he was a prisoner in. He knew about Amelia's children and the ones that died. She told him about Elensar, and when William asked about that evil incident in her cell, she denied it ever happened, saying he must have been dreaming it, but he wasn't so sure she was telling the truth. He also knew about the bottle of medicine she needed, but she couldn't have it by the Queen's orders; he knew even about the wizard Rotherkin who made it.

For the remaining night hours, William spent the final few hours summarizing his entire evening. Amelia watched William from the sidelines, ensuring he wrote all the information. When the writing was complete, Amelia asked William to draw a picture of himself from memory. It proved to be an intense challenge for William, who had to recall the features of his face without a mirror in his cell. Nevertheless, he persisted until he had produced several sketches of himself that were satisfactory to Amelia's standards. Finally, with all the records collected, William and Amelia concluded their session.

By the following early morning, that was the last time she would see or even speak to him. Celahir had come to William's cell and had brought four castle guards to take him away. William was probably confused and scared of what would happen to him, yet he knew it was his time to face the consequences of his actions.

Chapter 27

A Spell For The Shalimars Portal

Nestled within the rolling hills of a quiet countryside village was a cozy cottage that belonged to Rotherkin, overlooked by a canopy of trees, and surrounded by an emerald expanse. With four walls of rustic charm and windows glazed to capture the first morning light, this sunlit abode invited anyone to sit a spell. Inside, the motif of pastoral life continued with hardwood floors, timber beam ceilings, and exposed brick hearths that seemed to warm your soul with a comforting embrace. Vintage antiques and chests of rolling drawers offered ample storage that provided all the necessary everyday items. Squares of shabby-chic furniture beckon anyone to sink into them for an afternoon of reading and watching the bird's flit through the trees in their graceful dance. Here, it was easy to find moments of peace and relaxation in this peaceful home, away from the hustle and bustle of a city.

"A little early, aren't we?"

"I'm sorry, Rotherkin," replied Celahir. "That we've called at this unearthly hour, but it was urgent."

"I see you've brought the entire clan," Rotherkin, a wise and weathered wizard, peered at the four individuals standing behind Celahir. His eyes scanned each face, studying their expressions and gauging their intentions. A midnight mist swirled around them, adding an air of mystery to the scene.

"Yes. I'm afraid my refusal of this company here wasn't heard, for since their fathers and my harsh words, they now desire to help their mother's dilemma."

"It appears the wrongs of a mother can bring many changes."

"Yes, I am well aware of their actions," replied Celahir with a hint of frustration. "But I cannot fault them entirely. They are young and eager to prove themselves, just as their father once was."

Rotherkin nodded knowingly. "Indeed, the sins of the past have a way of shaping the future. Your refusal seems to have only fuelled their determination to right the wrongs done to their mother."

"You know of their doing!"

"Celahir, I know more than you think. However, for now, you should accept their sadness as repayment. Now, come, come into my house," the wizard opened his front door. The hour the royal family Orian entered Rotherkin's house was barely less than three minutes past midnight. Once everyone was seated, Celahir's nephew Alexander stood by the window.

"So, will you tell me why you've decided to have this meeting?"

"Secrecy," Celahir cast his eyesight to Rotherkin, who had just asked that question, "That's what I need."

"You've no fear of wondering ears hearing words," laughed Rotherkin.

"We will if we have a midnight stalker strolling our streets."

"These walls are so thick that even a wild stray borra couldn't smash through them."

"I should hope not!" uttered Lenith. "Even the thought of one sends chills down my back. Could you imagine the devastation, the horrors of seeing that happen, just—"

"You shouldn't worry," Lathlorn smiled. "It will never happen."

"Don't suppose their feet will never tread this way," Rotherkin gave him a glance with his brown eyes. "Your kind words to your brother are not protected words."

Lathlorn's smile faltered as he considered Rotherkin's words. He had always been optimistic, believing in people's inherent goodness and hoping for the best outcomes. But Rotherkin, with his piercing gaze and cynical nature, often brought him back to reality. "You may be right," Lathlorn admitted, his voice tinged with a hint of uncertainty. "We can never truly predict what lies ahead."

Rotherkin nodded knowingly, his expression softening just a touch. "Indeed, my friend. It is wise to remain cautious and prepared for any eventuality. The world is full of surprises, both pleasant and treacherous."

Lathlorn sighed, his mind wandering to the countless tales of unforeseen dangers befalling even the most peaceful realms. He knew that their idyllic haven was not exempt from such possibilities.

"It's true," Alexander joined in. "Only last year, for the first time in history, they trod upon the plains of Neatles. That frightened everyone; they were lucky to be pushed back before their feet touched Volarie."

"See what I mean," Rotherkin got up from his seat.

Celahir cleared his throat. "I wish to—"

As if he knew what he was about to say, Rotherkin interrupted him, "I know; the portal needs healing."

Celahir's eyes widened in surprise. He had expected resistance or scepticism from Rotherkin, but the wizard seemed one step ahead. It was as if Rotherkin had been pondering the same issue for quite some time. "How did you—" Celahir began, his voice trailing off.

Rotherkin chuckled softly, a knowing smile playing on his lips. "My dear friend, when you've lived as long as I have, you learn to anticipate certain things," his voice filled with a hint of wisdom.

"So can you do it," asked Lathlorn. "Can you close it, but from their side only, so those from the other side cannot gain access?"

"It's been long since I cast a spell like that. I'll need the portal in my sights."

"We have a human," uttered Celahir, "To pass through it."

"You have the human still!" Rotherkin looked shocked.

"We do, on one of our prison cells."

"A human, to pass through the portal? I've never done it that way before." Rotherkin's eyes widened with a mix of concern and curiosity. "Why do you need a human to pass through the portal this time? What purpose does it serve?"

Celahir took a deep breath, racing to find the right words. "Because," he began, his voice filled with determination and uncertainty, "The portal we are dealing with only goes to one other realm, the human one. So, a spell can only close it while a human walks through it."

"I've never heard of that before." Rotherkin's scepticism was evident as he furrowed his brow. "And how can we be sure this human can do it? What if it's all just a myth?"

Celahir paused for a moment, considering Rotherkin's valid concerns. He knew that convincing him would not be an easy task, especially concerning matters involving humans. But he also knew that time was running out, and they had to take a leap of faith. "I understand your doubts, Rotherkin," Celahir replied, his voice steady despite the uncertainty in his heart. "But we have exhausted all other options, and I have done the research. The ancient textbooks in our library speak of this unique connection between humans and that portal, saying only a human can close it permanently."

Rotherkin crossed his arms, still unconvinced. "And what if these texts are nothing more than folklore? We cannot risk everything based on mere legends."

"Then we will find that out after we have taken William from his cell to the portal."

"It's a shame we couldn't take Mother out of there as well at the same time," said Etheryn sadly.

Rotherkin turned his gaze to him and asked, "Have you spoken to her?"

"We're forbidden to cast our eyes upon her," Etheryn said.

"On whose orders does this cruel act come from!"

"Grandmother," synchronized the four kins.

"Then she's forgotten my deed; let bad judgment mist her mind!"

Celahir's mother may have made many mistakes, but that didn't make her any less his mother. Rotherkin's words, though, were too much for Celahir to take. He had never felt so angry and powerless before. In his desperate attempt to defend her honour, he recklessly lashed at Rotherkin, not caring about the consequences. Rotherkin, of course, was not impressed and practically dared Celahir to do something about it.

Celahir could feel his anger burning and was tempted to take him up on his challenge, but at the last second, he remembered the warnings his parents had drilled into him growing up, *'Never do anything without thinking it through first.'* "Don't speak unkindly of my mother!" he angrily replied, "Mother's words and actions were said and done in a moment of madness!"

"Madness is no excuse for such orders!"

"You must forgive her. She lays in a resting stage in her bedroom caused by heated words."

"Then this resting will bring about a turn in your family."

Lenith stood up and asked, "Do you see something coming?"

"I see many things from now, past, and future. But I'll not waste speech on a request of this subject. You've more pressing matters to arrange, the portal."

"The portal?" said Etheryn as if he'd forgotten.

"Yes, do you wish it closed?"

"Of course," Celahir said in a calmer voice, "Do you have a spell you could use?"

"I've got one. When do you wish it?"

"The sooner, the better," replied Lenith.

"Then give me time to learn the spell. Meet me later at the back of Volarie castle with this human today."

"You can do it today!" voiced Alexander in surprise.

"Of course, if one human walked in as yours did, this is an urgent matter that I must solve swiftly."

"Then today it is," Celahir gestured to the kin's to go to the door, "We will assemble with you when the time is ready."

"No; their mother will need their presence before this has finished." The kin's and Celahir looked at Rotherkin with thoughts that were plain to see on their faces. *What's he on about?*

"You don't need to know." Rotherkin smiled. "Just get your human out of his cell, or I'll meet you before you meet me."

So, they did. As they parted ways, Rotherkin hurriedly made his way to the ancient library in the basement of his house. He knew that time was of the essence, and he needed to find the spell to help them. For an hour, Rotherkin tirelessly searched through dusty tomes and fragile scrolls, but Rotherkin's determination never wavered; he was determined to find the solution. Finally, after what felt like an eternity, Rotherkin stumbled upon a worn-out book tucked away in a corner.

As he carefully pulled the book from its hiding place, a cloud of dust erupted into the air, causing Rotherkin to cough and blink rapidly. He wiped away the grime that had settled on the cover, revealing faded gold lettering that read '*Book of Polenua*.' Rotherkin opened the book with trembling hands, its pages crackling with age, words written in a language he had not seen in many years, their old Etherole tongue filled with intricate symbols and cryptic diagrams. Undeterred by the complexity, he delved into the book for a specific spell to close a portal. With unwavering determination, Rotherkin turned page after page, his fingers tracing the faded ink as if trying to absorb its wisdom. He knew that closing a portal required immense precision and understanding of the magical forces at play. It was not a task to be taken lightly, for even the slightest mistake could have catastrophic consequences. Then he found it. The text spoke of an intricate ritual involving a delicate balance of elemental energies and a profound connection to the ethereal realm.

Rotherkin's eyes widened as he realized what lay before him; this was no ordinary spell; it was a complex web of incantations and gestures that required utmost precision. With trembling hands, Rotherkin reached for his worn leather satchel, carefully retrieving his collection of arcane tools. Each instrument had been meticulously crafted over centuries, infused with his magic, and imbued with protective enchantments. He knew that only by employing every resource at his disposal could he hope to succeed in this task.

"Here we go again," Rotherkin sighed as he began to leave his library. As he stepped away, Rotherkin's eyes scanned his library, lined with towering bookshelves with ancient tomes and scrolls; this was his sanctuary, where he had spent countless hours studying and unravelling the mysteries of the magic. But now, duty called him beyond these familiar walls.

Chapter 28

Life Begin's to Fade

Elensar stood in a cold, dimly lit room atop a narrow, steep, solitary spire for almost an hour. He was on the brink of making a decision that could change the fate of his entire family. This spire room was the only place he felt he could be in deep thought without anyone disturbing him. He looked at his kingdom, full of proud cities and lush plains teeming with life. He thought of the people who lay beneath the clouds, their faith, hope, and courage to get through life despite its challenges. He closed his eyes and let out a deep breath.

"Your Highness, your presence is urgently required in the dungeons."

When those urgent-sounding words entered Elensar's ears, he turned around and saw a guard standing in the doorway. Elensar's heart skipped a beat as he registered the guard's grave expression. The dungeons were not a place he frequented often without cause to do so, and the urgency in the guard's voice only deepened his concern. Without wasting another moment, he followed the guard through the dimly lit corridors of the castle. The air grew colder, and an eerie silence enveloped them, broken only by their echoing footsteps. Thoughts raced through his mind, wondering what could have warranted such urgency.

"She's been refusing to eat lately, Your Highness," the guard told him as they fled to the lower levels. "The dungeon guards think she may have gone too far this time."

"Oh, Valar!" Elensar muttered, immediately recognizing the significance of those words. "Why didn't you force her to eat then," he angrily replied.

The guard glanced back at Elensar, his expression filled with guilt and remorse. "We tried," he explained, his voice laced with regret. "But Amelia is strong-willed and refused any sustenance we offered her. She claimed she didn't deserve it."

"Then why didn't you inform me earlier?" Elensar demanded, his voice filled with frustration and worry. "I could have intervened before it got this far."

The guard's eyes flickered with remorse as he tried to explain himself amidst their frantic escape. "Your Highness," he began, his voice tinged with regret, "We didn't want to trouble you unnecessarily."

Elensar's frustration grew, his brows furrowing as he struggled to comprehend the guard's reasoning. "Unnecessarily? Amelia's well-being is necessary," he snapped, his voice laced with anger and concern. "She is my wife, and her life is of utmost importance to me."

The guard lowered his gaze, realizing the gravity of their mistake. "I understand now, Your Highness," he murmured, his voice heavy with guilt. "We were wrong to assume that we could manage this situation alone. We underestimated the depth of Amelia's stubbornness and her refusal to accept help."

Elensar took a deep breath, attempting to regain his composure amidst the chaos surrounding them. He knew that time was running out, and they needed to get to Amelia before it was too late. They raced faster; the journey to the dungeons was short but mentally disorienting as Elensar tried to formulate the best way to save his wife. His plan was taking shape in his mind when he reached the dungeons and saw his wife, faded from her deprivation but still defiantly refusing to eat. Elensar could feel his temper rising, but he quickly calmed himself and reminded himself this was not the time for rash action. Elensar's worry and anguish were palpable in the air as he knelt by the bedside of his beloved Amelia. The royal guard had left her in the castle's coldest room, one with no light or comfort, and it had left the Elensar's heart heavy with despair. He gently placed his hand upon the brown blanket that covered her still body, calling out her name in a trembling, heartbroken voice. Still, there was no reaction. Her eyes were closed, and her skin was an unsettling shade of pale.

Enraged, he turned to face the guard standing near him, tears of regret and sadness clouding his vision, and shouted with a force that permeated the desolation of the room. "Why have you left my wife in the shadows!" His question echoed unanswered in the air as he tightened his grip on Amelia's blanket, his heart aching with grief.

"I didn't, Your Highness!"

"Didn't I tell you there are to be no shadows in here!"

"You did, I told the dungeon guards."

"Then where's the bloody light!" His voice trembled with frustration as he scanned the dimly lit chamber. The flickering torches on the stone walls barely provided enough illumination to make out the outlines of the cell. It starkly contrasted the opulence and grandeur that usually adorned the castle.

The guard nervously wrung his hands. "I—I don't know, Your Highness," he stammered, his eyes darting around for an explanation. "A guard down here earlier said they'd lit the lights, but it seems something is amiss."

"Find someone who can fix this immediately!" he commanded; his voice laced with urgency. "I want every corner of this cell lit up like daylight here."

"Yes, Your Highness."

"What are you standing there for? Go and get it sorted!"

"Yes, Your Highness," the guard turned and left the room.

Elensar's attention immediately returned to his wife, words spoken in a soft tone. "It's all right, my love. I understand if you don't want to talk, but I must insist you eat. Please, just a little something to keep your strength. I will make it for you if you'd like, or I could bring something from outside that you enjoy. I want you to be healthy."

His hand gave a few more gentle strokes to comfort her. He knew nothing he could do or say would make up for this injustice, but Elensar wanted her to know he had her back. Amelia shifted a little. Seconds later, she was motionless again. A hand moved to her face covered by the brown blanket; he pulled it downward. Elensar had a heavy heart as he surveyed the scene now before him. There, laid out before him on an old dirty rug, was the form of an older woman, her skin pale and her breath shallow, her hair like snow cut short and ragged. Tears welled up in Elensar's eyes as he looked down at Amelia, his hands lightly touched on her head. The sad truth that this could be their last transaction together suddenly sprung into his thoughts. At that moment, the guard returned to the room; he heard the guard gasp and saw him drop the candles to the floor.

Elensar yelled at him. "You—" he yelled louder, "What's happened! What have you done here!"

"Your Highness, I knew nothing of this; it's not my job to—" His voice halted as Elensar's figure rose and approached him.

"You," a hand reached out, grabbed him by the neck, pushed him to stand against the stone-cold wall, his face inches away from the guards, "If you think I'm going to believe lies, you'd better think fast!"

"I tell no lies!"

"Yet you've shown me nothing to prove otherwise!"

"I can't give you proof other than what I've said—"

"That you've no hand in this; it's so easy to lie when faced with danger, isn't it!" he replied angrily, "Now try to prove to me otherwise."

"I can't!"

"Then you must pay the consequences of lying to a royal!" Elensar squeezed his neck tighter.

Hearing the commotion coming from the cell, a group of guards quickly made their way down the long, narrow corridor, and upon entering the cell, one of the guards immediately rushed over and firmly grabbed Elensar around the waist, carefully but firmly yanking him away from the guard he had been attacking. The guard then pulled him swiftly into the hallway. "Your Highness," one guard attempted to say, "Reathern knew nothing of this: he's—"

"I don't care!" Elensar screamed again, striking a foot out to kick one of the guards near him, "Get your hands off me!"

"Grab his arm!" shouted a guard behind him, "Watch out!" Another guard, Korlern, stepped forward and grabbed Elensar's arm.

Elensar screamed in pain but fought back with as much strength as possible. He was determined to break free, but the guards held tight, not wavering in their grip. No one seemed to flinch as Elensar's struggles intensified, except for one guard who stepped forward to help Korlern. Finally, Elensar stopped fighting and looked at the guards in exasperation. He was exhausted, and he hadn't taken notice of how many guards had surrounded him. "I don't care!" he muttered angrily as the guards continued to keep him in their grasp, "You can't hold me down forever." Someone struck him from behind, hooking him by a foot around his knee. He had no idea what was going on as he was flung up against a guard before being quickly spun around and held captive again.

"Your Highness, please!"

Elensar freed himself, but before he lunged at another guard, they sent him crashing to the ground with the flick of a guard's leg. He rose swiftly, "Come on! Let's see what you've got!"

One guard grabbed him, spun him around, and trapped him to himself by threading his arms under his armpits. Now placed into a locked standing position, Elensar flicked his head back and cracked the guard's nose, making the guard scream in pain.

"That's right, you!" he shouted while struggling to be freed. "Play with me; you get hurt! Badly!"

"If you'd just behave," they ripped one of his arms backward, "We wouldn't have to do this, would we?"

While the guard held Elensar's arm, another guard came over and kicked Elensar in the knee; he lunged forward at them again. That sudden movement caused more than just one guard to respond; now, five held him in their grasp. With a surge of adrenaline, Elensar summoned every ounce of strength within him. He twisted and turned, desperately trying to loosen their grip. But the guards were well-trained and persistent in their task. Their combined force was overwhelming, rendering him powerless against their hold. Elensar's resistance and the guards' resolve to subdue him intensified. They tightened their grip on his arms, causing sharp waves of pain to shoot through his body. Yet, he refused to give in; he couldn't afford to let them win.

"You won't be released until you calm down!" One of the guards snarled, his voice laced with frustration.

Elensar's eyes burned with defiance as he glared back at the guard, his breaths coming in ragged gasps. Elensar's chest heaved as he struggled against the firm grip of the guards. The pain from the knee strike radiated through his body, but his determination to break free only intensified. With a surge of adrenaline, he mustered all his strength and attempted to wrench himself out of their grasp. "Let me go!" Elensar growled, his voice strained with defiance. His eyes blazed with anger and desperation as he fought against the overwhelming force restraining him. Each guard held on tightly, their combined strength making it nearly impossible for him to break free. "Get off me!"

"Shouting will accomplish nothing!" They forced Elensar to kneel on the stone floor, his head pushed forward by a hand on the back. "If you want to be released, you must calm down!" The guards were relentless, their grip on his arms unyielding.

Elensar felt his arms ripped upwards again; this time, it hurt, making him scream in pain. As his scream echoed through the room, he could feel the intensity of the pain intensify. The agonizing torment seemed to fuel his anger, igniting a fire within him.

"It's not our doing," one guard said, which was anyone's guess. "When we checked on her, we found her like this!"

"You're a liar! You are all liars!" Again, they pulled Elensar's arms upwards, making him scream even more loudly.

"You need to calm down!" One guard ordered. "We're just following orders," another guard said, trying to justify their actions. "We don't make the rules here."

Elensar's eyes darted from one guard to another, his face contorted with pain and anger. He struggled against their restraints, desperate to break free from their grip. "You expect me to believe that?" Elensar spat, his voice filled with defiance.

The guards exchanged uneasy glances, unsure of how to respond. They understood Elensar had every right to be furious. But they also knew that their own lives depended on following orders. Elensar had always been a passionate individual, but this outburst seemed different. An unsettling determination in his eyes made them question if they should just let him go.

Elensar lay on the cold, stone-paved floor in the dungeon, forcedly held down by the guards. He felt utterly helpless and barely hanging on to his last hopes. Through an open cell door, he could see the figure of Amelia, asleep on her bed, unmoved since he had seen her last. A tear streamed down his face as he said his following words. "You knew of this; that's why you wouldn't let me in, wasn't it!"

"You weren't allowed in because the Queen ordered it," a guard near him said.

"Then you should've disobeyed her instructions!"

"We can't go against orders from the Queen."

"Elensar, is that you!"

Amelia's voice entered his ears, making his eyes dart to her cell doorway. Its open position gave him a view of her trying to lift her head.

"Elensar, they've taken William!" she raised her head to see what was going on; lifting it had been heavy, so it fell against the mattress. "Please, please, where are you!"

"Valar!" Elensar cried; Amelia's weakened, frail words limpened his struggles, "Please, just let me go to her!" He gave one more effort to free himself, "Let me go, I beg of you, please!" They released him quickly. He went straight into the cell, straight over to the straw bed. "My love, I tried everything to set you free," and he had. He had used every means possible to have her released- beseeching the guards, the cell keeper, and even his mother. "I should have just come to you, taken you out of here myself," he cried, lifting her to himself, "Valar, if only I knew, I swear, I'd have come earlier!"

"Elensar, I can't see."

"It's the darkness that shuts your view out, that's all," he turned his head and shouted to the guards, "Give her light!" The guard quickly fetched the light from a candle and handed it to him; in return, he held it near to gaze upon her old face. When he moved it from side to side, she wasn't responsive to it. He sighed and placed the candle on the floor.

"Elensar, I can't breathe in here!"

"Speak not like this," he cradled her to his chest, "Don't disappear from me," he looked at the guards, "I'm taking her out of here!" he wrapped her up in his arms, picked her up, "Don't halt my steps."

They didn't, not even when another guard came rushing down the long corridor and stopped before him. "Your Highness, the Queen, your mother, she's dead!" the guard exclaimed urgently.

Elensar merely stayed quiet, taking in the news with a stony face. In the background, he could hear scurrying around, whispering voices coming from the cells as he passed them, reminding him why he was there. He was here to ensure Amelia's safety. With an almost satisfied voice, he raised his chin and said, "Good, I'm glad she is!"

Chapter 29

Farewell William

The bridges he had seen crossing over the dry riverbeds from high up in the sky while flying were now nothing more than rusting pieces of metal. Paths he'd seen when he first arrived no longer joined the collapsed buildings, he had seen but were piles of rubble. The fields once filled with corn, wheat, and barley were now large burnt fields, void of any life. Had something happened here that William didn't know about while locked up in the dungeon? William's eyes shifted to the sky, and he noticed a strange sight. The sky was empty of any birds or other animals. He felt an odd sense of emptiness but saw the oak tree surrounded by smaller trees in the distance. The branches of the trees were full of colour and life. How could this be when everything else around him looked dead? He knew this was the same oak tree they had flown over a few months ago, and he couldn't believe the transformation. He had never expected to see such destruction, yet here it was.

"You," William heard that call, making him turn his attention to look behind. He saw a figure around his height but portlier in stature. On his face, he had a long beard with metal beads threaded through strands of facial hair. He watched the figure dismount from his horse, walk toward him, then ask, "What's your name?"

"William Defer," he replied, his voice steady but curiosity evident in his eyes. The figure studied him momentarily, his piercing gaze searching for something beyond a name.

"William Defer," the stranger repeated as if testing the sound of the name on his tongue. "A strong name indeed. My name is Rotherkin. Tell me, William Defer, do you know why you are here?"

"Home, you're sending me home."

"And you know how this will happen?"

"I do, through a portal." Today, William was to experience dimensional travelling for a second time. He was nervous but in a different way from the first time. William had stepped through the portal once before, daring to explore the unknown on the other side, bringing information he thought would save them from intruders. But this time would be different. This time, he was going home.

"You're right, you will be going through a portal," said Rotherkin. "But also, half wrong."

"What do you mean I'm half wrong?" William furrowed his brow, confusion etched across his face. He had expected a straightforward answer, but now his words hung in the air, leaving William uncertain.

Rotherkin's eyes twinkled with mischief and wisdom as he leaned closer to William. "You see, my young human," he began, his voice laced with intrigue, "The portal you are about to enter will indeed transport you to another realm, your home. However, it won't be an ordinary journey."

A surge of curiosity coursed through William's veins as he leaned in closer, eager to unravel the mystery. "What makes this departure different?" he asked, his voice tinged with anticipation.

Rotherkin's lips curled into a mischievous smile before he continued. "This portal will transport your physical form and take your memories."

"My memories?"

"Yes. Did you think you would take the memories of this land with you?" Rotherkin's voice dripped with a sinister delight as he revelled in the shock on William's face. The mischievous glint in his eyes grew more pronounced.

"But—But why would you want my memories?" stammered William, his mind racing to comprehend the implications of Rotherkin's revelation.

"Your home is part of the memory of this land; therefore, you'll not be going home. Instead, you'll walk in your land with a new memory."

"A new memory, I don't understand!"

"Others have walked with a loss of memory in your world."

"That's probably due to a situation that caused them to forget."

"Not always."

"Not always?"

"Perhaps it was a spell cast to make them forget this realm."

"What are you on about? They walked into this land; you wiped their minds out of the memory of here?"

"Yes, you humans are so easily fixed."

William was perplexed. He had always known that some individuals had lost their memories after accidents, comas, or other life-altering situations in his human world. Still, he had never considered the possibility of intentional manipulation. As his mind raced to comprehend Rotherkin's revelation, William couldn't help but feel a sense of unease creeping up his spine. The idea that someone or something could deliberately erase memories of unsuspecting wanderers seemed sinister and powerful.

"But why would anyone do such a thing?" William finally managed to ask, his voice laced with curiosity and concern. "Isn't that a violation of one's free will?" William questioned, his brow furrowing with a mix of scepticism and apprehension. "To manipulate someone's memories without their consent. It feels like crossing a line."

Rotherkin's eyes fixed on William as if searching for something within him. "Free will is a complex concept," he replied, "Sometimes sacrifices must be made to safeguard the greater good."

A shiver ran down William's spine as he contemplated the weight of Rotherkin's words. "Well, you won't take mine so easily!"

"It's already starting."

"I feel no different."

"What's the last thing you remember?"

"I—" William scratched his head, "I can't remember now!"

"Do you remember him?" he pointed to a tall, blonde-haired male individual, beautiful to look at and dressed in a dark brown riding cloak, standing near the horses.

William watched as this exact figure started to walk towards them, his mind racing to recall any memories of him. But try as he might, he couldn't conjure up a single image or recollection. Frustration crept into his voice as he replied, "No, I don't remember him. Who is he?"

Piercing blue eyes met William's gaze, a hint of concern flickering across his face. "I am Prince Celahir of Volarie," he introduced himself calmly. "We have seen and spoken to each other before, but the forgotten spell has befallen you."

"Yes, it has," replied Rotherkin, "But he seems more stubborn in keeping something from me."

"I'm not!"

"Celahir, can you see anything hidden inside him, read his thoughts?"

Celahir stared at William for a few minutes. His piercing gaze bore into William's eyes, his mind reaching out to explore the depths of the man's thoughts. But as he delved into William's thoughts, Celahir encountered an unexpected barrier. It was as if a dense fog had settled within William's mind, obscuring his true intentions, and shielding him from prying eyes. Frustration flickered across Celahir's face as he realized that there was something more to this man than met the eye. His abilities were usually unparalleled, allowing him to unravel even the most complex minds. Yet here stood William, an enigma shrouded in mystery. With a deep breath, Celahir refocused his concentration, determined to penetrate through the fog that veiled William's thoughts.

Celahir probed deeper, searching for any hidden memories or concealed motives that might explain this peculiar resistance, and then something came forward, making him arch an eyebrow. "I see you still hold something back in your mind, William; perhaps it may feel like a distant memory to you."

"I—I—"

"I see it now," Celahir turned, then spoke to Rotherkin, "But he needs to tell me himself before I can utter it to you; otherwise, I'll just see it like a dream with lies inside it."

"I'll tell you nothing because there is nothing!"

Celahir turned to him, "Dig deep, William; you'll see it for yourself."

"I—I—"

"I know it's hard to believe," Celahir continued, his voice filled with conviction. "But trust me, there is something buried deep within you that you must tell me otherwise, you leave someone in danger."

"Someone?"

"Speak about what you've seen happening while in your cell."

"I've seen nothing."

"What did your eyes see?"

"I told you; they saw nothing."

Rotherkin turned, walked away, and walked to the portal carrying a bag in his left hand, a bag of magical instruments. As Rotherkin approached the portal, he slowly opened his bag containing various magical tools carefully chosen for their specific purposes, then placed them on the grass by his feet. Each item had been meticulously crafted and imbued with ancient spells, ready to aid him in sending William back home and permanently closing the portal on the human side from his side.

Celahir didn't follow him; instead, he said to William, "Why did you hold a dream vision in your mind of an old Amelia?" he walked up to him, "You don't have much time for that dream to linger, so tell quickly. What made you frightened Amelia wouldn't live for much longer?" William looked confused, so Celahir hinted to remember it: "I see a bottle, William, a special bottle."

Williams's eyes suddenly enlarged. "Holy cow! That's it! She's keeping a secret, a medical problem needing help. The Queen refused a magical bottle from the twins Elysium and Borthron."

"Their wizards?" Celahir asked, his curiosity piqued.

"No, not wizards," Williams clarified, his excitement palpable. "They are inventors, carriers of someone's deeds."

"Whose deeds?"

"I can't remember that. All I remember is Amelia liked that bottle, or does she need it," William was trying again to drag the memories of something he couldn't fully remember forward. When one of them did, it made him pant his following words: "Oh god! Does she need that medicine desperately, or was it the twins? Oh god, try to remember William, oh god! She'll die."

"She'll die!"

"The twins, the medicine, oh god, which one!" William's mind raced as panic set in. The weight of the situation bore down on him, his heart pounding in his chest. He desperately tried to recall the details, searching for clues to guide him towards the right decision. He closed his eyes, attempting to shut out the chaos around him and focus on what he knew.

"William, come on, which one?"

"Oh god, which one makes her live longer."

"Is it the medicine?"

"Celahir!" shouted Rotherkin. "Bring the human here,"

The portal appeared bigger before them all, like an opening to another realm. The sand, dust, grey, white, and black swirled around without thought or rhyme, creating an enchanting scene of a timeless void before them.

"William, is there any more you remember?" Celahir began quickly walking him to the portal. "Anything at all you remember?" Celahir asked again, his voice filled with urgency. He could sense the weight of responsibility on his shoulders, knowing their success hinged on gathering as much information as possible.

"No, only small snippets."

"Stand here," Rotherkin pointed to an area near the portal. "Step forward!" shouted Rotherkin as the wind picked up around them. "William! Come on; there isn't much time!"

William looked around as if he were afraid of going into the portal. So he should be, for the next minute, a crackling of lightning entered the portal he was supposed to enter. William stepped back in fright, then saw something. He noticed a single leaf floating in the wind, its bright red colour standing out against the grey and brown backdrop. If William had more time, he would have found out what had caused this, but he didn't have the time.

"Enter!" shouted Rotherkin, giving a quick shove on his back.

Just as Rotherkin did that to him, William remembered what he'd been trying to tell them. He turned his head around and shouted, "Your Queen! She visited Amelia in the cell; Amelia will die soon!"

William felt the energy ripple through his body as he stepped through, the portal sucking him in. It was like being swallowed into another reality, and he felt a mixture of fear and excitement as he began to fall through the darkness. Suddenly, a bright light filled the dark void, and William saw a breathtaking sight of the peaceful forest from a distance. Barely seconds later, William stood outside the portal; he took in the moment for a few more seconds.

The portal began to close behind William; he stepped forward and fell to his knees. Damp grass was under William's knees, but he didn't care. He spread his arms and kissed the ground, then wept so that a mixture of overwhelming joy and relief washed over him like gentle summer rain. For months, William had dreamt of this moment - the moment he would return to his homeland. The weight of nostalgia and longing had burdened his heart during those months spent in the cell, but now, as he knelt on the familiar soil, all those emotions converged into an indescribable sensation. As his tears mingled with the earth beneath him, memories flooded back to him like a vibrant tapestry. He recalled his home, Northline, with the red roof, the warmth and coziness of a soft bed, and the laughter of Tim, his apprentice, echoing through the halls.

With trembling hands, William scooped up a handful of soil, feeling its gritty texture slip through his fingers. It was as if he could feel the pulse of his homeland coursing through it, connecting him to every inch of this sacred land. The weight of his past struggles seemed to dissipate with each handful William held, replaced by a renewed sense of belonging. As he rose to his feet, William surveyed the landscape before him. The rolling hills stretched before him like an endless green carpet, dotted with wildflowers swaying gently in the breeze. The sights and sounds enveloped him like a comforting embrace, whispering tales of resilience and hope. He took a deep breath, inhaling the crisp air, then realized he wasn't standing in Cutton Folly forest; William wasn't in any forest. He was standing in the middle of a field!

Confusion washed over William as he tried to make sense of his surroundings. How did he end up in this vast field? He should have been in the dark, damp Cutton Folly forest! The towering trees and moss-covered ground seemed like a distant memory now. As he turned in a slow circle, William noticed something peculiar. There were no signs of civilization anywhere. No roads, buildings, or telephone poles were in sight. It was as if he had stumbled upon a forgotten corner of the world, untouched by human hands. A sense of both awe and trepidation filled his heart. The beauty of the landscape was undeniable, but the isolation made him feel vulnerable. He wondered how far away from civilization he was and if anyone would come looking for him.

"Hello," William called out for someone to hear him. No one replied. This time, he bellowed, "Hello!"

Still, there was no response. The echoes of William's voice faded into the vastness of the untouched wilderness surrounding him. The silence only deepened his unease, intensifying the feeling of isolation that seemed to suffocate him.

William took a moment to absorb his surroundings once more but in depth. Towering mountains loomed in the distance, their snow-capped peaks piercing the clear blue sky. Lush green forests stretched as far as the eye could see, with a river snaking through the valley below. It was a breathtaking sight that would have filled him with wonder under different circumstances. But now, standing alone in this unfamiliar territory, William couldn't help but feel a growing sense of dread. The realization sank in that he had been sent to the wrong location, far away from any signs of civilization or human presence.

Panic began to creep into his thoughts as he questioned his decision to explore this remote corner of the world, but he did. William moved one foot in front of the other and headed across the field he was in. The silence was deafening, broken only by the distant howl of a lone wolf. William's heart pounded in his chest, each beat echoing his growing unease. As he trudged forward, the ground beneath his feet became increasingly uneven and treacherous. With every step, William's imagination conjured up vivid images of wild beasts and unseen perils that awaited him. The once enticing allure of adventure now seemed like a foolish endeavour. Then, out of nowhere, a house came into view with a red roof that stood out against the bleak landscape of the nothingness around it. It was a beacon of hope amidst the uncertainty, a glimmer of civilization in this desolate place. William's eyes opened wider as he came closer; it was his red-roofed house! Northline.

The jubilation of seeing his Northline in the distance sent William's emotions into overdrive. As he stood there, overwhelmed by the whirlwind of emotions, William couldn't help but stop it from happening. His laughter filled the air with a sense of joy and release; just as quickly as his laughter erupted, tears welled up in his eyes, threatening to spill over, all to be repeated repeatedly until it suddenly stopped for a moment. Now, he was starting to run.

As William hurriedly made his way home, his laughter echoed through the stillness surrounding him. Each stumble and fall only fuelled his determination, as he knew he was finally nearing safety. With each step closer to his sanctuary, a sense of relief washed over him like a soothing balm. The adrenaline coursing through his veins mixed with an overwhelming joy that he couldn't contain. His heart pounded in sync with his footsteps, creating a rhythm that propelled him forward. As William approached Northline, his heart raced with disbelief and relief. How could it be? Yet here it stood, his sanctuary amid the desolation.

Memories flooded back as he stepped onto a path leading to the front door. It was as if time had stood still in this forgotten corner of the world. With trembling hands, William reached for the doorknob, half-expecting it to vanish like a mirage. But it held firm to his touch, and he pushed open the door to reveal a cold living room interior. As William stepped into the lonely living room, a chill ran down his spine, matching the frigid atmosphere that engulfed the space. The air felt heavy with abandonment, as if time had stood still in this forsaken place. Dust particles danced in the dim light that filtered through tattered curtains, casting eerie shadows on the worn-out, unfamiliar furniture. His eyes scanned the room, searching for remnants of his life that once filled these walls. A faded, unknown family portrait hung crookedly on the cracked wall, its subjects frozen in joy and togetherness.

William's heart sank as he realized that this room had once been a sanctuary for laughter and love, now reduced to a haunting memory not of his life but of someone else. For a moment, a thought did cross his mind. Maybe he had been gone longer than he thought, that instead of months, perhaps it was a lot of years. But then that would mean someone must have put his beloved house up for sale. Who would have done that? Tim? Perhaps he knew about those papers and his plans to find this secret world he'd just come from. Yes, it must have been Tim. William then got angry thinking all that; he had never permitted Tim to do that!

"Wait till I get a hold of you!" William angrily cursed him out loud. "I'll swipe more than your head this time!"

William continued walking around as if to dull the anger growing inside. The silence was deafening, broken only by the faint sound of wind whistling through cracks in the window frames. He cautiously moved forward, his footsteps echoing against the barren floorboards. A few old newspapers scattered on the floor; William picked one up out of curiosity. As he unfolded the yellowed pages, a headline caught his eye: '*Local Mystery Still Remains Unsolved; after two hundred years, this baffling case still haunts Cutton Folly's residents.*' Under this was a faded image of a male in his thirties with a dark beard.

William quickly dropped the newspaper out of his hand. His heart raced as he stared at the faded image, his face staring back at him from the pages of a newspaper that was two centuries old. Confusion and disbelief washed over him, leaving him with unease that seemed to seep into his very bones. How could this be possible? How could there be a newspaper article about his disappearance from two hundred years ago?

His mind began to run around, figuring dates out. He left in 2068 to seek the Shalimar out, so going by this paper, 2268 or possibly another one hundred years also added to that!

William's mind began to race with questions. Was this some elaborate prank? A well-crafted forgery? Or was there something more inexplicable at play? He couldn't deny the uncanny resemblance between himself and the man in the picture, down to the minor details. With trembling hands, he picked up the newspaper again, carefully examining every word and image on its fragile pages.

The mysterious vanishing of William Defer, a new resident who had seemingly vanished without a trace, leaving all belongings inside his house, was back in 2068. Rumours and speculations had swirled around William's disappearance for centuries. Some whispered of foul play, suggesting that he may have fallen victim to jealousy or revenge. Others believed he had stumbled upon something extraordinary—a secret so profound that it forced him into hiding or worse—

William couldn't go on anymore; it was too much. He fell to his knees in sudden despair; he was now alone. Tim had long passed on, and so had everyone he ever knew. Tim's mother who made a delicious steak and kidney pie. Tim's sister, Mary, who had a sweet spot for him. The lady in the garage who served him a sweet smile when he paid for his petrol, the young woman in the grocery store on the till who always tried to get his number. The older man who sat on the park bench every other morning, sharing stories of his youth. They were all gone, leaving William feeling like a solitary figure in a world that had moved on without him. As he knelt there, tears streaming down his face, memories flooded his mind. He remembered the laughter he shared with them all, the conversations that filled his days with warmth and purpose. Each person had left an indelible mark on his heart, reminding him of life's beauty and joy. Now, who was he to talk to, an empty house that now held no meaning to him?

Chapter 30

Amelia's Life Medicine

Celahir stood in his brother's bedroom with a guard by his side with bated breath, wondering what his brother Elensar would do with this information now he knew about it. The news of the incident at the portal and William's words before he slipped through the portal; *'Your Queen! She visited Amelia in the cell; Amelia will die soon!'*

Celahir's heart pounded in his chest while he replayed the rest of William's words to his brother. His mind raced, trying to make sense of the implications hidden within William's cryptic message. The weight of his words hung heavily in the air, filling the room with an eerie silence for a few moments afterward. Each sentence seemed to carry a secret, a clue that could unravel Williams's hazed message about Amelia, her medicine, the twin brothers Elysium and Borthron, and Rotherkin's involvement in it all. As Celahir continued speaking with Elensar, he couldn't shake off the feeling that someone other than the guard next to him, Elensar, and himself was listening to them talk. The guard beside him appeared on edge, his eyes darting nervously around the room. Celahir wondered if this unease was merely a reflection of his anxiety or if something more sinister was at play. His thoughts momentarily drifted back to his kinhood days when he and Elensar would spend hours exploring the hidden corners of their ancestral home. They had always been drawn to secrets and riddles, often losing themselves in tales of forgotten treasures and ancient prophecies. But now, it seemed they had a real mystery to solve. The guard shifted as if he were uncomfortable as Celahir spoke again. Celahir glanced at him briefly before returning to the conversation with Elensar.

Elensar's brows furrowed in confusion as he processed the information. "What do you mean medicine!"

"That's what William said, medicine."

"You're joking!" he started to walk towards his brother.

"No, I'm not!"

"You," Elensar asked the guard beside Celahir, "Did you know about this?"

"No, Your Highness, it's the first—" he would've said more, Celahir interrupted him.

"William said she was keeping a secret, a medical problem."

"The medicine was the cure?" Elensar's mind raced as he tried to make sense of the situation. Medicine? A secret medical problem? It all seemed so surreal. He quickened his pace towards his brother, determined to get to the bottom of this. As Celahir approached, Elensar could see the worry etched on his face. He repeated his word. "The medicine was the cure?"

"Yes."

For a second, Elensar turned to Amelia in their bed sleeping; he stared, her gentle breath rising and falling with each peaceful sound sleep. He couldn't help but think of her life's struggles; all he wanted to do was make her happy and healthy. He turned back, a sudden thought dawning on his mind, and said aloud, "It can make her live longer?"

"That's what he said."

"Where did this medicine come from?"

"William said it was from Elysium and Borthron."

"The twins cast a spell for her, not the medicine?"

"No, it's the medicine."

"But you just said—"

"Williams's words were misplaced."

Elensar sighed, "I didn't even know she was using any."

"Well, apparently she was."

He shook his head, turned to look at Amelia again, and turned back, "I don't understand why she didn't tell me?"

"I don't know, Elensar."

"If I knew, I could've helped her."

"How?"

"I could've given it to her while she was in the dungeon."

"I thought you weren't allowed to see her."

"I wasn't."

"Then how could you have given it to her?"

Elensar sighed, frustration etching lines on his forehead. He ran a hand through his dishevelled hair to gather his thoughts. "I have my ways, Celahir," he said, his voice tinged with a hint of secrecy.

Celahir raised an eyebrow, curiosity piqued. "What do you mean? How could you have given it to her if you weren't allowed to see her?"

"I'd have given it to the dungeon guards to give to her."

"Would they have?"

Elensar sighed heavily, "Yes, they would."

Celahir's scepticism deepened. "But even if they did deliver it to her, how could you be sure she received it? The dungeon guards aren't exactly known for their reliability or honesty."

"I gave them the bracelet Mother took away from her."
"And?"
"She's wearing it now."
"Your point is?"
"If I knew about this medicine before, she wouldn't lie there almost lifeless." Elensar's voice trembled with frustration and regret as he continued, "I should have found a way to get her the medicine sooner. It's my fault she suffered for so long."
"But you didn't know, though."
"No, I didn't, but I do now," he sighed deeply, "If I weren't so messed up right now, it'd make me wonder if she's keeping anything else from me." Elensar's mind raced with a whirlwind of emotions. The guilt gnawed at him, consuming, and clouding his judgment. "How many more secrets is she hiding from me?" He said with confusion. Elensar couldn't help but question everything now, wondering if Amelia was hiding any more secrets beneath the surface. "What do you think, brother? Does she have more secrets?"
Celahir replied instantly, "I would say no, brother."
As he watched her fragile form lying motionless on the bed, Elensar's heart ached with regret. He had always prided himself on being attentive and caring, but this incident had shattered his confidence. How could he have missed something so crucial?
"You're not the one standing in my shoes, Celahir, are you?"
"It's just simple confusion taking over, that's all."
"Pretty messed up confusion, more like."
"Then we need to get more answers about this medicine."
"From whom?"
"Amelia."
"I don't think she's in any fit state right now to answer questions."
"But if we let her sleep longer, it might do more damage."
Elensar looked at Amelia again, "I don't know," he replied almost heartrendingly, "Sleep might be the only thing keeping her with us." In his desperation and agony, Elensar was desperate to find some way of helping her that he had neglected to look at. He had been so stressed and desperate to find a solution he never stopped to examine the possibility that the simple act of sleeping could be just the thing to help her get better.
"Or it could send her to him much quicker than you expected."
"What!" he quickly turned his gaze back to Celahir.
"To Mahtan in Seaport Southern Shores."
Elensar's expression suddenly turned to anger. "I don't think so!" he clenched his fists, his anger boiling. The mention of Seaport Southern Shores stirred up painful memories and unresolved emotions. It was a place he had tried to forget that held the spirit of a lost loved one, Tilleryn.

Celahir observed Elensar's reaction, knowing the weight Seaport Southern Shores carried for him. He understood the depth of grief and longing within Elensar's heart. But he also knew that sometimes, facing one's past fear of a place was necessary to place that fear into good use. "The death sleep of old age might be her biggest enemy right now," Celahir replied. "So, you must keep her awake until we've found a cure."

"Damn right, I'm not letting her go to that place."

"Good, that is the attitude you need, brother."

"Then I'm going to have to pretend I know none of this."

"Everything if we're to find out the truth behind William's words. You'll have to pretend as if she told you for the first time."

"I don't understand why we have to pretend," Elensar's voice laced with confusion. "I don't like lying to her either."

"Think of it as helping her along the way to recovery."

"Then I will."

"Don't tell her what we discussed the other day, though."

"What?"

"That sovereign thing."

"Why?"

"She doesn't need to know about that."

"I have no secrets from my wife."

"I understand your sentiment, Elensar," Celahir said, his voice filled with concern. "But sometimes, keeping certain information from our loved ones can be for their good. The burden of knowledge can weigh heavily on someone struggling to recover."

Elensar sighed, conflicted by his brother's words. He had always prided himself on being open and honest with Amelia, believing that transparency was the foundation of their strong relationship. However, he couldn't ignore that Amelia's fragile state might be unable to handle the weight of the truth.

"I know you value honesty above all else," Celahir continued gently. "But consider this. By shielding her from unnecessary worries, you allow her to focus solely on her recovery. It's about protecting her mental well-being."

Elensar nodded slowly, realizing the wisdom in his brother's words. He had witnessed firsthand how Amelia's condition had deteriorated over time. He couldn't bear to see her suffer any longer, and Celahir's suggestion of shielding Amelia from unnecessary worries made sense to him. He knew that honesty was important, but in this case, it seemed like a necessary sacrifice for her mental well-being.

"Elensar, William has gone."

Those words made them both dart their sights to the bed in the room. They saw Amelia lying awake in bed, her frail body trying to move slightly. Elensar's observation of her state from where he stood filled him with a sense of helplessness. Amelia's once vibrant spirit seemed to have dimmed, and her frail body now bore the signs of old age. Elensar went to step forward towards her.

"Brother," Celahir had touched Elensar's arm. "I'll wait here if we need a speedy exit to get anything."

Elensar nodded, his eyes filled with determination. As he approached Amelia's bedside, his heart was heavy with concern. He gently took her frail hand, feeling the delicate bones beneath his touch. The wrinkles on her skin told stories of a life well-lived, but this was a lie, for it had happened in less than half a year. How could someone grow so old in so little time? He was here to find the answer to that question and reverse whatever spell, or disaster had been spun over his beloved wife.

"Elensar!" Amelia called out his name in a weakened way.

Her once vibrant eyes now held a glimmer of sadness, mirroring the pain he felt deep within his soul. Gently, Elensar took her other frail hand in his, feeling the delicate warmth that lingered. "Amelia," he whispered, his voice filled with love and concern. "I'm here, my love. What happened? Why is William gone?"

Her lips quivered as she struggled to find the strength to speak. Her voice was barely a whisper, but every word carried a weight that shook Elensar to his core. "They—They took him," she managed to say, tears welling in her eyes. "The darkness—It came for me."

"I know, my love, but it has gone now."

"Then can I not be released?"

"My love, you can walk by my side for eternity if you want."

"But the dungeons are dark; I won't see to leave it."

"No, my love," he whispered, his voice filled with tenderness. "You are not in your cell anymore. You are safe here with me, in our home." Elensar's words carried a soothing melody, an attempt to anchor her to reality. "Open your eyes," he leaned over, "See where you are."

"I can't!" she cried, "Can't see anything!"

He gently intertwined their fingers, offering comfort and security. "I understand," he murmured, his thumb caressing the back of her hand. "But trust me, my love, you are safe here. You have nothing to fear." He guided her fingers towards his face, encouraging her to explore the contours of his features. "Feel my cheek," he whispered, brushing her hand against his smooth cheek. "Feel the warmth of my skin beneath your fingertips." Elensar hoped that by engaging her sense of touch, she would begin to ground herself in the present moment. As she hesitantly traced the lines of his face, Elensar continued to speak in a soothing tone. "Listen to the sounds around us," he said, gesturing towards the gentle crackling of a nearby fireplace and the distant chirping of birds outside.

"I feel so weak, fragile; why's this happened!" Her head rested against his chest; her body slumped against him, "Rotherkin said I could stray life for longer."

"What do you mean stray life for longer?"
"He assured me my life could linger for longer."
"How?"
"Elensar, I don't know. Please, I'm tired, need sleep."
"It's the sleep of old death that wants you," his fingertips ran over her face, "Tell me of Rotherkin's words, what did you mean, '*Stray of life?*'"
"I went to see him—"
"Why did you see him?"
"He's a wizard," she yawned.
"And?"
"He knows things, medicine."
"Medicine!" he acted surprised, "What medicine are you on about?"
"Nice medicine," Amelia's eyes drooped, "Good medici—"
"Don't, don't slip!" His gaze shot across the room to his brother Celahir as if seeking help with his words, standing beside the guard.
Celahir didn't move from his spot. Instead, he said words to him. "Calm down, brother," Celahir said soothingly, his voice laced with concern. "Amelia is just tired. I know she's been through a lot, but you must be firmer if you want answers."
As the words sank in, frustration and confusion clouded Elensar's mind. How could he suggest being firmer with Amelia? She was already fragile, her spirit worn thin by her trials. The last thing he wanted was to add more pressure, but he knew he had to do it.
Elensar took a deep breath to gather his thoughts to find the right balance between assertiveness and empathy. "Amelia," he began softly, "I know you're tired, and I can see how much you've been through. But we need your help. We're all counting on you to shed light on what's happening." She didn't reply to him. He hesitated for a moment before shaking her to wake her up again. Her face appeared to have woken fully quickly, and her eyes opened. Elensar smiled weakly at her, not expecting her to notice it because of her blindness, then whispered in her ear, "The medicine, speak words to me about this medicine; tell me what it does or what it's done for you."
"But I've already told you about the medicine," Amelia replied hoarsely. "When I was in that place."
"What place?"
"Cell."
Elensar frowned, seemed confused, and repeated her words, "Cell?" That confusion suddenly deepened as Elensar tried to make sense of Amelia's words. How could she remember speaking to him in a place he had never been allowed to visit? Was it possible that she was confused or experiencing some delusion? Curiosity and concern filled Elensar's mind as he leaned closer to Amelia, studying her face for signs of distress or instability. "Amelia," Elensar began cautiously, "I understand

that you believe you were in a cell, but I assure you, I have never seen the inside of it. Can you try to explain what happened there? Maybe we can piece together the missing parts."

"Must we?" Amelia sighed heavily. "I don't want to repeat it all."

"I understand," Elensar said softly with defeat, knowing her tiredness and old age were causing her reluctance to talk in long conversations. "Then why don't you remind me where the medicine comes from, my love."

"Rotherkin buys it, or does he make it? I can't remember."

"Try to remember."

"Perhaps Hildernbyth's brother."

"Amelia, Hildernbyth is a place, you remember," he kissed the top of her head, "We stayed after we were married."

"Ah, I remember, last week, was it not?"

"No," he sighed, "It was well over a thousand years ago."

"You so sweet; you remember Star waiting for us; where is she?"

"Above us, looking down," he moved her so that he could see her blinded gaze, "Amelia, this medicine, tell us about it."

"I want Star," she sighed, "Elensar, I want to see her again."

"Don't say that; you'll see her, but not yet."

Her eyes moved their blind vision away from him, "If I tell you about medicine, will you let me go?"

He placed a small kiss upon her lips, "If you tell us about the medicine, you can sleep for a little while," his following words were mouthed silently to his brother, "Get ready."

"I went to the twin's house."

"And?"

"They gave me this medicine to make me more suitable for you."

"Did they make it, or did Rotherkin make it?"

"Rotherkin, brothers say he no more or make no more."

"When, when did they utter this?"

"I can't remember, before or after tho dungeons."

Then the twins must have the life medicine! He thought to himself*, No, they would've told me. Perhaps they were about to say to her to get it from Rotherkin. Oh, Valar! Rotherkin*!

"Go, Celahir!" He'd shouted. "Go to Rotherkin now!" But Celahir had already left the room and was halfway down the winding stairway before the bedroom door swung shut to its closed position.

As Celahir descended the stairway, his mind raced with urgency. He knew that time was of the essence, and he couldn't afford any delays. The fate of his sister-in-law Amelia rested on his shoulders, and he would stop at nothing to ensure her well-being. As he reached the bottom of the stairs, Celahir's eyes darted around the castle's bustling corridors. Servants hurried past him; their faces filled with concern upon seeing him. Without wasting a moment, he called out to one of them.

"Quickly! Fetch my horse, Fillion!" Celahir commanded, his voice filled with authority. One servant nodded and quickly scurried off to fulfil his request. While waiting for his trusted steed, Fillion, Celahir's mind wandered back to Rotherkin. He'd been in his presence barely less than six hours ago while at the portal. If only he had returned to Volarie, the castle with him after William's departure, he wouldn't have had to go and find him. As he now paced impatiently outside the back door of the castle, memories of their last encounter flooded his mind, and thoughts that made him wonder why, even after hearing what William had said at that portal, Rotherkin had gone back home.

"Your Highness," the sight of a tan steed, Fillion, was walking in front of Celahir, reinless and without a saddle. "Your ride is ready and waiting."

Celahir approached Fillion quickly and gently stroked his mane. The horse seemed calm and obedient, but it was merely a means of transportation. What they truly needed was Rotherkin. Celahir leaped onto his bare back, a hand grasping a few mane strands, his heels tapping against Fillion's sides, urging him forward. The majestic tan stallion responded instantly, his powerful muscles propelling them on with speed. As they galloped out from the small courtyard, then through the lush green meadows on the outskirts of Volarie city, Celahir could feel the wind rushing through his hair, invigorating his senses. Fillion was no ordinary horse; he possessed an otherworldly grace and an uncanny connection with Celahir. Together, they had traversed treacherous terrains and embarked on countless adventures in the past. Fillion seemed to understand Celahir's every command as if they communicated through an unspoken language. With each stride, Celahir could sense the energy emanating from Fillion's body, as if the horse possessed a hidden power unleashed. It was said by rumours, many years ago, that ancient spirits had blessed Fillion, granting him extraordinary abilities beyond any ordinary steed. It wasn't long before Rotherkin's well-lit house came into view; with determination in his steps, Celahir bid Fillion his horse to go faster to get Rotherkin and take him back to heal Amelia at the castle.

While all this had been going on, back at the castle, inside Elensar's bedroom, Elensar heard Amelia say, "Celahir's here?" said Amelia, lifting her head.

"He was, but he's gone now," he replied gently, retaking her hand. "Celahir will be back soon though."

She held her head against his chest, "Your brother here?"

"He wanted to help my love."

"Oh."

Her frail old body leaned into him more for a second as if she were falling asleep or the conversation bored her, but he had to keep her awake until Celahir returned. He gently stroked her thin, silver hair, feeling the fragility of her body against his own, and he knew time was slipping away. With a tender voice, he continued their conversation. "You know what he's like," he whispered, his words barely audible. "He thought his presence could make you smile; after all, he is the joker of this family, isn't he?"

"Yes," a faint smile tugged at the corners of her lips as she reminisced about Celahir, her eyes distant yet filled with warmth. "Celahir has a way of bringing light—" Her voice trailed off, and it seemed she had drifted into another time and place for a moment.

Elensar tightened his embrace around her frail form, desperate to anchor her back to the present. "Stay with me," he pleaded gently. "Amelia, tell me something."

"What," she mumbled that word.

"Anything; tell me something that makes you happy."

"Elensar, please, can I sleep, please."

"Not yet my love; why don't you speak of things to me that'll keep you from slumbering for a while."

"Not now, please," she closed her eyelids, "I'm tired."

Elensar gently brushed a strand of hair away from Amelia's face, his eyes filled with concern. "I understand that you're tired, my love," he whispered, "But talking about things that make you happy might help ease your mind and bring some joy to your weary heart."

Amelia let out a small sigh; her exhaustion was evident in her voice. "I suppose it wouldn't hurt to try," she conceded, letting another sigh escape. "Can I have water? My throat is dry."

He smiled. "Of course," his gaze lifted to the guard standing in the corner, "Can you fetch her some?" the guard nodded and walked out of the room.

"Elensar?"

His gaze lowered to his wife, "Yes, my love."

"I'm sorry for all the trouble I've caused you."

Elensar gently took Amelia's hand in his, reassuringly squeezing it. "Amelia, my love, you have nothing to apologize for," he said softly, his eyes filled with warmth and understanding. "You've been through so much, and I admire your strength and resilience."

"I know I've made mistakes," she continued, her voice barely above a whisper. "I never meant for things to turn out this way."

Elensar leaned closer, his voice filled with tenderness. "Life is full of unexpected twists and turns, my dear," he said gently. "We cannot always control the outcome of our actions or the circumstances we find ourselves in. What matters is how we face them together. And you, my darling wife, have caused no trouble, my love, just a little concern."

"But I have Elensar; I've done things in the past, stupid things," she admitted with a hint of regret. The weight of her past actions seemed to burden her even now.

"Now that I've time to forgive, they're forgiven."

"What do you mean," Amelia asked, a frown growing on her forehead. "Time to forgive?"

"I've offered Celahir the sovereign's sword."

"The sovereign's sword; I thought you were next in line."

"Indeed, I was next in line," Elensar replied to her with a hint of sadness. "But after much reflection and soul-searching, I realized that I need to be with you, care for you."

"But Elensar," she stammered, struggling to find the right words, "The sovereign's sword represents your rightful place as the future ruler. It symbolizes your duty to our people and the legacy of your ancestors. Are you sure about this?"

Elensar took a deep breath, his gaze unwavering as he reached out to gently cup Amelia's face. "Amelia, my love," he said softly, "I have spent countless nights pondering over my destiny and what truly matters in life. And every time, it led me back to you." Elensar paused for a moment before continuing. "Yes, I was next in line for the throne, but now Celahir will sit on it soon and be crowned king instead."

"Soon?" her voice sounded surprised and confused. "I don't understand. Where is your mother, Catreen, the Queen?"

Elensar tried to keep his angry thoughts about his deceased mother out of his following words to her. He took a deep breath, attempting to compose himself before responding to her question.

"My mother passed away unexpectedly," Elensar replied, his voice tinged with fake sadness. "Her sudden demise has left a void in our kingdom, and the responsibility of ruling will now fall upon Celahir."

That news woke her up, making her blind eyes widen with shock as she processed the information. "But—How? What happened to her?" she asked, her voice concerned.

Elensar hesitated momentarily, contemplating whether to reveal the truth about his mother's questionable actions and death. He decided she didn't have to understand the whole situation's complexity. "Mother just fell asleep and woke no more; that's all there is to answer your question."

"My god, Elensar! I'm so sorry!"

"Don't be sad; she had a hand in this doing that makes you lay here."

"But she was your mother!"

"She became no mother to me the day she cast you aside."

"Elensar, she was in your bloodline."

"Bloodline means nothing to me now, Amelia. Love and loyalty are what truly matter," Elensar replied, his voice filled with sadness and anger. "She may have been my mother by blood, but she never acted like one near the end. She abandoned me when I needed her the most."

He saw Amelia reach out and gently place her hand on his, offering him comfort. "I can't imagine how painful that must have been for you, Elensar. To feel rejected by your mother—"

Elensar nodded. "It was devastating, Amelia. But I found solace in knowing that true family is not defined solely by blood relations."

Amelia squeezed his hand tighter, understanding the depth of his words. "I don't understand you sometimes, but you're right."

"I am, and right now, my right place to be is here by my wife's side while Celahir stands in until you're better."

"He always was the helpful sort of person."

"I know. Now, while the guards are fetching your water, I'll tell you stories that came about in our life together," he pulled her to himself. "Will you listen to my words?"

"Yes."

"Then I'll begin with watchful eyes on you as I take us back to our visits to your favourite place—"

"Weath—"

He smiled down at her and laughed a little, "Indeed, Weath and our twins when they were barely a year old—"

Chapter 31

Mother's Favourite Fruit

"But this farmer Tilden, surely he wouldn't mind giving some to us?" asked Lenith.

"Are you mad!" voiced Lathlorn. "You remember the tales about him, don't you?"

Lenith looked at Lathlorn with a puzzled expression. "What tales? I've never heard anything about this farmer Tilden."

Lathlorn sighed, his eyes filled with caution. "Well, let me enlighten you then. They say that Tilden is not like any ordinary farmer. He's known for being fiercely protective of his crops and land. Rumour has it that he guards them day and night, even resorting to extreme measures to keep intruders away."

Lenith's curiosity grew as he leaned in closer. "Extreme measures? What do you mean?"

Lathlorn lowered his voice, creating an air of suspense. "Legend has it that Tilden has set up traps all around his fields, designed to catch anyone who dares to step on his property without permission. Some even claim he has enchanted the traps with magic, making them nearly impossible to escape."

Alexander nodded. "And he hates humans, and by now, I'm sure the whole kingdom knows about our mother."

"That's an understatement; he loathes them." Lathlorn's voice carried a hint of fear. "Rumour also has it that Tilden's hatred for humans stems from a tragic event in his past. They say he lost someone dear to him because of their greed and disregard for nature."

Alexander's eyes widened with realization. "So, he sees himself as a guardian, protecting the land from those who would exploit it?"

Lathlorn nodded solemnly. "Exactly. And if what they say about the enchanted traps is true, we must tread carefully."

Lenith frowned, contemplating their predicament. Desperation had driven them to consider seeking to creep into the notorious farmer Tilden's flourishing crops to steal a few of their mother's favourite fruit.

"I understand his disdain for humans," Lenith said cautiously. "But we have no other choice. It's the only place with the ones we're looking for."

"That's why you're the bait," replied Lathlorn talking to Alexander. "So, we can slip into his orchard and get the apples. In other words, we use his hospitality as a diversion for us. Now let's get going."

They let Alexander fly into the pebbled courtyard of farmer Tilden's dwelling, watched as he landed his horse, dismounted, walked to the door, and knocked upon it. When the door opened, Alexander's figure fainted before the farmer's eyes. As the farmer rushed to catch Alexander, his companions seized the opportunity to slip past him unnoticed. They swiftly approached the orchard, their hearts pounding with excitement and anticipation. The plan was simple yet risky - while the farmer was preoccupied with attending to Alexander, they would gather as many apples as possible and have a hasty retreat. The brothers scrambled through a hedge and a small field before leaping over a wooden fence. While their feet touched the soft grass of the area, they began running faster. It wasn't long before the three brothers spotted their destination, an apple tree with ripe, juicy fruit. A nearby stream's fast-flowing current made a gurgling noise, adding to the various sounds around them.

"Hay, you lot haven't forgotten about me, have you," laughed Alexander, running up to his three brothers in the apple orchard. "I'm here to help get Mother's favourite fruit too."

The three brothers turned around, their faces lighting up joyfully as they saw Alexander approaching. He was always eager to be part of any adventure or task; his blonde hair tousled from running, and his bright blue eyes sparkled excitedly.

"Of course not, brother!" exclaimed Lathlorn, the eldest among them. "We couldn't possibly forgot about you. We need all the help to gather Mother's favourite apples."

"We wondered how long it'd take for you to catch up," Etheryn replied, slapping him on the back after he reached them.

A camaraderie filled the air as they stood beneath an apple tree. The branches were heavy with luscious red and green apples, tempting them with their sweet aroma. The sunlight filtered through the leaves, casting dappled shadows on the ground. The next problem was to get the apples down from the tree. One of the brothers, Etheryn, decided to climb to the top of the tree but kept slipping from the slim branches onto the ground. He gave up in the end and left it to one of his other brothers to get their mother's apples.

"Great!" said Lenith, "Now, how do we get them?"

"Who's the lightest?" said Etheryn.

"Obviously," complained Lathlorn. "I'd have to say not you."

"Then it's between you and me," Lenith looked up to the tree.

"Do you want to draw stones," asked Lathlorn. "To see who gets the smallest one?"

"No, I'll go," he stepped closer. "Besides, this calls for a younger Shalimar's climbing abilities."

"Are you sure about that?" Lathlorn raised an eyebrow sceptically. "You know how clumsy you can be sometimes."

Lenith shrugged confidently. "I think I can handle it. Plus, I'm the only one who can fit through those narrow branches near the top."

Etheryn chimed in, a mischievous glint in his eyes. "If Lenith falls, we'll be here to catch him. Right, Lathlorn?"

Lathlorn sighed but nodded reluctantly. "Fine but be careful up there. We don't want any broken bones."

"Look, we have less than half an hour left here, so it needs doing quickly; no disrespect, Lathlorn; I am a quicker climber." Lenith began his ascent up the tall apple tree with a determined expression. He skilfully moved through the branches, using his agility to reach higher and higher.

"No offense taken," said Lathlorn, "But please, be cautious, and you Etheryn, not a word, all right?"

"Fine, fine," replied Etheryn, "But Lenith, watch out for snakes."

"Snakes!" Lenith turned a frightened gaze down to him; his heart raced as he glanced around the tree, half-expecting to see a slithering creature lurking in the branches. "There are snakes in this tree!" He had always harboured a deep fear of snakes, their sleek bodies and venomous fangs sending shivers down his spine. The mere mention of them was enough to send him into a state of panic.

"I didn't mean that," said Etheryn, "I meant it as a saying."

"What saying?"

"Don't scare yourself."

"Then don't use the word snakes," Lenith replied, "I don't like them."

"I'm sorry," laughed Etheryn, "I won't say another word."

"Then don't." Lenith looked higher up at the tree, trying to find a safer way up it. "Well, here goes." Lenith used the thick branches as steps, and after a few minutes of scaling the tree, he was near the top. He then reached down to grab the apples. He filled his hands with as many apples as he could, tucking the extra fruit into his pocket as his three brothers waited patiently at the bottom of the tree. Lathlorn, Alexander, and Etheryn watched as he started climbing higher. First, one hand grabbed a small branch sticking out, then Lenith seized another, and another, until he was in its highest branches, peering down at his brothers, who could not see his figure surrounded by the leaves.

"If you're nimble, don't wake the dog in the kennel; you can straddle the branches, pick the apples dangling over the stream."

Lathlorn turned an angry gaze to Etheryn. "You said you wouldn't speak anymore!"

"I didn't!"

"Then you must have," his angry stare had gone to Alexander.

"Not me either."

"Then who said that?"

"I did."

The three brothers turned their gazes up at the tree.

"Why are you speaking to yourself, little brother?" asked Lathlorn.

"I'm not speaking to myself," replied the tree, its voice gentle and melodic. "I am the ancient spirit of this forest, awakened by your presence and your quarrel." The leaves rustled as if in agreement.

Lathlorn's anger turned into confusion, his brows furrowing. "You—You can speak? But trees don't talk!"

Etheryn stepped forward, curiosity replacing his earlier annoyance. "What do you mean by 'awakened'? How is that even possible?"

The tree swayed gently in response, its branches reaching out towards them. "Long ago, when this orchard was young, someone cast a powerful enchantment; it allowed me to communicate with those who seek wisdom and understanding."

Alexander's scepticism lingered on his face as he crossed his arms. "And why would we need your wisdom? We are just four brothers trying to find apples for our mother."

The tree rustled its leaves, a soft chuckle escaping from its branches. "Ah, young ones, wisdom is not limited to those who seek grand adventures or unravel great mysteries. Sometimes, one can find the greatest lessons in the simplest tasks."

Alexander's scepticism wavered as he exchanged glances with his brothers. Lathlorn, the eldest, stepped forward and spoke with a hint of curiosity. "What kind of wisdom could you offer us? We are but humble people."

The tree's branches swayed as if contomplating its response. "You can learn much from nurturing and tending to the land in the life cycle."

Etheryn raised an eyebrow sceptically. "But how does that help us gather apples for our mother?"

A sudden hysterical laugh came from the tree, and then Lenith's face popped out between the branches, his words saying, "Holy Valar, can't you recognize your brother's voice? It's me talking, not the tree, you idiots!"

The three brothers, Etheryn, Lathlorn, and Alexander, standing at the base of the tree, looked up in surprise, their eyes widening at the sight of Lenith's mischievous grin.

"Lenith," Lathlorn angrily shouted at him. "For Valar's sake!"

Etheryn, the eldest brother, shook his head in disbelief. "By the Valar, Lenith! You scared us half to death," Etheryn exclaimed, a mixture of relief and annoyance evident in his voice.

Lathlorn angrily replied, "I'm going to whoop your arse when you get back down here!"

"I still need to get the apples—"

"Well, get your arse in gear and get them then!"

"Yes, sir!" Lenith playfully saluted him and then disappeared. He started moving along a branch; it began to wobble as his weight shifted.

"Lenith," one of his brothers called out to him. "Be careful."

"I know." By now, he was nearly upon an apple dangling within his grasp. "Be careful," he huffed out loud to them all, "I don't see any of you lot doing this," he said as his hand reached out to grab a green apple.

"Lenith, stop mumbling, concentrate."

Unfortunately, Etheryn's caring words made him look down on him. That gaze made him lose his balance. Lenith felt utterly out of control as he tumbled helplessly. He tried desperately to grab onto something to slow him down, reaching his arms out, grasping at branches, trying to slow his momentum. However, his actions were in vain, and soon, he found himself flying out of the tree and into the icy stream below. As he landed, he felt the apples in his pocket tumbling to the stream's surface, and he thought his embarrassment was increasing.

"Lenith!" cried Lathlorn, running to the stream edge. "Swim here, this way, quickly!" Lathlorn saw Lenith's arms beat up and down, his head descending a few times under the water, popping back up again, "Lenith! Fight it; fight the demons in the stream!"

Lenith couldn't. The current was strong, so he let it take him away from his brothers. By the time this happened, Alexander and Etheryn were by Lathlorn's side, running along the stream's bank, following Lenith's figure tossed about in the water. A few moments of fear passed as they chased their brother, and then Lenith reached out and grasped a branch dangling over the stream. The brothers pulled at the branch as Lenith clung to it and yanked him up on the grass bank.

"You idiot!" Lathlorn sighed, half laughing. "You're soaking wet."

"Thought I'd go for a dip," Lenith looked up, smiled, "Wash these clothes."

"Well, next time, warn us."

"I'm so sorry," Etheryn apologized, "I didn't mean to make —"

"Forget it," he sat up. "It would've happened even if you hadn't said anything," he sighed, looking upstream, "Do we have to go back again?"

"No," replied Lathlorn, looking down at him. "We've had enough excitement for one day, thank you."

"What about Mother?"

"We'll get something else for her."

"What about her wild roses?" Lenith was still shivering, soaking wet from the river, wrapping his arms around himself.

"Her wild roses are a good idea, but what about your soaking clothes?"

Lenith glanced down at his drenched attire, feeling the chill seep into his bones. He knew Lathlorn was right; he couldn't afford to catch a cold, especially after narrowly escaping the river's treacherous currents. Yet, his concern for their mother's happiness tugged at his heart. "Don't worry about me. Mother is more important; her roses, we could get them."

"I would have agreed if you were in dry clothes," said Etheryn. "But you're not and need to be out of them before falling ill."

"I'm not getting naked out here!"

"We didn't suggest that," Alexander laughed at his words. "I'm assuming he meant to find somewhere for you to change."

"And where would I get dry clothes?" Lenith asked, standing up. "From someone's washing line?"

Etheryn sighed, his patience wearing thin. "No, of course not," he rolled his eyes. "We'll go back home."

"I'm not going home looking like this!" Lenith protested.

"Then we'll find a store or a market where you can buy new clothes. It's better than catching a cold or worse."

Alexander chimed in, trying to lighten the mood. "Plus, it'll allow you to show off your fashion sense. Who knows? Maybe you'll find something that suits your style."

Lenith crossed his arms defiantly. "I don't care about fashion right now," he grumbled. "I just want to get warm and dry."

Etheryn nodded sympathetically. "I understand that, but we need to prioritize your health too. Trust me, finding dry clothes will make a world of difference."

"There is someone we could go and see," replied Lathlorn. "Mother's friend, Anlease. Her resident isn't far from here, is it?"

"Actually," replied Alexander. "That's a better idea—"

"Anlease!" uttered Etheryn. "Do you think she'd still welcome us?"

"There's no reason why she shouldn't."

"And precisely why are we going to see her?" asked Lenith.

"It could be something to do with changing you into some dry clothes."

"I'm going to wear her deceased brother Frethurn's clothes!"

"Well, it's better than walking around in wet clothes," Alexander reasoned. "Besides, Anlease has always been kind and helpful to us. She might have some spare clothes that would fit you, Lenith."

Lenith sighed, clearly not thrilled about wearing someone else's clothes. But the discomfort of wet garments outweighed any reservations he had. "Fine," he grumbled reluctantly. "Let's go see Anlease," he said, then started walking.

He saw Etheryn run past him a few seconds later, saying as he did, "Can I make a suggestion, Lenith?"

"What?"

"That you run," he called out loudly.

"Why?"

"Because farmer Tilden is coming up behind us."

"What!" That name made Lenith look around in fear.

The last person Lenith needed to see was him; they had just been trying to steal his precious apples! Lenith's heart raced as he glanced over his shoulder, hoping not to see the farmer. Farmer Tilden was known for his strict rules and relentless pursuit of thieves. Lenith knew all too well the consequences of being caught red-handed in his orchard, for he'd heard rumours of such cases before involving this farmer. Without wasting another moment, Lenith darted in the opposite direction, following Etheryn's lead. His mind raced with thoughts of escape routes and hiding spots as he pushed himself to run faster. He overtook Etheryn. The sound of running footsteps behind him echoed in his ears, matching the pounding rhythm of his heart; then Lathlorn passed him by, a big smirk on his face. "Why are you so happy?" he called out to Lathlorn.

"Because he lied to you," Lathlorn laughed hysterically, "Farmer Tildon isn't behind us," then he sped off.

"Why little—

"Hah, little brother," now it was Etheryn's voice he was hearing coming up behind him. "At least your clothes will be more comfortable and drier for us to wear if you die."

"Then you better run fast!" yelled Lenith, sprinting after him. "Cause when I get you, you're all so going to get it!"

"Catch me!" Etheryn snorted, "I'll laugh myself to death," he swiftly leaped over a wooden fence.

"Then you better stop laughing," Lenith leaped over the same fence, chasing him over the seedless field. "And stop running like a wounded animal."

"Hah, I see two wounded animals behind me!"

"In your dreams, you idiot!"

Lenith was almost on Etheryn, but just as he reached a hand out to grab him by the arm, Lenith fell into the field's dirt. His face smacked into wet soil; his vision clouded by the earthy mixture. Gasping for breath, Lenith struggled to push himself up, his heart pounding in his chest. He wiped the mud from his eyes, trying to regain focus on Etheryn's retreating figure. Determined, Lenith scrambled to his feet, ignoring the pain in his scraped palms. Ignoring the dirt clinging to his clothes and face, Lenith sprinted forward with renewed vigour. Each step sent tremors through his body as he closed the distance between them. But just as he was about to catch up again, he failed to notice a treacherous stone lying in wait, half hidden in long grass before him. His foot collided with it instantly, sending him hurtling towards the ground with a forceful thud. That second fall made Lathlorn stop, turn around, and help him up.

Next, they started running again, but by the time they did, Etheryn was already by the tall hedge, making his way through it. When Lenith and Lathlorn finally scrambled through the border, Etheryn was already there with Alexander.

"What on earth!" said Alexander, looking Lenith up and down, "Happened to you, you're all muddy!"

"Don't ask," he sent a scowl to Etheryn. "And I won't tell. Now, shall we get going?"

"Indeed," Lathlorn replied. "Of to Anlease's, it is then."

They did just that. First, four Flyers were mounted, horses with wings, and flown back down the dirt track that led away from farmer Tilden's private residence. As the Flyers soared through the sky, their majestic wings beating against the wind, they saw breathtaking landscapes below. The lush green fields stretched in all directions, with vibrant wildflowers swaying gently in the breeze. The distant mountains stood tall and proud; their peaks kissed by clouds. Then Tonlorn village came into view, the destination they had been heading to. The Flyers settled into a green field just behind Anlease's residence.

Her house was picturesque with thatched eaves and a white picket fence, surrounded by wildflowers, a beehive, and a small well at the side. It was a place of tremendous beauty and solace. The garden was the pride and joy of the house. The garden was alive in the spring and summer months with various wildflowers. The garden thrived under the owner's gentle touch; a green thumb evident in keeping it healthy. In the corner was a beehive, the bees buzzing around the garden and providing honey to enjoy. Near the side of the house was a well-used to water the garden and provide a home for some of the local wildlife.

Lenith knocked on a wooden door, waited a few moments, then knocked again. The door opened.

"Hello," Anlease's smiling face welcomed them. "Come for lunch, have we?"

"Anlease," voiced Etheryn. "Excuse my younger brother's appearance; we've had some trouble."

"I'd say a lot," she laughed. "What did you do, fight with a borra?"

"No," Lenith blushed, looked to the floor, and mumbled something.

"What did you say?" asked Anlease. "Speak up."

"I fell in farmer Tilden's stream."

"What were you doing there?"

"Getting apples for Mother," Lathlorn patted him on the back. "Unfortunately, it didn't work."

"So, you've come here for a change of clothes."

Alexander stepped a little closer. "If you've any to spare?"

"Of course," Anlease opened the door wider. "Please, come in," they passed by her. "You should've asked me to get those apples," she shut the door. "Perhaps this mishap might not have happened."

"I, my brothers, and I thought the apples were going to be easy to get," said Etheryn while they continued down the hallway.

"Don't listen to his words," Alexander voiced. "He's the one to blame for Lenith's accidents."

"Alexander, that's not nice," said Anlease as they entered the living room. "Accidents are accidents, no more than just that."

"Anlease," Lathlorn stepped up to her. "Before my poor brother freezes to death, do you have any clothes that would suit his body better than those wet ones he's wearing?"

"I'll get some." She turned away and started to walk to a closed door. "I think I've got some of Frethurn's old clothes still here."

Alexander watched how her hips swayed from side to side, hypnotizing him like someone dangling a watch in front of his eyes. He watched as she disappeared; he sighed loudly; his brothers heard that noise.

"What's the matter," Etheryn smiled. "Missing your love already?"

Again, another sigh escaped from his lips.

"If Father knew you were carrying on with her," said Lenith, shaking his head. "He'll go mad."

"He doesn't," Alexander voiced through his gritted teeth. "So don't say anything."

"Can I ask you something?"

"What?"

"How does she stay alive," asked Etheryn. "I mean, live for so long if she's human."

"I don't know the answer to that question."

Anlease entered back into the room. "What don't you know the answer to?"

"Nothing," said Alexander. "Did you get Lenith some clothes?"

Anlease entered the room and stood before him, saying, "I've got some trousers, a top, and some shoes." She had a folded bundle of green matching clothes and a towel on top of them. These clothes she handed over to Lenith. "These should fit you."

Lenith nodded. "Do you have some—"

"To change? Yes. Use the spare room; it's just through there," Anlease pointed to the door she'd entered. "Take a left turn; the door to that room should be in front of you."

"Thanks." Lenith walked from the room out of the door; instead of turning left, he turned right. The door opened, and he entered a bedroom. He stood for a moment, looking around the room. He was surprised at how many books and magazines were strewn about. On the wall overlooking the bed was a large painting of a sunset. The colours of the sky and the sun were so vivid that they almost made the painting glow. Lenith next walked across the room and went into the bathroom.

The house's occupant had recently decorated the room, and you could smell fresh paint as you entered. On top of the sink sat a small mirror with various cosmetics and brushes on a nearby shelf. Lenith's gaze travelled around the room, surveying for anything else interesting. There wasn't.

Lenith walked back into the bedroom, placed the clothes on the bed, then strolled towards the window. He stopped and saw the outdoors. Lenith saw a garden filled with vibrant colours of yellow, red, violet, and blue flowers. He remembered his mother and how she used to take great care of the garden. He couldn't help but smile in admiration at the beauty it held, and then something else in the room caught his eye. He moved towards a table and saw a frame with a picture of his brother Alexander and a few bottles of different shapes and colours; his attention shifted to them. He walked over, picked up the frame, smiled at it, then replaced it in its position. Next, his attention went to the bottles. He reached for a small blue bottle. Unscrewing the top, he held the glass bottle to his nose and sniffed. The pungent odours inside conveyed a strange concoction of suspicious smells. His face twisted as if uncomfortable with the scent before quickly replacing the bottle. Lenith then walked back into the bathroom, and while undressing, he sang as his wet clothes dropped to the floor. By the time his song ended, his figure had left that room, found the bathroom, his face and hands cleaned, and now he was entering the living room with a smile.

Etheryn whistled. "Who's a pretty Shalimar then?"

Lenith's reaction was a look of embarrassment.

"Now we've accomplished our mission," Alexander said from the sofa. "I think we should be heading back home."

"I suppose you're right," Lathlorn went to stand up.

"Thank you for letting me borrow these," Lenith smiled. "I'll return them washed."

"Don't worry about them," said Anlease. "I don't think I'll need to wear them; after all, I am a woman."

That remark made Etheryn and Alexander snigger loudly; Lenith scowled at them.

"Come on, you lot," voiced Lathlorn. "Time to go."

When Anlease opened the front door, Etheryn was the first to give her a small kiss on the cheek and leave. The next was Lenith, then Lathlorn, and lastly, Alexander. However, his kiss wasn't upon her cheek; it was upon her lips. Next, hands slid around a waist, guided away from the view of his brothers, pushed her against the wall, and lips kissed hers. By the time he released her, she was breathless, chest heaving, rising excitedly, hands pulling him back when he moved away.

"Will you visit again soon," she whispered. "My bed is cold."

Alexander briefly turned and glanced at his waiting brothers outside the front door. His gaze came back only seconds later. "You know I would if I could," lips touched hers once more.

"Can you not stay here? Let your brothers travel back alone?"

"I'd love to keep your company by my side in your bed. Would you desire my company permanently or in mine?"

"Yours?"

"Your sight, your love, I can't cast it away so easily, so I ask you now, will you exist by my side forever? For I shall never repeat it."

"Exist! What do you mean?"

"Live with me, live with my family, live as my family."

Anlease bit her lip. "If you desire my company, tell me one thing to persuade me to come."

Alexander hated it when she did this, but he understood her insecurities. "You'll have warmth when you need it, smiles, tears, loyalty, love, but above all, you'll have memories to fill your mind, memories of anything you want to keep."

"And you'll give me those memories?"

"Yes."

"Who's to say I can't get those memories from here?"

"With this I offer you, you'll have more to remember."

"Even bad ones?"

"Bad comes with good, good—"

"Come on," Etheryn had walked back into the hallway, "Why are you taking so long?"

"We were speaking," said Alexander, smiling.

"Ah, love between lovers," said Lenith, coming in, "Is such a sweet sight to see, even more so when it's one of my brothers."

"Are we going or not!" shouted Lathlorn, his figure still outside.

"Yes."

Lenith, Etheryn, and Alexander turned to walk out, but before they left, Alexander stepped up to Anlease and asked, "Will you give me an answer before I go?"

"Then my answer is yes; I will come and live with you."

"Then I'll be back for you soon." Alexander's figure quickly joined his brothers, Etheryn, Lenith, and Lathlorn, and they stepped forward.

When they reached Volarie castle, dismaying information was cast into their pointed ears upon their entrance by someone.

"Your Highness's, where have you been!" Lord Howden said in desperation. "Everyone has been looking for you!"

Alexander's heart sank as he exchanged a worried glance with his brothers. Lord Howden, the trusted advisor to their father, rarely displayed such desperation. Something grave must have occurred in their absence. "We apologize for our sudden disappearance," Alexander replied, his voice laced with concern. "We were unaware that anyone was searching for us."

Lord Howden's eyes darted between the four princes before he continued, his voice trembling slightly. "Your father—Prince Elensar—Has been asking for you all for hours. The healers are doing everything they can while they wait for Rotherkin, but your mother's condition worsens by the hour."

Shock rippled through their bodies like an icy current. Their mother had always been a pillar of strength, vitality, wisdom, and compassion. The thought of her lying helpless in bed sent shivers down their spines.

"Take us to her immediately," Etheryn demanded, his usually calm demeanour replaced by urgency.

Without wasting another moment, Lord Howden led the siblings through the grand halls of their ancestral home. The tapestries that once adorned the walls seemed to blur into a haze as they hurriedly passed, their hearts pounding with worry. As they sprinted up twisting stairs, memories flooded Alexander's mind - memories of a happy kinhood spent within these very walls. The castle's grandeur seemed to fade into insignificance now, overshadowed by the impending doom that awaited them in their parents' room. Reaching the top floor, they burst through the double doors and found themselves in a dimly lit corridor. The air was tense as they hurriedly approached their parents' chamber. Each step felt like an eternity as they desperately sought answers.

Chapter 32

A Sorrowful Loss

It was one of the most heartbreaking moments that he had ever experienced in his life. His wife was lying in his arms, her chest heaving slowly, her breathing getting shallower and shallower with every passing second. His heart ached as he watched a few tears trickle down her cheeks, understanding what would happen soon. Elensar's eyes drew away from Amelia's coming death face. The room was silent, half-lit by a few candles struggling to stay alive. The room's curtains were deep blue, a slight breeze fluttering those inwards, the carpet on the floor soft, uncrushable. His gaze also saw his four kin as they entered and walked to reach their dying mother lying in his arms. "Where have you been?" Elensar's voice trembled as he uttered those words, his eyes filled with relief and frustration.

Lathlorn, the eldest of the siblings, stepped forward with a sombre expression. His voice was laced with regret as he spoke, "We were caught up in our battles, Father. We never meant to be absent when she needed us most."

Etheryn nodded in agreement, eyes glistening with unshed tears. "We should have been here," he whispered.

Alexander, the stoic and reserved one, stood silently beside them. His usually composed demeanour cracked slightly under the weight of guilt. "I failed her," he admitted quietly.

Lenith's mind was regretful as he replayed their stupid attempts to get her the favourite apples she dearly loved; they'd wasted moments that could have been spent with their mother instead.

"It doesn't matter now, you're here," Elensar looked down at their mother. "He's not here yet," he said sadly, "Not back with Rotherkin even after all this time, and the healers, they have given up their hope to cure her back to what she once was. All have failed."

"Father," voiced Etheryn. "They will come."

"It's too late."

Lathlorn lovingly touched his father's shuddering shoulder and whispered, "Have faith, Father."

"Faith!" he looked up, "Where was faith while your mother was locked in the dungeon? Where was faith when your grandmother spoke against her? Where was it when Star died? Where was it when your sister Sarath was born without breathing?" he looked back down at Amelia. "Faith has no name or importance here anymore. It has vanished—" He could go on no more, his head lowered against Amelia's.

"If you've nothing else left to cling to, Father," said Lenith. "Trust in Uncle Celahir."

His head rose; his eyes looked to his youngest. "You're so much like me, with hope still drawing you in, but—"

"Mother always taught us time is precious, even for us," said Alexander. "You remember when she would tell us to write in our journal books every day so that we never forgot anything," his three sons nodded. "Did we not fuss, moan about it," again, his sons nodded. "And what did Mother always say back to us?"

"You can have memories longer," answered Etheryn, "If written down in permanent ink."

"Unless, of course, you rubbed out something," said Lenith. "You remember Mother used to moan at us for rubbing out some of our words?"

"Exactly, exactly. Father," said Alexander. "We still have time to rewrite this chapter of Mother's story,"

His response was a small whimper.

"Father," uttered Etheryn. "Mother will still be able to look down upon us, perhaps even with our sis—"

"I don't want her watching us from above," he mumbled.

"She'll be with Star," uttered Lathlorn. "She'll look after Mother."

"I don't want your sister, sisters, looking after your mother. I—"

"You remember when Star was alive, how mother said she was too wise for this world, that she was meant for other things," said Lenith. "Are we all not meant for other things? Do we not have another life to lead once this one is over," he raised his head slowly. "Mothers will be starting again. She'll be waiting for us just as Star would."

The body of Amelia shifted a little as if the conversation they'd been having stirred her awake from a deep sleep. "Why do you speak—"

"You wake. We thought—I thought," Elensar's voice sounded half cheerful, half saddened. "Look, see, your el—children," he saw her trying to look around; seconds later, her head fell heavily back.

"But Star isn't here."

"She is mother," Lathlorn sat on the bed. He would've continued, but the bedroom door opened, and Celahir and Rotherkin entered.

"Why have you taken so long!" Elensar shouted at Celahir.

Celahir walked into the room. "I apologize, Elensar," Celahir said calmly, his voice filled with a hint of exhaustion. "We encountered unforeseen obstacles on our way back."

Elensar's anger softened as he glanced at his frail wife lying on the bed. "It doesn't matter now. Just be here for her." His voice trembled with a mix of grief and desperation.

Celahir nodded, understanding the weight of the moment. He approached Lathlorn and gently touched his shoulder, offering silent support. Rotherkin stood by the doorway, his eyes filled with concern.

Lathlorn looked up at Celahir, gratitude shining in his tear-filled eyes. "Thank you," he whispered hoarsely.

"Of course," Celahir replied softly. "Your mother would want us all to be here for her."

"What about the medicine?" asked Elensar, his gaze on his wife's now sleeping face.

"It's unavailable," answered Rotherkin. "I've got something else that might work."

"Then hurry, hurry."

"Eu não ver nenhuma morte aqui, contudo algo umas configurações mais desastrosas na espera," uttered Rotherkin in his own language.

"What did you say?" asked Celahir.

"Eu não ver nenhuma morte aqui, contudo algo umas configurações mais desastrosas na espera. You didn't say it was this bad," Rotherkin said quietly to him; well, that sentence he'd uttered wasn't entirely correct, but he wasn't going to tell what he said because sheer chaos would've taken place in the room.

"Rotherkin," Elensar said to him, "She needs your help, can you?"

"Lay her down."

Lathlorn rose from the bed and went to stand next to his brothers. Elensar gently laid Amelia down and placed her head on the pillow. Next, Rotherkin moved closer, placing a hand on her forehead as if checking to see if a fever was present; his hand moved to cover her heart next, his eyes closed, and his mouth muttered something.

Elensar tried to see what he was doing, "Are you doing it?"

"Shh, I'm hearing the heartbeats of a feeble woman."

"Oh, Valar! Oh Valar," said Celahir, a hand covering his mouth.

"Shh," Rotherkin moved his hand away from Amelia, raised it into the air. *"Você éo assediador forte da sombra, o sem nome, mas eu sou mais forte, assim que seja ido mim digo, seja ido deste quarto. Ir para trás às sombras das costas do sul das mortes do porto e esperar um quando mais por muito tempo—"*

"What's he saying?" Etheryn whispered to Lenith, "I can't understand his words."

"I think," said Lenith, whispering. "He said something like *Your strong shadow stalker, Collector, but I'm stronger, so be gone, be gone from this room. Return to the shadows of the Seaport Southern Shores and wait a while longer,* but I can't be sure."

"Is that the wizard language he used?"

"Yes."

"Shh," said Lathlorn. "You're distracting him."

"Quiet!" Rotherkin turned an angry gaze to them.

"Sorry," whispered Etheryn.

Rotherkin turned his head back to the bed, *"Porque o mandar vir, que o chamou para a frente prematuramente para reivindicar esta vida."*

"What's he saying now?" whispered Etheryn.

"*Why have you come,"* Lenith whispered into his ear, *"Who's called you forward prematurely to claim this life?'"*

When Rotherkin's words finished, Amelia opened her eyes. Her blinded gaze stared at the bedroom door. "Look! I see Star, Star!"

Elensar hurried to the bed and sat on it. "Stay here, stay with us!" his arms cradled Amelia. "She isn't here; she isn't waiting for you!"

"I want Star," her head rising toward the door, "Can't you see!"

Elensar's gaze turned towards the door; he saw no one standing there. When his eyesight travelled back to Amelia, he passed a vision of their four sons trying not to cry. "I see no one except our sons. Do you see them, do you see your sons, do you see us? Do you see your family?"

"I only see Star."

Lathlorn's tears fell down his cheeks. "Do you wish to go to Star?"

"Just to say hello to her again."

"Amelia," Celahir cried. "If you go, you won't come back!"

"She mustn't go," Elensar's gaze turned to Rotherkin. "You said this spell would work!"

Rotherkin's gaze went to the floor. "Her words are too hungry to meet her daughter."

"It hasn't worked, has it?" Elensar turned to look at Celahir, "You!"

Celahir stepped forward. "Don't do this, not now, not—"

"Stop it!" shouted Rotherkin, "Both of you!" Elensar and Celahir turned their gazes to him. "Will you let me finish the spell, or will you continue this argument?"

Elensar turned his head back to Celahir. Another angry look pierced into Celahir's eyes. "So be it," he angrily said to him, "If there's a later, that'll be the time!"

"Stop this bitterness!" Rotherkin shouted; his angry words shocked them. They held looks of a surprised reaction. "Now, will you let me begin once more?" Rotherkin still had that angry look upon his face. They nodded. Rotherkin started once more. *"Eu não posso lutar de encontro a um senhor. Eu não tenho nenhum poder para tal prevenção, ajudo me agora nesta hora da necessidade."*

"Lenith?" whispered Etheryn.

Lenith sighed and whispered, *"I can't fight against a lord. I've no power for such prevention; help me now in this hour of need."*

After Rotherkin's words ended, he appeared to be waiting for something to happen; it didn't. It made him sigh aloud before saying, *"O senhor Elrohir ganhou sua noiva."*

"The lord Elrohir has won his bride," whispered Lenith before Etheryn had the chance to ask him.

"Why are you saying the name of Elrohir," Elensar had spoken this. "It is Lord Mahtan that has caused this,"

"For that is his true name," replied Rotherkin. "The name he uses in Seaport Southern Shore, Elrohir."

"Oh, Valar!" whispered Etheryn.

"What did you say!" Elensar cried to Rotherkin.

"It's too late."

"Then fix it, for Valar's sake, fix it!" Amelia made a sound as if it was hard to exhale the air from her lungs. Elensar cried into her hair, "Celahir, why didn't you come earlier!" he looked at him, "Did you not have the time given to you!"

"Elensar," Celahir went to step forward again because Elensar's face held a look of rage; it stopped him. "I used that time as quickly as I was allowed."

"Then you wasted it; she's no more!" Elensar's gaze turned to Rotherkin. "Please, fix it, please, I beg you!"

"O término está aqui, ele toma com mãos fáceis. Uma noiva para um senhor nas costas do sul."

"Lenith?"

"No, Etheryn!" Lenith gave him a stern look, "This is too much sadness to translate!"

"Please!"

Celahir stepped up to Etheryn. His mouth went by his ear, "Your mother lies dying!" Celahir whispered angrily, "And you wish Lenith to do this! He will not do that if he knows what's good for him!"

"Wait, Star, I'm coming, momma is coming, but wait a minute, I have to say goodbye first—Please wait!"

Celahir turned towards the bed; Amelia struggled against the death's grip in Elensar's arms; that sight made his heart almost die.

"Wait!" Elensar's frightened gaze turned to someone else. "Rotherkin!".

"Eu sou pesaroso, perdôo me."

"Let us know what you're saying!" Lathlorn cried, tears falling down his face. "Mother, stay, please, Father, help her!"

"I've failed!" Rotherkin sighed.

Just as Elensar's reddened eyes turned back to gaze at Amelia, the lamenting calling song known by all, he began to sing in a wretched voice. When he'd finished, the calling song appeared not to work. Perhaps Amelia's heart was too frail in beats to respond, so his hand slipped to her face, a tear fell from her blinded eye smeared away, and he sang a song, the ray of life song.

'An hour, a minute, and a second of prayer, the words you say in your hour of need, answered, as it should be. Cruel is the hand of fate. Cruel is the cry unheard; cruel is life itself, but a life without emotions is cruelty itself.'

Elensar never finished the song, for Amelia had whispered, "Elensar, let me sleep."

"Sleep, my love," he weepingly replied. "But don't go to him."

"To whom?" asked Amelia's voice faintly, then her eyes closed, and her body fell limp against him.

"To the deceiver, Elrohir," Elensar cradled her tightly; she gave no word to say, release his grip.

"Elensar, I'm sorry," Celahir whispered.

Elensar's head didn't rise, but his voice did ask, "I'll have you as a brother again tonight if you can give me peace of mind to say she won't go to him?"

"Elensar," Celahir sighed. He wouldn't be his brother tonight, for Amelia's mind was empty when he said, *To the deceiver*. "I say again, I'm sorry."

Hearing him say those words caused Elensar to raise his head quickly, glance at him, then at Amelia. His trembling hands reached for her pulse, hoping against hope that it would beat beneath his fingertips. But there was nothing. Silence engulfed the room as he realized the unthinkable - Amelia was gone. Elensar looked as if he were in shock, then words came out, "No, no, no," then slightly louder, "No, no, no. Please, Amelia, come back to me. Don't leave me," his voice cracked with grief, and his heart shattered into a million pieces.

The room seemed to close in on Elensar, suffocating him with its emptiness, and that's when his emotions started to build up. Step by step, a sob, a shudder, a wailing, and the most heartbreaking sight happened. Elensar collapsed over her lifeless body, convulsing with the weight of his anguish. The room, once a sanctuary, felt like a prison, trapping him in a whirlwind of despair. Each breath became harder to take as tears streamed down his face, mingling with the sweat that coated his trembling skin.

"Elensar, brother," Celahir called out to him.

Elensar's heart clenched at the sound of his brother's voice. He slowly lifted his head, his eyes red and swollen from the torrent of emotions that had consumed him. Celahir stood before him, his face etched with concern and sorrow.

"Please, Elensar," Celahir pleaded, his voice filled with compassion and urgency. "You cannot let her death consume you like this. She would not want to see you suffer." With great effort, he saw Elensar push himself up. "Her love is still here; she'll go to him, but she'll still love you too."

There was silence for a few seconds, then Elensar replied, "Of course, she'll love me!" his words cast in a heated tone, "I'm her husband, her true lover; now you've made me angry with your words, so get out of this room before I cast a hateful blow to your face!"

"You've every right to be angry, but your sons and I grieve!"

"Your grief for my love isn't stronger than her family's grief, so don't play all heartbroken in front of me!" His sight went back down to his deceased wife.

"Elensar, it wasn't just you who loved her deeply; I loved her too; she was my sister-in-law, my friend, a lo—" Celahir saw Elensar raise his head slowly while someone else was giving Celahir a shocked look; he didn't see that one; Celahir only saw Elensar's face once he'd raised his head fully up. Unknown to him, Celahir was a Shalimar with quick reflexes when using missing words, so accusing him of being his deceased wife's lover wouldn't be cast out from Celahir's lips. "A loyal friend, who I shall lovingly miss," said Celahir quickly, hoping to rectify his misplaced words.

"Get out!" Elensar screamed at him.

"Elensar!"

"If you truly loved her, you wouldn't have lingered at Rotherkin's dwelling for so long!"

"Elensar, please!"

"Get out!"

Rotherkin walked up to Celahir, grasped him by the arm, and pulled him to the door. "Speak later when today has gone."

"But he needs me!" Celahir protested as Rotherkin shoved him through the open door.

"If you linger in the same room, he'll not lament as he should."

Celahir turned to look at his brother and said before he closed the door behind himself. "Elensar, you're not without help in grieving; I'll be there for you if you need me."

But Elensar wasn't paying any attention to him now. He clung to Amelia like she was a precious gem against his chest. Celahir knew his brother's life would never be the same without her. For Elensar himself, he refused to let go. His whole world seemed contained in this moment of sadness, as if time stood still and all happiness washed away. All his life, he had searched for something special to fill him and leave him wanting more. But he had not expected to find such a thing in Amelia, but he did. He wished he could have had the capability to turn back time and rewrite their history to a better conclusion, but even that was too late now.

Elensar buried his face in Amelia's white hair and clung to her tightly as if his life depended on it. It was true; his life would never be the same without her. She would not be there to see him crowned King and her his Queen, to feel the wind upon her face, to smell the aroma of cut grass, to feel the ocean breeze against her skin, or to feel the warmth of his arms surrounding her. Then he thought of ways to end his life, a way to be with Amelia in the afterlife. He considered taking his own life or recruiting someone's help in the task, but he knew that the guardians of Seaport Southern Shore would punish such methods. In his grief, Elensar became desperate to seek any magical remedy but soon realized such measures were futile. He slowly grasped that the only way he could be with Amelia was either through time or chance.

This possibility was too much for Elensar, and he howled out in pain as if his world had just died before him. Tears streamed down his face, and he silently pleaded to the guardians in Seaport Southern Shore to keep Amelia's soul safe until he arrived to claim her back as his wife again. But for now, in this world, he was living in, nothing would ever be the same for Elensar, and he knew it and couldn't do anything to stop it from happening. Then, out of nowhere, he sang, singing with so much emotion that his four kin's, still standing by his side, began weeping.

"When I laughed, you made me laugh more. When I cried, you eased the sorrow from me. When I was confused, you made the day more comfortable to see. When I was hurt, you brought happiness to me. But now you're gone, who will do all that for me? What is life if you're not here to share it with me?

Can you see what I am without you? Can you understand what it feels like to be heartbroken? Can you walk away and forget everything we ever did or wanted to do? Can you live without love, for it's like a lifetime without air?

I am a male that's lost his smile. I am a male that's lost his will to live. I am a male doomed to die alone in old age. I am a male without his soul mate. I am alone and without love. What is life if you're not here to share it with me?

Can you see what I am without you? Can you understand what it feels like to be heartbroken? Can you walk away and forget everything we ever did or wanted to do? Can you live without love, for it's like a lifetime without air?

You've opened a window and shone your light onto me. You've shown me the morning, and my love for you will continue to burn bright. You've taught me how to love again. You've given me hope when all else failed. But now you've left my heart to sadness and tears. What is life if you're not here to share it with me?

Can you see what I am without you? Can you understand what it feels like to be heartbroken? Can you walk away and forget everything we ever did or wanted to do? Can you live without love, for it's like a lifetime without air? What is life if you're not here to share it with me?

That heartbreaking song had been the first song Elensar had sung to his wife so long ago, used to win her heart back to him. It was a song that spoke of the strength and passion of true love, of a love so powerful that it can save even the broken-hearted. It had caught his wife's attention, and her eyes softened before tearing up. He knew then without a doubt that she was the one for him and that this love would never end. So, when Elensar was grieving, he reached for that exact song. That song spoke of the beauty of true love—a love that had never once left their side, even in the most trying times. A love so strong that it could lessen the pain and make the tears slow down. It reminded Elensar that, despite everything, his love for Amelia would survive.

To be continued……

Milton Keynes UK
Ingram Content Group UK Ltd.
UKHW022202221223
434840UK00015B/708